A STORM HITS V~~

David Gaughran is the author of *If You Go Into The Woods*, *Transfection*, and *Let's Get Digital: How To Self-Publish, And Why You Should*. Born in Dublin, he currently lives in Stockholm, but spends most of his time traveling the world, collecting stories.

Praise for *If You Go Into The Woods:*

"There are definite shades of HP Lovecraft in both stories … punchy, entertaining reads with a bit of mental gymnastics thrown in, you can't go wrong with this one."—Jenny Mounfield, author of *The Ice-cream Man*.

"The writing in this story is top-notch. The writer has a strong, clean voice. He's able to sustain an air of mystery and suspense without it feeling cheap."—Sarah Nicolas, *SIFT* Book Reviews.

Praise for *Transfection:*

"I recently bought and read *Transfection* and I'm happy to say it is terrific."—JA Konrath, bestselling author of *The List*, *Stirred*, and *Disturb*.

"I laughed out loud at some of the antics as I was reading … yet another well written and, dare I say again, thought-provoking, tale from David Gaughran."—Heather L. Faville, *Doubleshot Reviews*.

Praise for *Let's Get Digital: How To Self-Publish, And Why You Should:*

"Even with my background as an indie writer, I picked up several valuable tips… simply the best book about the e-book revolution I have read."—Michael Wallace, bestselling author of the *Righteous* series.

"Credible and comprehensive. I'd recommend it to any writer who is considering self-publishing or anyone interested in the current state of publishing."—*Big Al's Books and Pals*.

DAVID GAUGHRAN
A STORM HITS VALPARAÍSO

A STORM HITS VALPARAÍSO
ISBN-13: 978-1468182033
ISBN-10: 146818203X

Editor: Karin Cox
Cover Design: Kate Gaughran
Map Design: Jared Blando: theredepic.com
Print Formatting: Heather Adkins

Cover shows Carte de l'Amérique (1740) by Benard Direxit (map); Illustration from Voyage of Discovery 1791-95 (1798) by George Vancouver (seascape); Combate de San Lorenzo (late 19th century) by Angel della Valle, 1855-1903/Museo Histórico Nacional, Buenos Aires (horseman). Author photograph © 2011 Neil Mitchell Photography: neilmitchellphotography.com

E-book edition published December 2011
Print edition published January 2012

This first paperback edition was printed by Createspace

ArribaArribaBooks.com
AStormHitsValparaiso.com

Copyright © 2006-2012 David Gaughran

All rights reserved. No part of this publication may be reproduced, stored in a retrieval system or transmitted, in any form or by any means without the prior written permission of the author, nor be otherwise circulated in any form of binding or cover other than that in which it is published and without a similar condition being imposed on the purchaser.

Si hay victoria en vencer al enemigo, la hay más cuando el hombre se vence a si mismo. If there is victory in overcoming the enemy, there is a greater victory when a man overcomes himself—**José de San Martín**

Contents

1: A Storm Hits Valparaíso 1
2: The Sea Wolf 6
3: A Pact in Blood 13
4: The Haunting Eyes of Robado Vivaldo 19
5: El Desertor 22
6: The Mountain That Eats Men 25
7: The Prostitute 30
8: The Flight of Diego 37
9: The Trial of Admiral Gambier 41
10: The Quilombo 43
11: The Field of the Dead 49
12: A Call To Arms 52
13: Death in the Andes 56
14: The Proctor and the Marshall 58
15: Madam Feliz's Gambling House 67
16: Everything Turns to Ash 72
17: Jorge and the Gauchos 78
18: The Stowaway 85
19: María de los Remedios 89
20: A Prisoner's Lament 101
21: Kitty 107
22: El Salar de Uyuni 112
23: The Mounted Grenadiers 117
24: Café Malquerida 126
25: The Battle of San Lorenzo 133
26: A Secret Meeting 139
27: An Accidental Rescue 142
28: The Sharp Shooter 153
29: Playing the Market 157
30: The Sickness of San Martín 161
31: Indictment 168
32: The Governor 175
33: The Battle of Rancagua 183
34: Exodus 187
35: Escape 194
36: The Whorehouse 197
37: A Case of Mistaken Identity 204

38: The Congress of Tucuman 210
39: The Irish Don Juan 214
40: The Price of Freedom 217
41: The Archimedes of the Andes 220
42: The Man of Many Titles 226
43: Release 235
44: The Crossing of the Andes 239
45: The Battle of Chacabuco 244
46: The Return 250
47: Homecoming 253
48: The Surprise of Cancha Rayada 256
49: The Battle of Maipú 260
50: Napoleon 267
51: The Coward San Martín 270
52: Cochrane the Pirate 275
53: The Traitor San Martín 282
54: The Expedition to Peru 285
55: The Esmeralda 291
56: The Long March 295
57: The City of Pizarro 300
58: The Protector of Peru 304
59: The Guayaquil Conference 309
60: Return to Valparaíso 316
Epilogue 321
Acknowledgements
Historical Note
About the Author
Sample: *Transfection*

For Gabháin "Hammer Hands" Neary.

1: A Storm Hits Valparaíso

Catalina Flores de la Peña's tongue got her in more trouble than any other part of her body, even though there were far more likely candidates. However, as soon as anyone brought these to her attention, they realized why most men preferred to admire her from the dusty corners of her father's tavern, rather than approach her directly. So legendary was her temper that the mayor ordered her father to keep her upstairs when dignitaries came to visit the tavern, fearing a repeat of the night she broke the magistrate's nose.

When she was confined to her room, customers tended not to linger; there was no one to hasten the hours between the first *pisco* and the fall of night. Watching her glide between tables—flirting with one man, berating another, eyes flashing one moment, soft and kind the next—was one of the more pleasant ways to avoid thinking about the weather on Valparaíso's long winter nights.

Her father—Don Flores—was a stern man and no one was quite sure of his first name. One customer swore his uncle grew up with Don Flores in Pucon, and that he was called Ignacio. Another insisted his brother once loitered outside the confessional and heard old Father Guido refer to Don Flores as Ricardo. Catalina's father never let on, happy to give the men something to talk about other than his daughter. And anyway, the majority of his patrons were content simply calling him Don Flores, the honorific reflecting the distance he kept from them.

Don Flores' low opinion of his fellow man resulted from years of seeing them at their worst, for he slept when he wasn't working and he worked when he wasn't sleeping. His daughter was spared this judgment. He showered her with all the love and affection he withheld from the rest of society. When Catalina was old enough, he insisted she work at the bar so that she would form the same useful opinion of humanity that protected and comforted him in equal measure.

*　*　*

Catalina could feel his eyes—watching her. She tried to ignore him, but every time she looked, there he was. Most men had the decency to look away when she caught them, but this Spanish *puerco* just went on staring, with the faintest hint of a sneer at the corner of his lips.

Something about him kept her on edge. She tried to put him out of her mind; she had troubles enough tonight. The crew of the *Esmeralda* had descended on Valparaíso with no good in mind. Their ship had docked, needing repairs, and they were taking advantage of several days of unexpected shore leave before continuing on to Lima. It had been a long voyage from Spain. The sailors hadn't seen port during the journey across the Atlantic, down the barren coast of Patagonia, past the frozen wastelands of Tierra del Fuego, and around Cape Horn into the Pacific. The Chilean rebels had no ships worthy of the name, and their forces had withdrawn on sight of the frigate; their one paltry cannon was no match for the *Esmeralda's* forty-two guns. The Spaniards had secured the waterfront in under an hour, encountering no resistance. Sentries were posted at each street corner, and the sailors who escaped guard duty were determined to make the most of this opportunity.

Toward midnight, the bawdy crowd began to clear, following the musicians down the street, looking for whores and gambling tables. An hour later, only one table was left: Spanish sailors, drunk,

A Storm Hits Valparaíso

shouting insults. Except for him; he just watched. She tried to shake it off, hoping they would be gone soon. Instead, they called for another drink.

"Very well, *señores*," said Don Flores, as he poured the *pisco*, "one more, then we close."

Catalina placed the drinks on the table, grateful the night was nearly over, already thinking of bed. As she turned to leave, the *puerco* grabbed her arm. "I hope you are not going to throw us out on the street just yet. It's still early."

Catalina glared at him. "Let go of me, *puerco*, or you'll be out now."

He pulled her down onto his lap, grabbing her breast. "*Chica*, the night's only beginning—" He stopped short, her cold metal blade pressed against his throat. The bar fell silent—a silence quickly shattered by his companions jumping up from their chairs, upending the table in their haste. Catalina pulled the *puerco's* head back, exposing his sweaty neck. One of the sailors edged closer. The tip of her dagger nicked the *puerco's* skin, drawing a small bead of blood.

"Stand back lads," he cautioned.

Catalina turned to his companions. "You two, leave."

They paused. The *puerco* gave a slight nod, the knife still firmly at his neck. Eyes on Catalina, his companions staggered backward to the door and stepped outside. Her father hurried to her side and eased the knife from her fingers. With his other hand, he twisted the *puerco's* arm up behind his back and marched him after his companions.

"You tell that bitch this isn't finished." The *puerco* struggled. "I'll be back for her."

Don Flores threw him out the door, bolting it shut. He sighed then looked at his daughter. "Go to bed *mi hija*. It has been a long night. Tomorrow we can clean."

Catalina nodded and went upstairs.

The next morning, the air thick with stale sweat and tobacco, Catalina drummed her fingers on the bar as she surveyed the damage. *This day isn't going to improve in a hurry*, she thought. Last night's crowd had been rough. Aside from dirty glasses and plates, she had smashed bottles and broken chairs to contend with. At

3

least her regulars knew the rules—and occasionally respected them—but those animals, they had no respect for anything. She cursed as a glass slipped from her hand and shattered. A groan came from the doorway outside. *Pedro*, she thought, a smile sailing through the storm of her face.

Every night, Pedro Villar fell asleep in the doorway of the bar with a flower in his hand, intending to profess his love to Catalina. Every night, his courage would falter, leaving him slumped outside, cursing his cowardice and mourning his solitude. Every morning, Catalina sent him home to his mother—a stern woman who put a raw egg in his coffee as punishment for his nightly excesses.

Catalina opened the door and shooed Pedro away with the broom, unmindful of the heart she broke a little more each day.

"Pedro Villar?" Her father appeared as she was re-locking the door.

Catalina laughed. "Who else?"

"He has too much interest in you for my liking."

"That drunk would chase a *burro* in a dress."

Her father grunted. "Catalina, put down that broom. I want to talk to you."

"What is it, Papa?"

"I'm sending you to Santiago for a few days, to your aunt. I don't want any argument. It's not safe for you here."

"But Papa, we can't let—"

"Sergeant Eduardo came by last night, after you went to bed. He is worried about these sailors. They are hot-headed and foolish enough to do something stupid." Don Flores took a bottle of *pisco* from the shelf, cleaning the label with his thumb before pouring himself a healthy measure. "He can't protect us. His hands are tied. None of his men can enter Valparaíso while there is a Spanish warship in the bay." He emptied the contents with one gulp. "He feels it would be best if you visited some relatives until the Spaniards leave town."

"But this is my home."

"I have made my decision, Catalina. Just for a few days, until these sailors leave." He raised his hands, as if to brook any further discussion.

"Papa—"

"That's enough!"

Catalina continued cleaning in silence. There was no point arguing; her father's mind was made up. She had no siblings to share the burden of her father's protectiveness, no mother to soften his resolve; she was going to Santiago.

2: The Sea Wolf

Lord Captain Thomas Cochrane waited in the musty, oak-paneled corridor and wondered what the next few hours would bring. He had been summoned for a meeting in Admiralty House, near Whitehall, by the First Lord of the Admiralty, Lord Musgrave. He had no doubt they had received his report warmly—the mission had been a success; however, he also knew he had enemies within the Royal Navy. As an M.P. he had long fought against naval corruption, allying with the more radical elements in Parliament. In short, he was not expecting a warm welcome.

Members of the naval establishment were notoriously cautious. Cochrane felt their conservatism had not only held him back, but also impeded England's progress in the war with France. How he longed for a leader like Napoleon Bonaparte—someone who respected daring and inventiveness in commanders rather than being suspicious of it. His superiors were pompous old farts who valued procedure and protocol over courage and verve.

He unfolded the article from the *Naval Chronicle* his uncle had kept for him:

Seeing what Captain Cochrane has done with a single ship upon the French shores, we may easily conceive what he might have achieved had he been entrusted with a sufficient squadron of ships and a few thousand military hovering over the whole extent of the French coast, which it would take a considerable portion of the army of France to defend.

The Admiralty might be narrow-minded, but Cochrane knew they were keenly aware of the public mood, and knew how important this was to their political masters. The door opened and a liveried servant summoned him inside. "Sir, if I beg your pardon, the Lord requests your presence."

Cochrane rose, folded the newspaper cutting into his pocket, and entered the room. It was a grand, ornate chamber lined with portraits of dead kings and forgotten battles. Much of the space was taken up by a solid mahogany table at which Lord Musgrave was seated with a number of documents scattered in front of him. A blazing fire filled the room with heat, despite the sun streaming in from the ceiling-to-floor windows opposite.

Lord Musgrave gestured for Cochrane to sit and began leafing through his papers. "Well, I must say, events were concluded in a most satisfactory manner in Fort Trinidad. Napoleon's armies will have been delayed for weeks, if not longer."

Cochrane said nothing, his eye drawn to the outsized wind dial above the mantelpiece. He wondered if it still worked.

Lord Musgrave coughed, drawing his attention. "I won't be too fulsome in my praise; we don't want you losing your head." He locked eyes on Cochrane. "Press attention can lead one to get ideas above one's station."

Cochrane bit his lip, attempting to stop his displeasure registering on his face, as Lord Musgrave continued. "That being said, we have a ... situation at present that could benefit from your, shall we say, unconventional approach. As you may have heard from the latest naval dispatches, the French have taken advantage of some rather strong winds and have broken through our blockade at Brest. Eleven battleships and a number of frigates got through. This means—"

"Napoleon is free to attack British shipping."

"Indeed. As you have gathered, the situation is perilous in the extreme." Lord Musgrave's eyes darted toward the back of the room. "Stevens, if you don't mind." The servant unfurled a large map of France and placed it on the table, securing it with three silver paperweights. "As luck would have it, some of their ships took damage in the storm and regrouped here, in The Basque Roads, just north of Rochefort-sur-mer in the Bay of Biscay."

"Do we have any vessels nearby?"

Lord Musgrave nodded. "Admiral Gambier is some distance offshore, observing their movements, but is without sufficient numbers to launch an assault. He has suggested waiting for reinforcements or until the French leave the sanctity of the port. The shore batteries are causing him some concern."

Cochrane couldn't hold back any longer. "But if we wait, the French will have repaired their fleet. We can't let this opportunity slip through our fingers. While Gambier is sitting on his hands—"

"Enough!" Lord Musgrave rose to his feet. "We know you prefer a direct approach, which is why you were summoned. If you calm down, I would like to hear your thoughts on how we should proceed."

Cochrane inhaled, collecting himself. He decided to change tack. "I think Admiral Gambier is correct: a direct attack would be disastrous." He pointed at Rochefort-sur-mer. "I'm wondering why the French would choose to shelter here. I'm not worried about their shore cannon, but my instinct tells me they have afforded themselves a greater level of protection than we realize. If I were commanding the French, I wouldn't have docked here, unless my suspicions are correct."

"Which are?" said Lord Musgrave, growing a little irritated by Cochrane's grandstanding.

"I suspect the French have erected a boom across the mouth of the bay, from here,"—Cochrane traced a path across the map—"to here."

"A boom? Are you sure?"

"Almost certain. And if I am right, it will block all access to the port, only leaving a small gap to let ships pass through. It would prevent our fleet from attacking the harbor, because as they slowed down to pass through one by one they could be easily picked off by the shore guns here, and here."

"Are you suggesting we should draw them out somehow?"

"Not in the least. Quite the opposite, in fact. I have been working on a modified fireship that should be able to blow a hole in the boom wide enough for an attack to proceed. With a few of these explosion ships, as I like to call them, we will be able to cause sufficient damage to the boom to allow an attack." "And if you are wrong about the boom?"

Cochrane smiled. "Well then the explosion ships shall just sail right in and blow up the French!"

It took a few moments for the audacity of Cochrane's plan to sink in. Lord Musgrave slowly arched an eyebrow. A smile flickered at the edge of his lips. "Tell me what you need."

* * *

Three weeks later, Admiral Gambier waited aboard his ship for his visitor to arrive. He was not amused. The last thing he needed was this hotheaded Scot, Cochrane, charging into what was already a delicately-balanced position. How could the Admiralty send in this backward fellow, this impudent pup, to assist him? He had several well-educated, better officers, good Navy men, and this uncouth ruffian from some godforsaken glen had a hare-brained scheme to get himself in the newspapers again. He seethed as Cochrane approached.

"You may have been sent here by the Admiralty on special assignment, Captain Cochrane, but I want you to be clear on one thing: I am the Commander-in-Chief of the Royal Navy Fleet in the Bay of Biscay, and you take your orders from me."

Cochrane stopped just short of Admiral Gambier and saluted. "I apologize for my presence, sir, particularly as you seem to find it so odious. I did attempt to refuse command of the fireships." Admiral Gambier's mouth fell open in shock as Cochrane continued. "Unfortunately for both of us, Lord Musgrave ordered me to accept. I will be on my ship if you need me."

Admiral Gambier was taken aback. He had never been spoken to in such a manner, certainly not by a subordinate. He gathered himself. "One moment, Captain Cochrane. I gather you have convinced the Admiralty that we should use fireships in the attack. In your haste, you have failed to take account of one extremely pertinent fact: the French have erected a two mile-long sturdy wooden boom at the mouth of the harbor. Doubtless, this is anchored with heavy chains." Gambier paused to let this sink in, before continuing in a shrill tone. "If you choose to rush headlong into self-destruction, that is your own affair. But it is my duty to take care of the lives of the men, and I will not place the crews of the fireships in palpable danger."

Cochrane smiled at Gambier. "Do not worry yourself. I will take care of the boom. Just make sure the fireships are released when you get my signal."

Gambier's face darkened as he watched Cochrane climb down to his gig. Everything he had heard about this wastrel Scot was correct. Fuming, he entered his cabin, determined to rein in this upstart.

Back aboard the *Imperieuse*, Cochrane made preparations with his Quartermaster. "For each of the explosion ships, I need fifteen hundred barrels of gunpowder, the same amount of ten inch shells, and three thousand grenades. Before these are placed aboard, reinforce the hulls in the rear as well as both sides. This should focus the blast forward. When this is complete, I want all of the explosives placed carefully in the hold and bound together."

"It's like one giant floating mortar."

"Exactly!"

"How much of a fuse will you need, sir?"

"Longer than usual. I'll need ten minutes to get the men far enough back. I am expecting quite a bang. Now get me those supplies."

* * *

By the evening of April 11th, conditions were perfect: both wind and tide were heading in the direction of the port. Cochrane had meticulously assembled twenty-two fireships as well as three of his explosion ships. Admiral Gambier cautiously had the flotilla of fireships drop anchor eight miles from the coast, while Cochrane—with Lieutenant Bissel and a crew of just four men—began piloting the first of the explosion ships toward the giant boom. The two other ships would be timed to strike the boom moments later.

On the deck of the first explosion ship, Cochrane addressed his crewmen. "Listen up, we only get one chance at this. If we mess

A Storm Hits Valparaíso

it up, it could cost us our lives." Cochrane paused, glancing at each of them, making sure his point was understood. "When I give the order, I want everyone off this ship. Only when you are all safely in the gig will I light the fuse. Once the fuse is lit, we have less than ten minutes to get as far away as we can. The wind and the tide will be against us, so I will need everyone pulling their weight. Understood?"

The men knew it was a dangerous mission, but had readily volunteered. Cochrane had worked his way up the ranks and commanded a great deal of respect among his men. They knew he would never order anyone to take a risk he would not take himself, and that he was not yet ready to die. "Aye, Captain."

Resuming his position at the prow, Cochrane clenched his jaw and drummed his fingers against the wooden rail, his eyes fixed on the horizon. If he misjudged the distance, the vessel would explode harmlessly before it reached the boom. If the fuse burned too quickly, he and his men would perish. If the explosives failed to ignite, half of Admiral Gambier's munitions stockpile would fall to the French, and the boats laden with precious gunpowder could be turned against them. They were close, but Cochrane waited; too many things could go wrong. If only he had an opportunity to test the explosion ship first. But he didn't have that luxury. It was time.

"To the gig. Go!" The men rushed to the rope-ladders, scrambling down into the small gig tethered to the ship's side. Cochrane lit the fuse and paused, wanting to make sure it caught. There was something else at the back of his mind, something he couldn't quite remember ... he shook his head, ran to the rope-ladder, and clambered into the gig, grabbing the remaining oar.

"Row! For God's sake, row! I don't want to be anywhere near this damned thing when she blows." They had only put sixty yards between themselves and the ship when Cochrane stood in panic, nearly toppling the gig. "Back! Back!" he screamed, his arms flailing. "We must go back."

The men held on to his legs, attempting to steady the gig. "Captain, the fuse is lit. We must press on."

Cochrane glowered at the crewman. "Turn around, that's an order."

The men were even more scared of their Captain than of the imminent explosion. Moments later, Cochrane was back at the ship, scaling the rope-ladder.

The crewman stared at each other. The only sound came from the waves slamming into the side of the gig. Just as one of them was about to speak, Cochrane appeared, sliding down the rope-ladder and landing awkwardly in the boat. From inside his coat, a pup's head appeared. Cochrane smiled. "We couldn't leave a man behind lads, even if it was only wee Blackie."

The men didn't know whether to laugh or cry, but they knew they had to row. They worked hard, but time and tide were against them. Wave after wave crashed over the small boat, knocking the frightened rowers—their eyes shut tight against the stinging salt—into one another, each stroke sapping the strength from their aching arms. Desperate to put some distance between themselves and the ship, mortal fear propelled the men forward. Cochrane urged them on, his exhortations cut short by slapping mouthfuls of brine.

Then the sky ripped itself apart. A fireball tore through the heavens and the little boat trembled, as if in anticipation of what was to come. The resultant wave threw them forward at a frightening speed, but somehow their vessel remained upright as debris and shrapnel whizzed over their heads.

The sea now calm, Cochrane stood, his face tinged red by the fire raining from above. Nobody was looking at the shattered remains of the French boom; all eyes were fixed on the point where the remnants of the explosion ship had landed.

"Good God," said one of the crewmen, "if he hadn't gone back for Blackie, we would have snuffed it."

Cochrane turned to face the boom, the boat rocking gently under his feet. As he surveyed the broken, twisted remains of the French defenses, his chest tightened. No longer could they ignore him. Finally, they would give him the ships to win this war. "Perhaps a little less gunpowder next time," he said.

3: A Pact in Blood

In northwestern Argentina, in the foothills of the Andes, remote settlements consisted of just one or two houses separated by hours of hard riding. Only an occasional wayward merchant—seeking shelter from the elements, before continuing on to the markets of Tucuman and Salta—brought news from the outside world.

Inez Ramírez de las Rozas always considered herself luckier than most. After all, she had a faithful, hard-working husband, enough animals that food wasn't a constant worry, and two strong sons—although, in truth, only Jorge was her own. Her sister died in childbirth over seventeen years ago, and little Diego's father, gripped by a grief so consuming that he couldn't even hold his son, had abandoned him. Inez had raised Diego as her own, thankful that the Lord had seen fit to let her sister live on in this little boy.

She worried about him, though. There was too much of his father in him. Jorge was a good, serious boy. But Diego? His head was in the clouds. Often she would see him gazing off into the distance, lost in a world of his own making. It was worse on the rare nights a traveler passed through. Diego would pester them from the moment they arrived. Tucuman, Salta, Buenos Aires— Diego wanted to know everything. The buildings, the clothes, the food, the mechanical contraptions; it was impossible to get the boy to sleep afterwards, as he lay there in a fevered state of excitement, imagining these exotic places. On those nights, she would lie awake worrying, picturing Diego whispering to Jorge and putting crazy notions in his head.

She worried Diego would leave one day, just like his father. It was not that he wasn't a hard worker, and he was as good, if not better, than Jorge with the horses. What she had come to accept was that, just as Diego had been given to her by the grace of God, he might be spirited away again. After all, someday he might wish to find his father. His real father. Her greatest fear was that Jorge would go with him—*that* she couldn't accept, and she didn't care whose will it was.

She had made the mistake of letting her husband, Miguel, take Diego to the market at Tucuman one spring. Inez knew it would only fire the boy's imagination, but Miguel was stubborn, especially where Diego was concerned. Miguel had hoped that seeing the noise and filth of the city would scare him a little, put some of his dreams to bed. But Diego was fascinated, plaguing Miguel with questions on the two-day ride home. Sighing, she collected the last of the eggs from the chicken coop then crossed the yard to watch the two boys saddle up their horses.

"I'll race you to the top of the hill." Diego spurred his horse.

Jorge kicked his horse and sped after him. Miguel had sent the two boys to track down a mare that had escaped during the night. He could have done it himself, but the boys were good riders, and he suspected they knew where the horse was anyway. He shook his head in dismay as he watched them in the distance, grappling for each other's reins.

"Those boys," Inez said, smiling as she walked toward him.

Miguel's face hardened. "I heard Diego creep from his bed last night. He lets those horses out just so they can go off for the day."

"Miguel, they are young." She put her hand on her husband's arm. "They need a little excitement."

Miguel frowned and silently disagreed. He knew Diego was a bad influence on Jorge. He vowed to keep that boy under control.

A Storm Hits Valparaíso

* * *

"Diego if we don't find this horse soon, we are going to be in big trouble." As the sky darkened, Jorge began to worry, remembering the strange look on Papa's face as they were leaving. "I'm sure he knows what you are up to."

Diego slowed his horse. "I haven't lost one yet. Come on, let's keep going."

"Yes, but this time you didn't tie the rope properly. She could be anywhere." They zigzagged their way up the steep slope.

Diego followed Jorge's gaze across the crest of the foothills until his eyes fixed on the granite wall beyond. Sometimes, when he looked at the mountains that encircled the smaller, flatter hills of his home, he could almost feel them closing in on him. Most mornings, when he went out into the yard, he swore they had inched closer in the night and he cursed them for taking another sliver of his freedom. But on mornings like this, he didn't care; it seemed like the green hills would roll on forever, and he would never reach those grey mountains, no matter how fast he rode.

As they crested the hill, they spotted the black mare munching on some thick grass at the edge of the woods. "There she is, I told you!" Diego charged down the hill, drew up beside the startled mare, and dismounted. He approached her carefully, putting his arms around her neck and whispering in her ear. As Jorge drew up beside him, Diego turned. "I should be more careful next time. Maybe choose one of the older horses who won't stray so far."

"What do you mean next time?"

Diego tethered the mare to his horse. "You prefer chopping wood and cleaning up pig shit?"

"No, but..."

"Don't worry; I'll wait a little before we do it again."

"Two months at least, promise."

Diego laughed as he climbed back into his saddle. "If you insist."

* * *

The two boys got a good scolding from their mother when they returned home. Then Miguel boxed their ears and sent them to bed without any dinner, promising further punishment in the morning. Inez was more relieved than angry by the time she saw the two dirty shadows approach the fire. *Miguel is always too hard on them*, she thought, *especially Diego*. She promised her sister in her prayers that she would raise Diego as her own, and that is what she did. But the truth was that Miguel never really got along with her sister, and had little respect for her sister's husband, especially after he left so suddenly.

"You are too soft on them," said Miguel when she returned to the fire after bringing the boys some *empañadas* and making Diego swear to behave.

"They need to eat. And why do you think Diego does it? Well?" She continued without giving her husband a chance to reply. "Ever since you told him we weren't his true parents, he has been doing everything he can to prove himself to you."

Miguel looked up. "What are you talking about? I told him what he needed to know. He's a man now."

"He was only sixteen, and for the last year he has doubled his work around this place, trying everything to please you."

Miguel poked the fire. "I don't see what you mean. I told the boy he would still inherit half the farm."

Inez placed her fists on her hips. There was no use talking to Miguel when he was in a mood like this. Stubborn as a *burro*, and smells even worse, her sister used to joke. He always closed in on himself when she brought up the subject, but she could never forget what he had done to Diego that day.

In the beginning, Miguel had been full of love for Diego, thankful that God had blessed their union with a child, even if it wasn't strictly their own. But almost a year later, when Jorge was born, Miguel grew cold toward Diego. It still shocked her to recall what Miguel had said to Diego that day a year ago, or rather the way he said it. She always knew Diego had to be told, but surely not like that. She had held him for hours afterward, as he cried for the mother he could never know and the father he would never meet; it broke her heart. Her face grew stony remembering, and Inez turned away and left her husband by the fire.

A Storm Hits Valparaíso

***

Later that night, Jorge and Diego were lying awake when Miguel entered their room, carrying a brazier. The glowing embers illuminated his face, and Jorge could see that he was still angry.

Diego sat up. "Papa, please don't punish Jorge. It's all my fault. I let out the horses, I convinced him to keep quiet about it."

Miguel grabbed Diego by the arm. "I want you to stop this. I am sick of you getting *my* son into trouble."

Jorge winced at his father's words and wished there were something he could do. Diego spent the night unsuccessfully stifling sobs.

***

Two weeks later, Jorge was shaken awake from a deep but dreamless sleep. He sat up, wiping the sleep from his eyes with the back of his hands. "Before you start, I don't care what you say, we are not letting a horse out tonight. You promised, remember?"

Diego waved away his objections. "It's not that. I have something special to show you. Or at least, I was going to." Diego pouted playfully. "I'm not so sure now."

"All right then."

The two boys slipped on their boots and overcoats and tiptoed out into the yard. At the large beech tree on the far side of the *campo*, Diego stopped. "Close your eyes."

"What?"

"Just close them, Jorge."

"Good. Now, I know it was your sixteenth birthday last month, and I didn't give you a gift."

"Is that what you woke me to tell me? I knew that already," said Jorge, still annoyed at being pulled from bed.

"No, you fool. I want to give you your present."

After scrabbling through the undergrowth, Diego removed a piece of tattered cloth. He unwrapped it. Inside was a knife, its sharp blade glistening in the moonlight. "*Feliz cumpleaños.*"

17

Jorge turned the knife over in his hand. "It's so heavy ... it's beautiful."

The two boys stood in silence for a moment before Jorge sat down with his back to the trunk of the tree. Only half listening to Diego babble on about some story he had heard, Jorge thought about his brother. *Cousin*, he corrected himself, silently. It didn't seem right that Diego wasn't his brother anymore. Diego had been his brother his whole life; someone can't just take that away. He knew it must be even harder for Diego; he had lost a lot more. Slowly, a plan formed. Jorge looked at Diego and then at the knife. "Do you remember the traveler who came by during the harvest?"

Diego's face lit up. "Of course! How could I forget? Why?"

Jorge splayed his left hand. "Did you see his scar? While you and Papa were cleaning his horse, he told me about it."

"He said it was a burn."

"It wasn't. He told me he and his friend made a pact when they were young, and they sealed it by cutting their hands and mixing their blood. It means they are friends for life. Brothers. Blood brothers."

Diego eyed the knife. "But we are already brothers."

"Not real ones," said Jorge, a little too quickly. "Sorry, I didn't mean that. Listen, being blood brothers is more important and it's forever. Come on, let's do it?"

"I don't know. I'm not sure. How ... I mean ... do I cut myself or do I cut you and you cut me?"

Jorge handed the knife to Diego. "Don't worry. Just make a small cut here. We only need to mix a little bit—it still counts."

Diego trembled as he held Jorge's left hand. "Don't blame me if it hurts."

"I won't. Just be quick."

Jorge winced as Diego drew the blade across his palm. "Diego, give me your hand. Hurry! We have to do it before all the blood drips away. Come on. It's not that bad."

Diego handed him the knife and held out his left hand, closing his eyes. He stifled a shout as he felt the cool metal slice his skin. When he opened his eyes, Jorge was beaming at him. Pressing their palms together, they both felt the warm, sticky blood mingling, binding their fate together.

4: The Haunting Eyes of Robado Vivaldo

Zé had heard stories of the *quilombos* all his life: hushed tales around the fire, history passed in whisper, victories sung in secret, defeats silently mourned. In Brazil, there were only two roads to freedom for a slave—meeting your slave price with stolen or borrowed gold, or the *quilombo*. Death of the master only brought freedom for a lucky few; most slaves were passed down the family tree like a pocket-watch.

The slave-owners had tried to spread stories that all the uprisings had been quelled, all the runaways returned to chains or dead. But everyone knew the *quilombos* were still out there, existing as tiny communities of runaway slaves who lived in secret in the *sertão*, the vast, barren Brazilian interior. Many *quilombos* survived for only a few months before having to move on. Most slaves lasted only a few years before they were captured or killed. But most would take a few years of freedom over a lifetime in chains. That's why the price on Zé's head was so high—escaped slaves had to be recaptured and returned so the others couldn't dream, so the others would accept their place in the great scheme of things, their role in keeping sugar prices low for whites—that, and because of the blood on his hands.

Zé had been on the run for three nights now, making his way inland under the cover of darkness. By day, he lay as still as possible, waiting for the sun to set. Every time he closed his eyes, he saw the face of the man he had killed, for Robado Vivaldo would not let him sleep; those cold, dead eyes haunted him. Instead, he inhabited the eerie twilight of the insomniac—tracing the sun's slow progress in a sweeping arc across the sky, counting the seconds, minutes and hours until he would be hidden by the cloak of night and free to move again. They would still be looking for him when the sun went down, but at least he would be harder to find. He knew they would be looking for him, because there was a price on his head.

Most men have a vague notion of their own worth. Some count it in property, some count it in chickens, yet others in good deeds done or worse deeds avoided. Zé knew he was worth six hundred and seventy-six *mil-reais*. At least he *was*, before he killed Robado Vivaldo. It might be double now; an escaped slave was worth a lot more, but only when caught.

That was the price of his freedom: a price he could never afford. And now, he was here. Free, but trapped. Imprisoned by the glare of the sun and the watchful eyes of the slave catchers. He hadn't eaten in three days. Zé was used to going without food, but his strength was beginning to fail. Each night he made less progress, but he couldn't allow himself to lose hope, just as Robado Vivaldo wouldn't allow him to sleep.

Old Falcão's voice came to him again. *Follow the direction of the setting sun and keep going. Don't worry, they will find you before you find them. Only travel by night. Be careful, the slave catchers will be looking for you too.*

* * *

Zé woke with a start. The sun was high in the sky; he needed to hide, fast. He scanned his surroundings, spotting some brush in a gully not far to his left. Keeping low, he scurried toward it. Every snapped twig made him flinch as he eased under the foliage. As he lay down, a wave of nausea swept over him. Falcão's voice drifted back to him once more. *I will delay them as long as I can, but you have to leave, Zé. Now! If you don't, they will kill you. Go! Run! Stay off the roads and away from any villages. And stay out of sight. Go!*

Zé's shirt was torn, his back lacerated from the whip. He had cleaned the blood from his face and hands, but it still covered his clothes. And that face, he would never forget that face. He probably would have stood on that spot forever, still standing over the dead body of Robado Vivaldo, if his friend, old Falcão, had not grabbed him and broken the spell. When they came for him, he would have still been standing there, frozen by the awfulness of the act he committed.

Follow the setting sun... Falcão's words echoed in Zé's head like the voice of a spirit. *Keep to the edge of the field and then cut through the trees. I will delay them as long as I can.* Zé wondered what punishments were inflicted on Falcão for that act of kindness. He wondered what other crimes he would have to answer for when the time came. He stared at the deep cuts around his knuckles, made when he struck Robado Vivaldo over and over. The hands of a killer. Zé closed his eyes. He wanted to see the face of his victim again; he wanted to suffer.

Blessing himself, Zé asked God for forgiveness.

He got no response.

5: *El Desertor*

In the harbor of Cadiz, the crew of the HMS *Eagle* was becoming restless.

"Sir?" The First Officer approached the Captain, whose eyes were fixed on the dock. "What shall I tell the men?"

"Tell them to wait, as ordered." The Captain knew he was running out of excuses. "Just take care of it, will you."

"Sir, if I may, the men are beginning to talk. The Spanish authorities are starting to ask questions, and we're short on answers."

The Captain turned around. "What I am about to say must remain in the utmost confidence." The First Officer nodded. "When we docked on Tuesday night, an emissary of Sir Charles Stuart came to see me."

"The Crown's man in Cadiz?"

"Precisely. It was intimated that Sir Charles wishes to transport a special cargo—a passenger—to England. He should have arrived a couple of hours ago, but we were warned to wait at all costs."

"How will we know who it is?"

"I venture he will announce himself to us. Besides, he shall be carrying a letter bearing the seal of Lord Macduff."

"That means—"

"Exactly—it comes from the top. Now find a way to keep these men quiet. Tell the Spanish we found a hole in the hold or a rip in our sails. Tell them we lost a man overboard; even better, throw one over. That should delay things a bit."

The men had been away from home for more than a year and the Captain knew that any delay, especially this close to their return, was excruciating. He was in the midst of thinking up a further round of excuses when a carriage thundered down the dock. Leaping from the carriage even before it drew to a halt, a cloaked figure then hurried up the gangplank and handed the Captain a letter sealed in heavy red wax. The Captain brought the stranger into his cabin, away from the curious eyes of his crew, and opened the letter.

I'm afraid I must dispense with the usual pleasantries. As soon as you receive this letter, bring the man below deck. He is not a prisoner, but you must insist that he remains out of sight until you are out of Spanish waters. He is to be treated with the utmost courtesy. Please extend to him every comfort at your disposal. He is very important to us. I must insist that you do not enquire as to his identity. Further, I depend on you to dispose of this letter immediately, and in secrecy. Your esteemed friend, Lord Macduff.

The Captain grunted and immediately brought the stranger below deck, posting a guard outside his quarters. "No one is to enter or leave this cabin without my express permission," he instructed his First Officer before making his way to his own cabin, where he sat in his chair and began to tear the mysterious letter into ever smaller pieces. Above deck, the crew's confusion turned to joy as the order to cast-off was given.

* * *

Below deck, in his cabin, José de San Martín removed his long black cloak, and placed it on the chair beside the writing desk. At the washbasin, he cleaned the grime from his face, looked at his reflection, and mouthed one word: "Deserter." As Lieutenant Colonel in the Spanish Army, he had men shot for doing what he was doing tonight, but, unlike them, he wasn't running from a fight: he was running toward one.

San Martín reached into his cloak and removed a weather-beaten envelope. It had been given to him by Sir Charles Stuart, the British diplomat in Cadiz who had arranged his departure. Reaching for his dagger, he weighed the envelope in his hand before sliding the blade through the seal and removing the envelope's contents: a succession of letters, all penned by Lord Macduff. Scant light from the flickering candle barely illuminated the desk and San Martín had to strain his eyes to read them. There were letters of credit, entitling him to funds, and letters of introduction to various personages of note, intended to facilitate his introduction into London society. He held each of them over the candle, watching as they caught fire; he didn't plan on staying long in England. Throwing the burning letters out of the porthole, he watched the sea fall away beneath him as the ship skipped through the waves.

The lights of Cadiz were soon out of view. He would never see them again. Not unless he were caught, and then only to face a firing squad. Spain had been his home for twenty-six years and he had only distant memories of Argentina; he was just a small boy when his family emigrated.

San Martín felt a sudden pang of guilt; he would never see his father's grave again, nor would he ever again see his mother. She was ill in Galicia, being tended to by his sister. They weren't sure how long she had left. His three brothers were still in the service, but he told them all nothing, hoping ignorance would shield them from retribution.

He hoped they would understand.

San Martín sat down at the writing desk and reviewed his plans once more. He was satisfied. Once in London, he could organize passage to the land of his birth. Only then could he begin to fulfill his greatest dream: independence.

6: The Mountain That Eats Men

Once, Potosí was the center of the world—the merchant capital of América. The wealth generated by its silver mine was so vast that the rich had trouble spending it. They tried to squander it by dressing their slaves in Florentine satin. Bodyguards sported swords from Spain and daggers from Turkey. Scriveners scribbled on parchment from Genoa. The competing fragrances of spices from the Malay Peninsula filled the marketplace, where jewelers, masons, and weavers tempted the newly minted nobles with wares from faraway lands. But by August 1811, Potosí was cowering in the shadow of its past, no longer the richest nor the largest city in América.

The city's fortunes, like those of the miners, were tied to the dwindling mine. The *Cerro Rico* still yielded its precious metals, but grudgingly. More-enterprising merchants had long since left for Rio or Panama, and more-ambitious nobles had departed to Lima or Santiago. Potosí no longer provided a quarter of the Crown's revenue, but it provided enough, and the Spanish guarded it jealously. The Indians hadn't left; they couldn't. They were the fuel that powered the mine. Plucked from their villages to work as slaves, their families followed. Encamped on the southern base of the mountain, in a series of ramshackle huts that had sprung up to supply the mine, they waited and hoped.

Deep in the bowels of the *Cerro Rico* came a loud bang, followed by a deep rolling rumble. For the miners of Potosí, that meant only one thing. Pacha dropped his hammer and looked up. The low ceiling seemed to be shaking free from the gnarled wooden struts. Dust streamed into his eyes and choked the already thin air, but the roof was holding, for now.

"We have to get out of here." Pacha grabbed Chikan—who was on all fours, spitting incantations and blessings—by the neck. "*Pachamama* is awakening."

Moving as quickly as they could, they tried to keep to the rotted wooden slats of the track, all the while listening for the distant thunder of the ore-cart that could crush them without losing momentum. They scrambled up the first ladder, knowing their only chance of surviving a roof collapse was to get as high up as possible.

Pacha had been working in one of the most dangerous parts of the mine, the deepest tunnels. Three hundred years of intensive mining had bled most of the silver from Upper Perú, with thousands dying each year to feed the rapacious Spanish throne. Slaves imported from Africa couldn't cope with the extreme altitude and died in huge numbers before Spain turned to the natives. Pacha, like most Indians of his age, was taken from his village and forced to work in this pit of tears for six straight months. Six months without seeing his family, without breathing clean air. Six months without seeing the sun. The Spaniards' relentless thirst for precious metals pushed the Indians deeper and deeper into the mine. Those who survived the meager diet, the grim conditions, and the sadistic guards, were plagued with the fear that keeps all miners awake at night: a cave-in.

The few lucky enough to survive six months in the mines were haunted for the rest of their lives, knowing it was not skill, perseverance, or faith that spared them, but the whims of fortune. However, most of these men suffered the cruelest fate of all: the slow, coughing death that claimed the miners of Potosí. Before the silver ran out altogether, Potosí would claim eight million souls.

A Storm Hits Valparaíso

As he made his way upwards, Pacha knew something was afoot. The guards had disappeared; miners were streaming from adjacent tunnels. They had all heard the noise, but there was no word of a cave-in. As they approached the mouth of the mine, the group slowed, making the painful transition to the light they hadn't seen for months.

Pacha shielded his eyes, waiting for them to adjust, and kneeled down to pat the earth, murmuring a prayer. The city of Potosí spread out beneath him, in the shadow of the *Cerro Rico*, into which the mines had burrowed deep. Just below him, creeping up one side of the mountain, Pacha could make out the edges of the maze-like town that was home to the miners' families.

"Look!" Chikan grabbed his elbow and pointed southwest to where a large army was camped on the outskirts of the city. But Pacha's attention was drawn to the ramshackle buildings. His wife and only son were there. Pacha made his way down toward them, along with the other miners. As they approached, an anxious crowd intercepted them.

The children playing in street reveled in the commotion. Their faces bright, they ran toward the miners, tugging at their tattered clothing. Behind them were the hardened faces of the women: mothers calling the names of dead sons, wives searching the crowd for dead husbands. In the doorways, the old men sat, nodding greetings as Pacha passed, adding him to their short list of survivors. As he fought his way through the crowd, he saw his wife. Alone. No child at her hand. His chest tightened. He called her name and she turned.

"Pacha! You are alive!" She pressed her face against his, blackening herself with soot from the mountain that eats men. He kissed her and held her tighter, feeling his worry drain away, only to rise again immediately.

"Where is my son?"

"He's with my mother. He's safe. And he has gotten big. Big like his father."

* * *

The party that night was more like a wake. Each embrace was followed with furtive glances toward the widowed, the bereaved, and the orphaned. Pacha's head was spinning, and not just from the amount of *aguardiente* in his stomach. Yesterday he was a prisoner of the mine; today, he had his wife on his knee and his son at his feet. The bottle reached him again and he took another swig, passing it to his right. Everyone was talking about the army from the south that had run the Spanish from Potosí. Pacha went looking for Chikan, finding him in the middle of an argument with two of the older villagers.

"You want to turn your back on your people and go and fight for the *Kastillas*?"

"We should go and hear what they have to say. After all, we wouldn't have escaped the mine if it wasn't for them."

"We wouldn't be in the mine if it wasn't for them."

"Let's see what they have to say. It can't do any harm."

The argument continued, in circles, for most of the night.

* * *

The following day, Pacha stood with the others in the Plaza Antigua. They were all feeling ill effects from the night before, all except Chikan, who was snoring in the shadow of the fountain. Many had come simply out of curiosity. Everyone wanted to see the Indian who was fighting the *Kastillas'* war. Stories of the short-haired Quechua man in the strange uniform had brought a large, if somewhat bawdy, crowd.

There was a gasp as the man entered the square on a large black stallion. Swinging his feet out of stirrups polished brighter than any Potosí silver, he leapt from his saddle and handed the reins to a young boy, pressing a coin into his hand. A table was brought out from an adjoining building and the man climbed up, held both his hands aloft, and waited for the crowd to settle. Chikan woke with a start when the horse leaned over him to drink from the fountain.

At first, most of those gathered weren't paying much attention to what the man was saying in his strange accent. Instead, debate raged about how he might have received the long, curved scar that started under his right eye and stopped just short of the corner of his mouth. Then the man smiled and his scar and his mouth became one, giving him the lopsided grin of a lunatic. Everyone stopped talking immediately.

He was from the mountains far to the south—past the Salt Plains—and he told them his army had come to fight the *Kastillas*. He spoke of the battles they had already fought and of the many more they were yet to win. And he warned them the Spanish would be back, with more men and more guns. He pointed at the *Cerro Rico*, asking the crowd if they wanted to die in there. Then he asked them if they wanted to kill the men who had put them there.

"Are you willing to fight? Are you willing to stop the Spanish dragging us into the mines while they rape our wives and daughters? Will you join me and fight for our freedom?"

The crowd roared its assent.

7: The Prostitute

Catalina had been subjected to the same speech, in one form or another, since she arrived at her aunt's basement apartment. She bit her lip as her aunt continued. "I don't know what your father was thinking, having a young girl like you work in that dirty bar of his."

Catalina's father had given her a letter to deliver explaining her surprise appearance in Santiago. She doubted the embellishments were her father's, but her aunt needed little encouragement to find drama in the smallest of matters. Despite her initial reluctance, Catalina was excited. She hadn't seen Santiago since she was a child, and even today the city filled her with a sense of wonder. If she could escape the smothering attentions and haranguing tongue of her spinster aunt, she might even get to satisfy some of that curiosity.

"I'm not surprised there was trouble; I'm just shocked it took this long. You just be glad that you are here safe, with me." Concepcion de la Peña was two years older than Catalina's father and felt compelled to bring the superior wisdom these years bestowed on her into every interaction with her brother-in-law. She never approved of her late sister's choice of husband. She herself never would have been foolish enough to marry a tavern owner.

A Storm Hits Valparaíso

Indeed, she never married at all, although whether this was because of the shadow of a lost love on her heart, or a natural extension of her piety, no one knew, or dared to ask.

Rather than seeing this situation as an imposition or obligation, Concepcion saw it as an opportunity: a chance to undo the malevolent influence of that depraved drinkers' den. She could see Catalina was headstrong and liable to get herself in trouble without direction or guidance; she decided to keep her close.

Catalina sensed it was best to go along with the batty old woman, to keep her mouth shut and gain her aunt's trust. So, for the first four days at least, she bit her tongue, clenched her jaw, and tested her restraint like never before. Days were filled with lectures on knitting, sewing, darning, embroidery, comportment, manners, etiquette, and religious affairs.

Her patience was rewarded on Tuesday morning. A lady on the second floor went into labor; Concepcion was called in to assist. Catalina was given money and sent to the church around the corner to ask the priest to say a mass for the health of the mother and of the child she was bringing into the world.

As Catalina raced down the street, she realized that, for the first time since her arrival in Santiago, she was outside, alone, without her meddlesome aunt. Shielding her face—as if anonymity would protect her from the sin of her deceit—she hurried past the church. She spent the day wandering the wide streets, which were decorated with independence banners; exploring the crowded plazas of the city; and ignoring the cat-calls of the soldiers guarding the municipal buildings. Remembering, with some guilt, the lady giving birth, she lit a candle in the Iglesia San Francisco. As the sun set, Catalina began to retrace her steps but soon got lost amid the darkening streets. It was quite late when she eventually found her aunt's apartment, well past the time her aunt turned in for the night.

Catalina let herself in the unlocked door, praying she wouldn't have to deal with her aunt until the morning. Her hope was dashed when she saw Concepcion sitting in her rocking chair, knitting, with a steaming jug of coffee at her ankles.

"Sit down, Catalina." Her aunt didn't even drop a stitch. "As I am sure you are aware, your father asked me to take care of you, keep an eye on you, make sure you were safe."

"I know. I'm sorry. I got lost."

"You got lost?" Concepcion paused. "The church is just around the corner."

"Yes I know, but after mass I decided to take a walk. It was so stuffy in that old church. Before I knew it, I had wandered too far."

"So you went to mass."

"Yes."

"What was the sermon about?"

Catalina was caught off guard; her face colored. "One of the parables."

"Which one?" Concepcion paused in her knitting for the first time and looked directly at her niece.

Catalina held her aunt's stare. "The one where Jesus forgave a sinner."

Concepcion stood, knocking over the jug of coffee. "Liar! You didn't go to church. I went down there. Father Vasquez said he hadn't seen you since last Sunday."

"No, I didn't."

"Where did you go then?"

"None of your business."

"How dare you! I take you into my care, feed you, and look after you, and this is how you treat me? You go wandering this town of tramps and thieves and gypsies, leaving me here worrying all night—worrying about how I am going to tell your father you were walking the streets like a painted lady, or that you were found dead in an alley."

"What am I supposed to do? You keep me like a prisoner here. You never give me a second alone."

"All I want is what's best for you, Catalina."

"No you don't. You want to turn me into you, closeted away in the dark. You sit here in your room and knit and pray. I want to be out there! I want to live. Not stay in here with you and grow old and die. Alone."

Catalina stopped and looked at her aunt. Concepcion had drawn back within herself, suddenly old and frail, shocked by the vitriol in her niece's outburst. Catalina attempted to apologize, but Concepcion waved her away and walked slowly out of the room.

A Storm Hits Valparaíso

Catalina realized she couldn't stay there any longer. She wouldn't be able to leave for Valparaíso until tomorrow, but if her aunt's resolve hardened before dawn she might wake to find a bolt across her door. Despite her fear of venturing out at night alone, she packed quickly, deciding to go back toward the main plaza, hoping to find a boarding house that would take her in at this late hour.

* * *

The clerk looked up as she cleared her throat. "Yes? How can I help you?"

"I need a room—clean, quiet and cheap."

"Certainly. We have a vacancy. But let me make something clear. First, no trouble, or you'll be out. No excuses. Second, money up front."

Catalina counted out the required coins and slid them across the desk.

"There's one last thing: I get ten percent."

"Ten percent of what?"

"Your takings." The clerk looked at her knowingly.

"I have no idea what you're talking about."

"Of course you don't." He smiled. "Look, it's ten percent or no room. Are we clear?"

Catalina resented the insinuation, but she was at breaking point. This was the third boarding house she had tried. Blood was splattered all over the corridors in the first. In the second, the manager had tried to fondle her after letting her into the room. "Very well, ten percent," she said, just to keep him happy. "Give me the key. I can find my own way."

Her room was at the end of a dark, foul-smelling corridor. Placing the lamp the clerk had given her on the bedside table, she sat down on the bed and looked around. The room was bare, apart from a cracked mirror on the opposite wall. Catalina walked to the window and opened it, letting the chaos of Santiago wash over her. Closing her eyes, she took a deep breath.

"Close that mouth, *chica*, or I'll give you something to chew on!" A group of drunken young men down on the street were staring and whistling at her.

33

"In your state, you would have trouble finding your little *pito*." She crooked a little finger at them and smiled, and they went on their way, somewhat deflated by her acerbic reply.

As she closed the window, Catalina heard noises from the room next door. Raised voices. A fight. Something smashing. A scream, and then nothing. A door slammed and Catalina heard someone stomping down the corridor away from her, punching blameless doors. A man's voice shouted curses until silence descended, punctuated only by the staccato sobs of a woman.

"Hello? Are you all right?" Catalina called through the wall. The only response was a low, keening moan.

Catalina opened her door and checked the corridor. It was clear. She went to the door next to hers and knocked.

"*Bastardo!*" said the voice behind the door. "You got your money. Leave me alone!"

"I'm sorry. I just wanted to see if you're all right."

No response.

"Please, my name is Catalina. I'm from the room next door. I just wanted to check if you needed help."

"One moment."

The woman took so long to open the door that Catalina began to wonder if she was going to at all. When she did, Catalina understood why. She had been badly beaten. Her face was bruised, her right eye was cut and swollen, and her lip was bleeding heavily. She wore a low-cut blue dress, which had been torn, and her right arm hung limply at her side.

Catalina had seen enough bar fights to know what to do. She sat the woman down on the edge of the bed and brought the lamp up to her face to take a closer look at her wounds. Despite the cuts and bruises, and despite being ten years older than Catalina, the woman was stunning. She began to speak, but Catalina interrupted her. "Let me stop the bleeding and then we can talk."

Ripping the bed-sheet into several small pieces, Catalina gave the woman a strip to hold against her burst lip and began cleaning the woman's wounds, dabbing at the drying blood around her swollen right eye. "You are going to have a few nasty bruises, but aside from that, you should be fine. What's your name?"

"Teresa. Thank you for doing this."

"It looks like you got a bad beating."

"I'll be all right, as long as he doesn't come back to finish the job." She winced as she dabbed at her lip again.

"Well, as soon as I get you cleaned up, I'm taking you to my room, in case that *bruto* returns."

Teresa nodded. Catalina finished dressing her wounds and led her out the door. In the corridor, Teresa hesitated, but Catalina calmed her and brought her into the room where she sat on Catalina's bed and took a deep breath.

"I knew he was trouble." Teresa was fighting back tears. "But it was getting late." She dabbed her lip again with the makeshift cloth. "He was drunk. Stank of *aguardiente*. And he seemed nervous, shifty." Pausing, Teresa put the cloth down and Catalina took her hand. "There was something off about him. He wanted to do something I charge a little extra for." Her voice trembled. "He didn't have the money for it, so I told him no."

"Then he started to cry." She looked up at Catalina. "Can you believe that? Told me it was the only thing he liked. I told him to find the money or it wasn't going to happen. Then he hit me." Her hand flew to her swollen, blue-black jaw. "So I called him a *maricón*." Teresa attempted a smile, wincing as her cut re-opened. "That may have been a mistake." Glancing at her bruised face in the broken mirror opposite, she shook her head and said, "Now I won't be able to work for at least a week. I didn't used to have to go with such *culos*. I used to be better than this. I used to laugh at the girls who had to work these dumps." She looked at Catalina. "I'm sorry. I didn't mean anything by that..."

Catalina cut her off with a nervous laugh. "No, no, I'm only spending the night here before I return to Valparaíso tomorrow. I had a fight with my aunt and had to leave."

"Do you have family there?"

"My father."

"You're lucky. I have no one. At the start I didn't care—I didn't need anyone. I had it all." Teresa attempted another smile. "Money, jewelry, masked balls, high society, well-paying clients. Men with connections. Men who couldn't treat me too badly because they didn't need the scandal."

"What happened?"

"Ha! I shouldn't laugh, but I still do. It was Carnaval. All the top army men and high-ranking bureaucrats, the cream of Santiago society, gathered in the Captain-General's palace for the night. All the wives and girlfriends had been banished. It was one hell of a party. I was the main attraction, the centerpiece. Six strong, handsome Indians, naked to the waist, carried me above them on a giant salver. I was the feast, trussed like a pig on a shining plate of Potosí silver. The Captain-General wanted the first bite. I was only tied loosely, more for show than anything, so I propped myself up on my elbows as he was undoing his pants. I wanted to see the most powerful *pito* in Chile. Then he took it out, and I laughed! My God, I have never seen a smaller one—thin too, like a worm."

Catalina laughed too, partly out of shock at what she was hearing.

Teresa continued. "Well, that did it for me. I'm lucky one of the officers took pity on me before the Captain-General killed me. I've never seen anyone so angry. I still think it was worth it, even if I have to work the streets for the rest of my life. Those *bastardos* are so pompous."

When Teresa eventually dozed off, Catalina rose from the bed and went to the window, staring out into the darkness until her eyes became heavy. With the lamp blown out, she lay down beside Teresa. Sleep overcame her almost instantly. The next morning, when she woke, Teresa was gone.

8: The Flight of Diego

As winter began to bite, the snow capping the Andean peaks spread to the foothills below. This season was a time of survival, nothing more: animals had to be slaughtered or buried, paths cleared, and food rationed. Outside, the only light piercing the black cloak of winter was the faint glow of a waxing moon. But inside their simple mud-brick home, Inez and her family were huddled around the light and warmth of a small fire. A wisp of smoke escaped from a small hole that served as a chimney, and a stooped entranceway kept out the worst of the weather. Inez, well wrapped in several blankets, lay on her side, coughing.

"Diego, come here," Miguel, his tone urgent, beckoned. "Take my horse and go to the doctor's house. Bring him here as quick as you can."

Frightened, Diego did not bother responding, instead hurrying to saddle the horse. Inez had been sick for several days, but today her condition had deteriorated. No matter how many blankets they wrapped her in, or how many cups of *mate* they gave her, she still complained of the cold—when she was conscious. The rest of the time she slept fitfully, her body hot with fever.

Miguel was worried. He would have fetched the doctor himself, but he feared his wife might die in his absence. He wanted Jorge nearby in case Inez passed away before help arrived. The doctor was far away and always busy at this time of year.

"Keep dabbing her face." Miguel handed a cloth to Jorge. "And don't let that water boil over. I'll be back in a moment."

Outside, Diego was mounting his horse. Miguel checked the girth strap, tightening the cinch. "Hurry," he said, slapping the horse's flank. "We don't have much time."

The light was poor and the snow more than a foot deep, but Indio was a good horse and Diego knew the ground well; he set off at a gallop. A slow trail of smoke rose from a distant farmhouse further down the valley, where horses huddled together for warmth against the building. Diego tugged sharply on the reins to keep Indio going straight, but he was only half paying attention; his thoughts were occupied by his mother's condition. She was usually the first up, but this morning she had not risen at all. They had carried her to the fire, but even then she had shivered.

He slowed Indio at the top of the hill and frantically scanned his surroundings, trying to decide which route would be quickest. Then it came to him—the brook! He could jump that, easy. He wheeled the horse around and pressed on back down the hill.

As the brook came into view, Diego spurred Indio on. The horse gathered speed. Crouching low and gathering the reins together, Diego pressed his thighs firmly against the saddle, feeling Indio's powerful haunches bunch beneath him.

They jumped.

Indio's hooves hit the soft snow on other side—hard. The horse buckled and fell, sliding into the icy brook. Diego was thrown clear, his head breaking his fall just before the rest of his body slammed into the snow. He could feel its wetness begin to eat its way through his clothes. Groaning, Diego brought his hand up toward his sodden face and brushed his eyes clear. His head was spinning and parts of his body were alternately aching and numb. Behind him, the horse let out an unnatural scream. Diego struggled to his feet but fell once more, crying out as he landed on his swollen left wrist. He propped himself up on one knee. The world began to steady itself. Wrist throbbing, he hobbled toward his stricken horse, which thrashed in the snow.

The horse was kneeling on its forelegs, struggling to get up; one of its back legs was twisted uselessly beneath it, clearly broken. Diego put his arms around Indio's neck and his tears soaked into the horse's tangled mane. He knew what to do. Removing his knife from his belt, he whispered an apology before slicing Indio's throat. Indio kicked and screamed as Diego held him down; the steaming blood ate through the snow like acid. Diego cleaned the blade and replaced it on his belt, apologizing to Indio a final time before covering the horse's head with the saddle blanket.

The doctor's house was still a few hours ride away, much longer on foot, and Diego knew it would be quicker to go back and get another horse. Something glinted on the ground—one of the stirrups, with the strap still attached. It must have snapped when he fell, allowing him to be thrown free. If it hadn't broken, he realized, Indio probably would have been crushed him, and they would have both frozen to death. Picking up the stirrup, he fashioned it into a sling for his wrist. Then, holding his left arm for support, he began running toward home, following the bank of the brook.

*　*　*

Two hours later, Diego burst through the door. He was just catching his breath when he saw the blanket drawn over his mother's face.

"Where's the doctor?" asked Miguel, his face ashen.

"Not ... here," said Diego, between gasps. "I fell ... had to come back."

Miguel stood up, dropping the cloth he held. "I give you this one thing to do. One thing. And you can't do it right. *Idiota.*" Miguel noticed the blood on his clothes. "What's this, eh?" He squared up to Diego.

"Papa, wait..." said Jorge.

"I was jumping the brook," said Diego, "I don't know what happened. Indio fell. I think he broke his leg. I had to—"

Miguel slapped him across the face. "You stupid boy! What were you thinking?"

"It's not my fault." Diego untied the stirrup from his shoulder. "The strap broke. I was thrown."

Miguel snatched the stirrup from Diego's hands and shoved him against the wall. "*Bastardo*. I should never have trusted you." He shoved him again.

"Leave him alone," cried Jorge.

"Keep out of this!" Miguel shoved Diego once more.

"It's not my fault."

"Stop saying that, or by God I will—"

"But it's not my—"

Miguel whipped Diego across the face with the stirrup, cutting him on the cheek. "*Bastardo*."

Trying to block Miguel's blows, Diego fell backward, cowering against the wall.

"Papa stop, please stop. Papa, please." Jorge threw himself on his father, grabbing his arms and pulling him off Diego.

"Get out." Miguel dropped the stirrup. "I never want to see you again." He grabbed Diego by the shoulders and shook him. "Do you hear me?" His lips were flecked with spittle as he yelled, "Get out!"

"Papa, no!" cried Jorge.

"Now, Diego. Leave!"

Diego stood against the wall, his cheek bleeding, his whole body shaking. He looked at Miguel, then at Jorge, and walked out the door, into the night.

9: The Trial of Admiral Gambier

The *Naval Chronicle*, August 3rd, 1809.

Today witnessed a most extraordinary decision at the end of an unprecedented and lengthy court martial aboard the HMS Gladiator. *The case principally involved one of the most distinguished officers of the Royal Navy, Lord Admiral John James Gambier. The protagonist was the Radical M.P. for the City of Westminster, and Captain of the Royal Navy, Lord Thomas Cochrane.*

Lord Gambier was acquitted of all charges relating to accusations he had neglected to destroy the French Fleet at The Basque Roads when it was within his means to do so. This case was most unusual in that Lord Gambier had personally requested the court martial after Lord Cochrane recently protested a Motion of Thanks to Lord Gambier in the Commons. This Motion was proposed after the Navy dealt a crushing blow to Napoleon's forces at The Basque Roads in the Bay of Biscay, causing weeks of repairs to the French Fleet and untold damage to the confidence of Bonaparte's sailors.

In his speech against the Motion, Lord Cochrane opposed it on the grounds that Lord Gambier had "not only done nothing to merit a vote of thanks, but has neglected to destroy the French Fleet when it was clearly within his power to do so." Lord Gambier requested that this allegation be the basis of the court martial he submitted himself to.

He had claimed his reputation was being besmirched by his colleague's repeated questioning of his actions during the engagement at The Basque Roads.

Lord Cochrane complained Lord Gambier had failed to press home his advantage.

In detail, the allegations were thus: Lord Cochrane alleged that, after he had blown apart the boom protecting the French Fleet, Gambier failed to follow with an attack on these ships, many of which had run aground. Lord Cochrane contended that Gambier failed to respond to his repeated requests to send ships to assist him in engaging the French in any meaningful way. Lord Cochrane claimed that the French could have been easily destroyed had he been given the requisite support. He further argued that the failure to do so constituted a dereliction of duty on Lord Gambier's part and that he had unnecessarily put the lives of British sailors at risk, and indeed Britain's soldiers and citizens, by unnecessarily prolonging the war. Lord Cochrane took particular exception that the Motion of Thanks was being proposed in the House of Commons to a man who, he felt, had done nothing but hinder the operation's successful conclusion.

After eight days of testimony and evidence, the court decided the following:

"Having heard the evidence produced in support of the charge, and by the said Right Honorable Lord Gambier in his defense, and what his Lordship had to allege in support thereof; and, having maturely and deliberately weighed and considered the whole, the court is of opinion that the charge has not been proved against the said Admiral, the Right Honorable Lord Gambier; but that his Lordship's conduct on that occasion, as well as his general conduct and proceedings as Commander-in-Chief of the Channel Fleet in The Basque Roads, between the 17th day of March and the 29th day of April, 1809, was marked by zeal, judgment, ability, and an anxious attention to the welfare of His Majesty's Service, and doth adjudge him to be most honorably acquitted. The said Admiral the Right Honorable Lord Gambier is hereby most honorably acquitted accordingly."

Lord Cochrane's future in the Royal Navy is now in some doubt. The allegations he made were most serious, and were proved to be utterly unfounded. Lord Gambier is not without friends nor influence, and will no doubt seek to prevent Lord Cochrane from bringing any further disgrace to himself or his fellow seamen. At the time of writing, it has been confirmed that Lord Cochrane has been stripped of the command of his ship, the HMS Imperieuse, and has been struck from the Navy List.

10: The Quilombo

Zé heard a twig snap behind him. He whirled around. Two figures emerged from the shadows and walked slowly toward him.

"*Tranquilo, amigo.*" The smaller of the two showed his outstretched palms. "We mean you no harm. We're here to help."

"Are you all right?" the taller one asked. "There's blood all over your shirt."

Zé could make out the slave-mark on the man's forehead, the scar glistening in the moonlight. "I'm fine. It's not my blood."

"Not yours?" The tall man locked eyes with him.

Zé held his stare. "No."

"I'm César," said the smaller man, breaking the tension, "and this is Ignacio. Here, have some water."

"I'm Zé," he said between gulps. "How did you find me?"

"We weren't looking for you. We were following them—the catchers. We guessed they were hunting someone. No one gets within half a day's walk of the camp without us knowing. We have to be careful." Ignacio turned to César. "*Vamos.*"

The camp consisted of eight or nine simple huts but had the feel of permanency. César brought Zé some fresh clothes. He changed and joined César and Ignacio in the small clearing between the huts.

"How long has all of this been here?"

"Almost four years," said César with pride.

"We had to move from our last camp because we weren't careful," Ignacio said, handing Zé a bowl of rice and beans. "But we are now. We take turns making sure no one gets too close. We were watching you for several hours."

"How did you get out?" César said.

Zé finished his mouthful and looked away. In the last few hours he hadn't thought about Robado Vivaldo and the life he vanquished. "I escaped from a sugar plantation near Olinda."

"How?"

"I took my chance."

"Whose blood was on your clothes?" asked Ignacio.

Zé put down his bowl and swallowed. "Robado Vivaldo, my master." Zé paused. "I killed him."

Ignacio shook his head. They finished their meal in silence before Zé excused himself and collapsed on the offered bed.

When he woke a few hours later, Zé couldn't move his arms or legs; he was tied fast. He struggled against his bindings but it was no use, they were too tight. His eyes began adjusting to the darkness and he heard voices, arguing. Then the voices stopped and the door opened. Ignacio and César entered.

"Zé, I'm sorry, but you have to go back," said Ignacio. César stood to his left, shifting uncomfortably.

"Why have you done this? Why am I tied up?"

"You must go back," insisted Ignacio. "You are too dangerous. They will be looking for you. They won't stop. We can't risk them discovering the camp."

"You tricked me!"

"We had no choice. If we kept you here, you would put everyone's life in danger. You must understand that."

"They will kill me. Please!"

"We are taking you to a man who will bring you to Salvador. There, if you admit to your crimes, they might be lenient."

"Might? You are sending me to my death!"

"We have to protect our people. I'm sorry. We leave tomorrow." César and Ignacio left Zé to the darkness of the room and the bleakness of his thoughts.

* * *

"Keep moving," said Ignacio, pushing Zé ahead of him on the path as they left the camp. A small boy waved from a doorway as they passed. Zé, his hands tied behind his back, could only nod glumly in response.

They spent the next few hours walking west. When the sun began to set in front of them, they turned and headed south, walking all night and breaking only briefly before moving on. Zé was grateful when the sky began to lighten and they had to stop and find somewhere to hide. César and Ignacio took turns watching him throughout the day, sleeping in shifts, waiting for the sun to set. Zé sat with his hands bound behind his back, staring into the distance. He was still awake when César took his place for the second shift. After some time, César spoke. "I'm sorry about this, I wish we didn't have to do it."

"You don't have to do it. You can let me go."

"No, I can't. When they took me in, I agreed to live by their rules. I can't break their trust. They saved my life. And now, I have a child."

"That was your son waving?"

"Yes. He's two. Born here in the *quilombo*, free."

"So was I," said Zé, "a long way from here."

"You mean you were taken across?"

Zé nodded.

"Was it bad? How did they catch you?"

Zé flinched.

Noticing, César said, "Sorry about all the questions. It's just, well, I was born here. My father, he never talked about it. Then, when we escaped..." César kicked a loose stone. "I never saw him again. He said he would tell me when we were free. But now he's dead. Dead or recaptured."

They both fell silent. After a moment, Zé spoke. "Untie me."

César looked over to where Ignacio was sleeping.

"If you want to hear my story, untie me," Zé pleaded.

César thought for a moment, took a dagger from his belt and cut the bindings, and then sat down opposite Zé.

"I was fourteen, I think, when they took me." Zé rubbed at his scar, the slave-mark over his heart. "They came by day and took us from our hut—me, my father, my mother, and my sister. My father tried to resist, but he was knocked to the ground. I don't know what happened to my mother and my sister. We were separated. They carried us to another village in large nets. Many of us were beaten. Two of the men with me didn't make it. Then we traveled on foot for many days, with little food or water. When we reached the sea, they took us to a large stone building. That's when they put us in chains—the chains I wore until three days ago. We waited days, weeks I think, locked in a dark room with many others—thirty or forty, all chained to the walls and the floor. Never let out, not even if we were sick, not even to go to the toilet. At least half of the men in that room were carried out dead." Zé stopped, shaking.

"Here." César handed him a leather canteen.

Zé took a drink and continued. "One day, we were all taken outside. It was difficult to see what was happening; my eyes were stinging from the sun. We were stripped naked and doused with water. Then we were led toward the ship. To the right was a long line of men, heads bowed; to the left, women were being stripped and washed. I looked for my mother and my sister, but couldn't see them. Then I reached the ship. They began chaining us together by our arms and legs, and then they took us down into the darkness where we were chained to the floor, crammed into a space not big enough to sit up in. Above me was another row of people, and above them, more. And the rats..." Zé shuddered.

"So many died during the journey." Zé leaned back on his elbows, disturbing a small rock. "We didn't get fed every day. When we did, I had to fight the men I was chained to for scraps of food." He shifted backward a little, carefully moving his right hand behind him, feeling for the rock. "If you were sick, you didn't get fed. If you were really sick, they threw you overboard; that was how my father died." His fingers grazed the hardness of stone. It was the right size. All he had to do was wait.

"A man chained to me also died that way. There wasn't enough room to unchain prisoners below deck, so all eight of us were dragged up on deck so they could remove the chain linking us and throw him off. We were forced to watch as they pushed him over the side."

César leaned back against a tree trunk.

"I didn't see the sunlight again for many weeks," Zé continued. "When I did, we had arrived. They washed us and gave us our first proper meal in months." Zé picked up the rock. It was the right weight. He could smash César's face into the tree before César even knew what was happening. "Next, we were taken in groups of five or six to be sold. Some rich man prodded my muscles and inspected my teeth, measured me with his hands. He never once looked me in the eye." Behind his back, the hand holding the rock trembled as Zé lifted the rock, clutching it tightly. "He was my new master." With a cry, Zé dropped the rock, his whole body shaking. "It's his mark I will wear on my chest until I die," Zé said, kicking the rock away.

* * *

César leaned over Ignacio. "*Amigo*, are you awake?"

He didn't move.

Satisfied, César moved over to where Zé was sleeping. Putting his hand across Zé's mouth, he shook him awake. Zé opened his eyes.

"Shhh." César put a finger across his lips and quietly led him away.

"What are you doing?"

"I'm letting you go," he said. Before Zé could respond, César raised his hands and continued. "I have to do this. For me, for my son. If I don't, I'm no better than the slave catchers."

"I don't know what to say."

"You should keep going—to Salvador. Ignacio would not believe you'd head in that direction. You can get on a ship and get out of here."

"I'm not getting on a boat, never again."

"Listen—"

"I'm not doing it."

"Come on, Zé, think. You can't go back to the camp, you will die if you try to stay out here on your own, and you certainly can't stay in Salvador. Getting a ship is your only option. Creep on at night, stay hidden for as long as possible. It's your only chance."

"There has to be another way."

"This is your only chance. Think!"

Zé nodded. "Thank you, César. I'll never forget this."

11: The Field of the Dead

South of Potosí, by the Desaguadero River, Pacha had been drifting in and out of consciousness for several hours. The periods of oblivion were a relief, respite from the searing pain in his back where he had been sliced by an enemy bayonet.

It was dark when he finally came to, although the full moon gave him more light than he wished for and illuminated the bodies all around him—pale, twisted, rotting corpses of soldiers from both sides. All were united now in death. Some faces were frozen in pain, and he could read the final blow in their countenance; others were more serene, as if content they could mumble a final prayer before being vanquished. Most still had their eyes open and seemed to implore him to explain the inexplicable. But they all stank.

The battle had begun at daybreak. Pacha and the rest of his detachment had marched forward with nervous excitement. Some had seen action before, but many more were new recruits like Pacha and Chikan, men with barely a month's training under their belts and who were completely unprepared for the horror that was about to unfold. Pacha's unit was pinned down from the beginning. The Spanish, with their heavy guns, led the Argentines into a trap and slowly picked them off. Pacha's commander realized the only option was to charge the higher ground and attempt to capture or destroy the Spanish artillery; they died in waves. The Argentine forces were completely routed, beating such a hasty retreat that they were unable to collect their injured and bury their dead.

* * *

Pacha tried to lift his battered body up, but it was no use. He could barely move his arms, let alone prop up his torso. He lay still, trying to gather some strength. Occasionally, a groan would rise out of the sea of dead, but Pacha didn't call out, not knowing if it issued from friend or foe. He had heard what happened to Spanish prisoners. If lucky, it meant a quick death; the other possibilities didn't bear thinking about. Instead, Pacha stared at the corpses, charting their decomposition between blackouts.

Just when he thought about trying to move again, he heard voices: two men were picking their way across the field of bodies, collecting weapons, ammunition, and whatever else they could find, and occasionally kicking and prodding the piles of corpses. Pacha kept his head down, viewing the procession through half-closed eyes. One mumbling shadow was dispatched with a dagger thrust. They came closer.

"This one's still breathing," said the first.

"Kill him," said the second.

Another shadow was finished off. Pacha shut his eyes and slowed his breathing. He could hear their boots squelching in mud thick with the blood and entrails of the fallen. He opened the slit of one eye. Something flickered right in front of him. Four feet away, an enemy corpse opened its eyes and looked directly at him. Closing his eyes again, Pacha held his breath. He heard a moan. The injured man was trying to give him up. If he were seen, Pacha would surely go the way of the others.

The two scavenging soldiers come closer, close enough that he could hear them breathing. Pacha's lungs were burning, the air in his chest expanding, pushing out against his rib cage. He couldn't hold it in any longer. He carefully exhaled through his nose.

"Hello? Can you hear me?" asked the first soldier.

A Storm Hits Valparaíso

"He's alive," said the second.

"He looks all right. Let's get him out of here."

"Grab his legs."

The injured Spaniard moaned louder. Pacha dared to open his eyes again, just a little. The soldier was trying to lift his arm, trying to point at Pacha!

"I think he's trying to say something. What is it?"

He moaned again.

Pacha's heart was beating so loudly he was afraid the two soldiers could hear it.

"Don't worry, we'll get you fixed you up."

Pacha struggled to hold his breath as the soldiers' voices grew fainter and he heard them stumbling and tripping through the field of the dead. When their voices became distant, Pacha allowed himself a few deep breaths and opened his eyes. They were gone. Despite the occasional moan of the dying and the ever-intensifying smell of the dead, Pacha eventually drifted off to sleep.

He awoke with cracked lips and a dry throat. Some of his strength had returned, but he was slow to use it. As soon as he opened his eyes he was horrified by what he saw—death worsening with time. It was just him. Him and the dead. That field would stay with him for the rest of his days. He would remember it when he was sad and when he was happy, and every time he sought the silent refuge of sleep it would be there, waiting to ambush him in the night and torment him anew.

Knowing he wouldn't survive another night on the battlefield, he lifted his head up slowly, stifling a moan, and scanned his surroundings. Supporting himself on a discarded rifle, he finally got to his feet, a little unsteady at first. He checked the faces of the men around him to see if any of them used to be Chikan.

Then he began walking.

12: A Call To Arms

San Martín arrived in London in December 1811 carrying just a small suitcase; twenty years in the Spanish Army had trained him to travel light. In his nondescript lodgings near Regent's Park, he unpacked his only possessions: a change of clothes, a small wooden box, an old book, a figurine, and the well-worn letter his mother had written just after his father's death. A knock on the door interrupted his thoughts.

"Can I get you anything, Sir? Some food, perhaps?"

"Summon a carriage. I'll be leaving shortly." San Martín picked up the figurine. General Solano: his mentor. He'd had the likeness carved in Cadiz, to remind him of the man he had come to consider a friend—to remind him of the tragic consequences of making the wrong decision. He sighed as a knock on the door announced the arrival of his hackney.

The driver pulled up at 58 Grafton Way, the Palladian home of estranged Venezuelan poet Andrés Bello, but also the meeting point for a group of exiles plotting the liberation of América. A servant led San Martín upstairs, took his overcoat, and ushered him into the reception room, where he was pleased to see a blazing fire fending off London's bitter December cold. San Martín was introduced to Bello, and three fellow Argentines: Manuel Moreno, Tomás Guido, and Carlos de Alvear, all of whom greeted him warmly. His reputation as a brilliant military commander had preceded him, and he was the highest-ranking officer to desert from Spain thus far.

"Lieutenant-Colonel, we are so glad you could join us," said Bello, inviting him to sit.

"Please, call me José."

"Very well. It's good to see you made it safely, José." Bello indicated an empty chair. "Please sit."

The servant returned with a decanter and placed glasses in front of each man. When the wine was poured, Bello dismissed the servant, stood, and raised his glass. "To our esteemed compatriot, José de San Martín."

San Martín stood. "To América." He had been to such meetings before, in Cadiz, but they had involved a lot more suspicion and intrigue, the penalty for treason against the Spanish throne being death. Here, however, one was able to speak freely, without fear. The thought warmed him, and he felt his cheeks flush.

Carlos de Alvear walked to the center of the room. "In November last year, Argentine forces struck at the monetary heart of the Spanish Empire, seizing the mines of Upper Perú. After they won the Battle of Suipacha, town after town welcomed them: Cochabamba, Oruro, and most importantly, Potosí."

San Martín examined the grim faces of the others. Bad news was coming. Alvear continued. "A few months ago, a large Spanish force was dispatched from Lima. The Royalists defeated the Argentine army at Huaqui on the Desaguadero River. Our Patriots were forced to retreat to Argentina, suffering terrible losses. All previous gains have been reversed. I believe Andrés has news from Venezuela."

Andrés Bello stood. San Martín knew little about him, but gathered he had some connection with one of the leading Venezuelan revolutionaries: Simon Bolívar.

"The news from Venezuela is mixed, I'm afraid." Bello placed his glass on the table. "The revolution is under threat, and a counter-revolution is underway in some cities. The population's support seems evenly split between the Patriots and the Royalists.

The political situation is extremely turbulent." He paused. "And, a Spanish attack is considered imminent. The government the Patriots installed had to extend significant self-rule to each city to win their support, but Bolívar warns certain cities cannot be relied upon when the inevitable Spanish invasion comes."

Ignoring the murmuring among the group, Bello continued. "As you know, since Chile declared its independence last year the country has been in turmoil. There have been coups and counter-coups. Various factions are vying for control. There is also the possibility that some of them will side with the Spanish should it prove advantageous."

"I am sure Spain will attempt to exploit these weaknesses when the reprisal comes," agreed San Martín.

"And that is expected soon enough," said Alvear. "Now that the Royalist forces from Lima have beaten back our invasion of Upper Perú, they will soon turn their attentions to Chile and Venezuela."

"After that, they will be free to put down the insurrection in Argentina," said San Martín.

"Yes. And the war will be lost."

"This is why I think we must wait for British help." Andrés Bello interrupted. "Without regiments of experienced troops, we cannot hope to succeed."

"The British are too bogged down in the war with Napoleon," said Alvear.

"Then we should turn our attention to the Americans. They have expressed an interest in exclusive trading rights with the colonies."

San Martín wasn't a particularly tall man, but when he stood his military bearing commanded everyone's attention. "Gentlemen, each of us has but one dream in our hearts: the liberation of América. To free our people from their colonial masters. While we sit here talking, people are fighting, and dying, for freedom across our continent. You talk about waiting for British or American help, I say no!"

San Martín looked around the room. A strong gust of wind rattled the sash windows. "You want to exchange the shackles of one master for another? We are standing in the house where

Miranda waited ten years for promised British help before giving up and returning to Venezuela with Bolívar to fight." San Martín put down his glass. "While the Spanish and French are committing troops to fighting each other, now is the time to claim our freedom. It's the perfect time to strike."

He could see them nodding. He was winning them over. "The people of Buenos Aires showed an appetite for the fight when they repelled the British four years ago. Let us not waste ten more years talking and waiting. Let us go now and fight, and win, a country of our own."

San Martín paused. They were smiling now. "It has already begun, gentlemen. We can either sit here in our comfortable surroundings, or we can go and fight, standing shoulder to shoulder with our brothers to win our freedom."

San Martín lowered his voice. "There is a ship leaving in three weeks for Buenos Aires, the *George Canning*. I'm taking it. When I arrive in Buenos Aires, I will pledge my allegiance and my sword to the revolutionary government. Who is with me?"

13: Death in the Andes

Sitting on a fence in the foothills of the Andes, Jorge stared at the fallen snow. Only yesterday, Miguel had cast Diego out of the house, and Jorge was wondering if his brother were ever going to return. He had tried to speak to Miguel about it, but his father just ignored him. Jorge could not focus on Diego without also thinking of his mother. Both his mother and his brother gone. Tears welled, but he forced them back with some difficulty as Miguel emerged from the house and stood in front of him, silent.

They had buried Inez together, her corpse wrapped in a white sheet. They hadn't called a priest. Jorge had asked Miguel about it, but his father just walked outside and grabbed his shovel. When Miguel tried to dig, his spade skipped against the icy earth. Jorge, seeing his father's struggles, helped him break the frozen ground with a pick axe. They dug together—grieved together—the incessant snow mocking their efforts, filling the hole quicker than they could work. Even when no longer able to dig, his father refused to rest, instead aimlessly scooping snow out of the grave with his shaking hands.

Eventually, Jorge broke through the hard, icy crust. Shin deep in the hole he stood, holding his cup of steaming *mate*, letting its heat burn his skin and warm his bones. Finally, when the grave was finished, they placed a blanket over the hole and secured it with rocks to prevent the snow from filling it in. It was as if they had done this a thousand times before. They buried Inez the next day, silently, like strangers.

The months that followed were difficult. Death's hand had enveloped the farm, squeezing all life out of it. It was as if time had stopped. Miguel had become withdrawn and had begun struggling with work. He had trouble getting in and out of his saddle, which meant Jorge had to accompany him wherever he went. Miguel's pride refused to acknowledge Jorge's presence, so his son became his silent shadow, picking him up when he fell over, tying knots he had forgotten, and carrying him to bed when he passed out beside the fire with a bottle of *aguardiente* gripped in his hand.

The few people who visited after Inez's death could not lift the gloom from the house. A thin layer of sorrow settled like dust over their lives, but still Jorge went about his work. Dying animals had to be slaughtered, horses had to be fed, fences had to be repaired. The daily toll become too much for Miguel, beaten into submission by life and death, anger and guilt.

It soon became clear that Miguel would not make it through the winter. Each day he took another step toward the grave. His walk became stooped; his arms, weak. He began tilting his head forward, leaving his face permanently in shadow. It seemed he was giving up, little by little, with each passing day.

After he buried his father, Jorge decided he was unable to begin a new cycle of life on the foundation of so much death. As soon as spring came and the snows began to melt, he would sell the remaining animals, board up the house, and leave. On the day he set off for Tucuman, he knelt beside his parents' graves for a silent prayer. His duty done, Jorge took out the knife Diego had given him, walked around to the front of the house and carved his name on the door.

14: The Proctor and the Marshall

The post-chaise driver opened the door. "Lord Cochrane, gentlemen, we have arrived at Falmouth."

"Excellent work, young man." Cochrane descended from the carriage, reached into his pocket, and took out several coins. "This is what we agreed, and here is a little extra for making good time. Ensure these horses get a good rest before you head back. That was quite a clip you were going at."

"Thank you, sir, very generous of you. Thank you, gentlemen." He nodded at Cochrane's three companions as they emerged from the carriage. "I'll fetch your trunk."

"Smith, Jeffries, help the boy," Cochrane instructed.

The driver untied the ropes holding the luggage, which Smith and Jeffries offloaded to a waiting porter. When finished, the driver clambered back into his saddle, doffed his cap, cracked the reins, and trotted away.

"Now lads," said Cochrane, "let's find this boat."

"Sir?" said Lieutenant Bissel. "If you don't mind me asking, where are we going exactly?"

"The Mediterranean," said Cochrane, with a mischievous smile.

"But, Captain, sorry to keep pestering you. I thought you didn't have a command."

"You're right, Bissel. I don't." Cochrane was still smiling.

"Sir, you're not planning to..." Lieutenant Bissel lowered his voice "...you're not planning to steal one?"

"Don't worry, everything is above board. We will be traveling in my private yacht. Look, there she is, boys." Cochrane pointed at a small boat. "The *Julie*."

"Captain..."

"Bissel, look, all of you, come closer. Now listen, no more Captain, a plain sir will do, at least until we get aboard. I'm traveling as an M.P., not as an officer." Cochrane looked over the three men. "Bissel, you can be my Permanent Undersecretary." The other two smirked. "Smith and Jeffries, you can be his Parliamentary Assistants. When we're at sea, I'll explain the plan, but I want to get out of the harbor without any fuss. Understood?"

"Aye, Captain. I mean, yes, sir."

Cochrane took one cabin and retired for the night immediately. Bissel, Smith and Jeffries were to share the other, but stayed up on deck drinking rum, mulling over their last battle in The Basque Roads, and despairing at the subsequent court martial.

"We could have ended the war there and then, but Gambier was too afraid to get his hands dirty," insisted Smith, handing the bottle to his left.

Bissel took a swig. "The Captain had no chance at the trial. Half the judges were Gambier's friends."

"At least the public are on his side," said Smith.

"I wonder if he should have held his tongue." Jeffries took the bottle.

"The Captain would never do that," said Bissel. "And how is anything supposed to change if no one speaks up?"

"The newspapers have been clamoring for the Admiralty to give him another command, talking up his record," said Jeffries.

"I don't know if that will help," said Bissel.

Silence followed until Jeffries turned to Bissel, seeking to change the subject. "You've been with the Captain some time now, Lieutenant, you must have some stories."

59

"You can drop the Lieutenant for now." Bissel looked out to the horizon. "Captain Cochrane is the most able officer I've ever served under. That's part of the reason I've been holding out. I've been hoping he'd get another command so I could serve under him again."

"Go on," said Smith. "Tell us a story."

"All right." Bissel cleared his throat. "One time ... my word, it must be about ten years ago now. He was only twenty-four or twenty-five, but just as mad. It was his first command, a small brig, the *Speedy*. We'd taken damage from a Spanish frigate that wouldn't give up the chase. At night, we managed to give them the slip and pulled into a small cove, thinking the Captain was going to order some repairs. Instead, he had half the crew painting the ship."

"Painting?"

"Aye. We had a hole in the stern the size of an ox, but he wanted the ship painted like a Dutch neutral. After a few basic repairs, we hit the open sea, heading straight for Plymouth. Of course, the Spanish frigate appeared, bearing down on us and not even bothering with any grapeshot, knowing our guns can't trouble her."

"She was going to board you?"

"We had neutral colors, but they weren't taking any chances. When she got close, the Captain hoisted the yellow quarantine flag!"

The three men laughed.

Bissel slapped the table. "She couldn't turn around quick enough!"

"I'd say you got a few funny looks at Plymouth."

"Certainly did. He flew the Dutch flag the whole way in, to make sure we would have an escort, as he put it, 'like returning heroes.'"

"Go on, give us another, we still have half a bottle left."

Bissel smiled. "A few years later, the Captain was given the *Pallas*. Thirty-eight guns. A crew of over two hundred. And she must've been near seven hundred ton. They were good days. In a few weeks we'd taken prizes worth more than a hundred thousand pounds."

Smith let out a low whistle.

"But on our way home from the Azores we were surprised by three French ships. With their larger sails we knew they could catch up in an instant. It was a dark, heavy sea, a strong starboard wind—a storm rising, you see. The Captain piled on the sail, but then orders us to start tacking, slowing us down. Pretty soon, two of the French ships were within a half-mile either side; the third was a little further off. All of them were preparing to fire. The Captain gave the order: every sail on the *Pallas* was hauled down."

"Hauled down?" said Smith. "At that speed?"

"Wait." Bissel smiled. "At the same time, her helm was swung around to take her across the path of the storm."

"That could snap the ship in two!" said Smith.

"If we were any larger, it would have," said Bissel. "The French shot past. Our hull was creaking like it was going to rip apart. We hoisted sail again, quick smart, and sped off in the opposite direction at thirteen knots. Took the French several miles to change course; they were too big to pull that stunt."

"And you got clean away?" said Jeffries.

Bissel nodded. "Clean away."

"A hundred thousand pounds," said Smith laughing. "No wonder you're so loyal to the Captain."

"Well," said Bissel, "prizes aren't what they used to be."

"And that's the reason for this mission," said a voice from behind them. Cochrane had come up on deck. The men made to stand, but Cochrane waved them down. "I'm sorry for the subterfuge, but as will become clear, it was necessary. Now we are safely at sea, it's time to let you know where we are going: Malta."

"Malta?"

"This is a somewhat unorthodox mission and, as you may have guessed, not one sanctioned by the Admiralty, but you'll get full pay from my own pocket."

The men looked surprised.

"Let me explain. You may have noticed we haven't been getting our fair share of booty lately. And it's not just our crew; every sailor in the Navy will tell you the same thing. Some joke that it's just the Captain keeping more for himself, but I assure you my share is falling too."

"Why is that, sir?" asked Bissel.

"It's complicated, but the answer lies in Malta. You see, tradition declares that how we share the prizes we capture is arbitrated by a neutral party: the Prize Court in Malta, which is presided over by two men, the Marshall and the Proctor. I have information that something is amiss, that these men may be keeping an unfair portion of what is rightfully ours."

"How?" asked Bissel.

"Well, the Proctor and the Marshall both charge fees for deliberating on each case and for deciding the share each crewman gets. The problem is, their fees for consulting each other have risen sharply. It seems they find it harder and harder to agree, at a great cost to us and to every other seaman in Britain." Cochrane smiled. "I just want to convince them to get along a little better. Do I have your backing?"

"Aye, Captain."

* * *

Cochrane, wearing his full naval uniform, stood outside the Prize Court in Valetta, alone. There were several Naval vessels in harbor; Cochrane had sent Lieutenant Bissel to inform them of what he was doing, knowing he would have their support if anything went awry. As a precaution, he ordered Smith and Jeffries to stay close to the yacht in case he needed to leave in a hurry.

As he entered the reception of the Court, he saw a clerk standing behind a high counter and making notes in a ledger. Cochrane waited for a moment.

Without looking up, the clerk spoke. "Can I help you?"

"Perhaps. If you take your nose from that book."

The clerk looked up, a little embarrassed as he noticed the Captain's insignia. "Apologies, sir. How may I be of service?"

"I need to make an appointment to see the Marshall and the Proctor."

"Of course. The Marshall and the Proctor are meeting each other as we speak; that should take all day."

"It's a matter of some urgency.

"They should be free after lunch tomorrow. I'll make an appointment for you to see Mr. Jackson at two o'clock, and the Marshall at four o'clock."

Cochrane went to leave but turned back to the clerk. "I do apologize. I appear to have gotten mixed up. Can you give me those times again?"

"Of course. You are meeting the Proctor at two o'clock and, yes, Mr. Jackson at four o'clock."

"I thought I was meeting Mr. Jackson at two o'clock."

"You are."

"Forgive me. And at four o'clock?"

"Mr. Jackson also."

"Look, I need to see both the Proctor and the Marshall," said Cochrane, getting a little annoyed.

"Mr. Jackson *is* the Proctor *and* the Marshall."

"He holds both offices?"

"Yes," said the clerk, turning back to the ledger. "A suitable replacement for the late Marshall has not yet been found."

"And I suppose Mr. Jackson is in charge of finding this replacement."

"Well, he is the ranking official in the Prize Court."

"And he can't see me now because he is busy consulting himself?" Cochrane smiled. "Ingenious. Can you show me where his fees are displayed?"

"I'm not sure we have a copy of the fees here."

"A copy of the Prize Court's fees must be publicly displayed by Order of the House of Commons, of which I am a member. I demand to see it."

"I'm afraid it is under review."

"Is it now?" Cochrane raised an eyebrow.

"Yes. In fact, that is why they are meeting today."

"Let me make sure I've got this right. Mr. Jackson has called a meeting with himself to see if he is going to increase the amount he is charging himself for such meetings."

"If you want to put it like that, sir, but I assure you everything is above board."

"We shall see. Where is this meeting taking place?"

"I'm afraid I'm not aware," said the clerk.

"Where is Mr. Jackson's office?"

"Which one?"

"Either!" Cochrane thumped his fist on the desk. He noticed the clerk's eyes flicker to the large wooden doors to his right and moved toward the door.

"I'm afraid you cannot enter Mr. Jackson's office without his permission."

"Which one?" said Cochrane, smiling. He entered, shutting the door behind him before the clerk could scurry around from behind his desk. Grabbing a chair, he tilted it under the door-handle and looked around. He was in a short corridor with two doors leading off it and a smaller door at the very end. The first two doors led to offices, and a quick scan of both revealed little. The Proctor and the Marshall agreed on one thing: neatness. Cochrane couldn't find the list of charges anywhere. The only item of interest was a large scroll that seemed to contain a list of Mr. Jackson's charges on a recent case. Cochrane concealed it inside his breeches and then opened the last door. To his disappointment, it was just the lavatory. However, on the back of the door a piece of paper was pinned up: the list of fees. Stuffing it inside his shirt, Cochrane closed the door just as two guards burst into the corridor, followed by the clerk and a small, immaculately dressed man.

"That's him, Mr. Jackson," the clerk pointed at Cochrane, who was immediately restrained by the two guards.

"Captain Cochrane,"—Mr. Jackson approached him—"you have been found in contempt of court."

"Nonsense!" said Cochrane. "How could I have offended the court when it isn't even in session?"

"Take him away."

"Can I ask one thing, Mr. Jackson?"

The guards paused.

"Are you giving this order as the Proctor or the Marshall?"

Mr. Jackson stamped his foot. "Take him away!"

* * *

Cochrane heard footsteps approaching. Hurriedly taking the package passed through the small, barred window, he untied the makeshift rope from the iron bar and put it under his bed, along with the package, then grabbed the chair from on top of the bed and replaced it at the desk just as the door creaked open.

The guard entered the room, his lamp bouncing shadows on the walls on both sides of the cell. "Lord Cochrane, you are going to get me in trouble with all this behavior."

"I would never dream of it. Sorry if my stumbling around woke you. I couldn't find my chamber pot in the dark. I shall endeavor to be quieter."

"Lord Cochrane, I have even less interest in guarding you than you have in remaining in captivity. All I ask is that you play by the rules. Now, hand over the contraband."

Cochrane said nothing.

"Please, I don't want to subject you to the indignity of a search. Hand it over and the matter will be forgotten."

"Well, if you must know, it's merely a bottle of scotch I intended to share with you, so that we might civilize this unfortunate situation we find ourselves in."

"Let me see it."

Cochrane reached for the package under the bed, removed the wrapping, and handed it over.

The guard took a close look at the label. "This is indeed a fine bottle." He smiled. "I'll fetch some glasses."

Three hours later, the bottle of scotch was empty and the guard was asleep at his desk. Cochrane removed a loose brick from the wall and took out a hidden file. He worked as noiselessly as possible, fearful that the sawing would awaken his guard. For three nights now, Cochrane had been secretly filing away, but within a half-hour he was done. Taking his bedsheets, he tore them into long strips, tying them end-to-end. As he fastened his makeshift rope to the only bar that remained intact, he heard the guard awakening. This time, Cochrane couldn't hide his subterfuge. Tossing the rope out the window, he pulled himself through the gap in the bars.

A shout came from outside his cell. "Cochrane?"

He gave the rope a sharp tug. It seemed like it would hold his weight. Pressing the soles of his feet against the outside wall, he began lowering himself down.

Cochrane tried not to look down, knowing the drop was about twenty feet onto stone cobbles. The guard was shouting. It wouldn't be long before he called for help. Cochrane quickened his pace. Feeling the knots loosening as he made his way backward down the wall, Cochrane dropped the last eight feet onto the street and made for the harbor.

15: Madam Feliz's Gambling House

Tall, dark-skinned *mulatas*. Small girls who could out-drink the toughest fighter. Blonde girls with sad eyes and silent scars. They were all here for one purpose: to encourage the drinking men to gamble, to convince the gambling men to drink, and to tease all of the drinking gamblers and gambling drinkers into losing an hour of their time on one of Madam Feliz's sodden bedspreads. It was a rough place, loved by staff and patrons alike, but hated with equal passion by the wives and priests who couldn't compete with the watered-down drinks or the rigged roulette table.

Today was a special day: the first Saturday of spring, when farmers from the hamlets around Tucuman brought their animals to market. Special, too, because it was Diego's birthday and he was determined to have a good time. He was finished work for the day. The slop-buckets were empty. The filthy bedsheets had been changed. The blood had been wiped from the walls. Now his real job started.

At first, he felt bad about stealing. But things were different here. People didn't help each other, and when he had been hungry long enough, his moral objections had disappeared. Still, he restricted his targets to the wealthy. Diego took a certain pride in relieving the dandies, fops, and playboys of a small portion of their assets. In a sense, he felt he was correcting some kind of natural imbalance. Besides, he told himself, what he took would be a fraction of what they would waste in the gambling houses and brothels.

Diego got what he needed in the second tavern he passed through, spotting the man as soon as he walked in: tall and well-dressed, the crowd parted before him in sartorial deference. The man asked for wine and tobacco.

Diego waited.

Two ladies appeared at the man's side and introduced themselves.

Still Diego waited.

He waited until the wine had flushed the gentleman's cheeks, until the girls had begun to break his resistance. Then he saw his opportunity. One of the girls had draped herself around the man's neck, the other had unbuttoned his jacket. Diego crawled through the raucous crowd and paused at his target's feet. Within a minute, he was outside, one pocketbook richer, and running. Five minutes later, he was home.

Madam Feliz let him sleep in the cellar in exchange for menial tasks. Most days, he finished work before sunset and was free to wander the streets of Tucuman. Like most Spanish colonial towns, Tucuman was laid out in a straightforward grid of wide streets; however, Diego felt more comfortable in the side streets and shadows. These alleys enabled him to earn a living, to escape a pursuer and, sometimes, to find a place to be alone. Few residents braved these side streets, for Tucuman was a city like any other. It was inhabited by those in their fine dresses and jackets and horse-drawn carriages, and by urchins, pimps, thieves, and hookers. There were those who owned the city by day, and those who controlled it by night. One of the latter was Madam Feliz.

Diego had been just ten days in Tucuman when he met Madam Feliz in her basement. He had broken in to escape the cold, seeking somewhere dry to sleep away the night. Taking pity on the boy, and impressed that he hadn't helped himself to any of her stock, Madam Feliz offered him a job. Here, Diego had carved out a kind of life for himself. It was not what he imagined when he yearned to escape the mountains, but it wasn't altogether miserable. Besides, for someone with nimble fingers and quick feet, there was money to be made. With money, he could travel to Buenos Aires, Santiago, or Rio de Janeiro—maybe even Europe.

He often thought about Jorge. When spring broke, he combed the streets, searching for his brother's face in the crowds. On days like today, he would walk to the market, wondering if Jorge had made the trip down the mountain. He would mingle with the farmers, listening as they called out livestock prices and patting the horses as they stamped in their stalls. He would pity the mules their burden of produce, and would sit at the edge of the square until the last of the farmers left, lost in thoughts of Jorge, absently rubbing the scar on his left hand. After sunset, he would work the taverns of Tucuman, stealing pocketbooks, jewelry, watches, anything. Mostly, Diego kept to himself, turning in once his night's work was complete. But tonight he was celebrating. He was eighteen years old.

Madam Feliz's always amazed him. Never had he imagined such places existed. He loved watching the patrons around the roulette table. The careful ones would play only until their first win and then take a girl upstairs. The real addicts could win ten times on the trot, always letting it ride one last time until they invariably lost. They would usually try to talk one of the girls into doing it for free, which the girls sometimes put up with for a few minutes if they were bored.

He took a seat at the bar.

"Diego, how are you?" asked the barman, shaking hands.

Diego smiled. "It's my birthday, and I want a drink."

The barman smiled back. "The water pump in the square is working, no?"

"Come on, I want a real drink..."

"Just joking." The barman laughed as he pulled a bottle down from the shelf. "Let's see if this can put out some of that fire, eh?"

Diego took some coins out of his pocket, but the barman shook his head. "No charge, little man. *Feliz cumpleaños.*" He poured the clear liquid into Diego's glass.

69

Picking up the drink, Diego looked around. He was eighteen years old, he had money in his pocket and a drink in his hand, and from where he was sitting he could see at least seven girls in various states of undress. *I love this place*, he thought. Smiling, he took a sip then flinched as the *aguardiente* burned down his throat. In the corner, another patron leaned against the wall to vomit. Diego silently corrected himself: he loved this place at night, not in the morning when he walked into the aftermath.

"That's him!" The mark Diego had relieved of his money stood in the doorway with a group of policemen. "Him! At the bar—the boy."

Diego slipped off his stool and bolted for the back door. He heard a loud crash behind him as he slid out into the alleyway then sprinted away as fast as he could.

Several hours later, Diego crept back into the cellar. Madam Feliz found him there the following morning and woke him gently.

Diego sat up, rubbing his eyes. "I'm sorry, I didn't mean to cause trouble, to bring the police here."

"Diego, the police are always here." She smiled. "The problem is, this time they had their uniforms on."

"What happened?"

"Aside from all the customers running out, some of them leaving hefty bills, the police shut the place down and made such a mess."

"I'm sorry."

"They also took two of my girls: Esmeralda and Esperanza."

"What for?"

Madam Feliz snorted. "Do they need a reason? I got Esperanza out, but Esmeralda threw a drink in the policeman's face when you were making your escape."

"I'm sorry. I promise I'll never cause you problems again."

"I'm afraid it's not that simple."

"What do you mean?"

"That pocketbook you stole belonged to the son of a rich and powerful man. They know you work here. They said they would give me Esmeralda ... if I gave them you." Diego didn't know what to say. "Don't look so glum. I'm not playing their game. I've never let them push me around, and I'm not going to start

A Storm Hits Valparaíso

now—I'm too old." Madam Feliz took out her purse. "But you can't stay here; they'll be back. Take this money and go somewhere, away from here. Send me a message and I'll let you know when it's safe to return. These things usually blow over soon enough." She embraced him. "Now go, but be careful. They'll be looking for you."

Diego picked his way through the side streets and alleyways, keeping to the shadows cast by the rising sun. Block by block, he made his way down to the market, hoping to hide among the morning crowd while he came up with a plan.

"Thief, stop!"

Diego didn't turn around to see who had shouted; he didn't need to. Sprinting toward the market, a policeman hot on his heels, he turned and cut across the plaza, coming around the rear of the stalls. Looking back to see how close his pursuer was, he caught his foot on a loose cobble and crashed to the ground. He felt a boot on his neck.

"Don't move."

16: Everything Turns to Ash

Most merchants made the trip down to Valparaíso with a light load. They didn't always shift the goods they brought from Santiago, and they needed to leave as much room as possible for the imports that would sell well on their return to the capital. Despite the profit to be made, few were willing to make the journey. Recent political upheaval across Chile meant the road wasn't as well protected as before, and bandits needed little invitation to pounce. Merchants tended to travel in convoys, sharing the cost and protection of an armed escort.

It was in one such convoy that Catalina found herself. Sitting quietly as the convoy wound through the gentle foothills of the giant mountains that cut Chile off from the rest of the world, she kept a lookout for a glimpse of ocean. Ever since she was a small child, she was fascinated by it—so forbidding, yet so full of possibilities. It seemed limitless. Her father used to take her down to the harbor, reading aloud the exotic-sounding ports painted on the ships' hulls. As she grew older, she enjoyed viewing Valparaíso from above. Perched on one of the hills that encircled the bay, she would watch seagulls hover over the tiny fishing boats while the sunlight bounced off that endless ocean, reflecting onto nothing.

A Storm Hits Valparaíso

Some days, she would sit there until the sun was swallowed by the horizon, taking the heat of the day with it and leaving her to scurry down the hill toward the warmth of her father's bar.

The mood among the assorted merchants brightened as they crested the final hill and saw the port of Valparaíso shimmering below. The end of the journey was in sight. The return trip was a couple of days away, and there was plenty in Valparaíso to distract the merchants in between. There was relief, too, at reaching the sanctity of the town. Daylight assaults on convoys were becoming more common. During the trip Catalina had heard plenty of nervous talk about the trouble in the south spreading to Santiago. There were mixed feelings about the revolution. Many thought war would disrupt business, but others argued it could increase the opportunity for trade and that prices might rise if Spain lost its monopoly on trade with the Colonies. Almost all agreed, however, that any revolution was doomed to fail. The Chileans may as well have been an island race, for the Andes were as sure a barrier as any ocean and there simply weren't enough men willing or able to fight the inevitable Spanish invasion.

All such talk ended at the sight of the crescent-shaped bay of Valparaíso. Catalina had made the trip before, but the sight always caught her by surprise, as if she had reached the edge of the world. She knew she would be in trouble, remembering her father's explicit instructions; despite that, she was glad to be home. As they made their descent, the view of the town was swallowed up by the outlying buildings, and Catalina gathered her things. She disembarked at the main square, which was already crowded with traders cutting deals, forming alliances, and teaching the unwitting an expensive lesson. Dodging the crowds, she made her way inland from the seafront, down the adjacent thoroughfares, intending to cut back to the coast nearer the bar.

When Catalina turned the corner, she noticed something strange: a large crowd gathered outside her father's bar. She got closer. Heads turned. Then she saw why. A few blackened, warped wooden struts stood smoking in the embers of what should have been her home. All that was left was the charred frame of the bar, still smoldering. Crying out, Catalina dropped her bag and fell to her knees.

* * *

Doña Rozilda was one of those women who never seemed to do anything at all—that is, until there was a crisis, when she became the only one who seemed to know what needed to be done. When she saw Catalina helpless outside the bar, she moved into action. Picking the girl up, she led her to her house, two streets back from the waterfront. After bathing Catalina and helping her into fresh clothes, Doña Rozilda put her to bed with a cup of *mate*. It was only four o'clock, but she needed time to think and to plan the wake. Already she was besieged with requests for information about the funeral. Catalina needed to be away from all of that.

Doña Rozilda decided the wake would take place in her house; no one would object. An altar could be placed in the living room, and the kitchen could be used for entertaining and refreshments. The fire had been so fierce that there was no question of an open coffin, so she would not need to prepare for that.

The following day brought a string of demands. Priests had to be instructed, storytellers summoned, food prepared, relatives informed, black clothes dug from musty chests, and poor young Catalina had to be attended to. That was the easiest task of the lot. She never left the bed, lying there with her eyes open, unresponsive to any entreaty, only moving to accept a cup of *mate*.

Catalina was lying there impassively, true; but her mind was crawling all over itself with a thousand insidious thoughts. Anytime she thought about beginning to speak, her mind objected. What was the point? What could she say? Since seeing the ruined bar, her mind had closed in on itself. She was afraid. Afraid to speak. Afraid to move. But most of all, afraid to feel. She remembered falling to her knees outside the bar. Then she remembered feeling nothing at all. No sadness, no pain, no loss, but in its place a narcotic numbness. She was afraid to go downstairs and talk to all of these sad people, for she had no tears, or at least none she would allow herself to cry. She knew that if she started crying now, she might never stop.

A Storm Hits Valparaíso

On the morning of the second day, Doña Rozilda entered the room, placed a black dress and shawl on the bed, and gave sleeping Catalina a kiss on the forehead. She awoke with a start, gasping, and Doña Rozilda jumped back, shrieking. They both laughed, but stopped as soon as they started.

"I didn't mean to startle you, Catalina. I've left you some things. We leave in an hour."

* * *

Si en la hora de mi muerte. Catalina sat at the front of the small church as the prayers washed over her. *El Demonio me tentare.* Her father's body, in a coffin covered by a blanket of candles, was just behind her right shoulder. *Porqu'el día de la Cruz.* She stared at the large crucifix behind the altar. *Dije mil veces, Jesús.* Christ's eyes closed in pain; his mouth fixed open, as if in a scream; his hands torn from struggling against the nails; his face wet with red tears, blood from his crown of thorns.

Five of her father's customers shouldered the coffin, with the final place being taken by Sergeant Eduardo. No other relatives had arrived in time for the service; the trouble in the south was making travel impossible. The coffin was lowered into the grave. The priest said a few words. Then Catalina had to endure half the town's commiserations.

Later, back at the house, Catalina drifted off, lulled by the rhythmic hum of competing novenas. When she awoke, she finally had enough strength to join the funeral party downstairs. Silence greeted her when she entered the kitchen. Sensing her discomfort, Doña Rozilda leapt up and squeezed her hand, guiding her toward the food. The conversation began again, and Catalina felt the mourners' eyes turn from her. Well-meaning friends and customers sought her out, mumbling a sentence or two, not really knowing what to say, then shuffling away. From their platitudes and sympathies, a story emerged.

The night before Catalina's return had been a quiet one—normal enough, many said. About two hours before dawn, the call had gone out: the tavern was on fire. A chain of men passed endless buckets of water from the shore, but it was all they could do to stop the fire spreading. By sunrise, the fire was out, but the bar was gone, and Don Flores was dead. Everyone knew who was responsible, but there was nothing they could do. The murderers had already set sail for Lima.

Catalina stood and listened and nodded and waited while the minutes ticked by and she could leave again. When she could, she went upstairs to the room Doña Rozilda had provided for her and waited for it all to start again. Each day, the house played host to slightly less grief, and slightly more drinking. Catalina patiently waited for the end of the nine-day wake so that she herself could begin to mourn.

In the end, the wake took place as all wakes do—tears were shed, songs were sung, tales were told, and sleep was as rare as laughter. Catalina played the role of sorrowful daughter, but inside she felt nothing at all. She would save her tears for when no one could see them. The morning after the final day, Doña Rozilda shooed away the last of the hangers-on. Now that all the traditions had been observed, the last thing she wanted to do was turn her house into a surrogate home for patrons of the lost tavern. Catalina snapped out of her torpor the following day. On the first day, she cried. On the second, she raged. On the third, she lost the strength to be angry and cried some more. On the fourth, she grabbed the small bag containing her only surviving possessions and left the house without saying goodbye.

"You're leaving?"

She was walking down the street, toward the main square, when a voice called out to her. She turned to see Pedro Villar, keeping his distance.

"Yes." Catalina walked toward him. "There is nothing for me here now."

Pedro put his hands in his pockets then took them out again, folding his arms. "Where will you go?"

"Santiago." There was another pause. Catalina lifted her bag. "I must be going..."

"Wait." Pedro put his hand on her arm. Taking a small pouch from his pocket, he handed it to her. "It's not much, but you will need something to get you started."

Catalina shook her head. "Pedro, I can't."

A Storm Hits Valparaíso

"Please, take it." He pressed the small pouch into her hand and closed her fingers around it.

Catalina met his eyes. "I don't know what to say."

"Don't say anything, just go, and don't look back."

"Thank you."

"Remember, you always have a friend here in Valparaíso."

Leaning forward, Catalina kissed him softly on the lips. "I'll never forget you, Pedro Villar." Without another word she turned and left. She didn't look back.

Philosophers say that sadness and happiness can only be defined in opposition to each other. Like light and dark, one can be said to be the absence of the other. But in that moment, Pedro Villar felt sadder and happier than he had ever been—than he ever would be. He watched her walk the length of the street before she turned away from the shore. Pedro stood for a while after she disappeared, hoping that perhaps she would come back and say something else. Hoping, too, that he might taste once more the lips he would never touch again.

17: Jorge and the Gauchos

The market was quiet; Jorge was struggling to sell anything, giving him far too much time to think. He had already halved his prices but had no interested buyers. All the farmers were telling the same story. It had been a hard winter, prices were down, and everyone was worried they wouldn't make enough to buy seeds for the planting season.

The war was affecting business, they said. The northern merchants—from Salta and Jujuy—hadn't reappeared since before winter. Those from the south were afraid to come to Tucuman in case the fighting spread down into the city. The Argentine army had already retreated from Salta after its failed campaign in Upper Perú, and there were fears they were going to pull back as far as Cordoba, leaving the population of Tucuman at the mercy of the Spanish.

Some had already deserted the town. The few stragglers that had escaped the Spanish net around Salta had been spreading stories of retribution against those who supported the Patriots. Rumors of rape and torture by the Spanish were making people very uneasy. No one wanted to buy livestock in times of such uncertainty, especially not if the animals were going to be seized to

A Storm Hits Valparaíso

feed the enemy. Even after hearing all this, Jorge was determined not to return to the farm. He couldn't.

A few of the farmers packed up and left. Jorge considered doing the same, until one of the older farmers wandered over. "Not much luck today, eh?"

"No, Señor. Nothing."

"Me too. Would you like to join me for a cup of *mate*?"

"That's very kind of you, Señor." Jorge followed him across the square.

The old farmer poured out two cups, handing one to Jorge. "Say, I think I know your face. Where are you from?"

Jorge paused for a moment, a little uncomfortable. "A farm about a half-day's riding from Raco."

"Ah, the mountains. Some nice land up there, but hard work, I hear. Me, I'm from just outside the city, but I remember your face. I never forget a face. You've been here before, right?"

"Yes, Señor, with my father. Before..." He looked down, kicking the dirt.

"I'm sorry *joven* ... has he passed away?"

"Yes Señor, just recently."

"I'm sorry for your loss."

Jorge didn't know what to say, so he thanked the old farmer for the *mate*. "Señor, it doesn't look like I am going to sell anything today. I better start looking for somewhere to stay."

The old farmer leaned in close to him. "Hold on, you'll make your sale."

"What do you mean?"

The man looked around. "Keep this to yourself, yes?"

"You have my word."

"I'm only telling you this because you are on your own." He glanced at Jorge's scrawny, pitiful animals. "And you look like you could do with some help."

Jorge nodded.

"The only people doing any business at the moment are the army."

"The Spanish army?"

The old man shushed him. "No, no, our boys. An officer comes along toward the end of the day and buys up what he can—

79

soldiers need to be fed after all. That's why I'm telling you to wait. Now, you must keep this quiet. If everybody knew, and they all waited, you mightn't sell any of your sorry bunch. Usually, he comes when most of the others have gone so you will have a good chance of getting rid of what you have for a decent price."

Jorge thanked the old farmer for his advice and returned to his animals, and to scanning the crowd for his brother. He had looked for Diego all day, but he didn't even know if he was in Tucuman. Thinking of something, Jorge went back over to the old farmer.

"Señor, my brother is missing. I wondered if you might have seen him. Maybe you recognized him; sometimes he came here with my father." Jorge gave a short description of Diego.

The old man shook his head. "I'm sorry. I see so many people every day. I only recognized you because you were in front of me with the animals." Seeing the disappointment on Jorge's face, he said, "Why don't you tell me what happened."

Jorge took a deep breath then explained.

"How long ago was this ... when Diego left?"

"About three months ago, Señor."

"And he never came back in all that time?"

"No."

"You never heard from him again? A message? Nothing?"

Jorge shook his head.

The old farmer thought about this for a moment. "Well, I'm guessing he didn't have too much money, right?"

"No. Nothing."

"And if he had gotten a job in one of the farms around Raco, you would have heard something, right?"

Jorge nodded.

"Well, he must be here in Tucuman somewhere." The old farmer clicked his fingers. "Maybe with the army."

"The army?"

"*Claro*. The army is recruiting. He could have joined."

Jorge thought this over for a while.

"Say, what are you going to do when you sell all these animals?" the old farmer asked.

"I'm not sure."

A Storm Hits Valparaíso

"You should join the army! They need strong young men like you, especially if you can ride a horse. Maybe you will find your brother there. The pay is not so great, but you get fed, and somewhere to sleep."

"Maybe..."

"Look," said the old farmer, pointing. "Here is the officer I was talking about. I bet if you explain the situation, he'll buy all your animals just so you sign up." He laughed and clapped Jorge on the back.

Jorge walked back to his animals, dazed. *That crazy* viejo, he thought, *but maybe he's right*. The army officer walked around the market, prodding animals, haggling with farmers, and exchanging pleasantries. Then he stopped to talk to the old farmer. Jorge overheard him asking about the rumor of the army abandoning Tucuman and retreating to Cordoba. Jorge couldn't hear the reply—the officer spoke quietly—but the old man laughed in response. He pointed over at Jorge, and the officer sized him up before striding over.

Jorge signed up immediately. He had asked about Diego, but the officer told him he spent so much time in the storehouse and at the markets that he rarely got a chance to meet new recruits. But there was no work in Tucuman, especially for farmhands, he insisted. Everyone looking for a job was being sent to the army. The officer wished him luck, giving him a docket Jorge could redeem at the army camp the following day in payment for the livestock.

There was quite a commotion when Jorge arrived. Soldiers were marching in formation and hammering filled the air. Sleeping quarters were being erected, supplies were being delivered, and at the edge of all of this activity was a sea of white tents. He had never seen so many people in one place. Jorge was separated from the other recruits and put with the other *gauchos*, most of them from Salta. He guessed it was because he arrived on his horse, and they were *campesinos* like him. Talking to the *gauchos*, he realized there were people here from all over. The *comandante* was from Buenos Aires, the *capitán* from Catamarca. There were soldiers here from Cordoba, Rosario, Punta Gorda—everywhere.

The training was tough, but Jorge enjoyed it. He was learning to ride hard, in formation. The *capitán* would shout something, and they would have to change positions. Sometimes they would have to bank sharply to the left, pulling the reins as hard as possible while staying tightly together in formation. Other times, they would have to spread out in one thin line. The most difficult was when they had to scatter. When the command was given, the idea was for everyone to spread out in all directions and make for what the *capitán* called cover, which was really just the forest. Usually, this resulted in everyone bumping into each other and getting thrown.

The *capitán* was getting frustrated. He made them practice over and over again, even though everyone was tired and the horses were thirsty. One of the *gauchos*—whom everyone called Negrito because he had a black mark on his face like a giant freckle—suggested splitting everyone into groups of six and practicing first, before trying it all together. By the end of the second day, this seemed to work. The *capitán* was pleased. It got more difficult when the *capitán* began firing his *pistola* above their heads. Then, some of the men would drop down, clinging to their mounts, terrified. The horses liked it even less, some throwing their men and fleeing. Most of the horses got used to it eventually, but some had to be put with the pack mules. The horses considered this an affront, but still seemed to prefer it to the sound of gunfire. Eventually, the men grew braver, most not flinching when the guns were fired. Although, if any of them said they had gotten used to the sound, they were lying. No one ever does. When training finished for the day, Jorge would comb the camp, looking for Diego. He spoke to the *gauchos*, the officers, the stable boys, the soldiers, the musicians, the laundrywomen, the cooks and the *putas*, but nobody had heard of Diego from Raco.

One night, when he returned from one such search, the *gauchos* were excited. The *capitán* was happy with their progress. In appreciation, he had given them some fresh beef, which they cooked on a big fire to the side of the tents. Jorge had a drink of *aguardiente* and thought again of his family. Whenever his mother and father argued, Miguel would stay up late on his own. On a nice night, he would sit in the middle of a field, drinking a bottle and singing *campesino* songs, shouting at no one in particular. During winter, he sat around the fire, and his voice would carry in to where Jorge and Diego slept. When the singing stopped, Diego would sneak out and steal the bottle, trying to get Jorge to drink some. He tasted it once but spat it out straight away. It was disgusting. But Diego would force himself, sometimes even getting sick in their room. Jorge would take the bottle from his sleeping brother's fingers and put it back beside the fire, near Miguel's snores.

But tonight, the *aguardiente* tasted just fine. Plus, all of the others were drinking it and he was sick of being called *joven* and *chico*. He was a man now. He didn't drink that much, though; it made his head spin. Later, when the others were drunk, they tried to convince him to go to the *putas*. Jorge refused. But the next day, he listened when they talked about their exploits and argued over dice and cards.

The morning after the party, one of the *gauchos* still lay in bed when they were supposed to already be at training. Esteban was the hairiest man anyone had ever seen. Naturally, the others called him *El Lupo*, but never to his face. Most of the men were sick, but El Lupo was still snoring, his head the only part of his body he managed to get into his tent the night before. The *capitán* was furious, waving his arms and screaming and shouting, but still El Lupo snored.

This was how Jorge got promoted: he was the only man who could climb into his saddle on the first attempt that morning—many of the others were still drunk.

"Empires have been built on less," said the *capitán*.

That didn't fill Jorge with confidence, but neither did the taunts about what El Lupo would do when he woke up and saw the *joven* had taken his place. But they never found out; when they returned from training, El Lupo was gone.

The *capitán* called Jorge for a meeting. "*Joven*, training has been going well but I had to get rid of El Lupo. Don't worry. He has gone to another regiment. We can't throw out someone his size." The *capitán* laughed and slapped Jorge on the back. "But, *en serio*, there is a new *comandante* coming from Buenos Aires. He has sent word that we need more troops, and we have to find them wherever we can. Tomorrow you are coming with me to the jail."

"Sir?"

"I know! This *comandante* has some crazy ideas, but you know, maybe if these *hombres* are in for killing Spanish soldiers then they are just the kind of *hijos de putas* we need, eh?

18: The Stowaway

Zé sat at the first-floor window of an abandoned dockside building, waiting. He had been watching the ship all day. The stevedores were still loading goods on board, but it looked like they would be finished before long. As night fell, the loading ceased and the workers departed.

From his vantage point across the street, Zé examined the ship once more. The gangplank directly across from him connected the boat to the dock and was guarded by two men. A third man paced the deck above, occasionally calling down to the others. Zé had to get aboard before the ship left, but couldn't see how. The ship was moored with several stout-looking ropes, but there seemed to be no way to get to the gangplank or the ropes without being spotted.

Zé watched and waited. As night progressed, the guards began to relax. The pair guarding the gangplank shared a surreptitious drink and the guard on deck found somewhere to lie down. Zé's hopes were rising. If the other two dozed off, or passed out, he might be able to sneak past them or hoist himself up one of the mooring lines.

His thoughts were interrupted by someone approaching the guards. The figure was just out of sight, but the guard on deck appeared from his hiding place, and the other two were whistling and calling. It was a woman. Zé could see her now: a tall *mulata* walking toward the two guards, swinging her hips. He couldn't hear what she was saying, but he could guess.

Zé saw some money change hands and the *mulata* pointed across the street, directly to the building Zé was in! He began to pace, struggling to think. There was no way out. His only hope was that they wouldn't come upstairs. Zé resumed his position, seated at the window.

The guard reached the door and called back to his friend, "*Amigo*, call me if anyone comes."

"Don't worry, I'll tell them you've gone for a piss. Don't be long. I want my turn." The first guard laughed and pinched the *mulata* on the bottom, for which he received a playful slap in the face. Grabbing at her roughly, he kicked open the door and threw her inside.

Zé could hear them below, shouting at each other. If they came upstairs, he was done for. He loosened the catch on the window as quietly as possible. There was a crash downstairs and the *mulata* screamed. Zé looked out the window, seeing the remaining two guards dashing for the building. This was his chance. He opened the window and looked down. Two of the guards were inside, fighting with each other on the ground floor, but one of them remained in the doorway, repeatedly looking back toward the ship.

Only when the third guard dashed in to intervene did Zé climb out onto the window ledge and lower himself down. Hanging from the lip, he dropped down into the empty street. Stifling a groan, and hoping the fighting inside had drowned out the sound of his fall, Zé paused, his back against the wall just to the side of the door. He decided to take a chance. Bent low, he ran toward the ship and scurried up the gangplank, as light on his feet as speed would allow.

As he reached the deck, he heard the fight spill out onto the street. He threw himself to the ground to the right of the gangplank, out of sight of the guards. Stopping for a moment, catching his breath, he listened. The *mulata* had escaped while the guards were fighting, and now the first guard was trying to reclaim the price he had paid from the other two. From his vantage point, Zé could see a staircase leading down into the belly of the ship. The problem was, it was on the other side of the gangplank. He waited until the guards were all looking away before making his move. Crouching low, he darted to the other side then paused once more. The argument was dying down, and they hadn't spotted him, but it was only a matter of time before the third guard resumed his post on the deck. Zé crept down the stairs and was pitched into darkness.

He knew he wouldn't be safe until the ship was far from Salvador, so he settled in to a dry, quiet place between some bundles of sugarcane and a crate of coffee beans. Zé laughed. A ship took away his life; now a ship was giving it back to him. *Free again*, he thought, *but trapped again*. He shook his head. His hand reached for his slave-mark, the sign that would follow him for life, the sign that he was owned by another, branded like an animal. Without papers, he knew that if they docked in Brazil again he couldn't escape. But then again, they could be going anywhere, maybe even to Africa.

Zé shook his head, telling himself not to worry, but worrying was the only thing that kept him from darker thoughts. Thoughts of César, risking his own expulsion from the *quilombo*. Thoughts of old Falcão, who was probably beaten to death for covering his tracks while he escaped the sugar plantation. Thoughts of his family; he did not even know if they were dead or alive. And thoughts of Robado Vivaldo, the man he killed with his bare hands.

At the end of his first night at sea, Zé had mapped out his immediate surroundings and begun to learn the rhythms of the ship—the creaking of a sharp turn against the tide, the footfalls he must evade. Zé was careful, but eventually the crew began to separate his movements from the sounds of the night. On the third day at sea, he was woken with a sharp kick to the ribs and brought before the Master-at-Arms.

"What have we here then?" he said, looking Zé up and down.

"A stowaway, sir. Found him in the hold."

"What's your name, son? *Como se chama?*"

"Zé."

"Hmm. Runaway slave, I'm guessing."

Zé just stared, breathing heavily through his nostrils.

"Thought so. Well, you're in luck. We won't be stopping again until Buenos Aires." The Master-at-Arms waited for a response, but Zé was silent. "Not very talkative are we." He turned to one of the sailors. "Have you searched him?"

"Yes, sir. We found nothing. He doesn't appear to have stolen anything."

"Very well, Zé. We are putting you ashore at the next port. Until then, you earn your keep. Got it?" The Master-at-Arms waited again, but Zé didn't respond. "For God's sake! Bring me someone who speaks Portuguese!"

Another sailor was brought to translate. In responding, Zé got very animated. The Master-at-Arms quickly cut him off. "Enough! Now, translate this. I don't care who you are. All I know is that I've another mouth to feed, and three slack guards to discipline. Now, we are going to put you ashore at the next port: Buenos Aires. Until then, you work. We will feed you, but if you steal anything, you'll go overboard and you can swim home. That is, if you can swim. Got it?"

After all this was translated for him, Zé nodded.

"Any questions?" asked the translator.

"Where is Buenos Aires?"

The translator laughed, and then translated for the others, who laughed too.

"About three weeks south of here, depending on the weather," said the Master-at-Arms. "And it's not in Brazil if that's what you are worried about."

"What happens when I get to Buenos Aires?"

"Well that, my son, is up to you, or should I say, up to the port authorities. Now someone get him a mop, and for God's sake give him some food before he falls over."

19: María de los Remedios

As soon as he stepped off the *George Canning* at the port of Buenos Aires, San Martín was arrested and accused of treason and of being a spy in the service of the Spanish Empire. Despite the protests of his well-connected fellow passengers, he was immediately hauled away by soldiers.

After a short carriage ride from the docks, he was taken to the *Cabildo* where the soldiers handed him over to another set of guards. All of San Martín's entreaties were met with stony silence, but he noted that his weapon had not been taken. Bristling with rage, he was marched down a corridor and into a large room with a desk in the center. Behind the desk sat three men, who immediately stood and dismissed the guards.

"What is the meaning of this?" asked San Martín. "Yes, it is true. I was a Lieutenant-Colonel in the Spanish Army, as you well know. But, as I am sure you are also aware, I have deserted and have pledged my sword to the cause of liberty in Argentina—"

"If I may interrupt, Lieutenant-Colonel," said one of the men.

San Martín nodded.

"First of all, let me introduce myself. My name is Bernardino Rivadavia." He gestured to the man on his right. "This is Juan

Martín de Puerreydón, and on my left here is Feliciano Chiclana. Since we deposed the Viceroy, we are the Triumvirate in which the people have vested sovereignty until a formal declaration of independence can be made. I apologize for the commotion at the docks, and for the rough handling of the guards. It was necessary, for reasons that will become clear momentarily, if you will be kind enough to indulge me a little."

"Go on," said San Martín, his anger fading to curiosity.

Bernardino Rivadavia continued. "I would like to formally welcome you to Buenos Aires on behalf of the Triumvirate, and on behalf of the Argentine people. We are distinguished by the presence of such a decorated Lieutenant-Colonel in our midst, and we are well aware of your desertion from the Spanish Army and your efforts to contact us. Let me say that your bona fides are above reproach, and once again, I apologize for your arrest. As I have already said, it was necessary."

"Necessary," snapped San Martín. "You keep saying that, but I haven't heard an explanation yet."

"Your anger is understandable, Lieutenant-Colonel," Juan Martín de Puerreydón spoke up. "But you see, the *George Canning* returns to England in a few days, and we decided it would be advantageous to let the crew, and thus the British, believe you had been arrested."

"I see."

"So, if you don't mind, we are going to have to keep you out of sight until then. It will give us time to get acquainted and to discuss our plans. If you accept, Lieutenant-Colonel, we would like to recognize your rank from the Spanish Army and place you at the service of the Argentine people."

"Nothing would please me more," said San Martín, smiling.

"Excellent," said de Puerreydón.

"But I have a few conditions."

"Conditions?"

"Yes. But before I get to that, I will need a full update on the current situation."

"Have you been briefed at all?"

"The last I heard, the Army of the North's initial successes in Upper Perú had been completely reversed after the defeat at

Huaqui on the Desaguadero River. We had been forced back to Salta."

"There have been some developments. Please take a seat."

Feliciano Chiclana handed San Martín some papers. "The situation has deteriorated further. Please, read."

San Martín looked over the dispatches. The Army of the North had suffered further defeats, and morale was low. In addition, Spain was rumored to be sending an expeditionary force, twenty thousand troops to definitively quell the revolution and re-establish control over the colonies.

"Now that you have been appraised of the situation, could you give us your thoughts?"

"I can say this with absolute surety. Your military commanders are not without integrity, nor your men without spirit, but your methods are completely outdated."

"How do you mean?"

"Forgive me for being frank, but I believe this to be of the utmost importance, and time is of the essence."

"Go on."

"In your initial military successes, in the incursion into Upper Perú and so on, there were several factors in your favor." San Martín checked them off on his fingers. "Number one, the element of surprise. Number two, the freshness of your troops. Number three, the receptiveness of the local population to your cause."

"Agreed."

"Now, all of those factors are turning against you. The Spanish are no longer on the back foot and are well prepared against further attack. Your troops are depleted and the survivors weary, disheartened by recent losses. The people of Upper Perú are still on your side, but you need further successes to keep them there. If they see the war turning against you, they will switch sides to avoid retribution from the Spanish. The problem is, with each new battle, you are further out-manned, out-gunned, and crucially, out-thought."

"What do you propose?" asked Rivadavia.

"We will never beat the Spanish if we just march toward them and fight them in open battle. Even if we somehow manage to kill ten thousand of them, twenty thousand more will be stepping off a boat in Lima or Montevideo. We need to fight a new kind of war, and for that we need a new kind of soldier. I want to create a regiment of these soldiers, the likes of which have never been seen in América—cunning, ruthless, and most importantly, mobile. I want complete control, from the creation of the regiment to its deployment in battle. These are my conditions and the only circumstance under which I will accept command. I don't mean to be so forceful, but I submit to you that it is our only hope. With several of these regiments, we will beat the Spanish; I give you my word."

There was silence for a moment before Rivadavia spoke. "Lieutenant-Colonel, your proposal is intriguing, and I, for one, am interested. However, there is procedure to be followed, and we must discuss the matter further before we commit. We will be requesting further details."

"Of course." San Martín nodded.

"In the meantime, as I mentioned, we will have to keep you out of sight for a few days. You will be staying near the cathedral, at the home of Don Antonio de Escalada."

* * *

María de los Remedios de Escalada was sitting in her bedroom, brushing her hair and staring out the window, when she heard her name being called. She went to the door to find her mother hurrying toward her, a frantic look on her face. María knew that look.

"Start getting ready for lunch; we have a guest."

"Who is it? Not another suitor, I hope."

"I don't know who it is, but he must be important. Your father ordered everyone to be here, smartly dressed. I'm running around making all sorts of preparations."

"Jesúsa," María called her maid. "I have to get ready for lunch, mother says we have an important guest coming."

The maid hurried to the wardrobe, before turning back to María. "Another suitor?"

"Mother didn't say. I imagine so."

"Don't look so glum, you might actually like this one."

María groaned.

The maid selected a dress, smoothed it down, and then handed it to María. "You know, you are sixteen next month, and some of your friends already have a husband."

"I know."

"Your family only wants what's best for you. You know that."

"I know. I just wish ... oh, I don't know."

Just before one o'clock, her mother called her once more. After checking her reflection in the mirror, María left the bedroom.

"Ah, there she is." Her father gestured as she came down the staircase. "Don José," he said, turning to the man standing next to him, "allow me to present my daughter, María de los Remedios. María, this is Lieutenant-Colonel José de San Martín. He has just arrived from Europe and he will be staying with us for a few days."

María curtsied. "I am honored to meet you Lieutenant-Colonel." She offered her hand.

"The honor is all mine, Doña Remedios," said San Martín, lightly kissing her hand. "I must insist you call me José."

María blushed and then realized she was staring. She tried to think of something to break the awkward silence. "Don José, you are from Spain?"

"No. Actually, I was born here in Argentina—a small town called Yapeyú, in Corrientes province. My father was Governor there, but took my family to Spain when I was still a boy."

María's mother interrupted. "There will be plenty of time to talk over lunch. I'm sure the Lieutenant-Colonel would like to bathe after his long journey. Lieutenant-Colonel, let me show you to your room. I'll have someone bring your trunk."

María watched as he walked upstairs. An impressive figure, and those eyes: she couldn't decide if they were beautiful or not. Either way, they were unsettling.

When San Martín came back downstairs, Don Escalada noticed he was wincing.

"Are you all right? You seem to be in pain?"

"Oh, this is just an old wound. It plays up when I am inactive for too long. Three months on that small vessel didn't help. Don't worry, I have medication, but it is best taken before bed. I'll be fine."

"Was it from your time in the Spanish Army?" said Don Escalada's son, Manuel.

"Don't be rude, Manuel," Doña Escalada chided, ushering everyone toward the dining room. "Keep your questions for after the Lieutenant-Colonel has eaten."

"It's all right, Doña Escalada," said San Martín, sitting down, "and please, call me José, all of you. Yes, it was from my time in the Spanish Army, fighting Napoleon."

"I want to enlist," said Manuel, "and so does Mariano." He looked across the table at his brother.

"Very good," said San Martín. "It's a noble pursuit for a young man to serve his country, and Argentina will need the help of as many young men as possible."

María coughed, blushing when all eyes turned to her.

"Mother thinks I'm too young," admitted Mariano, as Doña Escalada shot him a warning glance.

"Some of your mother's fears are justified," said Don Escalada. "At the moment, the finances of our new country are in such a pitiable state we can't even afford a rifle for every man that enlists."

"Really?" San Martín put down his fork.

Don Escalada wiped his mouth with a linen napkin. "Frankly, yes. After we expelled the Viceroy and took control, Spain had no standing army in Argentina, just a militia force—local men. Naturally, they came over to our side straight away, but the militia's armory simply cannot cater for the numbers that have since enlisted. With our system of tax collection in such disarray, it's a problem that won't be quickly solved."

San Martín frowned. "That is unfortunate."

"What age were you when you joined the army?" Manuel asked.

"Young." San Martín's eyes met Doña Escalada's. "Perhaps too young. I was eleven when I joined as a cadet in the Murcia Regiment."

"Did you see any action?"

"Not for a year or so, not until I was sent to North Africa. After that I was mostly fighting the French."

"Were you ever taken prisoner?" Mariano stared at the Lieutenant–Colonel admiringly.

"Only once, thank God, by the British. Luckily, I was exchanged shortly afterwards for an English sailor."

"Enough questions, boys," Doña Escalada interrupted. "The food is getting cold."

Toward the end of the meal, María plucked up the courage to speak to him again. "Don José, do you miss your home town, Yapeyú? Do you plan to visit?"

"Yes, one day. Although, I'm not sure if I will get the opportunity for some time. Not until this war is over." He paused for a moment, as if struggling to recall something. "I was only six or seven when my family moved to Spain. In fact, we spent a couple of years here in Buenos Aires before my father transferred, so I was very young when I left Yapeyú." San Martín wiped his mouth. "I remember a wide, lazy river and lots of trees and flowers. And the heat! In my memories, the sun is always shining, even though I know it must have rained a lot. Just before we left, my father took me out into the forest. He was carrying a small wooden box and a shovel. We came to a clearing where he dug into the earth and filled the box with the soil of Yapeyú. My father instructed me to keep the box with me always so I would never forget where I was from."

"Do you still have it?" María asked.

"Yes. It's upstairs. I took it everywhere with me: Spain, Morocco, France, England, and now here. I'd like to go back to Yapeyú and see if I can find the spot. Maybe after the war. Maybe I'll settle down there."

María's mind drifted as she watched San Martín speak. He seemed far less stuffy when he got excited about something—like now. His eyes were shining, and her father liked him, she could tell.

"Tell us a story about Napoleon," Mariano pleaded.

"Well, did you know that he is very short?"

"Really?"

"Yes. He even needs to be helped into his saddle!"

Mariano laughed. "I don't believe you."

"Well, you should. I met him once. I had volunteered to serve as an infantry marine and was serving on a frigate that docked in Toulon in the south of France. He inspected our detachment. He stopped right in front of me, probably curious about my different uniform, and read out the name of my regiment from my jacket button. His head only came up to my chest!"

Don Escalada laughed along with the boys, and then stood. "That was a wonderful meal, my dear. Now you will have to excuse us, the Lieutenant-Colonel and I have some important business to discuss."

The two boys murmured complaints.

"Don't worry, you will get the chance to hear more war stories; the Lieutenant-Colonel will be staying with us for a few days. Don José, would you care to join me in the library?"

* * *

Don Escalada poured two snifters of brandy and handed one to San Martín, inviting him to sit. "These generals are Patriots," he said, "but you have to be careful how you deal with them. They have won some important battles. We need to win people around to your way of thinking, not fight them. Don't forget, some of them have had lengthy military careers too, some longer than yours, and they won't take kindly to being talked down to."

"I agree," said San Martín, "and I respect what has been achieved to date. I understand that we should proceed with caution. I don't want to step on anyone's toes. Having said that, I am more concerned with the progress of the war than wounding someone's pride."

"Why don't you tell me a little more about this regiment, how it will be constituted, and so on. I'm intrigued."

San Martín swirled his brandy around the snifter. "As I was saying at the *Cabildo*, the regiment must be impeccably well trained. Discipline is paramount and mobility will be key. My first commander had a saying: the three most important factors in the quality of an army are training, training, and training. We got so sick of hearing that, but he was right. It was no accident that

Napoleon swept across Europe so dramatically—his troops are the best drilled on the Continent."

"And he is a superb tactician," said Don Escalada.

"True, but most of his theories are based on a very simple set of ancient principles."

"Go on."

"First, you must excuse me a moment, there's something I want to show you."

San Martín placed his glass on the table and left the library. He bumped into María on the stairs as she rushed past him, muttering an apology and continuing toward the front door. Back in his room, San Martín took a battered old book from his suitcase. Then he returned to the library and handed the book to Don Escalada.

"What's this then? I'm afraid my French isn't what it used to be."

"It's *The Art of War*, written by an ancient Oriental general named Sun Tzu. I believe it's from the 6th Century BC but was only translated into French about thirty years ago. It hasn't yet been translated into Spanish, or English for that matter."

"What does it say?"

"It outlines a simple set of principles for military commanders that, if followed, will assure victory. Some are common sense, like 'All warfare is based on deception', but there are some intriguing insights here, too. Let me give you an example." San Martín took the book from Don Escalada. "He says here: 'Thus one who is skilful at keeping the enemy on the move maintains deceitful appearances, according to which the enemy will act. He sacrifices something that the enemy may snatch at it. By holding out baits, he keeps him on the march; then with a body of picked men, he lies in wait for him.'"

"Fascinating."

"Yes, indeed. Not only are his ideas relevant today, but I believe they are particularly applicable to the war we will have to fight."

"You think Napoleon is applying these principles?"

"I'm sure of it. Take Napoleon's Chasseurs, for example. They are the perfect example of Sun Tzu's mobile force. It is exactly this kind of unit we will have to create if we are to beat the Spanish."

"We should print a copy for every commander in the army and make it compulsory reading," suggested Don Escalada.

"Perhaps," said San Martín, "in time. But not all men are as open as you to new ideas and theories. I think it would be best to codify these principles in a model regiment, which we can then replicate across the army. Many commanders can only see the practical value of an idea when it is actualized; they have the lives of their men to think about after all."

"I see your point. So how would this work in practical terms? What do you need?"

"You can't change an entire army at once," said San Martín, "and it would be foolish to try. I want to start with one squadron; let's call them the Mounted Grenadiers. They will be the best: men who are equally comfortable with gun, saber, lance, and dagger, and all skilled horsemen, disciplined and tough. This squadron will serve as a template, a model, and the best officers will create further squadrons until we have a regiment of these men."

"This will take time," said Don Escalada.

"Yes, it will. But it's the only way we can win this war. At the moment, we are trading victories with Spain in the north, at great cost to us in terms of men and munitions. They can keep doing this—gradually weakening us—until reinforcements arrive. And when they do, they will crush us. They could have twenty thousand men here in a matter of months. We can't waste any more resources."

"Don't worry," said Don Escalada, "you'll get your squadron. The Triumvirate was impressed with your ... purpose. We need more men of action."

There was silence for a moment. "Is there any word on when a formal declaration of independence will be made?" San Martín asked.

"We are independent in all but name, for now at least."

"Yes, but you cannot underestimate the positive effect on morale for our troops and for the people. Imagine marching into battle under our own flag, defending our country—our own sovereign, independent country."

"I agree. It's something we should move toward at the earliest opportunity, but a Congress will have to be convened. Naturally, all sorts of factions will be vying for control."

"Of course."

"Now, José, I had another reason for wanting to speak to you alone. If I may be so bold, I have a request for you. Assuming you get approval of these proposals, and I'm confident you will, I know my sons are keen to enlist. I would feel far more secure knowing they were under your command."

"I will be glad to have them, and I give you my word I'll take care of them. I need many more like them. For the officers, I need men of the highest caliber—men with integrity and honor, men schooled in mathematics and military history. For the infantry, all I need is to find those in whose hearts freedom beats strongest. I don't care if these men aren't from good families, or even have a criminal past, as long as their hearts are pure and they are willing to dedicate themselves to the liberation of América."

"You're a good man, José. I am glad you returned home. Forgive me for asking such a personal question, but why have you never married?"

"I have been considering my return to Argentina for a few years now. My focus was entirely on that. Military life hardly affords one the opportunity to meet a potential wife. I had thought that perhaps I would meet someone when I came home."

Several hours later, a servant knocked to inform them that dinner was ready.

"Just when I was getting hungry. Come José, I have a special bottle of wine I have been saving. I think you will like it."

San Martín followed Don Escalada into the dining room, where the smell of beef filled his nostrils. Doña Escalada, Manuel and Mariano were already seated, but there was an empty chair.

"Is María not joining us?"

"I'm not sure where she is," said Doña Escalada. "She seems to have left with Jesúsa and hasn't returned."

"That's unusual."

"I waited as long as I could, but it was getting late. I didn't want the food to be spoiled. We'll begin without her."

Just as Doña Escalada finished speaking, the front door slammed. María ran into the room, her face illuminated by a smile. "Mama, Papa, sorry I'm late." She waved a piece of paper excitedly then handed it to her father.

"Where were you?" asked Doña Escalada. "We were worried."

"You shouldn't have been; I had Jesúsa with me."

Don Escalada started reading. It was a list of names—women's names—and at the top was María de los Remedios de Escalada. The page was full. "I don't understand María, what is this?"

"It's a list, Papa. A list of women."

"I can see that, but for what purpose?"

"All of the women on that list have pledged to buy a gun."

It took a moment for what María had said to sink in. When it did, Don Escalada's eyes widened, and San Martín smiled.

"The women of Argentina can help the revolution too, Papa."

20: A Prisoner's Lament

Diego lay on the bed, his skin sticking to the tattered leather. Another bad dream. He stared at the window high above him. This time, he had been in a cage, his body twisted and contorted. The cage wasn't tall enough for him to stand up in, or wide enough for him to sit and was on a cart, surrounded by cages of chickens, being rolled toward the market in Tucuman. He was covered with feathers and chicken shit. Every time he cried out for help, people just laughed. When he had awoken, scratching his skin and screaming, he was back in his jail cell.

Diego's cell was only marginally larger than the cage of his nightmares, the sole relief being the high, vaulted ceiling and the window far up on the wall across from the door. Opposite his bed were his chamber pot—the smell of which filled the room—and the heavy door keeping him captive. There were two slots in the door, but both could only be opened from the other side. One was at eye level and was covered by tight wire mesh. The other was at ground level, and through it Diego received his food and passed out his chamber pot.

Diego sat up in bed and a wave of nausea coursed through him. Soon, he was on his knees, retching and coughing into the pot of his own filth. The guards were supposed to take it each morning, when the prisoners got their bread and water, but they often didn't bother. After wiping his mouth with the back of his hand, Diego threw himself against the door and pounded. The grille opened and a shadowed face grunted a warning. "Any more of that and it's no food tomorrow."

Diego bit his tongue, fearing losing his meager rations. Protesting was futile. Despite his restraint, he didn't get fed the next day anyway. Nor did they take his chamber pot out. The guards laughed as they passed an empty plate into his cell, and all week the rancid stench of the pot caught in his throat and burned his eyes. When they finally did remove it, they berated him for his filth and punished him with more missed meals, but at least the smell was gone.

A few days later, the terrors of the night moved to another cell, and Diego was haunted by something altogether more perplexing. It started with a face—a woman's face surrounded by long, wavy brown hair. At first, the picture was hazy, but each night it became a little clearer. First, her light brown skin and elegant slender arms, next her mocking black eyes and full red lips. It was as if Diego willed her into existence, night after night, detail by detail. She came to him every time, even those rare evenings when he wanted to be left alone. It was always the same face, sometimes talking, although he could never make out the words.

"*Puta!* Who is this girl? She's killing me!" Diego was sure he had never seen her before, failing to match her face with that of anyone from his past. She was neither the first girl he kissed, Juanita Calvos; nor was she María de las Moras—the farmer's daughter he met last year at the *feria*. It wasn't Esmeralda either, the *puta* from Madam Feliz's brothel. She never let him kiss her, but that had never stopped him trying.

Diego opened his eyes, shouting curses before calming himself. Esmeralda had promised him a birthday present, but he had to do that stupid robbery and get caught. *Hijo de puta!* But, it wasn't Esmeralda who invaded him every night and drove him crazy. It wasn't anybody he knew, or had even ever met. He lay back on the bed and closed his eyes, letting the mysterious dark-haired girl pull him back toward sleep.

A Storm Hits Valparaíso

Diego woke late in the evening, the sleepy sun already stealing the light from his cell. He had forgotten to leave his metal plate at the door; he would have no food again tonight. *Que tortura!* He shook his head. *What an idiot*, he thought, *now I'm going to be awake all night because I slept all day. The whole night awake, with no food and no water.*

Diego began pacing the cell in a vain attempt to tire himself out. It wasn't working, but at least his mind drifted to something other than the *puta* who terrorized him in his dreams. What came in her place wasn't entirely welcome. The ghosts of his past: Inez, wrapped in a blanket beside the fire, close to death; the horse Indio thrashing in the snow, its leg broken; Miguel, eyes wide with anger, beating him; Jorge hysterically pleading, only to be shoved away; and two faceless ghosts who always came to Diego—the mother who died giving birth to him, the father who abandoned him.

"*Hijo de gran puta*," he said, wiping a tear from his eye. He was sweating now from all the pacing, so he stopped, caught his breath, and slumped against the wall of his cell, staring at the window opposite. It was the only window and was set high up in the wall; even when standing on the bed beneath it, the bars were out of reach. The ledge was slanted toward him, so even if he could reach that, there was no leverage to haul himself up.

A small bird perched on the other side of the bars. It stared at Diego and ruffled its feathers, as if it might fly away at any moment. Diego tried to stay perfectly still. The bird took one tentative step toward the inside of the cell and then stopped. Opening its beak wide, the creature shook itself like a dog: body first, then head. Diego held his breath. The bird fixed its eyes on Diego once more. Then it turned and flew away. Diego watched as it flapped furiously, first to gain height and speed, before relaxing and spreading its wings wide, arcing upwards, over the building, out of his field of vision, and away.

Diego stripped the bedding and bundled it in the corner of his cell, and then pulled his bed out bit by bit and quietly rotated it, so the bed would be perpendicular to the wall under the window. Lifting up one end, he propped it against the wall beneath the window ledge and tried to wedge it in place. He looked at his makeshift ramp. *Maybe this will work.* Putting one foot on the bottom strut, he tested his weight. It held. Then another; it seemed to be working. Step by step, he inched up the wooden slats of the bed toward the window. It was holding. By the time he reached the top, the bed was creaking a little, but steady.

Reaching the window, Diego just missed the sun, which had slipped behind the block of cells across the courtyard. He tested the first bar, yanking it as hard as he could: solid. He tested the second: solid. He tested the third, pulling with all the strength he could muster, not caring anymore if the bed beneath him would hold. Nothing. He stopped, sweating, his chin resting on his chest.

Turning his attention to the cracked plaster at the bottom of the third bar, he picked at it with his fingers. He needed something sharp. Searching the room, he spotted a rusty, loose screw in the bed frame and was able to work it free. Climbing back up, Diego set to work. After scraping away some of the loose plaster, he surveyed his progress. He continued. Ten minutes later, after only getting down an inch or so, he hit a dead end. It was pointless. The rusty screw was disintegrating in his hands, there was harder stone under the loose plaster, and the bar was still solidly in place. He tried working on the other two bars, but they yielded even less.

With his cell now shrouded in darkness, Diego felt defeated. His anger rising, he pulled at the third bar with all his might, inadvertently kicking the bed from under him. It clattered to the concrete floor, upending the chamber pot and leaving Diego hanging from the bar, his feet pressed against the wall.

Shouts rang out from the corridor outside his cell. The grille opened. A voice barked an order. One by one, the locks ground open. His door was thrown open, only to be blocked by the bed. The door was kicked, the bed scattered, and three guards stormed in. They stopped momentarily, surprised to see Diego hanging from the bars, and then one of them grabbed his right leg and tried to yank him down. Diego held on. Later, when he looked back on this moment, Diego wondered why he held on for so long. Perhaps just reaching the bars was a kind of freedom—one he wasn't going to give up easily. A second guard grabbed his left leg. Still Diego tried to hold on. But it was futile; his hand ripped free from the iron bar, and he collapsed on top of the two guards. Diego's last memory, before the third guard drove a knee into his face, was looking across at his stinging left hand, the hand that had held on for so long. His scar—the scar his blood brother had given him—was torn open and his hand was red with blood.

"Jorge," Diego mumbled, before everything went black.

When he awoke, Diego felt pain everywhere. One eye was completely closed over and his nose didn't feel quite right. The only way he could breathe was by opening a small crack at the left-hand side of his swollen mouth and gasping. That hurt too, rattling ribs he was sure were broken. Despite the pain, he would have laughed if he could, but the best he could manage was a wheezy cackle, followed by a coughing fit he did his best to restrain. A blob of red mucus flumped over his lip and landed on his chin.

Lying on the floor, he lifted his head to gauge how far away his bed was, but it was gone. The guards must have felt a beating was not sufficient punishment. No chamber pot either. Diego lay there for a long time, staring at the ceiling.

The following morning, the grille on his door opened. Diego instinctively tensed.

"Where is the prisoner?"

"Open this door immediately."

Then another voice: "You don't want this *muchacho*, he's trouble."

"Open it. Now!"

Diego heard the locks turn one by one, then the door creaking. He rolled over on his side, giving the door room to open fully.

"Why has this prisoner been beaten?"

"I told you, he was trouble. He was trying to escape, sir, and then he resisted ... he resisted us."

Diego tried to speak and was kicked in the ribs. The pain was unbearable. And then, with his broken nose, three broken ribs, and six broken fingers he turned his head and opened his one good eye. Lying there in his own piss and shit and unable to move, Diego had a vision: his brother Jorge standing over him, with some stranger beside him and one of the *hijo de puta* guards who had beaten him, looking worried. Diego smiled and then closed his eyes. This was even better than that *puta* of his dreams.

He heard someone say: "We can't take him. He's a mess."

"*Capitán*, this is my brother. I will vouch for him, whatever his crime."

"I don't know, Jorge. Look at him."

"Sir, he is the only horseman I know that is better than I."

Diego felt someone pick him up, and then he blacked out again.

21: Kitty

Cochrane sat in the drawing room of the townhouse he shared with his wealthy uncle. Basil was the only family member with any real money, and he always had a fondness for his nephew. Unfortunately for Cochrane, this sentiment was now driving Uncle Basil to find him a bride, and Cochrane wasn't getting much say in the search. In fact, the entire concept of arranging such a match revolted him. It was against everything he stood for; besides, the women were so dull. However, he was currently enjoying Uncle Basil's largesse and had been made heir of his considerable fortune, so he felt compelled to humor him, if not necessarily to see the process through. In his heart, he knew it was not going to end well, but he also knew that dwelling on it served no purpose other than making him gloomy.

Cochrane stared out the window. Seeing that it was a fine day, he decided to go for a walk to clear his head. He turned right out of his door and headed up Green Street, toward Hyde Park. As he turned into Grosvenor Square, he spied two sailors in high spirits on the other side of the road. He was about to call out to them when he thought better of it. The last time he tried that it became quite embarrassing. It started innocently enough—small talk about the vessels they had served on and the progress of the war—but when they enquired as to his identity, the sailors became quite excited, loudly imploring him to continue his crusade and causing quite a scene. They had pressed him on when he might get another command, which depressed him and left him in a foul mood for days. This time, he just tipped his hat and wished the men well.

It was a strange sensation, he thought: a Captain being jealous of ordinary seamen. But that's what he felt. He didn't know if he would ever have another command. His friends had been urging him to keep up hope, but the truth was that he had rattled too many cages. The farce of the court martial had fingered him as an insubordinate, and the fallout from his trip to Malta and the uncovering of the scandal there had him blacklisted by the Establishment. Even his uncle Alexander, a Vice-Admiral, couldn't help him.

Uncle Alexander was urging him to lie low, to stay out of the press, to break his ties with the Radicals in the House of Commons, and to end his noisy fight against naval corruption. In short, Uncle Alexander was asking him to give up everything he believed in, to become another toad, another flunky, and to keep his mouth shut. He simply couldn't do it, even if it meant he would never have another command.

Cochrane made his way into Hyde Park, taking a seat on an empty bench. Angling his face toward the sun, he tried to clear his mind of such depressing thoughts. It was pointless. He couldn't help tormenting himself. Would his family really be happier if he went along with all of their plans? Would they be happier if he married someone he didn't love and toed the line just to get another command? What kind of man would that make him?

The only person giving him any support was his youngest uncle, Andrew Cochrane-Johnstone. Uncle Andrew was the only reason Cochrane wasn't considered the black sheep of the family. And while there was something dubious about some of Uncle Andrew's past, Cochrane felt a strong bond with him—one that went beyond normal family ties. Uncle Andrew had urged him to stick to his guns, counseling that if he abandoned his principles for the sake of advancement he would never be at peace. Cochrane valued this advice. He also valued the help Uncle Andrew had given him with his finances, advising him to invest in a number of stocks to bolster his meager income.

All of these thoughts were floating around Cochrane's head until he was snapped back into the present by the sight of a woman—a girl to be exact, a schoolgirl. On the other side of the pond, a teacher was leading a line of schoolgirls toward him. They could only have been sixteen or so, but there was something about one of the girls that caught his eye. He couldn't stop staring. She had an unusually dusky complexion and moved with a grace that belied her age. But that wasn't what caught his attention, or at least not what kept it. As the snake of schoolgirls passed, he got a better look. There it was. A glint of something—a fire, a hint of mischief—right behind the eyes. It made him curious. As she caught his gaze, he swore he saw the faintest hint of a mocking smile, directed at him.

Intrigued, Cochrane followed at a distance, certain he was being inconspicuous. But when the teacher called a halt, he was caught by surprise. He saw the girl turn and notice him again, so he pretended to look away, catching her eye at the last moment. Too flustered to continue following, he was relieved when they eventually turned out of the park.

For the next few days, her face was all he could think about—especially with all the dowdy dowagers' daughters Uncle Basil was introducing him to. He returned to the park daily, hoping to see her again, but she did not reappear, at least, not until the following Friday. This time, Cochrane was ready.

As the line of schoolgirls entered the park, headed by their teacher, Cochrane waited to see which way they were walking. Then he set out in the opposite direction, around the pond. The girl took the same position in the line as last time, second from the end. Cochrane followed them, on the other side, until they turned toward him. He tried to keep his pace slow, his eyes elsewhere: the pond, the grass, the sky, anywhere. When he reached the line of girls and passed the teacher, he looked up and caught his target's eye. As he passed, he pressed a note into her hand and marched away triumphantly.

He wasn't so confident the next day, waiting in the park. The note was simple: Saturday, 3 o'clock. Perhaps he should have elaborated, written something romantic. When he thought about it, it sounded more like an order than a love letter. *Well*, Cochrane thought to himself, smiling, *let's hope she obeys*.

It was almost four when he saw her walking away from him with a studied nonchalance. He hadn't even seen her pass. He cursed himself and stood, before thinking better of it. After all, she had seen him and still continued walking, he thought, deciding to wait for her to pass by once more. About twenty minutes later, he spotted her and was determined to strike up a conversation. Rising from the bench, he doffed his hat. "May I walk with you a while."

The girl stopped. "Well, I can't be seen walking with a man who does not even have the manners to introduce himself. Think of the scandal." She grinned before abruptly turning and resuming her walk.

Cochrane caught up with her and mumbled an apology, which made her laugh. "Forgive me, Madame. My name is Cochrane, Thomas Cochrane, and I would be privileged to make your acquaintance."

She stopped. "Very well. I'm Kitty. Just Kitty."

"Well, it's a pleasure to meet you, Just Kitty."

She laughed.

"Would you permit me to walk with you for a moment?"

"Well, Mr. Cochrane, we won't get very far in a moment," she said, her eyes twinkling.

"In that case, would you permit me to walk with you for a while?"

"We'll see how the moment goes."

They commenced walking, commenting on the fine weather. Kitty stopped. "Excuse me, did you say 'Thomas Cochrane'?"

"Yes, I did, Madame."

"Lord Thomas Cochrane?"

Cochrane bowed. "The one and same, at your service."

"Well, well, the dashing sea captain himself."

"Not so dashing anymore. I've been grounded for some time."

"How fortuitous."

"How so?"

"It would have been difficult for us to meet at sea, Lord Cochrane. For one, I can't swim."

"Fortuitous indeed."

"Lord Cochrane, are you not afraid of gossip, escorting me around the park like this, unaccompanied?"

"Not one bit."

"Splendid."

* * *

Over the following months, Cochrane and Kitty spent a lot of time together, growing ever closer. Cochrane was forced to hide the relationship from Uncle Basil, knowing he would never approve, for Kitty was no strategic match who would restore wealth and prestige to the Cochrane name. She was the illegitimate daughter of a Midlands businessman and a Spanish dancer, orphaned by their refusal to acknowledge her. And so Uncle Basil was never told, continuing to match Lord Cochrane instead with *his* idea of suitable ladies. Cochrane planned to elope, knowing he would probably lose his inheritance. It was far from rational, but he didn't care.

22: El Salar de Uyuni

Pacha couldn't see the wound on his back but he knew it was festering. He had been walking for four days straight, stopping only for increasingly feverish sleep. He had struck out to the south, in the direction he presumed Chikan and the rest of the Argentine forces would have gone after the defeat. He had thought of attempting to return home but suspected it might put his family in danger. Also, Spanish cavalry were harrying the retreating troops; Pacha knew he wouldn't be safe until he got further south, but he was also nervous about going in that direction. He knew what lay south of here: *El Salar de Uyuni*—the Salt Plains. It was said that strange things happened in there, that men who entered were never the same again. Still, he thought, it couldn't be worse than the mine, and he had survived that. Plus, he didn't have much choice. While wearing his Argentine uniform he couldn't risk approaching a village, not until he got further south. Again he cursed himself for discarding his weapon.

When Pacha reached the edge of the Salt Plains, he was apprehensive. First, he attempted to circle around, now unsure of his plan. That proved impossible, and soon the eerie white surface surrounded him as far as he could see. The reflection of the sun on the salty ground was so intense he had to tear a sleeve off his shirt to bandage his head and protect his eyes.

The further he progressed into the endless white expanse, the more he began to worry. He had only a little food and water left, and there was no sign of either being replenished. By the time the sun reached its peak, he had stripped almost completely naked, unable to take the ferocious heat reflected from every surface. Two hours passed before he realized what a mistake this was and had to retrace his steps to find his discarded clothing. He dressed slowly, cursing his foolishness and his burned skin.

When the hated sun finally dipped beyond the horizon, a vicious cold set in. Pacha realized he was going to have to keep moving as much as possible, resting when only absolutely necessary, if he were going to survive.

On the second day, he began to hallucinate. At first it was small things, shadows playing at the corners of his eyes. Soon, the slow rumble of the wind became secretive whispers; his breathing, loud and forced, echoing around him, bouncing off the nothingness that enveloped him like a mist. He would see things on the horizon, but they would disappear as he approached them.

When he first saw the outline of a person slumped over in the distance, he dismissed it as another trick of the mind. Slowly shuffling southward, he tried to focus on his feet. But every so often he would sneak another glance. It seemed to be real. As he got closer, his eyes began to make out what he was seeing. He quickened his pace, breaking into a run.

Soon, Pacha stood panting before the body. It was definitely real, and whoever it was had been dead for a long time. The clean, bleached skeleton was covered by tattered, faded clothes and dull metal armor. The skull lay apart, inside a helmet in the shape of a jaguar's head. Pacha remembered the stories his grandmother told of their descendants, the Incas who fought the Spanish long ago. He had no doubt he was looking at the remains of one such warrior. Beside the corpse lay a wooden sword, its copper-edged, serrated blade reflecting the blinding sun.

Pacha was transfixed by the corpse. Sitting opposite it for hours, he half-hoped he could divine the fighter's story, perhaps draw some of his strength while avoiding his fate. When the sun set,

Pacha knew he had to begin walking again. He stood, taking one last look at the remains of the once-proud warrior.

After Pacha began walking away, he had a sudden, overpowering urge to return and pick up the sword. He fought this temptation at first, sure that doing so would desecrate the Inca's memory in some way. However, he quickly convinced himself that he would be carrying on the legacy of this fighter, that it would be what the warrior would have wanted. When he picked up the sword, his whole arm tingled. It had a good weight, was well-balanced and, while the blade could have been sharper, was still in fine condition. Pacha headed south once more, the sword in his outstretched hand leading the way.

By the time the sun had risen again, Pacha was so thirsty he had stopped caring about being hungry. His lips were cracked and his throat was parched. He was getting dizzy, his vision was blurred, and he was beginning to wonder how long he had left. The sword became very heavy. For a moment, he considered getting rid of it, but this, he felt, would have been a bigger crime than taking it in the first place. Pacha slowed his pace and was contemplating a rest when he heard a voice coming from right beside him.

"I'm not sure if you're going the right way."

Pacha dropped the sword in fright. He stared in shock, and then began circling it on the balls of his feet, as if it were a snake waiting to strike. He stopped and shook his head. Slowly, he picked up the sword, examined it closely, cursed himself, and then started walking again.

"I said, I think you're going the wrong way."

Pacha dropped the sword again.

"If you are going to keep doing that, I'm not going to help you," said the sword. Pacha looked around, but there was nothing to see—nothing except for the white earth around him and the sun burning in the sky. "I must be going crazy," he said.

"I must be going crazy, trying to help someone who doesn't want to be helped," said the sword.

"Hello!" Pacha whirled around. "Hello!"

The sword sighed. "I'm down here. And it's just you and me out here, in case you haven't noticed."

"What kind of trick is this? I can hear you, come out."

"Look," said the sword, "you have a wound in your back. It's infected. If we don't clean it, you're going to die. Now stop spinning around, shouting like an idiot, and listen to me." The sword paused. "That's better, now pick me up."

Pacha obeyed.

"Good, now turn to the right and start walking. We don't have a lot of time."

It took Pacha some time to pluck up the courage to ask, "How ... how can you talk?"

"That's a good question," said the sword. "I'm not quite sure. I suppose I never really tried before I met you. It's hard to remember. I'm very old, and I have been on my own for a long time."

Pacha puzzled over this for quite a while. "Maybe you are a magic sword."

"Maybe, but I'm not quite sure what that is. I do know I'm an Inca sword."

Pacha thought for a moment. "My grandmother used to tell me stories about the Incas. They were great warriors. Before the *Kastillas* came, we were free, living in great cities on top of the mountains. Now everything is destroyed."

"I don't remember much. I think that before you picked me up I had been lying there for a very long time. I don't know for sure, but I do know where you need to go."

"Where?"

"See those hills in the distance, slightly to your right?"

It took a moment for Pacha's eyes to adjust.

"Aim for them."

"And what will I find when I get there?"

"I'm not sure, but I think I will remember when we're there."

It took most of the day to reach the base of the hill, and when they did, Pacha found the sudden incline a struggle. A rocky outcrop cast a shadow large enough to fit him. "I need to get some rest," he said.

"Good," said the sword. "I need to think."

* * *

Pacha was woken by the cold, and stood quickly, stomping his feet to get his blood flowing again. He picked up the sword.

"I think I remember the way. Keep climbing, up to your right."

A full moon provided some light, but Pacha still found the rough terrain hard work and stumbled on a few occasions. Having only one hand free didn't help, but he didn't dare discard the sword now. After two hours, the ground leveled out, rising only gradually in front of him. "Where now?"

"Straight ahead," said the sword, "just over this hill."

Pacha sped up, finding it easier going on this flatter ground, and soon reached the crest. On the other side, lower down, was a large lake.

"Water!" Pacha ran down the slope toward the shore.

"No! Wait!" said the sword. "Wait! It's not safe."

Pacha ignored the sword's warning.

"Stop! It's poisonous!" shouted the sword.

Pacha skidded to a halt. "What do you mean it's not safe?"

"Take a deep breath if you don't believe me."

Pacha filled his lungs, and then coughed. The air had a burnt, acrid quality. "What's that smell?"

"It's the lake. The water is poisonous. Don't drink it."

"Then why did you bring me here?"

"Your wound. You must clean your wound or you will die."

Calming himself, and feeling a little deflated, Pacha walked to the edge of the lake. Closer to the shore, he could feel heat coming from the water. Forgetting his anger, he stripped bare and placed the sword on top of his clothes. He put a toe into the water. It was hot, very hot. After a minute, he managed to get a whole foot in, then another. Soon, his body was submerged. He scrubbed his entire body clean, then made his way back to the shore and dressed.

Then Pacha lay down beside the sword and fell into a deep, deep sleep.

23: The Mounted Grenadiers

Zé disembarked in Buenos Aires, attempting to lose himself among the sailors on shore leave. He was feeling a little dazzled; the few words of Spanish he had picked up on the voyage didn't seem to help in this chaos. He kept his head down, but soon realized there was no one to question him, and that people here were free to come and go.

He was free.

Zé had been so worried about being questioned or arrested that he hadn't really considered what to do otherwise. With nothing but the clothes on his back, and with nowhere to go, he was going to have to find a way to survive, and fast. In every direction there were signs of activity—ships being loaded and unloaded, passengers boarding vessels, pickpockets working the crowd, hawkers selling food, prostitutes, policemen, soldiers. There was so much activity that Zé couldn't even think straight.

He tried to get his thoughts in some kind of order. First of all, he needed food. To eat, he needed money, and to get money he needed a job. He tried approaching some men who were loading crates, but they sent him away, as did the crew at the next ship, and the next. Eventually, an old sailor who spoke Portuguese explained to Zé that Argentina was at war and that the only people hiring were the army.

It took most of the day for Zé to find the address the old sailor had written down for him. Zé couldn't read, and when he stopped to ask for directions, most people shooed him away, thinking him a vagrant, which, he supposed, he was. He only got lucky when he approached a smartly dressed soldier and was taken directly to the recruiting office. He paused before going in, wondering if he was doing the right thing and worried he might be asked for his papers and imprisoned, or maybe even sent back to the plantation. Then Zé pushed the door open.

In the end, it didn't matter; they didn't care who he was or where he was from, as long as he signed up. The recruiting officer gave Zé a short speech on the army and the war, which he only partly understood. Spanish wasn't that different from Portuguese, but everyone here spoke so quickly, chopping words, running one sentence into the next. Only one part was easy to understand. The penalty for desertion was mentioned several times: *muerte*. Death. This gave Zé some cause for concern, but he would be paid and fed and have a place to sleep, and—most importantly for Zé—after two years' service he would become a citizen of Argentina. A citizen! With papers!

Zé was given another address to report to the following day, and the officer advised him to improve his Spanish, saying one day it might save his life. He spent the rest of the night wandering the city, his stomach rumbling, trying to tire himself out so that he could sleep.

The camp was several hours' walk west, in a field beside a river delta. The training was exhausting, but Zé soon adjusted. The food was good; more importantly, it was free. Zé had a comfortable bed in the barracks and plenty of free time, but most evenings he was too tired to do anything. When the weekends came, the camp emptied as most men returned to the city to see their families or girlfriends, or to go drinking. Zé preferred to remain in the barracks. He had no money, and didn't know anyone in the city. Besides, he didn't care for the city—it was too noisy and dirty. It was more peaceful out here, especially when he had the camp to himself. Usually, he was able to cajole one of the black cooks into knocking something together for him, and he liked to wander the grounds on his own and think.

One day, he met a boy called Frederico working in the stables. He couldn't have been more than fourteen, but one day Frederico had turned up to enlist claiming he was an orphan. The army refused to accept him on account of his age. He kept pestering them, and when he explained he had worked as a farmhand, they gave him a job looking after the horses until they found someone more experienced to take over. As time went on, Frederico became a fixture in the camp; there were so many other things to worry about that they never got around to replacing him.

Zé and Frederico became friends straight away, kindred souls in a way. Neither had many friends; Frederico was isolated in the stables, and Zé kept to himself. Soon, Zé was spending every weekend down at the stables, and some evenings too. At first, he helped Frederico clean out the stalls and feed the horses in exchange for some Spanish lessons. Frederico was glad to have the help and it was nice having someone to talk to. Plus, with two people doing the work, he could spend more time riding the horses, which was important to him. When he was old enough to enlist, Frederico wanted to join the army's new elite regiment, the Mounted Grenadiers, which took only expert horseman.

"Why do you want to join the Mounted Grenadiers so badly?" Zé asked him one day. "You have it good here."

"It's simple. They're the best. They have the best officers, the best equipment and the best training. I don't want to sign up to be killed; I want to survive. The way I see it, the best chance of that happening is with the Mounted Grenadiers. Besides, a man on a horse is much harder to kill than a man on foot."

"Really?" said Zé, eyeing one of the beasts.

"Which would you rather have charging at you?"

Zé laughed.

"It's something you should think about."

"What do you mean?"

"Do you *really* want to be in the infantry when all this starts? Riding is easy. I could teach you."

Zé shook his head. "I don't know."

119

"Well, you help out here all the time, the horses seem to like you, and your Spanish is getting a lot better. Why not?"

"I could give it a try."

Frederico seemed to know everything about the Mounted Grenadiers. He explained to Zé that they were modeled on Napoleon's feared cavalrymen and that the *comandante* was a real tough nut. They had all sorts of rules, which Zé couldn't fathom. Everyone who joined was given a nickname—or war name as they called it—and they were forbidden to answer to anything else. They were never allowed to duck from danger, which seemed to Zé to be the only sensible thing to do. Also, they could never refuse to fight a duel—whether it was just or unjust—and they must never strike a woman under any circumstances, even if provoked. They carried a long, curved saber with them at all times, and some claimed it could split a man's head like a melon.

The *comandante*'s name was San Martín, Frederico explained, and he was a Lieutenant-Colonel who had spent twenty years in the Spanish Army before coming home to fight his old masters. It hadn't escaped Frederico's notice that this would have made San Martín younger than Frederico when he enlisted, and this antagonized him. However, for now he was prepared to be patient, focusing on improving his riding and befriending the Grenadiers he met, learning as much as possible from them.

As for Zé, his training continued, and he was made part of the 7th Battalion of Infantry. There were a few other black faces around, but none in his unit. Most of the men kept to themselves, which suited him. He and Frederico spent the majority of their free hours riding, and Zé soon became reasonably proficient, despite some early setbacks.

One Saturday, Zé called down to Frederico as usual, and saw him frantically scrubbing the stables. "You look busy. Need some help?"

Frederico looked up. "Make yourself scarce. The *comandante* is coming. This is my chance to impress him."

* * *

A Storm Hits Valparaíso

San Martín and Don Escalada approached the stables, sending an orderly ahead with instructions to saddle up a pair of horses.

"The stables are a little smaller than I would like, but they seem to be well run." San Martín looked up. "I just hope this rain holds off."

Frederico walked out with the mounts.

"You have some fine animals here," said Don Escalada.

"What's your name, son?" San Martín asked.

"Frederico, sir."

"And who's in charge here?"

Frederico paused. "I am, sir."

San Martín laughed. Frederico was confused.

"I think he's serious," said Don Escalada.

"I am serious, sir."

San Martín frowned. "Frederico, you are doing a fine job. I would like to have a talk with you when I get back."

"Yes, sir. I'll be here all day, sir."

After the horses were saddled, San Martín took Don Escalada on a tour of the camp.

"José, you're running a fine operation here," said Don Escalada. "There are rumors you are going to make Colonel soon."

"Well, it's as I said, a soldier is made in the barracks, not on the battlefield. We need to drill this into people."

"And the Grenadiers? My boys only speak highly of you."

"They are fine boys, Don Escalada, but I don't think the Grenadiers are quite ready yet."

"Reinforcements are going to be needed in the north soon, and there's talk of an assault on Montevideo."

San Martín chose his words carefully. "Infantry will suffice for the siege of Montevideo, and the *gauchos* in the north are proving themselves, I hear."

"They are, but the recent defeats involved heavy losses. We can't make up the shortfall with recruits alone."

San Martín slowed his horse. "The northern campaign is bleeding us dry. They invade, take Salta. We just about hold Tucuman. We drive them out, invade Upper Perú, get as far as Potosí. We can't hold our ground and are chased all the way back down to Salta again. We can't keep doing this. They can send five thousand troops from Lima whenever they want. The entire Army of the North would struggle to reach that figure, even before the recent losses. We need a different strategy before we run out of men altogether."

"I know, José, I know."

"Is it true General Belgrano disobeyed the order to retreat to Cordoba?"

"That's what I heard."

"Thank God," said San Martín. "Holding Tucuman stopped the Spanish in their tracks."

"It was an important victory. Cordoba would have been next, and they could have been here in less than a month. But, as I said, José, prepare to lose some men; reinforcements will be needed."

"I understand. I will give what is needed, but I would like to keep as many of the Grenadiers here to train up new squadrons. The 7th Infantry, too. They are still a little raw."

"I'll see what I can do."

"Thank you." San Martín gathered in his reins and stopped his horse. "There is something else I wanted to ask you."

"Anything, José."

"This ... is a little different. It's a personal matter. As you know, I have been spending some time with María."

"Yes," said Don Escalada, smiling. "She is quite fond of you, as is my wife."

"Thank you, you are too kind. If I may, I would like to ask you, sir, for her hand in marriage."

Don Escalada beamed. "I would be delighted, José. You will be a fine addition to the family."

"Thank you."

"Come to the house for dinner tomorrow and we'll discuss everything."

"Perfect. There is just one last thing."

"Yes?"

"If you don't mind, can you refrain from saying anything to María? I would like to ask her myself."

* * *

A Storm Hits Valparaíso

When San Martín returned to the stables with Don Escalada, Frederico could hardly contain his excitement. The *comandante* seemed to be in a good mood, laughing and joking. This would be the perfect time to ask him about enlisting in the army and maybe even about joining the Mounted Grenadiers. But when the *comandante* dismounted, he left without another word.

It was a glum Frederico that Zé found later, taking shelter from the rain in one of the empty stables. Zé sat down in the hay beside him and started talking about the latest news from the battle in the north.

"I wish they would let me enlist," said Frederico. "I'm sick of sitting around here with the horses while you learn how to fire a gun. Next you will be sent off to the front and I'll still be here, kicking my heels."

"I would be happy to trade places."

"Why? Are you afraid?"

Zé's silence filled the stable.

"Are you worried about getting killed?"

"No," said Zé, finally.

"What then?"

Zé paused. "I'm worried about killing."

"What do you mean?"

"I've killed before."

Frederico leaned away from Zé, who put out a hand to calm him. When Frederico recoiled, Zé stood and made for the door. "Don't worry, Frederico. If any man on this earth deserved to die, it was he. Killing him gave me life. Even so, I wish I could take it back."

"I don't understand."

Zé opened his shirt and showed Frederico the slave mark burned onto his chest. "I was a slave. This is the mark of my master: the man I killed."

Frederico's mouth fell open. "They branded you like cattle."

"Me and many others." Zé pointed to his forehead. "Some got it here."

"My God."

"Robado Vivaldo—that's the name of the man I killed, my master in Brazil. I killed him to escape." Zé walked to the door.

123

"I'm sorry, I should never have spoken of this." He shook his head and walked out into the rain. After a few steps, he looked over his shoulder. To his relief, Frederico hadn't followed. He hadn't intended to tell Frederico anything; he didn't want anyone else to know. The fewer people who knew about his past, he decided, the less he would be reminded of it—the less he would be trapped by it. Zé cursed himself for making this slip, but he was tense. In fact, the whole atmosphere in the camp was tense.

It would only get worse.

* * *

By the middle of the year, entire battalions were being sent to the northern front. The men knew this meant that battalions had been wiped out, and any man posted there treated it like a death sentence. Rumors flew around the camp of roads lined with impaled heads and of prisoners being shot. Someone told Zé he was lucky, that any black soldiers captured were spared and enslaved. *Maybe blacks weren't worth the price of a bullet,* he thought. Zé decided that day that he would never be taken alive; if he were to die, it would be as a free man.

There were some lighter moments in the gloom. The number of Mounted Grenadiers was growing. Officers from the original Grenadiers had trained new squadrons until there was a whole battalion of them. Everyone took pride in that. The Mounted Grenadiers could really make a difference against the Spanish. San Martín, the *commandante,* was promoted to Colonel, and there was a large party at the camp to celebrate his marriage to a local girl from a rich family, Doña María de los Remedios de Escalada.

Toward the end of the year, the men of the 7th Infantry began speculating on what 1813 would bring—the year they would be sent to the front. There was a flurry of excitement around the camp in February when the *comandante* took a squadron of Grenadiers to intercept some Spanish ships sailing up the Paraná River. Everyone else was wondering whether they would go next. For some, the wait became too much. They did not want to go to the front, but waiting was almost worse. Everyone's preference was to be sent to fight in Montevideo, where they would be close to their families and girlfriends.

They were to be disappointed.

24: Café Malquerida

It had been just over a month since she had started working at Café Malquerida. Catalina knew she was lucky to have found a job so quickly on returning to Santiago. Upon fleeing Valparaíso, she'd had only the few coins Pedro Villar had given her and had spent most of that securing lodgings. The café owner had seemed friendly enough. Catalina explained her experience, and he said she could work that night to see if she was suitable. While she was working, he had asked her plenty of questions. Perhaps he could sense she was hiding something. Eventually, he had asked her if she had run away from home. Catalina had leaned her broom against the wall and taken a seat opposite the owner. In a cool voice, she'd told him of the Spanish sailors and the fire that had killed her father.

The owner patted her hand. "Don't worry, you'll find no friends of the Spanish here."

She soon learned that the café was a home, of sorts, for malcontents. Most of the regulars were old men with long lists of grievances against the Spanish and with sons and nephews fighting the Royalists in the south. People talked openly of revolution and pledged their support for independence. Developments in

A Storm Hits Valparaíso

Argentina and Venezuela were discussed in excited tones. They seemed to be faring better than the Chilean effort under the Patriot leader Bernardo O'Higgins. The Patriots knew their grip on the capital was tenuous. Much of the population had Royalist sympathies, and the Spanish had many spies in the city. Many Patriots worried that if the fighting spread in this direction, the loyalty of the citizens could not be assured.

The Spanish, aware the café was a meeting point for old revolutionaries and younger agitators, had placed a spy in their midst. The regulars simply tolerated the spy, who was so consistently and prodigiously inebriated that his Spanish paymasters disregarded his reports anyway. Besides, he was the only decent singer in the group, blessed with a soulful voice that moved even the hardest of hearts. One night, the spy had a lapse. Instead of the patriotic laments he had learned by rote, he burst into a Royalist marching number about the birth of King Ferdinand.

"Don't worry about him," the owner of the café reassured Catalina. "He gets so drunk he can't even remember where he was the night before. We all know he's taking the Crown's peso, but really, he is harmless. And we are careful. Besides, if we rumbled him, they would replace him with someone else, someone who might actually be effective."

Aside from the incompetent spy, Catalina's customers rarely caused her concern. Naturally, she was subject to various attentions—after all, the clientele were not made of stone—but she was able to handle it with humor and grace and, where necessary, scorn. She dealt with everyone equally, but the regulars couldn't help noticing that when the occasional Chilean soldier visited, their *cazuela* had a nice, juicy piece of *carne* in the broth, instead of the usual stringy *pollo*.

One evening, a few weeks after she started work, Catalina was in the café, cleaning, when she heard a knock on the rear door. The owner—returning from the stockroom with a tall, disheveled man with darting eyes—told Catalina to draw the blinds. The man seemed uneasy and whispered to the owner.

"She can be trusted," the owner replied, looking at Catalina.

The stranger's reply was inaudible, but the owner bristled. "Raul, please. Sit. Catalina has been working for me for a while now. Please, you're safe."

The stranger eyed Catalina suspiciously while the owner poured two *aguardientes*, handing one to Raul.

Catalina resumed her tidying, and her eavesdropping. From the few words she caught, it seemed that the fighting was going to spread to Santiago, and Raul was here to prepare for that in some way. Catalina heard him say he needed somewhere to stay, and then the owner reply that there was an apartment they used, but that he would have to go and get the key. Raul wanted to go with him, but the owner insisted he wait, asking Catalina to stay until he returned. "If someone knocks," he instructed, "don't answer. I'll use the back door."

Once the owner left, Raul walked behind the bar and took a clean glass from the shelf.

"How long have you worked here?" He invited Catalina to sit, indicating the chair beside his and offering her the glass.

Catalina hesitated before accepting. "A month, more or less."

Raul grimaced. "And he says you can be trusted."

"I can."

"He's taking a risk; I don't like risks."

"How dare you," said Catalina, eyes flashing.

Raul snorted. "For all I know you could be working for the Spanish. It wouldn't surprise me. A pretty girl like you can get a man to say anything once she—"

He was cut short with a slap. Catalina stood. "You know nothing about me."

Raul rubbed his face. "I know you're stronger than you look."

"You will get another if you say anything like that again."

"I was only joking around."

"Some things shouldn't be joked about. The Spanish took everything from me, everything."

"I'm sorry, I didn't—"

"They killed my father; burned him alive. Destroyed my home. They would have killed me too, but I got away..." Catalina bit her lip, blinking.

Raul bowed his head. "I'm sorry, Catalina. I had no idea." He looked back toward her, clenching his jaw, as if unsure whether to say something. Then he drained his glass and grimaced. "I grew up in the south, in Arauco. My father was a fisherman—a simple, peaceful soul, and thin too, like a bird. My mother was his opposite: a big, boisterous woman whose laughter filled the room." Raul rubbed his face again. "She had a temper too."

Catalina allowed herself a brief smile and sat back down at the table.

"When my father returned with the day's catch, my mother would go out to sell it while he fixed his nets or slept. He wasn't much for other people anyway, but my mother could talk the ears off a *burro*."

Catalina laughed as Raul poured himself another drink.

He nodded to her glass. "You haven't touched yours."

Catalina took a small sip, and cursed, nearly spitting it out.

"It's tough stuff, isn't it? Most girls don't like it."

Catalina fixed him with a stare, picked up the *aguardiente*, and drained it. Her eyes watered as the fiery liquor burned her throat. She slapped the table in pain, cursing again.

Raul roared with laughter.

Catalina slid her glass over to him. "Again."

"If you are sure."

She nodded, and Raul refilled her glass. As she went to pick it up, Raul put his hand on hers. "Slow down *tigre*, this is powerful stuff."

Catalina left her glass on the table, noticing Raul's hand, the sensation of it lingering for a moment.

"Now, where was I? My mother," he continued. "She wasn't the argumentative type, as such, but she never backed away from a confrontation. One day, she got into a row with a customer—some serving girl who accused her of selling bad fish. This girl worked up on some *hacienda*. There had been a big *fiesta* on the Sunday and half the guests got sick. The *hacendado* went crazy, threatening to fire the staff—you know what these rich types are like. After questioning all of them, my mother's fish got the blame, so this serving girl wanted a refund and was making all sorts of crazy threats."

Raul smiled, but there was no joy in it. "My mother was having none of it. Of course, her fish came straight from the sea. And what she didn't sell, we ate at home. She wasn't going to let her reputation be questioned, and she gave the serving girl a piece of her mind. I don't know exactly what she said, but it was enough to get the attention of the *hacendado*, who came down with a policeman the next day to arrest her. We only found out when someone came to the house to tell my father she was being taken away."

Raul stopped to take a drink, and wiped his mouth with the back of his hand. "My father flew into a rage—I've never seen anything like it—and ran up to the market with a knife in his hand. He was stopped before he got anywhere near the *hacendado*, but as he was being hauled away, he made several threats against the man's life. My mother was released later that day, but they held my father for months. He died before he went to trial."

Catalina began to speak, but Raul held his hand up. "Wait," he said, "there's more. But first, drink with me." They raised their glasses and emptied them in unison. "My mother went downhill quickly after that. She stopped eating, stopped going outside. She refused visitors and couldn't talk to me without bursting into tears. I started avoiding her. Eventually, when I couldn't take it anymore, I went to live with my uncle. I think she was relieved anyway. I think I reminded her too much of what she had lost."

Raul paused for a moment, clearly upset. "I tried to visit her as often as I could, but I was thirteen or fourteen, just discovering the world. I was trying to get past my father's death, but she just wanted to hang on to it, as if it was all she had left. I remember being very angry with her." Raul locked eyes with Catalina. "I even remember blaming her, hating her even. I said some things that were very hurtful, and I stopped visiting as much. She died within the year." Raul coughed, trying to cover his breaking voice. "When she died, she was so frail ... I could have picked up her coffin in my arms and walked it to her grave. That broke my heart."

Catalina took his hand, and her eyes met his. Leaning toward her, Raul kissed her, tentative at first, then more passionately. As his hands moved from her face to her neck, she tensed, and then relaxed, deciding not to think, not to care—deciding to feel something other than the sorrow that shadowed her.

They were interrupted a few minutes later by the owner returning. Catalina slipped her hand from Raul's in time, but she could feel her cheeks burning from his stubble.

"Catalina, you can go now. I can finish up here," the owner said, turning to fetch a glass from the bar.

Raul leaned in to whisper, "Meet me around the back in five minutes."

Catalina got up, smoothing her dress, and said goodbye, meeting Raul's eyes for just a moment. Then she slipped out the front door, which the owner locked behind her. Outside, she leaned against the wall of the café, breathing heavily. Conscious of the sound of her breath and of her heart hammering madly in her chest, she turned down the alleyway.

* * *

The following morning, Catalina had been lying awake for some time—trying to come to terms with her situation—when she decided to act. First, she carefully disentangled her hair from Raul's hand, then she retrieved her scattered clothes and dressed. Tiptoeing across the wooden floor, she stopped at the door to check that he was still asleep.

Silence.

By the time she reached the street below, Catalina's head was pounding—partly from the amount of *aguardiente* she had drunk the night before, and partly from the questions she kept pushing from her mind. She tried to focus on getting back to her lodgings. Finally home, she locked the door and undressed, letting out the longest sigh of her short life.

What have I done? Catalina finally gave in to her own mental interrogation. *And why?* The second question was more difficult to answer. Perhaps she had just wanted to feel something. Something other than the gnawing numbness that was eating her from inside, turning her existence into one long, slow day on which the sun rose and fell arbitrarily and events occurred behind a screen of gauze.

131

And she had felt something last night, but she couldn't think about that—not yet.

Turning to examine her naked body in the mirror, she consoled herself with the knowledge that she didn't look any different—apart from a couple of bruises on her thigh. She didn't feel any different either. Blushing, Catalina looked away from the mirror and continued washing her body with her face turned. Then she dressed, and left for work.

25: The Battle of San Lorenzo

For months, Spain—taking advantage of its complete naval supremacy—had been undermining the Argentine defenses. The Spanish alternated between bombarding Buenos Aires and sacking towns on the navigable Paraná River. Batteries were erected to protect the cities of Rosario and Punta Gorda, but these only diverted attacks to more defenseless targets. In October 1812, the towns of San Nicolas and San Pedro were sacked. By December, the Argentine military commanders dispatched Colonel Rondeau to lay siege to Montevideo—the base for the Spanish sorties. Naval assaults became more frequent as the Spaniards desperately tried to divert the Patriots' attention away from the siege and to disrupt their supply lines to Montevideo.

At the end of January 1813, a flotilla of eleven Spanish ships left Montevideo, sailing for the Paraná River. San Martín was ordered to follow the flotilla, engaging them wherever they landed. Traveling under the cover of night, he took one hundred and twenty of his Grenadiers upstream, keeping his troops out of sight of the river itself. Disguised as a *gaucho*, he reconnoitered the Spanish ships himself, from a high bank.

On January 29th, the Spanish flotilla bypassed Rosario without attacking and anchored shortly afterwards on the island of San Lorenzo. The following day, a small force attempted to climb the bluffs that overlooked the river, but was fired upon by a rudimentary militia desperately awaiting San Martín's reinforcements.

The Grenadiers had been delayed by the capture of a prisoner on the river bank. He was taken to San Martín—still dripping wet—for questioning.

"Sir, we spotted him swimming ashore from the boat."

"Really, what have we here? A spy?" asked San Martín.

"Ha!" said the prisoner, with a crazy grin. "My name is José Félix—from Paraguay. I was being held captive on that ship you are following."

"Go on."

"They don't know you are here. I mean, they suspect there may be some defenses, but they are not sure. They only expect light resistance. They plan to take the monastery."

San Martín paused, locking eyes with the Paraguayan. "Why?"

"They think there's gold there."

"Then what?"

"Sail upstream, destroy the guns at Santa Fe, and sack the city."

San Martín turned to his Lieutenant. "Tell the men to saddle up." He turned back to the Paraguayan. "Was there anything else?"

"They don't intend to hold Santa Fe, just destroy it. Their aim is to continue upriver to Paraguay, to take Asuncion—my city. From there, they can make further attacks on your armies in the north."

"And how do you know all this?"

"They talked openly in front of me. They didn't think I would be crazy enough to attach myself to a bundle of sticks and throw myself into the river." The prisoner grinned once more. "They were wrong!"

San Martín laughed. "Wrong indeed."

"You are going to attack them, right?"

San Martín said nothing, just smiled as the prisoner said, "Give me a weapon. Let me fight."

"We'll see." San Martín nodded to one of the Grenadiers, who took the Paraguayan away. "Good work, Lieutenant. Make sure this man gets some dry clothes. If you find out anything else, let me know immediately."

"Yes, sir."

"And Lieutenant, make sure he is locked away somewhere when all of this starts."

With this news taken into account, San Martín pressed his men onward until they reached San Carlos Monastery.

* * *

San Martín approached the monastery door and knocked three times. No answer. He signaled for two of his men to circle around and look for another entrance, and knocked again. This time he heard footsteps. A metal slit opened. "Yes? How can I help you?"

"I'm sorry, Padre, for disturbing you at such a late hour, but I need your assistance."

"And you are?"

"Colonel José de San Martín, of the Argentine Army. We've been tracking a flotilla of Spanish ships up the river. I need access to your lookout tower."

"I'm sorry, Colonel, but that would be impossible."

San Martín set his fist against his palm, but held his tongue.

"The Franciscan Order is a peaceful one and cannot assist you in matters of war—we're not Jesuits." The monk grimaced. "Now, if any of your men need shelter or medical assistance, I'll be happy to—"

"Padre, our action here is purely defensive." San Martín cut him off. "These Spanish sailors—"

"This is Spanish territory, sir. I don't see why I should assist brigands."

"They mean to sack this monastery and use it as a staging post to attack Santa Fe. I don't need to tell you how many innocent people will die if we let this happen." San Martín leaned in closer to the door. "You may not recognize the sovereign Argentine

135

government, but when I'm finished with them, I'll be back, and I will recognize you."

There was silence before the monk said, "As long as no assault is launched from here. This is sacred ground."

"I give you my word."

"I will hold you to it, Colonel."

Several bolts slid open and the heavy door swung inward. San Martín entered without invitation. "I appreciate your assistance. Now, please show me the way. We don't have much time."

"Follow me."

From the lookout tower, San Martín watched the Spanish ships. They hadn't yet begun unloading troops, but he could see they were getting ready to do so. He surveyed the land. Between the wall surrounding the monastery and the edge of the high bluff overlooking the river, there was sufficient level ground for a cavalry charge. There was only one point where the Spanish troops would be able to climb up in formation—the perfect spot for an ambush.

San Martín withdrew his Grenadiers, keeping them out of sight behind the monastery buildings and dividing them into two columns with Captain Bermudez at the head of the right-hand column and himself at the other. He left the local militia inside the courtyard with orders to join the assault once it had begun. Just before dawn, San Martín took up his observation post again. Thirty minutes later, as the sun rose, the Spanish infantry disembarked. Three hundred in total, he estimated, more than double the number he had. As he left to rejoin his men, he saw the monk again.

"Colonel, forgive me, but you don't look like an ordinary soldier."

San Martín took off his poncho and removed his white farmer's hat. "That's the point, Padre," he said, smiling. He ran toward the orderly who held his reins, mounted his horse in a single bound, and galloped toward the rear of the monastery where the rest of the Grenadiers were stationed. Drawing his curved saber, he barked his instructions: urging his men to remember their training, not to fire a shot unless absolutely necessary, to fall on the enemy at top speed, and to trust their sabers.

For the first time in América, the war clarion of the Mounted Grenadiers was sounded. The two lines of cavalry charged forward from both sides of the monastery simultaneously, their sabers drawn, but the column led by San Martín was the first to fall on the enemy. The shock of their surprise attack stunned the Spaniards, who attempted to retreat and fire muskets. The clanging of swords filled the air as dust from the cavalry charge spread like panic. Through the haze, the Grenadiers made quick work of the enemy. Soon, the ground was littered with slain Spaniards.

San Martín heard a high-pitched scream of terror as his horse buckled beneath him. His mount fell heavily, landing on top of him as they hit the ground. Winded, he tried to ease out from beneath the writhing, snorting best, but his leg was pinned by its weight. He lay beneath his dying mount, exhausted and defenseless. The battle raged on around him. The Spanish troops, surprised by the speed and ferocity of the repeated cavalry charges, were in complete disarray. But San Martín was still vulnerable.

A Spanish soldier, seeing his opportunity, charged—bayonet fixed—but before he could reach San Martín, he was dispatched by the lance of a Grenadier.

"*Comandante!*" Spotting San Martín, one of the Grenadiers—Juan Bautista Cabral—set about freeing him, easing him from under his horse.

"Juan, behind you!" San Martín pointed, but it was too late.

Cabral fell, two mortal wounds causing his voice to bubble in his throat as he cried, "I die content! We have beaten the enemy."

One arm clutching his injured leg, San Martín hauled himself to his feet and tried to staunch the Grenadier's blood loss, but it was too late. Around him, the panicked Spanish retreated, only to be pursued by wave after wave of cavalry. The Grenadiers charged them relentlessly, bearing down on them again and again. Resigned to death, some of the Spaniards even threw themselves off the high bluffs into the river rather than face another deadly charge. The battle was only thirty minutes old when the Spanish retreated to their ship—protected, by its guns, from further attack. Forty of their dead littered the shores of the Paraná River.

The Franciscan monk was as good as his word. San Martín brought his twenty-seven wounded Grenadiers back to the monastery for treatment. Fifteen more had been buried that morning, and San Martín had then ordered his troops to pay similar respect to the Spanish dead, so the digging had begun again. In a final act of clemency, food and medical supplies were sent to the Spanish vessel to enable them to treat their wounded.

San Martín, still covered with the dirt of battle, sat in the courtyard of the monastery under the shade of a large pine tree and put the finishing touches to his report. Putting his pen down for a moment, he gazed up at the sky. The Mounted Grenadiers' first shots had been fired in battle—the first in a long war, he suspected.

He wondered if he would live to see the end of it.

26: A Secret Meeting

In a roadside tavern four miles north of London, two figures huddled over a table. A flickering candle barely illuminated the hooked nose of one, the white hair of the other, and the small pile of newspapers and pamphlets between them. They talked in whispers, occasionally glancing around for eavesdroppers, but the other patrons were more interested in the contents of their glasses and in the serving girls refilling them. The two men stopped talking altogether whenever someone came to top up their drinks.

A third man entered—expensively-dressed and wrinkling his nose as he sniffed the air. Wiping his face with a silk handkerchief, he scanned the room, walked to the table, and greeted the two others with a simple nod as he sat down. "What's all this about then?"

The man with the white hair handed him a newspaper article:

Lord Thomas Cochrane, Right Honorable M.P. for Westminster, rose in the House of Commons today to give his widely anticipated speech. The House was full to the rafters, and men were fighting for space in the galley. It was Lord Cochrane's first appearance in the House since the infamous court martial, but it was clear that, while his standing in the eyes of the Navy may have fallen, his popularity with the public-at-large is unabated. As he stood, somewhat dramatically, with a large tattered scroll in his hands, several jeers rang out from the opposite side of the chamber. Rumors had been circulating for several days about the content of the speech, but all that was known was that it was regarding naval corruption, and that it would be explosive.

"I have read all of this. He travels to Malta, uncovers the scandal ... there is nothing new here."

"Read the last paragraph," the white-haired man insisted.

Although not a classical orator, Lord Cochrane had the House transfixed. At the end of his speech, he marched up to the Speaker's Table, unfurling the scroll he had been holding throughout. It was a list of the charges that the Proctor and the Marshall of Malta—both being the same Mr. Jackson—had applied in one single case, and it stretched from the Speaker's Table to the Bar. The House was in uproar.

"And what of it? We were aware this was going on for some time. While it is unfortunate that it has been made public like this, it hardly damages us." The man smoothed down his silk shirt.

"It's more serious than that. This is being handed out in Plymouth." The white-haired man handed him a pamphlet.

"'Royal Navy—Rotten to the Core!' That's a little dramatic isn't it," said the expensively-dressed man, reading. "Oh, this isn't good. Listen: 'Sailors! Did you know that as you risk your life for Britain, the Navy plans to wash its hands of you if you get injured? A sailor who loses his arm is lucky to get a pension of £45. A clerk in the ticket office gets £700 a year for *risking* himself in the world of retirement. A clerk's annual pension is worth 16 of your arms.' Stirring stuff. Where did they get this from?"

"A speech Cochrane gave in the House some time back. You need to see this also—this one is being handed out in Southampton."

"'Cochrane—Scourge of the Naval Establishment!' Is he now? We shall see." He traced a gloved finger under the text. "Hmm, his Malta adventure, and his speech. Can we trace this back to Cochrane?"

"No," said the man with white hair. "But at the very least it appears that radical elements are appropriating the content of his speeches for their own subversive ends."

"Are we worried this will get wider support?"

"Well," said the man with a hook nose, "my sources have provided me with a draft of an article that will appear in tomorrow's *Times*. It's strongly worded, criticizes the war effort, contains a long list of setbacks, and calls for Cochrane's immediate reinstatement in the Navy. It even goes as far as to suggest that he was banished because he's getting to the heart of, what was it now ... ah yes, 'the systematic corruption that is enriching a small circle.'"

"This is a little more damaging," said the expensively-dressed man.

The man with white hair agreed. "In the past, we could count on him being shipped out every few months, but since the court martial he has been free to interfere in politics and has succeeded in allying himself with every radical element inside and outside of Parliament."

"We must take care of this," said the man with the hooked nose, "before it gets of out of hand."

"It's already out of hand," said the man with white hair.

"Agreed," said the expensively-dressed man. "But what's our approach? What's his weakness?"

"Money. He might like to dress his causes up in populist garb, but he's only looking to feather his own nest."

The man with a hook nose cleared his throat. "My sources tell me he has just been disinherited. It seems Uncle Basil had been trying, without success, to make a suitable match for him. Then he found out Cochrane had run off to Gretna Green with the illegitimate daughter of a Spanish dancer, some schoolgirl called Kitty. Cochrane never said a word to his uncle, who continued to pair him up with eligible ladies even after his illicit nuptials. It's caused something of a scandal."

"Excellent," said the expensively-dressed man. "He's penniless then. We can use this." He paused for a moment. "I presume you have a plan or you wouldn't have sent for me."

"Indeed we do," said the man with white hair, handing over a document. "All we need is your approval."

27: An Accidental Rescue

In February 1813, the commander of the Army of the North, General Belgrano, routed the Spanish at Salta, seized the city, and captured three thousand enemy soldiers. In an act of mercy, he freed them on the condition they remain unarmed—a decision that would later be regretted. General Belgrano pressed on into Upper Peru but was badly beaten at Vilcapugio in October. The following month, his army was almost destroyed at Ayohuma and was then chased all the way back to Tucuman, forfeiting Salta once more.

When General Belgrano asked Buenos Aires to relieve him of command, San Martín—promoted to General after his victory at San Lorenzo—was sent to replace him. Leaving his young bride in Buenos Aires, San Martín traveled across the deserted country, leading his Mounted Grenadiers and the 7th Infantry to bolster the shattered Army of the North. The journey gave him plenty of time to mull over the plan set forth by the Argentine commanders.

San Martín had been tasked with the recapture of Salta and with yet another invasion. The consensus among his commanders was that, to break Spanish power in América, they must take Lima—the grandest and most important city of all. To take Lima would end the war and guarantee freedom for the new republics.

But the only way to Lima was through Upper Peru, and taking it would be no easy task. Additional forces were sent to lay siege to Montevideo, preventing any further assaults on Buenos Aires or on the towns along the Paraná River. The Argentine Navy, under the supervision of the Irishman William Brown, was still in its infancy and could only be employed in limited defensive engagements. Capturing Montevideo would deprive the Spanish of a vital stop-off point for staging any invasion of Argentina, as well as giving Brown time to develop his naval force, which was still no match for the Spanish navy.

When San Martín arrived in Tucuman to take command, he despaired at what he saw: a weary army with defeat in its bones. The troops, their uniforms in rags, had little appetite for further fighting. Insubordination was rife and the quality of the officers was poor. San Martín's first order was to confiscate a shipment of thirty-six thousand pesos—a prize that had survived the ignoble retreat from Upper Peru to Tucuman. It was destined for the government coffers in Buenos Aires until San Martín seized it to pay and equip his men. It soon became clear that any notion of a quick reinvasion of Upper Peru was foolish, so instead San Martín set about retraining the men and fortifying Tucuman. The one bright spot for San Martín was the *gauchos*—farmers of the northern provinces who were renowned for their horsemanship and had been making life difficult for the Spanish; he immediately began devising ways to use them more effectively.

* * *

It had been almost a year since Diego and Jorge had seen each other. Jorge had grown taller, which he teased Diego about remorselessly; and that was new, too. Jorge had always been a gentle person, causing some to mistake his timidity for weakness, but now his gentleness had been replaced by steeliness, a creeping cynicism. Diego hadn't yet made up his mind whether that was a good thing.

Jorge now noticed a confidence in Diego that troubled him, bordering, as it was, on the cocksure. Both felt they had moved away from each other somehow, but neither knew how to put it into words; instead, it was communicated through teasing, snide remarks, and jokes at the other's expense. Where these actions had once bonded them, now they served only to separate them.

When Diego was freed from prison, Jorge was delighted to have his brother back—their difference in rank merely a source of mirth at first. Diego, his tales of Madam Feliz's Bordello popular around the campfire, was liked and respected by the men. Jorge, even with his skill as a rider, commanded only a grudging respect from some of them. Others—especially the veterans—resented such a young superior and secretly derided him and attempted to undermine his authority. Knowing he could only gain their trust on the battlefield, Jorge threw himself into the training exercises, rising before the others and running, in full uniform, in the morning heat. When finished training for the day, he went over to the infantry to practice with his saber. At night, despite sitting with the other men and listening to the tall tales, the hairy stories, and the bawdy jokes, he felt apart, separate. He rarely took the bottle that was passed around, and he never went to the whorehouse.

Jorge also volunteered for every patrol. It was his job to keep his men alive; he wanted to know every inch of the terrain around Tucuman and Salta. He didn't want to be surprised if the fighting moved his way. He thought of his parents only rarely, and Diego didn't mention them either. It seemed they were both creating new worlds to replace the one that had been ripped away from them.

Diego sensed this growing chasm, but misinterpreted it, thinking Jorge's promotion had made him aloof, cold, snooty even. Sensing it too, Jorge responded by volunteering Diego for the patrols.

"Can't we just ride in peace?" Diego snapped one morning on patrol when Jorge was droning on about edible berries and soft ground. He shook his head for a moment, partly in exasperation at his brother, and partly to clear away the fog of a hangover.

"I'm trying to teach you."

"Always trying to teach me something, I'm sick of it," Diego said. Lectures on the terrain, potential points of attack, the advantage of higher ground, and when to hold and when to charge bored him.

"Diego..."

"I know you're my brother, but come on. Let's just be quiet for a while."

Jorge pulled his horse in front of Diego's, blocking him. "For God's sake, I'm trying to keep you alive."

Raising his head, Diego met Jorge's eyes. In an instant, he recognized the loss of his brother, and the changes in them both, for what they really were. Tears welled in Diego's eyes, but he fought them off as he silently raised his left hand. The scar stood out proudly. He and Jorge stared at each other in silence for a full minute. Then Jorge nodded, turned his horse, kicked it, and set off at a gallop. "Catch me if you can!"

Diego, smiling, let him get a little ahead before setting off in pursuit. For ten glorious minutes, they were children again—boys from Raco who knew nothing of pain or war or death.

When Jorge eventually drew up alongside Diego, who had already dismounted, Diego was still smiling.

"You know, Diego, I only let you win because you were in such a foul mood."

"Ha! That's funny because I tried to let you win, but you were so slow, it was impossible!"

After sharing some bread, they resumed their patrol in silence, until, after a few hours, Diego said, "Jorge, this might sound really strange, but I have been having this dream."

"What kind of dream?"

"It's about a woman."

Jorge laughed.

"Don't laugh. This is different. It's strange, I've never seen her before ... I mean ... it's not someone I've ever met."

"Are you sure it's not one of those girls from the whorehouse?"

"Ha! No. They visit me sometimes too, but this is different; she is different. It started in prison. Every night. It was torture."

"And you are sure you have never met her?"

"Certain."

"That is strange."

"I know. I wish I knew who she was. I mean, I'd like to meet her."

"You think she is real!"

"Don't make fun."

"I'm not making fun, it's just..."

"I know. It's strange."

Minutes passed, with only the hoof beats of the horses to break the silence, before Jorge spoke. "Diego, do you believe in God?"

"You know I don't like talking about that nonsense."

"Well then, what do you believe?"

Diego smiled as he slapped his horse's neck with a flick of the reins. "I believe this horse has tried to throw me twice today. I believe this saddle is chewing my ass. And I believe the *capitán* is going to kill us for getting lost again."

"We're not lost," said Jorge. "Give me that map again."

But they were. They knew they were north of Salta, but they couldn't find any landmarks to pinpoint their position and it was impossible to ascertain how far they had traveled in this difficult terrain. Camp was a couple of days ride from Salta itself, and they had been riding north since morning, encountering only the odd farmer.

The *capitán* had been tasked with expanding the network of *gaucho* outposts that comprised the vanguard of the Army of the North. While the Spanish still held the city of Salta, the land surrounding it was under rebel control. As soon as the Royalists took control of the city, the local population fled, partly out of fear—stories of severed limbs lining the road to Upper Peru were commonplace—but also to continue the insurrection. Some made their way to Tucuman and enlisted in the regular army, but most of the *campesinos* melted into the countryside along with their horses and weapons. Hiding their cattle, harrying patrols, and burning crops, they prevented any meaningful reconnaissance of the defenses of Tucuman. These roving bands of rebels were organized into a tough, disciplined militia that pinned the Spanish down in Salta and prevented any relief for the troops trapped there. The tentacles of this *gaucho* network were not only choking Salta, but were also twisting up through the countryside toward the town of Jujuy and the border with Upper Peru.

"There must be gaucho outposts all around us," Diego said after they had ridden on for half an hour.

A Storm Hits Valparaíso

Jorge nodded. "Yes, but if we can't figure out where we are..." He glanced down at the map again. The outposts were not marked, for fear of maps falling into enemy hands. Although Jorge had memorized the locations of some of them, that was useless unless they could get their bearings. Eventually, they stumbled upon a stream. As the horses drank deeply and Diego refilled the water canteens, Jorge examined the map once more in the fading light.

Jorge heard a rustle in the bushes, but before he could react, two men appeared pointing guns.

"Don't shoot!" Jorge waved the map. "We're Patriots." After a quick explanation, the men lowered their weapons and rushed forward to shake hands.

"Come," one of the men instructed, leading them down a winding path away from the stream. As the thicket cleared, Diego and Jorge saw what resembled an abandoned farmhouse in the valley below—the outpost.

"Names?" the local commander asked, after they had tended to the horses and were presented to him.

"Corporal Jorge Ramírez, sir, and this is my brother, Cavalryman Diego Ramírez. We were patrolling north of Salta but got lost—until your men found us and brought us here."

"Well, it's not the first time. I suppose I should be glad we're so difficult to find. When did you leave your camp? Did you encounter any Royalist troops?"

"No sightings of the enemy, sir. We left camp two days ago, riding due north from Salta."

"Good. You should rest up tonight. Spanish patrols have become more frequent in this area. I think they are making a renewed effort to open the supply lines from Jujuy, and I don't want you two getting caught up in the fighting. I have some important documents for Tucuman. I would have had some of my men take them, but as you can see, we are a little short at the moment."

"Yes, sir."

"There's something else." The commander paused, scratching his chin. "A couple of our scouts were patrolling just inside the border of Upper Peru, near the edge of the Salt Plains.

147

They came across one of your regular infantrymen—alone and badly injured. He was quite delirious. At first we thought he had lost his mind, but he seems to be recovering. We have done everything we can for him here, but he needs to see a physician. Take him with you; escort him to Tucuman. He's still in a bad way, but I fear if he stays here any longer he may not make it."

"No problem, sir."

"One last thing. I recommend that you strap him to one of your horses. He is in no condition to ride, and he can get a little ... confused. There have been some violent outbursts."

"I don't understand."

"From what we have been able to gather during his lucid moments, he was one of the Indians who signed up during General Belgrano's campaign in Upper Peru. He was found alone, close to death, with a septic wound on his back and severe dehydration. Something may have dislodged in his mind. When found, he was raving about a talking sword; then he attacked them, claiming they had stolen it. He had to be restrained. I don't know if his condition is permanent, but he needs help. Now, I can't spare any horses, so you two will have to double up. While you are there, tell headquarters to send me some damn supplies!" With that, the commander stormed out, leaving Diego and Jorge to figure out what he had been talking about.

* * *

Pacha, in his delirium, remembered little of the journey south. He had been drifting in and out of consciousness, alternating between fear, paranoia, and listlessness. When they eventually reached Tucuman, he was taken to the military hospital, where his slow convalescence began. It was bewildering: he didn't recognize his surroundings or any of the people around him. Eventually, with nutritious food, clean water, and lots of rest, he began to recover. He was still weak and disorientated, but the violent outbursts had stopped.

When the doctors felt he was ready, they tried to explain how he had come to be there. Bringing in a large map, they pointed out Tucuman. Pacha was very confused. He was shown Potosí, far to

A Storm Hits Valparaíso

the north, and the great journey he had undertaken. They pointed to where the battle had taken place, indicating that he had somehow evaded detection by the Spanish and made his way to the edge of the Salt Plains, where he was found by a *gaucho* patrol. It took him a while to comprehend. When he realized how far away he was from his family, Pacha demanded to be discharged. It was refused. He flew into a rage, only calming when told that the Spanish had retaken Potosí and were fortified there. Even if he could find a way of getting home without being caught, he would be putting his family in danger.

"Remain with the army. Wait for the reinvasion," the doctor insisted.

"What about Chikan?" Pacha asked. "My friend. Did he survive?"

"We know nothing of him," the doctor lied, looking away, fearful of agitating his patient further.

Once he was physically able, Pacha was released from the hospital and sent back to training with the regular infantry. All they seemed to be doing was digging in around Tucuman, preparing defenses—that and more training. They didn't seem to be preparing for an invasion, and rumors soon began to circulate about its cancellation. As time went on, Pacha became ever more disillusioned—compounded when he learned the truth about his dead friend. He started drinking heavily, picking fights with the other men, and turning up late for duty. When reprimanded, he became insubordinate. When drunk, he would tell everyone that he planned to desert.

* * *

"Come." San Martín looked up from the maps on his desk on hearing his assistant's knock.

"Sir, there is a disciplinary matter regarding an infantryman. I felt we should bring it to your attention."

"The commanding officer can't handle it?"

"This soldier is on the verge of being jailed for extreme insubordination among other things. I'm not sure what to do. It's a special case, but he has become a disruptive influence."

149

"A special case? Do you know him?"

"I know of him. There are extenuating circumstances. He's one of the *indios*. He enlisted when we took Potosí but was left for dead after the massacre at Huaqui. Somehow, he survived and made his way south through the Salt Plains. We're not sure how he survived, but one of our patrols picked him up. He has family in Potosí, heard the rumors we're canceling the reinvasion, and has become disenchanted. We're worried he will desert and try to make his way home. Obviously, we can't let him fall into the hands of the Spanish. Even if he doesn't desert, he's affecting morale."

"One moment, did you say he was one of the *indios*?"

"Yes, sir."

"Bring him to me."

* * *

Pacha shined his boots for the third time. He had managed to wangle a fresh uniform from the Quartermaster and had made sure he was clean-shaven. A meeting with the *comandante*. Pacha had no idea what to expect or why he had been summoned, but everyone knew his reputation: a hard case. If he were to be disciplined, surely his commanding officer could have done it, which meant this was something different—or something worse. Pacha tried to put it out of his mind as he walked across the field. When he arrived, he was taken straight to the *comandante*. San Martín didn't even look up as he told Pacha to sit. Pacha had seen him before from a distance, but never this close.

Still without acknowledging Pacha, San Martín stood and moved to the window to look out at the marching troops. He cleared his throat. "Insubordination, fighting, disobeying orders, and threatening desertion—I could have you jailed for any of these offences." He turned from the window, locking eyes with Pacha. "Even for threatening desertion, I could have you shot." He paused, letting this sink in.

"I can't let this go on," he continued. "Not only are you setting a bad example to the other men, but you're affecting morale. Now, I know what you have been through, and I know you miss your family, but I haven't seen my wife in a long time either. If we don't win this war, I may never see her again. Do you remember why you joined up? Those reasons are more valid than ever."

San Martín sat down in his chair. "As the commanding officer of the Army of the North, I have decisions to make. Whether I decide to attack the Spanish in Salta or Potosí or Madrid, I will only take them on when and where we can win. I will not send my men to slaughter. Every soldier out there is precious; we can win this war only if I keep as many of them alive as possible. Now, I'm sorry but I can't send you back to your regiment, it would set a bad example."

"But—"

"I am going to give you a choice," San Martín cut him off. "It's either jail or ... the other option."

"What's that?"

"You work for me. But I swear, if you betray me, I will have you shot."

"What do you want me to do?"

"You are going to become a spy."

After they finished talking, Pacha excused himself and left. He knew he had little choice, but he wanted to get everything straight in his head. Anyway, the General insisted he take time to think about it. This way, he suspected, he might even have a better chance of getting back to his family. Pacha corrected himself—it was his only chance.

* * *

From his chair, San Martín watched Pacha cross the field. Then he called in his assistant. "Keep an eye on him."

"Yes, sir. Anything else?"

"No, that's it. You can go. I'll finish up here." Once his assistant left, San Martín let out a low groan. It was getting worse. He winced as he mopped his damp brow. Struggling a little, he stood and rested his hand on the desk before wiping his forehead once more. With some difficulty, San Martín hobbled over to his medicine cabinet and removed a vial that contained a thick, foul-smelling greenish liquid. He knocked back the contents in one go, grimacing and fighting the urge to throw up. Then he put the

151

empty vial in his right-hand desk drawer and slumped in his chair, eyes glazed.

28: The Sharp Shooter

Cochrane sat at his bureau poring over a map of the North Atlantic.

"How are the preparations going?" his young bride asked, watching him with a mixture of excitement and sorrow.

"My love, I apologize." He held a hand out to Kitty. "In all this commotion, I haven't even talked to you properly yet. I'm sorry. You know this is my first command in five years. And what a ship—the *Tonnant*—one of the finest in the fleet. This is my chance—our chance. I can restore the family prestige and put us on a secure financial footing. With a child coming, I must think of these things." Cochrane rested his hand on his wife's belly. "You aren't sorry I'm going, are you?"

"Thomas, no. If you even attempted to refuse this command, I would have knocked you out and dragged you onto the ship myself." She smiled. "But I am allowed to miss you."

"You are under orders to miss me," said Cochrane, taking her into his arms. "North America—not the most prestigious command, I know, but not the worst either. Now that we're officially at war, there might be some action. It's better than could have been expected, especially after all this time. I thought I'd be escorting packet ships for a few years. Then again, I didn't think I would be stuck on dry land all this time."

Kitty pouted. "Stuck here with your horrible wife."

"Stuck with my horrible wife." He kissed her.

* * *

"Thomas, come with me." Uncle Alexander grabbed Cochrane by the elbow. "I want you to meet that gentleman I was talking about."

"Who?" Cochrane was not much for dinner parties, but Uncle Alexander had used his influence to secure him the new appointment. He could hardly refuse.

"The marksman," said Uncle Alexander. "Ah, here he is."

"Admiral Cochrane, pleased to see you again."

"And you, Monsieur de Berenger." Uncle Alexander made the introductions. "This is my nephew, Lord Captain Thomas Cochrane. Thomas, this is Monsieur Random de Berenger—a man that proved most useful to us."

"A pleasure, Lord Cochrane," said de Berenger with a pronounced accent. "Your fame precedes you."

Cochrane bowed his head, but not before noticing that de Berenger was particularly ugly—the kind that could silence a room and slow the pulse of all those present.

"Now, Thomas," said Uncle Alexander, "Monsieur de Berenger was telling me about a pesky innovation those Americans have come up with. It's causing havoc—you really must pay heed before you ship out. Monsieur de Berenger, would you be so kind as to explain?"

"Of course. It is simple really, simple but deadly. The Americans are not short of expert sharpshooters. They got plenty of experience aiming at the British during the War of Independence, and of course, they always have the Indians. Lately, they have been putting marksmen on the spars of their vessels, with orders to take out the officers and work their way down the chain of command. This has had predictable results."

"Predictable indeed," agreed Uncle Alexander. "It's causing bloody mayhem, and it's clearly against the rules of war, but there's no point complaining to the Yanks."

Cochrane grunted. "How do we propose to counteract this? This is the first I've heard of it."

"That's where Monsieur de Berenger comes in, Thomas. He has a wealth of experience in training sharpshooters. He has offered to come aboard to school some of your men. The aim would be to nullify the American snipers, rendering their advantage void. What do you say?"

Cochrane paused. There was something about the man. He couldn't quite put his finger on it. "It's interesting, certainly interesting." He tried to buy time. "My only reservation is that the mission isn't too far away now. This doesn't leave us much opportunity to– "

"Which is why Monsieur de Berenger would depart Portsmouth with you," Uncle Alexander interrupted, "and train the men at sea."

"Lord Cochrane," de Berenger said, looking earnest, "it is more advantageous to train the men at sea anyhow. As you can imagine, firing a stock from the mast in high seas—at a moving target—is considerably different to hitting a mark on the range on a clear day."

"It certainly is." Cochrane took the opportunity to end the conversation. "Monsieur de Berenger, you have given us a lot to discuss. It was interesting talking to you."

Thanking both men, Monsieur de Berenger excused himself.

"Why did you give him such short shrift?" Uncle Alexander leaned in to whisper. "I thought the elegance of the solution would have appealed to your creative nature."

"It's not without merit, but let me ask you something: how much do you know about this man? French, is he?"

"French and German parentage, I believe. He comes highly recommended by Lord Yarmouth."

Cochrane snorted. "I wouldn't hold much stock with—"

"Now, Thomas," interrupted Uncle Alexander, looking around, "he was adjutant to Lord Yarmouth's sharpshooters for some time."

"He can be trusted?"
"Of course!"
Cochrane wasn't so sure.

29: Playing the Market

*N*apoleon *is dead! Napoleon is dead!* The rumor spread through London like wildfire. Hands were shaken, strangers kissed, and locals danced in the streets to the news of Bonaparte's death. Soon, brothers would be back from the front and lovers reunited. Despite the lack of official confirmation from the Government, the people were celebrating. They weren't alone. Parliament's hawks and England's generals could now turn their attention to fresh battles, recalcitrant colonies, and desired possessions—all in the name of George III. And the other king in town—the Sun King, the doyen of dandified fops, the exiled King of France, Louis XVIII—toasted his good fortune with white wine, celebrating his imminent return to the throne.

It had begun, like all things of dramatic portent, at dawn. It seemed every coachman arriving from the south had heard the news, but it didn't really gather full steam until after lunch, when a carriage bearing Bourbon brocades rattled joyously over London Bridge, down Lombard Street, and into the City of London. Amid triumphal cries in a foreign tongue, pamphlets were thrown to bemused pedestrians and startled urchins. "*Vive le Roi! Vivent les Bourbons!*"

Word spread at the speed of salacious gossip. Admirals were woken, servants roused from slumber, and meetings hastily arranged. Royal advisors clamored for an audience with the King, and George III summoned everyone he could think of. Businessmen, quick to see the potential, scrambled to cash in on this momentous news. The death of the tiny terror of France was cause for long celebration. Potters hatched plans for plates, and jewelers for pendants. Minters devised commemorative coins, and innkeepers calculated stock levels. Musicians formulated songs, and enterprising poets wrestled with rules of verse. And brokers hammered at the doors of the trading houses that had the temerity to keep to regular hours.

The brokers knew better than most that there was money in this. Already they were calculating margins, revising dividends, and estimating profit. They knew most of the focus would be on a stock called Omnium—wildly volatile, tending to exaggerate the market's movements, and heavily favored by margin traders who could get in and out quickly and make a profit before having to actually pay for the stock. Everyone knew that Omnium would shoot up, and everyone wanted a piece. The question was: how high would it go?

Omnium opened at twenty-six-and-a-half and was the immediate focus of heavy trading, mostly in one direction. Twenty-seven, twenty-eight, twenty-nine: it kept climbing as the palpitating traders licked their lips. Thirty: fortunes were being spent in eight different ways before they were earned. Thirty-one: the glee was universal, for everyone had bought in. Omnium hit thirty-two and showed no signs of slowing. Frantic runners competed with carriage drivers to pass urgent instructions to brokers—the whole town was watching the City. People who had bought already that morning piled in once more. Even the conservative traders, who had cashed out earlier, went in again. Guaranteed profit—so safe that people started buying the stock with money they didn't even have. Everyone was in up to their oxters. Then it started falling. Fast.

Napoleon lives! Napoleon lives! Everyone rushed to sell simultaneously. The problem was: no one was buying. The price dropped. Then dropped again. Then dropped some more. At the end of trading, it was back at twenty-six-and-a-half, as if nothing had happened. But something had happened: fortunes had been lost several times over. Traders were sitting on the floor, clutching their heads in their hands. Nobody wanted to go home. When the shock subsided, fear set in. As fear turned to anger, the word hoax began to circulate. Somebody had to pay, and someone would.

* * *

That morning, unaware of the commotion around the City, Cochrane went to his factory on Cock Lane to work on his patents. He had been there less than an hour when his footman unexpectedly interrupted. "My Lord, you have an unexpected caller at the residence." The footman paused. "An army officer."

Cochrane's mouth dropped open as the footman continued. "I have a hackney waiting."

On the journey back, Cochrane fretted. His brother was serving in Spain, fighting in the Peninsular War, and had been ill for some time. Cochrane feared the worst. He tried to console himself by thinking up any other reason an army officer might call, but failed. On arriving, he ran into the house—forgetting to discharge the hackney—and was surprised to find a man wearing the green uniform of a sharpshooter standing in the middle of the living room. "Monsieur de Berenger, forgive me," said Cochrane. "I was expecting someone else."

"I apologize for calling unannounced, Lord Cochrane, but I'm in a predicament and I need your assistance."

Cochrane shook his head in frustration. "I wish you could have let me know you were coming."

"I am afraid that wasn't possible." De Berenger straightened up. "I formally request permission to board the *Tonnant*."

"Excuse me?" Cochrane furrowed his brow. "Now? At this exact moment?"

"Yes."

"I'm afraid that's impossible."

"I know your uncle is anxious to have me aboard to commence training the sharpshooters."

"I'm aware of that, but why the urgency? Why do you mean to board now, for God's sake?"

De Berenger paused, not meeting Cochrane's gaze.

"Spit it out, man."

"I owe money." De Berenger cleared his throat. "Eight thousand pounds. And I've no way to repay it. I am in a bind. I beg you."

"Even if I was disposed to accede to your request—which I must say is highly unusual—I would need the permission of the Admiralty to take you aboard, as you are a foreigner."

"I know your uncle was most anxious to have me aboard."

"As I said, I am aware of that, but there's no way around it."

"So you cannot assist me."

"If you manage to avoid your creditors until we are ready to set sail, and assuming the Admiralty approves, I will be happy to welcome you aboard. Until then, I'm afraid there is nothing I can do," said Cochrane. Then, noting de Berenger's distressed mannerisms, he added, "Come now, you wouldn't be the first man to dodge the Debtors' Prison by lying low for a while. Pull yourself together."

De Berenger looked down at his uniform. "I can't return like this."

"Excuse me?"

"I have presented myself in uniform in the hope of boarding. If I return to my lodgings like this I will arouse suspicion."

Cochrane sighed, anxious to be rid of him, and asked him to wait. Most of his own clothes had been packed away, but he was able to find a broad-brimmed hat and a large greycoat he wasn't taking with him, and he brought them back downstairs. De Berenger thanked him, and left in a hurry.

30: The Sickness of San Martín

At the end of 1813, Zé and the rest of the 7th Infantry spent a month marching from Buenos Aires to Tucuman with the *comandante*, a couple of squadrons of Mounted Grenadiers, and one hundred artillerymen. Among the infantry, there had been scattered, furtive talk of desertion. A few men disappeared and were never seen again; whether they escaped or were shot, Zé didn't care. He wasn't risking it.

With time, the men's fears about being posted to the north evaporated. They believed in the *comandante*, and his recent promotion to general strengthened their faith. The more experienced troops pointed out the level of artillery and cavalry support, arguing they had always been outgunned in previous battles and never had the horsemen to switch the point of attack or disrupt the relentless cannon-fire. Their previous commanders had been buffoons, they said, catapulted into position on the strength of their family name. The *comandante* was different; they knew a military man when they saw one. He proved at San Lorenzo that he wouldn't ask his troops to do anything he wasn't prepared to do himself. It was also clear that he preferred to surround himself with officers who had risen through the ranks on the field of battle—inspiring trust and respect along the chain of command.

However, morale took a hit when they arrived at Tucuman and saw the traumatized troops garrisoned there. Hospitals full of wounded but empty of medicine. War amputees desperate for food, pressing for alms in the town square. It was a lot hotter there, too. The simplest movement seemed to unleash a torrent of sweat that drenched every part of the body—everywhere bar the throat, which was always bone dry, no matter how much water one drank.

The *comandante* was a bundle of energy in the beginning, giving an instant boost to the flagging spirits of the Patriot forces. He ensured everyone was well fed, had a fresh uniform and new boots, and most importantly for the men, had a functioning weapon. Construction began on an intricate series of defenses to the north of the city: the Citadel of Tucuman. While this bolstered their confidence in defending future Spanish attacks, it was clear the Citadel had a second purpose: closing off the most successful route out of the city. Desertion had reached chronic levels.

As for the rest of the Army of the North, their spirits rose as a further Spanish assault on Tucuman seemed less likely with each passing day. The only attacks on the Royalists were being carried out by the irregular troops—the *gaucho*s—with the occasional support from the Mounted Grenadiers. Numbers in the *gaucho* ranks were swelling, so the *comandante* began incorporating some of the younger, more promising *gauchos* into new Grenadier squadrons. Their horsemanship was already excellent, so training primarily focused on discipline and use of the saber.

* * *

Diego put on his clean uniform, taking great care everything was neat and tidy.

"Don't you have the day off today?" Jorge asked, watching his brother spend an inordinate amount of time shining his belt buckle.

"I certainly do."

"Of course. *Feliz cumpleaños!*"

"Thank you."

"Nineteen, eh?"

Diego smiled. "So I'm told."

"Why are you getting into uniform?"

"It's my first free day since we joined the Grenadiers; two months without a break. Today I'm going to enjoy myself."

"I've got sentry duty again—I can't join you. Where are you going anyway?"

"To do something I should have done a year ago." Diego winked and walked out of the barracks.

He was greeted at Madam Feliz's Gambling House like a returning hero. Everyone was still there: the barman, the croupier at the roulette table, and Madam Feliz, hovering, prodding the girls into action.

"Most of the rich pulled out of town last year," Madam Feliz complained when she joined him at the bar. "Most haven't returned yet. And, of course, the merchants are still staying away. Things won't return to normal until the trade routes to Upper Peru reopen." She put her hand on Diego's shoulder. "Any news of the reinvasion? I'm thinking of taking my show on the road. Tucuman has become a little small for my tastes."

Diego laughed. "You'll probably hear before I do."

"True, half the officers are regulars here. Without the army I would have gone out of business six months ago."

Diego raised his glass. "To the army."

As the *aguardiente* warmed his throat, he saw her: Esmeralda, as beautiful as he remembered. Without another word, he jumped up and intercepted her on the stairs. She gasped when she saw him, and then blushed. There was an awkward silence before Esmeralda spoke. "It's been a long time."

"One year to the day, exactly," said Diego.

"Ah, so it's your birthday!"

"You remembered."

Esmeralda stood back to look at him properly. "Look at you; this uniform."

"The Mounted Grenadiers," said Diego with a touch of pride.

"I like it. It suits you."

"Thank you. And you look great, Esmeralda, really beautiful..."

The silence was punctuated by a shout from the bar. "Take her upstairs, Diego, for God's sake."

Diego blushed, but Esmeralda took his hand and led him into one of the upstairs rooms. "No charge," she whispered, as she pushed him through the door.

* * *

San Martín examined the map of the Citadel once more. It was constructed with the intention of holding the city with a minimum of troops—far fewer than he had here at present. He hoped the new series of defenses would make Tucuman impregnable because he never wanted the Army of the North to be the situation again where they were ordered to abandon the city to the Spanish. San Martín knew the strategic value of Tucuman. Cordoba would be much harder to defend. If that fell, the revolution would be doomed. Tracing the map with one finger, he thought he spotted a weak point and was about to call in his assistant when there was a knock on his door. "Come!"

His assistant closed the door behind him and approached the desk tentatively.

"What is it?"

"The ... the..." the assistant struggled to get the words out. "The doctor is here to see you."

"I didn't call for him. What does he want? I'm busy."

"I did, sir."

San Martín glared at his assistant. "You called him?"

"Yes, sir."

"Would you like to explain why?"

"Sir, I've noticed you have been in increasing discomfort the past few weeks. When I asked about it, you said it was an old war wound playing up but that the doctor said you would be fine. Last week, when I was looking for some papers, I found an empty vial of some kind of medicine in your desk drawer—"

San Martín thumped his desk. "You had no business—"

"I was worried. I asked the doctor about your wound and he said he knew nothing about it. As far as he was aware, you were in fine health, as you had never been to see him."

"Then you told him about the vial."

His assistant nodded.

"And he insisted on seeing me."

"Yes, sir."

"Send him in. I'll be speaking to you afterward."

The assistant beckoned the doctor inside before slipping out.

"Sit down, doctor. I know what this is about."

"What are you taking, General?"

San Martín grimaced. "Opiates. I was prescribed them in Buenos Aires for a stomach ailment arising from an old battle wound."

"What dosage did he recommend?"

"I don't know," said San Martín. "He gave me the vials and said one should do the trick."

"And how often did he tell you to take it? How often are you taking it?"

"When I need it," San Martín snapped. "No more; no less."

"Can I see the vials?"

San Martín went to his cabinet and retrieved an unused vial, handing it to the doctor.

The doctor's eyes widened. "General, please tell me these aren't the opiates your doctor prescribed."

"No. That supply ran out a couple of months ago. This is from the hospital."

"It certainly is. This is field-strength laudanum. We use this when a patient is in extreme pain—when we are performing amputations. Pharmaceutical opiates, which your doctor would have prescribed, are less than half this strength."

"That might explain a few things."

"I'd say it does. Let me ask you this: in between vials, how do you feel? I can see you have watery eyes and a runny nose, both signs of an opium dependency. Are you having trouble sleeping? Sweating excessively? Do you have any cravings? Headaches? Loss of appetite? Any tremors? Nausea? Vomiting?"

San Martín looked down at his trembling hands.

"I know the signs, General," the doctor continued. "I knew as soon as I walked in. This kind of laudanum is strictly a temporary measure. In your case, I presume it was prescribed so

165

you could fulfill your duties because you refused to rest. But, I must warn you, it is not a cure for your ailment. Over a long period of time it would exacerbate your condition. I want to take your supply and move you to a lower dose immediately."

"That's impossible! Without the vials I am in too much pain. I won't have you—"

"General, you may be the commanding officer, but if I sign a certificate saying you're unfit for duty—"

San Martín thumped the table. "Don't threaten me, doctor. I can have you arrested right now, and we both know it."

The doctor paused. "You won't see out this war unless you listen to me. You have already developed a dependency, and your condition is worsening. Soon, the tremors will become constant, and you will have trouble signing your name. Then it will start to affect your heart. The next thing to go will be your memory. Do you need me to go on?"

San Martín took the vial, turning it over in his shaking hands. He knew it was getting worse, but had been ignoring the signs, too busy building the defenses around Tucuman and reorganizing the army.

"What do I do now?"

"What I would really like is for you to take a leave of absence, to convalesce in a more temperate climate, somewhere better for the constitution—perhaps somewhere in the south, in the mountains. But I know you won't agree to that. The next best thing is cut down on as much unnecessary physical activity as possible while we reduce your dose. Then we can look at treatment." The doctor stopped suddenly, aware that San Martín was no longer paying attention. "General?"

San Martín was staring out the window, distracted. "Sorry doctor, I was just thinking."

"Do we have an agreement?"

"Sorry?"

"You cut back, let me administer the medicine from now on."

San Martín nodded.

"I'll drop by every day to check on you."

The *comandante* did not respond.

The doctor stood "Was there anything else?"
San Martín turned to the doctor. "The mountains, eh?"
"General?"
"You said something about the mountains."

"Yes, well, a cooler climate. The crisp mountain air would be ideal for your convalescence if you want to *really* treat this ailment. Why?"

"I've always wanted to retire to the mountains one day, maybe work some land."

"Maybe when this is all over, General."

* * *

The announcement came three weeks later. It shocked everyone—the infantry, the Grenadiers, the *gauchos*, the townsfolk of Tucuman, even San Martín's assistant. The inspirational *comandante*, the General in charge of the Army of the North, the hero of San Lorenzo, the great hope of the Argentine independence—José de San Martín—was resigning his command with immediate effect. It was a blow to the men, and it didn't make any sense. Many were sure the decision would be reversed, that it was just political posturing, or that he was threatening resignation in order to secure more men, more resources, or authorization for the reinvasion of Upper Peru.

They were equally surprised by a second announcement. San Martín had been appointed Governor of Cuyo—a small, barely populated province far south of Tucuman. He would be taking up residence immediately in Mendoza, an unimportant provincial backwater on the slopes of the Andes. Some of the men, especially those closest to him, took the announcement at its word, noting the *comandante* had been more withdrawn lately. There were rumors that the doctor had been visiting him daily. In any event, all agreed that the long and hitherto distinguished military career of José de San Martín was over, despite his relative youth.

But they were wrong.

31: Indictment

The nature of the spectacular hoax was beginning to come to light. The Stock Exchange had been duped; now it would strike back. An inquiry examined the day's trading, discovering a small group of people had made profits on the volatile movement of Omnium: Andrew Cochrane-Johnstone; his broker, Richard Butt; as well as his nephew, the M.P. for Westminster, Lord Thomas Cochrane. All three men had sold their stock before the price fell.

Investigations also focused on uncovering the origin of the false rumor of Napoleon's death. Just after midnight, in the early hours of the day in question, a man wearing a scarlet jacket—the uniform of an officer of the general class—had hammered on the door of a public house in Dover, attempting to gain access. It was shut, but the inn across the street, The Ship, opened its doors to him. The man identified himself as Lieutenant-Colonel du Bourg, Aide-de-Camp to the British Ambassador in Russia, and explained he had discreetly landed by French cargo boat. He asked the innkeeper for some paper, sent for a messenger boy, and composed an urgent message for the Port Admiral. He told the boy to deliver the note immediately, with strict instructions to wake the admiral, as the message was of the utmost importance. Lieutenant Colonel du Bourg then set off in a carriage to London. The message was recovered and read:

Sir, I have the honor to acquaint you that the Aigle *from Calais, Pierre Duquin, Master, has this moment landed me near Dover to proceed to the capital with dispatches of the happiest nature. My anxiety will not allow me to say more for your gratification than that the Allies obtained a final victory; that Bonaparte was overtaken by a party of Sachen's Cossacks who immediately slayed him, and divided his body between them. General Platoff saved Paris from being reduced to ashes. The Allied sovereigns are there, and the white cockade is universal; an immediate peace is certain. In the utmost haste, I entreat your consideration and have the honor to be, Sir, Your must obedient and humble servant, R. du Bourg, Lt.-Colonel and Aide-de-Camp to Lord Cathcart.*

This impostor had stopped off at every coach house en route to London, spreading false news of the Allied victory and Napoleon's death. On March 4th, the committee inquiring into the fraud leaked two startling findings. First, Lieutenant Colonel du Bourg had taken a hackney from Lambeth to 13 Green Street—Cochrane's home. Second, Lieutenant Colonel du Bourg was none other than Monsieur Random de Berenger.

Less than one week later, Cochrane was asked to swear an affidavit in which he admitted to de Berenger's presence in his house on that day. Two weeks following that, a bundle of clothes was found in the Thames—the scarlet uniform of an officer, similar to the one worn by du Bourg/de Berenger on that morning. Finally, on April 8th, Random de Berenger was arrested at Leith while attempting to abscond on a ship to Holland. In his possession were banknotes that were traced back to Cochrane.

The Admiralty put Cochrane on compulsory leave from his captaincy of the *Tonnant* to assist the inquiry. The evidence against him was mounting, and the vultures were circling. The only relief from this pressure was the birth of his first child, a son whom he named Tom.

* * *

When Cochrane arrived home, Kitty knew immediately that something was wrong; he looked as if he was carrying a heavy

169

weight. When he saw Kitty cradling young Tom, Cochrane forced a smile.

"Tell me," said Kitty.

"How are you, my dear?" Cochrane leaned in to kiss his child.

"Don't be evasive, Thomas. What did he say?"

Cochrane looked down at his hands, and sighed. "I have been indicted."

Kitty gasped, then summoned the nurse, instructing her to put young Tom to bed. She turned back to Cochrane. "Tell me this isn't happening."

"I'm afraid so, my love. Yours truly, Uncle Andrew, my stockbroker, and our friend Monsieur de Berenger, as well as the three men that posed as Bourbon guards that day in the City."

"I don't understand."

"Neither do I."

"No, Thomas, I mean ... what are the charges? What's the link between all of you?"

"I made a modest sum on the movements of a stock called Omnium that day. Uncle Andrew and my broker, Mr. Butt, did considerably better. Monsieur de Berenger is known to me and called at my house on the day of the hoax and, of course, he has since been accused of being the prime mover in spreading the false rumor of Napoleon's death, which caused so much havoc on the stock market."

Cochrane opened the cabinet and took out a bottle of port, pouring himself a healthy measure. He sighed before taking a sip. "That rumor, of course, was made real by the appearance in the City of the three supposed Bourbon guards. So, from the point of view of the press—and, unfortunately, the Crown—it's quite simple. We were all involved in a conspiracy to spread this false rumor to profit in the stock market."

Cochrane drained the glass. "As for the charges, it seems to me they are making them up on the spot. As far as I can see, it's not an offence on the statute books, and such hoaxes have been common all over the world since stock-jobbing began."

"But you're not guilty!"

"I know that, Kitty. I know."

"Focus on that, not whether it's a crime or not."

"I know. I'm just trying to figure out how all this has come about. Heads must roll, as they say, and mine appears to be first on the list."

Kitty indicated to the bottle of Port. "I think I'll need one of those." Cochrane poured her a measure then handed her the glass. She took a sip. "This is ghastly."

"Not as ghastly as the Crown's attempting to pin this on me. Once you examine the assumptions this neat little theory is based on, my dear, it all quite falls apart. Any judge worth his salt will simply throw it out of court."

Kitty sat down, attempting to calm herself. She looked up at Cochrane, in hope. "You are that confident?"

"It's easy to be confident when you know you are innocent. The case is ludicrous!" Cochrane began pacing the room. "If I really had perpetrated this fraud, would I have Monsieur de Berenger call to my house on the day in question? In broad daylight, too! Furthermore, why did De Berenger feel the need to disguise himself? Before coming here, he changed out of the scarlet uniform he was said to have been wearing into the green uniform of a sharpshooter. If I was part of this conspiracy, that would have been unnecessary." He stopped in front of his wife. "And really, would I risk everything just as my reputation is being restored? I've been appointed Captain of the *Tonnant* for God's sake—the finest ship in the Navy!"

"Thomas, keep your voice down or the servants will hear."

"And why in blasted hell would I instruct my stockbroker to automatically sell my stock when it rose one point over the purchase price? Do people really think I would risk my reputation for such a measly sum?"

Kitty's eyes narrowed. "What of your enemies?"

"They wouldn't stoop this low. It's an oversight, a muck-up, a misunderstanding."

She paused. "It's more than that, Thomas."

Cochrane turned to pour himself another drink. "It's worse than that, you mean. I'm a scapegoat for reckless traders who have gambled with other people's money and lost."

"They are coming after you now; they've been waiting."

"Let them come. I've never run from a fight in my life."

Kitty stood. "But you are doing worse now!"

Cochrane's brow furrowed. "How so?"

"You're not defending yourself. These newspaper articles ... these charges."

"Kitty, listen to me." Cochrane placed a hand reassuringly on her shoulder. "I will fight this all the way. I give you my word. But I have to take the advice of my lawyer."

"Which is what? Do nothing?"

"No. He recommends—and I happen to agree with him—that I cannot rebut every leak from the inquiry. I must keep a dignified silence and await my day in court, and make my case then."

"But…"

"But nothing. For good or ill, this is the system. It's what I must do, no matter how painful it is for all of us. My lawyer has never seen me wrong, and I'm going to follow his advice to the letter."

"If you say so."

Cochrane drew Kitty toward him. "My love, don't be so alarmed. They have no case—none at all. And I have one of the finest legal minds in the country on my side."

They were interrupted by a knock at the door.

Kitty sat back down again.

"Enter."

His footman handed him a note and Cochrane thanked him, scanning the contents.

"What is it?" said Kitty, alarmed by his expression.

"The Crown has appointed the lawyer to lead the prosecution." Cochrane paused. "It's Mr. Gurney."

"Who? I know that name."

"It's my lawyer—they've appointed my lawyer."

*　*　*

The trial unfolded with grim inevitability as the weight of the Establishment came crushing down upon Cochrane.

Cochrane's defense was that the evidence was circumstantial. While his broker and his uncle had made exorbitant amounts that day, Cochrane himself made only a trivial sum. He had previously instructed his broker, Richard Butt, to sell his holdings of Omnium should they ever rise above his initial purchase price. Cochrane never revised that instruction; subsequently, Richard Butt sold Cochrane's stock at that point—at a much lower price than Butt or Cochrane-Johnstone sold at later in the day.

In addition to the modest financial gain, Cochrane had just been given a chance at redemption through his command of the *Tonnant*, so a motive for participating in this fraud was difficult to establish. And in terms of de Berenger, Cochrane argued that he would be foolish in the extreme to have a co-conspirator call on him on the day in question. He contended de Berenger's appearance at his house was proof that he had nothing to do with the conspiracy, as was de Berenger's need to change into a sharpshooter's uniform first.

The case against Cochrane was weak, but none of this mattered in the end. There were greater forces at work. Just before the trial, one of Cochrane's crucial witnesses—a household servant who could corroborate what de Berenger was wearing—was spirited out of the country, suddenly finding work with the Navy. The jury was handpicked by the Crown, and the judge was a political opponent of Cochrane's—Lord Ellenborough, an arch-defender of the Establishment.

The trial commenced on June 8th and the prosecution laid out its case. Cochrane's former confidant and lawyer, Mr. Gurney, did not conclude the prosecution case until ten o'clock that evening. To the surprise of all of those present, Lord Ellenborough insisted that the defense begin their case immediately, resisting protests that they should wait until the following day. The defense made their case over the next five hours, during which time much of the jury fell asleep, and only concluded at three o'clock in the morning. Lord Ellenborough summed up the following day in an incredibly biased manner, and after just three hours the jury returned a guilty verdict against all of the defendants. The result was a shock, but the sentence was astounding: a year's imprisonment and a fine of one thousand pounds.

Cochrane was then expelled from the House of Commons, dismissed from the Navy, and stripped of his knighthood. His coat of arms, helmet, and sword were kicked down the steps of Westminster Abbey. As a final humiliation, he was ordered to be placed in the pillory outside the Royal Exchange for an hour every day for the duration of his jail sentence. While the Establishment had closed ranks against Cochrane, the public was still on his side. Such was the indignation of the people at his being placed in the pillory, that the authorities, fearing a riot, were forced to cancel this part of his sentence, leaving Cochrane with the dubious honor of being the last person in Britain to be sentenced to the stockade.

32: The Governor

Mount Aconcagua—over twenty-two thousand feet tall—towers over the wine-making region of Cuyo. For centuries, its imperious, snow-covered face watched as Mendoza grew from a struggling settlement of twelve enterprising Spaniards in 1561 to a bustling center of ten thousand inhabitants in 1814. This hitherto unimportant town became the center of intrigue when San Martín arrived to assume the Governorship. The town's fortunes had been fading; fighting in Chile had eaten into its principal source of revenue—commerce with Santiago, over the other side of the Andes. This trade route was lucrative but extremely dangerous, for the only way to cross the Andes was by lonely trails through some of the highest, most treacherous mountain passes in the world. Those who traveled this route battled year-round snowstorms, without so much as a barn to provide shelter or a storehouse to replenish supplies. Merchants who braved the route with pack mules were richly rewarded, but the risks were so great that few tried. Only those most familiar with the mountains and their unforgiving ways would attempt the journey.

On taking office, San Martín's first priority was to replace the income from taxing this trade, which had comprised two-thirds of the town's revenue. Mendoza had little rainfall and much of Cuyo was arid, but an intricate irrigation system channeled the melting springtime snows into fertilizing the surrounding plains. As a result, vineyards and large landholdings had sprung up all over the province. After sending for his eighteen-year-old bride—María de los Remedios, or *Remeditos* as he called her—from Buenos Aires, San Martín set about restructuring the taxation system. He increased levies on wine and capital, as well as the church, and confiscated land from absentee Spanish landlords.

The rich were unhappy with these tax increases, but San Martín was more concerned about antagonizing the devout. The previous year, on assuming command of the Army of the North, the outgoing commander—General Belgrano—had cautioned that the Spanish frequently waged war from the pulpit, ordering priests to denounce Patriots as heretics, and threatening the faithful with the ultimate censure if they aided the rebels: God's eternal wrath. San Martín dispatched men to the churches of the province with instructions to observe the sermons, watching for any Royalist urgings. Reports of pro-Spanish pastors led to immediate cloistering of four. He wasn't taking any chances.

There was one particular priest San Martín was curious about. Padre Luis Beltrán's rambling, incoherent sermons had left several attendees confused as to where his sentiments lay.

"Which is he then: Royalist or Patriot?" San Martín asked one of his men, who had been sent to confront the priest.

The Lieutenant hiccupped. "I asked him, sir."

San Martín noticed the Lieutenant's breath reeked of wine. "And what did he say, damn it?"

"Sorry, sir." The officer leaned against the wall for balance. "It was impossible to talk to him. I think he might be insane. He kept rabbiting on about all sorts of things. I couldn't keep track. And he kept filling me with wine—it was hard to keep up."

"And his answer?"

"He said he was a Kabbalist."

"A Kabbalist."

"Yes, sir."

"What's that?"

"I don't know, sir."

"Well, I don't like the sound of it." He dismissed the officer, and recorded the obstinate priest's name in his journal. Padre Luis Beltrán. The notes in the margin indicated he was a native of Mendoza. *Well*, he thought, *I can't afford to have someone right under my nose preaching against me.* San Martín resolved to visit him personally.

In the meantime, San Martín cut all unnecessary expenditure—halving his own salary and asking his men to do the same—and disposed of the Governor's mansion. For his living quarters, he took a two-room apartment, neatly sidestepping accusations of hypocrisy from critics of his financial reforms. It suited him anyhow; he was used to the Spartan military life and had no inclination toward luxury. *After all*, he thought, *what use is a dining room when you eat lunch in the kitchen, standing up?*

Central to his plan was the raising of an army and he continually pushed Buenos Aires for more men, more supplies, and more money—aiming to create a formidable fighting force in Cuyo. The local men were a hardy bunch. Disciplined and fatalistic, they were perfectly suited for military work. While the local horsemen were no match for the *gauchos*, there were more than enough brave riders to form the beginnings of a cavalry. To this end, San Martín requested the transfer of a squadron of Mounted Grenadiers from Tucuman to help him train new recruits. The central government acceded, keen for him to continue forming further squadrons.

San Martín had to be careful. He couldn't push too hard or he would be forced to reveal his plan, and the political climate wasn't suitable for that just yet. Still, he kept some influential friends informed—such as his father-in-law, Don Escalada—so that they could pressure the government to bow to his requests. In lieu of having his demands met, he transformed the criminal justice system of Mendoza. Prisoners were given the opportunity of enlisting in the Army and earning their freedom, and custodial sentences for all but the most heinous crimes were replaced with fines. The resultant lower prison populations allowed San Martín to transfer guards to the army. Slave-owners were pressured to free their slaves, who were coaxed into joining the army with promises of citizenship.

Justice was often dispensed by San Martín himself, in typically pragmatic fashion. For making unpatriotic remarks, one farmer was ordered to bring one hundred and twenty pumpkins to the Army kitchen. Those pumpkins were needed, as San Martín continued to recruit among the local population. When Buenos Aires, or the local wealthy taxpayers, complained about what they saw as an unnecessary build-up of troops, San Martín argued that the troops may be needed as reinforcements elsewhere, pointing to the sacrifices other provinces had made. However, he had no intention of his troops being deployed elsewhere. He focused on stockpiling rations, munitions and equipment, and set up groups of volunteer women to sew uniforms. He had his men gather rifles, pistols, muskets, sabers, and clubs from any source possible. He constantly plagued contacts in towns both inside and outside Cuyo, asking them to send blankets, ponchos, salted beef, saddles, tents, bugles, money, blacksmiths, goatskins, and volunteers. Everything was meticulously planned to the last detail. And it had to be, for what he was attempting was unprecedented.

* * *

San Martín found the priest sitting on a low wall outside his church, apparently deep in thought. San Martín cleared his throat. "Padre Beltrán?"

The priest stood, and smiled. "General, I was wondering when you would come."

"Excuse me?"

"You have cloistered four of my colleagues."

"How did you hear?"

"We priests have a special communion in the brotherhood. An intricate network, powered by prayer, through which messages can be sent." Padre Beltrán smiled, pointing at the sky. "Once they are approved by the *comandante*, of course."

San Martín chose his words carefully. "Then I'm sure you've heard that they have temporarily removed themselves from pastoral duties to focus on bible studies and won't be giving sermons or hearing confessions anytime soon." San Martín smiled, still trying to get the measure of this man.

"Nicely done."

"Excuse me?"

"A political priest is like a religious general: a castle with sails."

San Martín wondered if the man was mad. "Padre..."

"General, I know why you're here. You have already cloistered four priests for preaching for Spain, and you are trying to decide whether I'll be the fifth."

San Martín was shocked by his forthrightness.

The priest raised an eyebrow. "Am I right?"

San Martín paused. "Yes."

"Well then, please, if we are going to talk of matters of such import, can we at least step into my sacristy and talk like gentlemen."

San Martín was genuinely confused at the turn events had taken. "As you wish." Having been in a priest's sacristy before, San Martín knew what to expect—an untidy repository for all the items not used in the church on a day-to-day basis—but this was something else altogether. Towers of books leaned ominously on either side of the entrance, extending down the length of the room. San Martín saw dusty, battered texts in Latin, Greek and French, as well as Spanish. On top of the books, which covered nearly every surface, were alchemical contraptions, burners, specimen jars, metallurgical tools, elemental charts, tweezers, hacksaws, clamps and a plate, on which was something San Martín assumed to be some leftover lunch until he realized it was the desiccated remains of half a frog. There were maps from all over the world—Brazil, New Spain, Walachia, The Spice Islands, and Manchuria, even one of an exotic-sounding port-town called Waterford. Some were new, but others were so ancient they looked like they would crumble at a touch. Straining to get a closer look, San Martín almost slipped and had to steady himself against a wobbling pile of books.

"Sorry, General." Padre Beltrán came to his assistance. "I would have cleaned up had I known you were coming." The priest managed to find two relatively unencumbered chairs, scattering debris off them with a swipe of his paw. He gestured for San Martín to sit in one and then disappeared momentarily, returning with a bottle of red wine. "God's—and Mendoza's—finest creation. You don't mind?"

"Not at all, Padre. I was just thinking that the last time I was in a priest's sacristy was on my wedding day."

"Your wife isn't with you, I gather."

"No, but she is on her way, traveling across the *pampas* as we speak. Quite an adventure for her, I should imagine. I don't believe she has ever left Buenos Aires."

"Man and wife shouldn't be separated. But in times of war, the abnormal becomes normal."

"True, but it's important to hold on to some sense of the normal, lest we forget who we are."

Padre Beltrán produced a hammer, driving a nail into the cork. Then, enclosing the nail in a vice-grip, he wrenched the cork free, splattering wine on his robes in the process. He rinsed two glasses, handing one to San Martín, who raised his. "*Salud*, Padre."

"To freedom." Padre Beltrán grinned mischievously. "I must warn you, General—sorry, I have been calling you General, you are still called that, correct? Even though you resigned from the Army of the North, that is still the correct title, yes? Or should I call you Governor?"

San Martín sipped his wine. "General is fine."

"As I was saying—what was I saying?—oh yes, I must warn you, General, I don't care much for sermons. I usually make them up on the spot anyway: the weather, the war, how to buy a really good horse in the market, infidelity—that's always popular—politics, the politics of infidelity, whether it's against God's Law to whip a slave who takes the Lord's name in vain. It really is whatever pops into my head on the day. But I can't have you take away the confessions, they are my lifeblood and the only thing that keeps me sane."

San Martín raised an eyebrow.

"I know what you are thinking," said Padre Beltrán. "Priests love confessions, they love pronouncing judgment on people, fire and brimstone, penance, all of that. But it's not like that for me. I'm different because I am weak." Padre Beltrán cocked his head to the side, as if trying to dislodge some bathwater from his ear. "Or am I stronger because I know I am weak? After all, Socrates said, 'wisest is she who knows what she does not know'. Although, why the 'she'? I hope he wasn't aiming that only at women, although God

A Storm Hits Valparaíso

knows with him, he did prefer the company of small boys after all. Anyway, my point is, I know my limitations. I may be one of God's faithful footmen, but I am a man, body and flesh, and I am weak. And when I hear confession it gives me strength, because I am not as weak as them. Well, most of the time. I usually don't count the children; some of them are so pious it really makes me worry for the future."

"Padre..."

"I'm sorry, Governor. No, we decided on General didn't we? I got a little distracted. This is nice wine, isn't it? Would you like some more? Of course you would." Padre Beltrán refilled San Martín's glass. "So, General, what's your plan?"

"What plan? I don't understand."

"Come now, a man like you doesn't leave a promising position at the height of his career to become a glorified administrator in a nowhere town like Mendoza without a plan. I see you are already recruiting heavily for the army. You've emptied the jails to that end. So, what's the plan? You must have a plan."

"I have no idea what..."

"That's all right, you don't have to tell me. After all, we're barely acquainted. Perhaps when we know each other a little better." Padre Beltrán suddenly stood. "Well General, I'll think over everything that you said. I know you're a busy man, so I'll let you get on with things. Just remember, if you need anything, anything at all, come to me." Padre Beltrán walked the dazed San Martín out the side door. "And if you have any news about how things are going in Colombia, let me know. I have a cousin in the Patriot forces there. His last letter insisted they have the bastard Spanish on the back foot, but I haven't heard anything since. That was eight months ago. I worry about him. All he wanted was a girl and a piece of land, and I pray he will live to fulfill his dream."

As the priest walked him toward the front gate of the church, San Martín asked what battalion his cousin was serving in, and promised to see what he could do.

"General, you can do great things here." Padre Beltrán put his hand on San Martín's shoulder. "You still have that fire; I can see it. They are saying you're finished, but I don't believe a word of

181

it. I'm sorry if I said too much, but I want you to know you have a friend here, and an ally."

San Martín wasn't sure what to say.

The priest continued. "After my unit was overrun near Talca, I took off my uniform and walked back here to Mendoza. But when I saw—"

"Excuse me, Padre, your unit?"

He saluted. "Lieutenant Beltrán, sir. Artillery, volunteer."

"Why didn't you say?"

"You never asked." Padre Beltrán's eyes twinkled. "Besides, my new boss outranks you."

San Martín said goodbye and walked toward his apartment, trying to collect his thoughts and feeling a little woozy from the wine the priest had forced on him. Padre Beltrán was an interesting man, that was for sure—and that was probably the only thing he was sure about.

33: The Battle of Rancagua

On the other side of the Andes, the Chilean revolution was floundering. Popular support for the Royalists was widespread, particularly in the south. From Peru, the Spanish could reinforce the Royalists at will. To compound matters for the Patriots, fratricidal disputes were endemic in their ranks. Coup after coup, one faction overthrowing another, had left the rebel forces disunited and weak.

In March 1813, a Spanish advance party landed in the south to arm the Royalists and foment discord. Heading north, the Royalist army of three thousand swelled as sympathizers flocked to the invaders. One month later, the junta governing Chile replaced the head of the armed forces—José Miguel Carrera, who claimed a pure bloodline back to the conquistadors—with Bernardo O'Higgins, the half Irish bastard son of the former Viceroy of Peru. Carrera took the news badly, imprisoning the messenger and refusing to relinquish power. He eventually relented, but from that day forth his jealousy of the popular, jovial O'Higgins became outright hatred. Four days into the new leader's command, Lima again reinforced the Royalists who now numbered several thousand. O'Higgins had but two thousand under his command, mostly raw recruits. A siege in Santiago seemed inevitable as the remaining Patriot forces abandoned the cities of the south and raced north to consolidate. To the surprise of many, just as the Patriots began to dig in, a truce was announced. Santiago rejoiced, relieved.

O'Higgins knew the truce was nothing more than an attempt to buy time, which was confirmed when yet another large Spanish force landed from Peru. Soon they had advanced to the Cachapola River, just fifty miles from Santiago. On September 30th, the Spaniards crossed, but instead of pressing on to Santiago, they followed the bank toward the town of Rancagua. The Patriot Army was split into three detachments, headed respectively by O'Higgins and the other two Carrera brothers—Luís and Juan José. Luís Carrera, ordered to hold the ground between the river and Santiago, retreated. Juan José Carrera, charged with blocking the Spaniard's path, lost his nerve and fled to Rancagua, pursued by the enemy.

O'Higgins was in a bind. He could join the retreating Luís Carrera and attempt to take some kind of stand in Santiago; however, this would mean abandoning Juan José Carrera and a sizable portion of the Patriot Army to near-certain death in Rancagua. His aides advised him to join the retreat, arguing he didn't have sufficient troops to save Rancagua and would merely be adding to the long list of dead. Ignoring this, O'Higgins rode into Rancagua with his men, taking a brave stand beside Juan José Carrera, who had continually undermined and opposed his leadership and had even engineered a succession of coups.

Rancagua was a typical mid-sized Colonial Spanish town. A succession of low buildings lined a grid of streets that radiated from a central plaza where the Patriots concentrated their men and their stores. Snipers crouched on rooftops and the streets were barricaded and covered by cannons. The odds were against the Patriots. The Spanish had nearly five thousand advancing on Rancagua while O'Higgins had less than two thousand now, many lacking any weaponry other than clubs. He ordered the Chilean flag shrouded in black, a clear signal to the men that this battle would be to the death.

The fighting was vicious. Cannon fire filled the air as bullets whistled in both directions. Battles were fought street by street and the enemy kept advancing, only to be repelled again and again by the desperate defenders. When they ran out of bullets, they fixed bayonets and charged. When the enemy got too close for bayonets, they drew their daggers. And when the daggers were knocked from their hands, they fought with their fists: punching, grappling, choking, and gouging in the mud and the blood. At the end of the first day of fighting, bodies lay heaped in all directions. O'Higgins—running low on men, water, and ammunition—estimated he could only hold out for one more day. He managed to get a message out to Luís Carrera, urgently requesting reinforcements. It was his only hope.

The following morning, the Spanish resumed their assault. The Patriots began to weaken and the Spanish closed in on the plaza. Suddenly, a shout came from the bell tower: Luís Carrera was approaching with reinforcements. The Spanish were forced to divide their men to prevent being attacked at their rear and, for the first time in these two grueling days, the momentum was with the Patriots. It did not last long. O'Higgins and Chile had been betrayed by the Carrera brothers again. Before engaging the Spanish, Luís Carrera halted his advancing column and retreated once more toward Santiago. After this cruel trick, all the fight went out of the Patriots. They were resigned to their demise, their arms heavier, their throats drier, their spirits crushed.

O'Higgins attempted to rally his men, but when his ammunition dump was set alight by a stray spark, his position became hopeless. He ordered the buildings surrounding the plaza be torched to provide a cover of smoke. Then he gave the final command for all who could to fight their way out. Abandoning their defensive positions behind the final set of barricades, the Patriots hurled themselves on the Spanish hordes, attempting to carve a path through the enemy, over the bodies of their fallen comrades. O'Higgins' horse was caught at one of his own barricades, then shot beneath him. The beast stumbled and fell as O'Higgins flung himself onto his assailant's mount, disposed of the enemy soldier, then led his new steed and his men down the main road out of Rancagua, swinging his sword at all he could see.

Fewer than five hundred made it out alive, among them O'Higgins and Juan José Carrera. After butchering any prisoners, the Spaniards entered the church, raped the women, and slaughtered the children. As a final insult—amid the riotous looting that followed—the Royalists torched the hospital, murdering the bed-ridden patients inside.

O'Higgins rode through the night to Santiago, forcing his tired mount the last few miles, determined to find out who had given the order to Luís Carrera to turn around. He suspected José Miguel Carrera, the man he had replaced, and who admitted as much when confronted in the Captain-General's palace.

"You should have broken out sooner," Carrera sneered.

O'Higgins' mouth fell open in shock.

"I had to preserve some fragment of the army. It was the only way we would be able to resurrect the revolution in the north, after ceding Santiago of course," said José Miguel.

O'Higgins couldn't believe what he was hearing. "You had no right—"

"You had no right to lead your men to certain death. As a result of your irresponsible actions, I have been forced to assume command, and the officers back me. I will need you to—"

O'Higgins cut him off. "I'm taking my men across the Andes, along with any civilians that want our protection, seeing as you are going to abandon them to the Spanish."

Carrera thumped the desk. "Coward! I will raise the flag of rebellion in the north—alone if I have to."

Holding his tongue, O'Higgins gathered his family and set off, at the head of a column of refugees, toward the mountains. José Miguel dispatched men to block access to the mountain passes, but once his soldiers saw the wretched state of those fleeing, they relented. Having second thoughts about continuing the fight on their own, the cowardly Carreras joined the rear of the refugee column.

34: Exodus

Outriders had gone ahead to brief the Governor of Mendoza, but no one warned the people, who soon experienced the visceral horror of war. They were not prepared for the wounded, the lame, and the mad, nor for the crying orphans and the starving women, and certainly not for the soldiers—the few veterans of the disaster at Rancagua, with the glazed eyes of failure and the inexplicable guilt of the survivor.

Many dropped in the streets leading into Mendoza, unable to carry on and hoping someone would take pity on them. They had braved the treacherous mountain passes from Santiago, fleeing from the rampaging Spanish, many without adequate provisions or clothing, let alone a mule to carry them. All the while, they knew many would not survive the crossing, but they also knew that staying behind would have meant certain death, as the ruthless Spaniards exacted retribution for the effrontery of Chile's proclamation of independence. So to the mountains they had fled, led by the survivors of the Battle of Rancagua, who rode ahead to beat down the heavy drifts of snow.

Patriot supporters knew Spanish revenge would be swift and merciless; there were enough Royalist sympathizers in Santiago to pinpoint them. Some chose to stay—a fatal error. Those who survived the interrogations, the beatings, the rape, the torture, the burning of buildings, and the random executions, were imprisoned in conditions that made death preferable.

Death came regardless. Some months after the rebels escaped, when the Spanish had taken full control of Chile, hundreds of prisoners were brutally massacred. Those who fled fared little better. It was October, the beginning of spring. Heavy snow blanketed the high mountain passes. The Patriot soldiers attempted to organize the refugees, which proved impossible, so instead they quickly prioritized a retreat to the mountains before the Spanish could pick them off.

Catalina was lucky.

"The Patriots were defeated," a bleary-eyed messenger warned the café owner. "The Spanish will take Santiago in a matter of days." He needed several shots of *aguardiente* to calm his nerves. "The Army is offering its protection to anyone who wants to cross the mountain passes to Mendoza." While this announcement caused a stir, after a short debate, it was clear that evacuation was the only logical course of action.

"We don't have much time," Catalina told the patrons. "We must gather our possessions and then meet here in the morning."

"Leave?" scoffed one of the older patrons. "Look!" He held out his arthritic hands. "I am too old to go anywhere. What would the Spanish want with an old man like me? Surely they will just leave me to kill myself." He smiled, lifting his glass shakily to his lips. Emboldened, several others also agreed, not wanting to abandon the only place they knew, hoping some clemency might be shown to the elderly. They were wrong.

The owner also refused to leave. "Catalina, you must go on without us."

"They know who you are. You can't stay here. "Where will you go?"

"North," he said, refusing to say more, no matter how much she pressed him. Soon, she was forced to leave, hurrying home to make what preparations she could.

The next morning, an officer came to the café to explain the plans for evacuation. "We can only protect those who come with us," he told them. "Those who stay risk the likelihood of bloody reprisal and death."

"But it's October," complained one old man. "We'll freeze to death."

The officer paused. "The journey will be arduous and the Army is very short on supplies. We won't be able to provide food or medical supplies. Wear your warmest clothes. Take blankets. Pack sufficient provisions for a two-week journey, and, if possible, bring a mule or a horse. We will assemble on the road to the town of Los Andes."

Catalina had spent what little savings she had on a thick llama-wool poncho, a warm blanket, and as much salted beef as she could carry. It wasn't much, but she felt fortunate when she saw the ragged refugees fleeing with nothing. She walked along the column, trying to find anyone she knew.

"Catalina?"

An arm reached out and clutched her own and she looked up, into the face of a woman.

"It's Teresa, remember? I met you in that awful boarding house a few months back. You helped me."

Catalina recognized her now. Her face had healed nicely, and she was very beautiful, as Catalina had suspected. The two of them hugged and kissed as if they were old friends.

"I am surprised to see you here," said Teresa. "You were going to go home, weren't you? Where was it again ... Valparaíso, no?"

Catalina said nothing, and Teresa had enough sense to change the subject. "I suppose I'm more surprised by the people who aren't here—either they're foolish or traitors."

But Catalina wasn't listening, distracted by the tears that rolled down her face. Teresa moved her away from the refugees. "Don't worry about walking for now," she soothed. "It will be easier once everyone else has flattened down the snow anyhow."

Catalina nodded and then told Teresa everything.

Just as they began moving again, a desperate woman with a pale, listless child came begging. Catalina took pity on her, giving her some salted cheese.

"What are you are doing?" Teresa admonished after the beggar had left. "She's never going to survive the crossing. You've just wasted precious food."

Although surprised at the ferocity of Teresa's outburst, Catalina knew she was right. They would freeze to death before they made it out of Chile.

The human train grew, winding its way through the foothills of the Andes, supplemented by late stragglers, opportunistic traders, and the families of the soldiers who lived in the outlying towns. It took them a week to reach thirteen thousand feet, the summit of the mountain passes, and the same time again to reach the outskirts of Mendoza, crossing five mountain ranges along the way. Many died from malnutrition, altitude sickness, and hypothermia—their bodies tossed into the ravines below. By the time Catalina, Teresa, and the last of the refugees descended, a camp had been set up at the edge of Mendoza. The Governor had promised the Chileans he had ample provisions to feed them all, and he wanted to maintain order in the city. What he didn't tell them was that he was sure the Spanish had infiltrated the refugees; he wanted to weed out the spies before they had a chance to report to Santiago.

* * *

San Martín's assurances didn't stop fights breaking out over the allocation of tents and the distribution of food. While the Chileans were able to put aside their internecine disputes while confronted with the common enemy of the Spanish, in Mendoza, kicking their heels, the scramble for power began anew. Spain had complete control over Chile; all they were fighting for was titular head of the army in exile. This wasn't even theirs to bestow, San Martín had already decided. Much to the chagrin of the Carrera brothers, about whom San Martín had received several unfavorable reports, Bernardo O'Higgins was recognized as the commander of the estranged Chileans. Sensing trouble, the Governor ordered the Carreras to San Luis, a small town far to the east of Mendoza.

José Miguel Carrera refused to comply, believing he had sufficient support among the soldiers and refugees to force the issue. San Martín surrounded the Carrera brothers and their backers with a thousand men, capturing them as they slept. The recalcitrant Chilean soldiers were sent to Buenos Aires, along with emissaries to explain the action taken. The Carreras were taken under armed guard to San Luis. San Martín had stamped his authority, and most Chileans were glad to be rid of the corrosive influence of the Carrera family.

A few days later, San Martín sat in one of the pews outside Padre Beltrán's confessional box. When the penitent left, the priest stuck his head out to see if any confessors were waiting. San Martín hailed him. "Padre, I have some bad news."

"Please, please, step inside the sacristy. I don't want to take the Lord's name here." The sacristy was more chaotic than San Martín remembered, with an unpleasant tang in the air that he couldn't quite place. A beaker had been knocked over and must have contained something acidic, given the path it had chewed through a pile of books. "Iguana piss," said Padre Beltrán, seeing San Martín wrinkle his nose. "I brought one in to open him up, but the poor sod came back to life as soon as the scalpel entered his back. He ran around hissing and pissing himself until I managed to shoo him out the door."

San Martín was lost for words.

"Never knew I had healing hands," said Padre Beltrán. "Must keep that quiet; I'm busy enough as it is." The priest brushed the acid-eaten books off the chair and handed it to San Martín. Looking at the unctuous ooze covering the seat, San Martín decided to stand.

Padre Beltrán poured two glasses of wine. "So, he's dead then."

"I'm afraid so."

"Do you know what happened?"

"His unit was wiped out north of La Puerta—an ambush."

Padre Beltrán blessed himself. "My cousin went to Buenos Aires when he was just sixteen, got in with some smugglers, ended up working the route between Jamaica and Venezuela. When the fighting broke out up there, he signed up straight away. I urged him to return home, but he met a local girl and considered it home. I thought about visiting him some day. Now I'll never get the chance."

"Their day of reckoning will come, Padre."

"Amen." They drank in silence before the priest spoke again. "General, can we be frank for a moment?"

"By all means."

"All these *chilenos* now up at El Plumerillo, they are not planning to stay are they? I mean, they are going to want to return to Chile at some point?"

"I would imagine so."

"And you are probably going to want to help them, yes?"

"In some capacity, yes. But my hands are tied by Buenos Aires. There is only so much I can do."

Padre Beltrán gave him a skeptical look. "I want to offer you my services."

"As chaplain?"

"Good Lord, no." Padre Beltrán blessed himself once more. "I had something else in mind."

Padre Beltrán outlined his proposal to San Martín, who said he would consider it and then bade goodbye, apologizing once again for the priest's loss.

* * *

Catalina—ejected from Teresa's tent while she earned a living—began looking around the camp for any of the former patrons from the café. She found not a single one. With some guilt she remembered her aunt, Concepcion, but could find no trace of her either. *They all either died on the way here*, she thought, *or risked staying in Santiago after all.* Eventually, tired of looking, she took to chatting to some of the Chilean soldiers who were awaiting their turn in Teresa's tent.

"I'll happily take you if she's unavailable," one of the men, and not the last, propositioned.

"You could never afford me," Catalina responded, shocked by the coarseness of her own words, and, more particularly, her own thoughts.

In the mornings, she would giggle with Teresa over a cup of *mate* as her friend's encounters were described in minute detail, sparing no one's blushes. The men's proclivities and perversities astonished Catalina; nevertheless, she soon found herself fantasizing about what it would be like to sleep with all of these strangers—all these *chilenos* who risked their lives to fight the Spanish.

"I keep dreaming about sleeping with all these men, wondering what it is like," she confided to Teresa one morning after a particularly tortuous dream.

"Well, if you are going to sleep with them," Teresa teased, "you might as well get paid for it."

35: Escape

It was long past sundown on March 6th, and the intermittent flicker of a lamp could be witnessed on the top floor. The King's Bench Prison's most famous inmate—Lord Thomas Cochrane—was getting his affairs in order. It wasn't a high-security jail, being home primarily to debtors and fraudsters, and Cochrane's status allowed him certain liberties. He was permitted to pay for the comparative luxury of a two-room cell, to arrange for the preparation of his own food, to use writing materials, and to enjoy a certain freedom with visitors. His wife and newborn son were permitted to share the cell with him, but Cochrane refused to let Kitty and the child suffer such degradation, despite his wife's initial insistence.

Putting the finishing touches to a letter to his wife, Cochrane folded it over and placed in the center of his desk, on top of the rest of his correspondence. He did not bother with an envelope, knowing, from nine months of experience, that the prison authorities would only rip it open anyhow. From under his mattress, he took the stout rope he had smuggled in. Securing it around his right shoulder, he wound another, lighter rope around his waist.

Getting out of the high, unbarred window of his cell and onto the roof was always going to be the easy part. Now, standing on the roof, Cochrane swore the distance between the building and the spiked wall below was greater than he remembered. He caught his breath for a moment, going over the plan one more time in his head. Taking the rope off his shoulder, he looked around for a suitable anchor point. A gargoyle fit the bill; Cochrane noted with amusement that it was somewhat reminiscent of Lord Yarmouth's wife.

Cochrane tied a running noose and stood at the edge, examining the distance to the wall and slowly feeding out sufficient slack. *This is it*, he thought, *no turning back now*. After ensuring the slack was free from encumbrance, he tossed the rope outwards, watching it sail past the perimeter wall before snapping back and coiling around the iron spikes on top. He laughed to himself, knowing no one would ever believe he got it on the first attempt. Kneeling again at the gargoyle, Cochrane pulled the rope taut and retied it, making doubly sure it was secure. He crouched in wait until he was sure the noise had not aroused any guards into patrolling, and then tested his weight on the rope. It was a fair distance to travel, and the sedentary nature of his confinement hardly prepared him for the exertion of dragging himself hand-over-hand. He was about halfway across when he nearly lost his grip, startled by distant barking. Pausing, he reminding himself that he wasn't on a mission—life had become one instead.

As he reached the outer wall and swung himself upward, Cochrane had difficulty avoiding the sharp spikes. One caught on the rope around his waist, fraying the rope a little, he noticed. It would have to do. Careful to keep the damaged end toward the bottom, and looking down for any passers-by, Cochrane secured the rope around one of the spikes and began lowering himself down. Some twenty feet before he reached the ground, the rope snapped. He hit the street with a thud. After lying there, dazed, for several minutes, Cochrane got up—bruised but unbroken—and limped in the direction of the safe house.

Kitty was under constant surveillance, which upset her greatly. The only news she had was Cochrane's letter—written just before he had absconded and telling her not to worry. Each day, the newspapers printed another claim about her husband's whereabouts. He was said to have fled to Jersey, or to France, or to be in hiding in an Apothecary's shop in Ipswich. Finally, he was rumored to have gone mad and it was said that the wardens had promulgated the false story of his disappearance to prevent a riot. The only real information the authorities had was gleaned from another letter Cochrane had left on his desk, addressed to the Speaker of the House of Commons.

Cochrane had been expelled from Parliament following his conviction, but had won the subsequent by-election—the voters of Westminster convinced of his innocence. The letter to the Speaker announced his intention to take his seat in the House. Inevitably, the news was leaked to the press. If anything, Cochrane's fame and popularity had increased since his trial and imprisonment. Many believed he was set up, paying the price for his intransigent anti-establishmentarianism.

Two week after his escape, Cochrane appeared in the House, causing uproar. The Bow Street Runners were sent for, to take him into custody, but he refused to recognize their authority within the chamber, forcing them to carry him out on their shoulders. Cochrane was held for three weeks in solitary confinement in a cold, damp, subterranean cell. The authorities relented and returned him to a normal cell—this time with no unbarred windows—only when he was diagnosed with typhus.

Two months later, toward the end of his sentence, news came from Waterloo: Napoleon had finally been defeated.

36: The Whorehouse

Diego stood in the shade of a willow tree, his back resting against the trunk. Surrounding him were the crumpled pages of a letter he had been trying to compose all afternoon. The scrivener looked up at him expectantly and then sighed.

"Technology has brought us cannons and rifles, sir." He handed the latest effort to Diego. "But still no easier way to communicate than struggling with parchment and quill, each sentence taunting our creativity."

Taking the paper, Diego crumpled it into ball then dropped some coins into the scrivener's hand. As he walked toward the *Cabildo*, several people hailed him, inquiring as to his well-being. *Pleasant people here,* he thought, *easy-going, more relaxed than Tucuman.* Immediately he felt guilty; the people of Mendoza had not yet had to deal with the pain and suffering and death that war brings.

It had been ten days since Diego, Jorge and an entire squadron of Grenadiers had arrived from Tucuman. He had to admit that whatever apprehension he had felt had quickly dissolved in the clear mountain air. He was far from the front here, which suited him just fine. Jorge felt quite differently. He had been annoyed that they were moving away from the center of the action, far from the land he had carefully reconnoitered and disrupting the relationships he had cultivated with more-senior officers. Diego did not understand Jorge's ambition to climb the ranks. The way Diego saw it, prestige was not worth making oneself a juicier target for the enemy. He was happy to be anonymous, hoping that would be enough to enable him to survive. Being away from the front and seeing more of the country was a pleasant bonus, even if Mendoza was a little quiet.

Diego spent his free afternoons wandering alone through the city. Jorge came the first couple of times, but as soon as he heard that the *chileno* refugees were camped just outside Mendoza, he spent all his of time there, questioning the veterans of Rancagua about the tactics the Spanish had used. Diego went only once, finding it boring. Now even these walks were beginning to bore him. His blood was hot, but he had no release. If only he could write that damn letter. Turning, he strode off in the direction of the scrivener.

* * *

Over in the Chilean camp, Catalina was cooking a fresh batch of *empañadas*. She looked up at Teresa and paused before speaking. "Teresa, why did you decide to..."

"Become a *puta*?" Teresa smiled. "You can say it. I know what I am."

Catalina blushed.

"And it wasn't that simple. I didn't just wake up one day and decide to become a prostitute. It happened more ... gradually."

Catalina let her friend find the words.

"I ran away from home, like you, but for different reasons. My father drank too much and had difficulty keeping a job. He used to beat my mother. Sometimes I wished he would strike me instead of her."

"Did he ever?"

"No! God, no. He wasn't a good man, but he wasn't a bad man either. He loved us. He just couldn't control his drinking. And when drunk, he couldn't control his temper. I think he thought he had failed us—I suppose he had in a way." Teresa took a hot *empañada*, jiggling it in her hands before leaving it to cool on the plate. "We didn't care so much if we had a nice house or new clothes, we just wanted the gentle father we remembered as small children. I am not sure exactly what changed him; I was too young to remember."

"How old were you when you left?"

"Fifteen. I got a job as maid for a rich family. Santiago was full of important people then. The Viceroy would visit from Lima and they would have these wonderful balls all over the city. I was quite a beauty then, before time had its way with me, and I liked to go out dancing."

"You're beautiful now." Catalina added another *empañada* to the sizzling oil.

"Well, you should have seen me then! Half the men in the city were chasing me, some of them very wealthy."

"And what happened? Sorry, I mean..." Catalina blushed.

"That's all right." Teresa nibbled at one corner of her *empañada* before answering, "As I said, it was gradual. Young men would take me out for dinner to nice restaurants. They would buy me presents—necklaces, dresses, rings—all on the promise of spending a night with me. I slept with them all, not really admitting to myself at first that they were paying for my body. Eventually, I was recommended as somebody's escort to a masked ball. I went, but I was shocked when he gave me a gold ingot the next morning and thanked me for my *services*. I wasn't sure what to think. A little embarrassed, perhaps. But after a few days I realized I could give up my job as a maid and live very comfortably."

"It was that easy ... to make that decision?" Catalina's eyes remained fixed on the pastries that fried in the pan.

"I figured I'd been giving it away more or less free for years—or at least for a nice dinner, a brooch, a bracelet. I was uneasy about it at first, sure, but it made sense in a strange way. And I got used to it soon enough."

"It's not what I expected."

"What did you expect?" Teresa laughed. "A dark, troubling episode from my past?"

"I don't know. The way you talk, it's like you chose it."

"I did choose it."

"I know. I just always assumed women were forced into it, one way or the other."

"Some are. But some of us choose this life."

"Do you have any regrets?"

"It's easier to have regrets when you have some hairy beast on top of you, sweating out his night's drinking."

Catalina laughed.

"No, not really. I wish I had put aside more money; done something with it." Teresa wiped a crumb from the corner of her mouth. "But I wasted it all on the high life. Although," she smiled, "I had a good time doing it."

* * *

When Madam Feliz arrived six weeks later, everything changed. Her full retinue, moving wholesale from Tucuman, arrived under the cover of a gypsy circus she had met on the road to Mendoza. She set about making connections and greasing palms, and leased a building on a quiet road in between the city and the Chilean camp.

Diego was promised a cut of the profits if he drummed up business, but soon realized his efforts weren't needed. Word quickly spread about the quality of the girls and the relatively unrigged roulette table. Madam Feliz insisted on sticking to her side of the bargain, even after Diego confessed that the soldiers had required little coaxing. She had been losing money in Tucuman, and Diego's letter had saved her from going under. Soon, the place was busier than it had ever been in Tucuman.

* * *

Trembling, Catalina fumbled with the clasp of her brassiere. She had never worn one before, but Madam Feliz insisted upon it.

His eyes widened. "And the rest," he said.

She unclipped her stockings, rolling them, one by one, off her legs and leaving them coiled like snakeskin on the floor. After a pause, she removed her knickers, letting them fall on top of the stockings.

"What did you say your name was?"

She paused. "Catalina."

The man smiled. "I'm Carlito. Now come here."

Catalina could smell *aguardiente* on his breath—and sweat-smothered cologne—but at least he was clean, more or less. She closed her eyes as he cupped her breasts and tried not to recoil from his touch. The rough brush of his whiskers on her nipples made her flinch. His hand on her thigh made her visibly jump.

"What battalion are you in?" she asked nervously, attempting to slow him down, at least until she got used to this.

"My original unit was destroyed in Rancagua." Carlito's eyes hardened and he let go of her. "They move me around so much now, I can barely remember, myself. Today it was the eleventh. Tomorrow, who knows?"

"You are *chileno*?" Catalina was confused by his accent.

"No," he said with a laugh, "*argentino*. A couple of units were lucky enough to be volunteered to go over and help out. Not that it made much difference." He picked at a loose stitch in the seam of his trousers.

Catalina felt herself warming to him. "What you did was very brave," she said, lifting his chin up with a finger and bringing his lips to hers.

"I just hate this waiting." He jumped up from his chair, his face suddenly dark. "I can't wait until I get another Spanish soldier in my sights. I won't wait this time. Bam! Not after seeing what they did."

Catalina's heart quickened as Carlito tore off his shirt and grabbed her, kissing her hard. She pulled back for a moment, and he pushed her toward the bed, but her foot caught in her discarded stockings and she fell backward. The crack of her head against the small bedside table was followed by a yelp of pain.

He rushed to her side. "Are you hurt?"

Catalina rubbed her head. "I'm fine. Really. I wasn't as bad as it sounded."

"I'm sorry. I'm a little nervous. I haven't done this for a while." He helped her up off the floor.

"That's all right. It's the same for me." He raised an eyebrow, dubious.

201

"No, really," said Catalina. "This is my first time." She had difficulty saying the word. "As ... as a prostitute."

Carlito picked his shirt up off the floor. "I'm sorry, maybe this was a mistake."

Catalina laughed.

"Why are you laughing?"

"You've already paid! I am going to have to do this some time, and you seem nice. I—" Catalina was interrupted by another kiss, this time more gentle. Running her hands over his torso, she slid them down to remove his trousers, and then playfully pushed him onto the bed. They both laughed as he dragged her down on top of him. Then he rolled over and disentangled his legs from his trousers while Catalina lay there, her heart pounding.

"Do you mind if I blow out the candle?"

Catalina shook her head. She made herself comfortable under the sheet, but as soon as he had extinguished the light, he pulled it off her and crawled on top of her. He was hard now, and she stifled a giggle at the sight. Kissing her neck, Carlito parted her thighs with his knee and, resting on his left forearm, reached down and touched her. Then, slowly, he gently worked himself inside her, each thrust reaching deeper and deeper, becoming increasingly more frantic. His kisses turned to bites; her caresses to scratches. Just as Catalina began to sweat, his body convulsed in a violent shudder and he slumped against her, his damp chest hair tickling her bare breasts. A minute passed like this. Then he kissed her once on the cheek and slid out—rolling over on his back—still panting.

A little later, when Carlito had left, Teresa knocked on the door. "How was it?"

Catalina let her in. "All right. He was nice. Nervous—but not as nervous as me. I was worried he could hear my heart rattling around in its cage."

"He wasn't rough? Some of them can be rough." Teresa eyed Catalina critically, looking for any change in her friend.

"No, he was gentle."

Teresa smiled. "Not too gentle, I hope."

They both laughed. "What's that for?" Catalina pointed to the lemon Teresa held.

A Storm Hits Valparaíso

Teresa cut it in half and handed it to her. "Squeeze this inside you. It should keep everything clean and prevent you-know-what." Teresa tapped her stomach, causing Catalina to bless herself. "Do you want me to show you?"

"No! I think I can figure it out."

"Just lie on your back and..."

Catalina laughed and pushed Teresa out the door.

"One last thing," said Teresa. "Madam Feliz said that if you want to leave it at one customer tonight, you can."

Catalina shook her head. "I'm fine. But remember: only soldiers."

Teresa laughed. "She knows. Don't worry, you've told her enough times. Come downstairs when you are ready. Take your time."

Twenty minutes later, Catalina went downstairs to get a drink. Teresa was gone, probably upstairs with a customer, so she introduced herself to another of the girls, Esmeralda. A young man in a Grenadier's uniform entered, roundly greeted by everyone. "Who is that?" said Catalina.

"Diego," answered Esmeralda in a cold voice.

"Who is he?"

Esmeralda clenched her jaw. "It's a long story."

"He's very handsome."

Esmeralda didn't reply. She walked over to Diego and threw her arms around him, nibbling his ear and shooting Catalina a look that required no deciphering. Just as his foot was on the first step, with Esmeralda leading him by the hand, he broke away and came to the bar to ask for a bottle, noticing Catalina for the first time. Their eyes met. Diego opened his mouth, as if about to speak, but no words came, only a gasp. He went on staring at Catalina. Before she could introduce herself, Esmeralda came between them, grabbed the *aguardiente*, and led him away.

Catalina slept with Diego the following night. When Catalina left the bedroom afterwards, Esmeralda glared at her. Catalina met her stare. *I'll have to keep an eye on this one*, she thought.

203

37: A Case of Mistaken Identity

As Diego spent more and more time at the whorehouse, Jorge grew increasingly estranged from his brother. When Diego had told him about his arrangement with Madam Feliz, anger had welled up inside him and he had stormed from the room. He had worked hard to become a man of standing, only to have Diego drag him down. *If mother were still alive, she would be very disappointed at the path Diego has taken*, Jorge thought, although it didn't really surprise him. Diego always wanted to experience everything, which usually trumped whether something was right or wrong. But what really annoyed him was that Diego was suddenly everyone's friend. Even the officers would stop to chat Diego, ignoring Jorge. He could bear it only by keeping busy, training and patrolling. There would be action soon; he wanted to be ready.

Two armies were swelling on either side of the Andes. The way he saw it, sooner or later one of them was going to be game enough to attack. Everyone said there was no way to get an army over the mountains in condition enough to fight, but there was a lot of talk of about the Indian routes to the south. Any army passing through there would have to get the Mapuche on their side, which wasn't easy. Even if they did, they would still be a long way from Santiago, and Royalist support was stronger in the south. The only other option Jorge could see was marching to Buenos Aires, sailing around Cape Horn into the Pacific Ocean, and attacking Valparaíso by sea. But that was a long, perilous journey, and the Spaniards had bigger, better, faster ships—and plenty more of them.

In Tucuman, he had contacts and would have been able to find something out, but Jorge had no friends here. Diego had tried to take him to Madam Feliz's a couple of times, but he always refused. One night, his brother entered the barracks drunk, waking Jorge by placing his hand over his mouth and beckoning him—just as he did when they were children. Rubbing his eyes, Jorge followed him outside. Diego was making very little sense, babbling on about some *puta* he had slept with. He said he was in love, that she was the girl of his dreams. After some time, Jorge realized that Diego meant this in a literal sense—that this *puta* was the girl who had haunted Diego's sleep all those lonely nights in prison. It didn't make sense to Jorge, but he humored Diego, letting him talk himself tired before removing his boots and helping him into bed.

A few days later, Jorge was disciplining one of the new recruits over the condition of his horse.

"What's going on here, Corporal?" one of his superiors, who was walking past, called to him.

"Sir, this Cavalryman hasn't been tending to his horse. Twice now he's neglected to clean his mount after returning him to the stable. I won't—"

The officer raised his hand. "Corporal, screaming and shouting won't get you anywhere." The officer picked up a cloth and dunked it in the bucket, handing it to Jorge. "Why don't you show him how it's done?" He clapped Jorge on the back. "Next time, try to be a little more personable. More like Diego."

Jorge couldn't believe he had been upbraided in front of his men. Maybe he was being a little harsh, but it was important. Yet what annoyed him most was the final comment. He fumed for the rest of the day, cursing his brother's sudden popularity.

As soon as he was off-duty, Jorge hurried to a small bar near the barracks. He didn't usually drink, but today he needed one. Still fuming, he didn't speak to a soul, instead sitting in the corner and drinking his *aguardiente*, flinching every time someone laughed. By nightfall, he was good and drunk—more than drunk. He hadn't eaten since breakfast and his stomach now held a lot more alcohol than he could handle. All he could hear were his superior's words repeating in his head, *More like Diego*. Angry again, Jorge paid his bill and left, walking without any particular direction in mind. Staggering down the road, oblivious, he walked and walked until he reached that moment of drunken clarity that gives way to the impulse of a radical decision. Ten minutes later, with the dangerous faux-sobriety of a man who has straightened up enough to think he is acting rationally, he stepped inside Madam Feliz's Gambling House.

Catalina spotted him as soon as he walked in, and sidled up to him.

"A drink," Jorge muttered. "That's all I want. Maybe to play some roulette."

Catalina sat him down at the table and stood back for now. Although she pretended not to, she noticed him stealing occasional glances over his shoulder at her. He lost again, and got to his feet unsteadily, the shot reawakening the day's drink inside of him. Catalina held out her hand, and he took it. Drawing him toward her, she whispered in his ear. He didn't respond, simply squeezing her hand. Catalina led him upstairs.

* * *

"Where is Catalina?" asked Diego when he entered ten minutes later.

"Upstairs, with another customer," Madam Feliz answered. Seeing his face, she took him aside. "What is it with you and this girl?"

"What do you mean?"

"Since you were with her, you've gone crazy. Every night you're in here, sniffing around."

"You don't understand."

"Of course I do—I've seen it a thousand times before. You're in love."

A Storm Hits Valparaíso

Diego said nothing, but Madam Feliz continued admonishing him. "I know you've been leaving presents for her, and I know she's been avoiding you. And, of course, Esmeralda is very jealous."

Diego looked across the room, where Esmeralda sat scowling. He pouted. "That's not my fault."

Madam Feliz placed her hand on his arm. "I know, Diego, but this won't do you any good. Take Esmeralda upstairs tonight."

Diego winced.

"Take someone else, then. Don't get caught up on one girl— it's not good for either of you. Be realistic. She works here; you're a soldier. There's no future in it, for either of you. Think!"

Diego grunted. Seeing the sullen look on his face, Madam Feliz relented. "If it's burning you up so much, go for a walk and come back when you cool down. I'll keep her for you. But I'm warning you, Diego, don't get attached."

Esmeralda watched him leave then raced over to Madam Feliz. "Where's he going?"

"Get back to work," Madam Feliz snapped.

When Esmeralda had sulked in the corner, ignoring the customers, for some time, Madam Feliz sent over a heavyset, bearded man. With some reluctance, Esmeralda took him upstairs. He stank and had trouble removing his boots. Esmeralda sat on the edge of the bed and yawned. When he asked about a drink, Esmeralda sent him downstairs.

On the stairs, Jorge rushed past, almost knocking the man over. At the bottom, Jorge crumpled against the banister, throwing up when he tried to stand again. He was carried out the front door into a ditch, and a boy was dispatched to clean up the mess.

Stepping over the vomit, the bearded man went to the bar and ordered a shot. Downing it in one go, he then lit a small cigar. By the time he had stubbed it out underfoot and finished another *aguardiente* he was a little shaky, requiring the help of the railing to climb the stairs. The booze was swilling around in his head as he got to the landing and reached for the door.

Catalina was washing herself when the doorknob rattled. Realizing she had forgotten to lock it after Jorge left, she ran to the door, hoping to secure it in time. She was too late. The door burst open and a bearded man stumbled in.

Startled by the naked woman charging toward him, the man raised his arm to protect himself, catching Catalina cleanly with his elbow. He stopped. She was out cold. He paused momentarily, unsure what to do. No one was coming, so he stepped out of the room and closed the door.

Esmeralda, wondering what was taking the bearded man so long, stuck her head out of the door just as he left Catalina's room. Thinking he had simply entered the wrong room, she pulled him inside, hoping to get this over with quickly. She had a few tricks to expedite matters, and she didn't hesitate to employ them, sending the now-satisfied bearded man downstairs and home, oblivious to the trouble he was about to cause.

* * *

Diego returned an hour later, having spent the entire time trying to convince himself that Madam Feliz was right. But all along he knew that he was coming back for Catalina. He sought out Madam Feliz as soon as he came in, tapping his foot while she arbitrated some dispute over a bet that was made too late at the roulette table.

"Wait here," she told him when he asked after Catalina. "I haven't seen her since you were last in. I'll go and find her."

She went upstairs and knocked. No answer. Opening the door, she found Catalina unconscious on the floor, naked and with a nasty looking black eye. Madam Feliz ran down to the bar for some ice.

"Who was Catalina's last customer?" she asked the barman.

"The drunk soldier who had to be carried out. He is probably still in the ditch where they threw him."

Several soldiers at the bar sprang into action—all had slept with Catalina, and all had fallen in love with her. By the time Diego pushed through the crowd, the soldiers had formed a semi-circle, all kicking Catalina's assailant. Infuriated, Diego squeezed in between two of them and began punching the drunken officer in the face. It was only as his second blow connected that he noticed it was Jorge. When he did, he slumped back, stunned.

Snapping into action, Diego tried to pull the rest of the men away, struggling to restrain them all.

"Away with you! This man is in no state to defend himself," Madam Feliz came out and remonstrated, ushering them back inside. They sloped away, complaining, spitting at Jorge's bloodied body. Diego picked his brother up out of the ditch and sat him on the roadside. He was groggy and incoherent, even after Madam Feliz and Esmeralda returned with a bucket of water and tipped it over him. Esmeralda noticed it wasn't the bearded man she had seen leaving Catalina's room.

She said nothing.

38: The Congress of Tucuman

When Jorge woke the next day in the infirmary, he had only a modest recollection of what had happened. Getting drunk. Going into the room with that *puta*. Then little else. His face was badly swollen, he was missing two of his teeth, and he was pretty sure he had broken his wrist.

Diego visited him in a rage. It was difficult to follow what he was saying. It seemed he was accused of beating up a prostitute, but not just any *puta*, the one he had slept with, and the one Diego was in love with. He remembered sleeping with her—well, he had some hazy memory of doing so—but he did not remember hitting her. Then again, he couldn't say for sure what he had done; his mind was blank. When he told Diego this, his brother spat in his face and stormed out, leaving him alone with his scourging shame.

Diego avoided Madam Feliz's Gambling House for days afterwards, eventually learning of Jorge's innocence from a friend. His anger barely dissipated. His brother had still slept with the woman he loved. They avoided each other, Jorge resentful of what he saw as Diego's corruptive influence, partly blaming his brother for his own night of abandon, which had ended so wretchedly.

And so the two brothers drifted further apart.

* * *

Up at the Chilean camp, tension was high. Refugees continued to brave the mountain passes from Santiago and reports of Spanish butchery multiplied with each arrival. There was a new Captain-General of Chile who was intent on crushing all dissent—real or imagined. Not the kind of man to get his hands dirty, he preferred to give a series of sadistic brutes free rein. Vincente San Bruno—whose name will forever be followed by a curse—was his most feared henchman, responsible for keeping order in Santiago. San Bruno relished devising brutal methods of disposing of anyone with the remotest connection to the rebels, drawing inspiration from the conquistadors, the Inquisition, and his own bloodthirsty troops.

One day, he opened the front doors of the city jail, instructing the wardens inside to open the cell-doors. Most of those inside were being held captive unfairly, their chief offence being related to someone in the wrong army, or owning the wrong flag. The prisoners were unsure what was happening, tentative in their first steps down the corridors. Their confidence increased as they made their way through the labyrinthine prison, presuming some kind of amnesty must have been agreed. But the sting was in the tail. As soon as the convicts walked free, they were shot for escaping.

The dual effect of these atrocities was to demoralize the Chilean contingent and spread fear among the citizens of Mendoza. People began speculating that San Martín was building up troops because the Spanish had made a pact with the Mapuche Indians, and could now attack through their lands to the south. San Martín knew he had to take decisive action; he announced a banquet to honor the Chilean Army in exile.

"To the first bullet fired at the oppressors of Chile on the other side of the Andes." San Martín raised his glass for the customary toast, drank, and then smashed his glass so that it could never be sullied by toasting another cause. Stunned silence filled the room, giving way to cries of "*Viva Chile!*" San Martín sat back down and smiled to himself, watching the rumor mill crank into action.

Many of the guests assumed this was confirmation of the Spanish plan to attack through the Indian-controlled southlands. Others swore there was a clear emphasis on the word "other" when San Martín said "the other side of the Andes", and that this could only mean one thing: that San Martín was planning to assemble an army, cross the Andes, and take Santiago. They were right, but this was only part of what he had planned. San Martín intended to free Chile, assemble a navy, and take Lima by sea—breaking Spanish power in América once and for all.

Before anyone could savor the thought of finally taking the war to the Spanish, reports trickled in from other parts of the continent. Spain, fresh from its victory against Napoleon in the Peninsular War, now turned its attention to its erstwhile possessions. The guerrilla movement in Upper Peru was vanquished. The Colombian revolution had been rolled back entirely and its leader, Simón Bolívar, had been forced to take refuge in Jamaica. A report was obtained from British Intelligence sources in Cadiz: General Morillo and twenty thousand crack troops were setting sail for Buenos Aires. To top it all, in November 1815, General Rondeau, now commander of the Army of the North, had been routed at Sipé-Sipé in Upper Peru, and what was left of his army had been chased all the way back to Tucuman. By the end of the year, Argentina was the only country yet to be re-conquered by the Spanish, and General Morillo was about to set sail to correct that anomaly.

The Congress of Tucuman, where delegates from all corners of Argentina were meeting in a constitutional assembly to decide the future direction of the country, was only a few months away. With the powerful Don Escalada to assist him, San Martín had considerable influence in choosing delegates. San Martín, and his friend General Belgrano, emerged as favorites for the post of Supreme Director, but San Martín did not want to be distracted from his plan. In his place, he was able to have another candidate elected, Juan Martín de Puerreydón, a supporter of both Belgrano and San Martín. His other wish was for Congress to issue a formal Declaration of Independence, which Argentina had yet to do. In an impassioned letter to the delegates, San Martín wrote:

How long must we wait to declare our independence? Don't you think it is ridiculous to mint coins, have a flag and a coat of arms, and make war against the very government that is supposed to rule over us? What is there to do but say it? Courage! Great undertakings are for men of courage.

His stirring words had the desired effect. On July 9th 1816, the Congress of Tucuman formally proclaimed Argentina an independent state.

39: The Irish Don Juan

Don Juan O'Brien left Baltinglass in 1811 as plain old John O'Brien, earning his new moniker in Buenos Aires not due to disproportionate amorous exploits, but to the residents' propensity to localize names, making even an Irishman from Wicklow sound exotic. Emigration was common in Ireland; some left to find work, some to escape a criminal charge, and some to avoid the terror of deportation to Australia. Many left to escape religious persecution; others to raise an army, hoping to return and free their native land. But O'Brien left Ireland at the age of twenty-five to plough a different furrow.

He was born into a family of farmers and shopkeepers, relatively well-off for Catholics who had to endure the savagery of the Penal Laws. His father passed away when he was just sixteen, bequeathing him some commercial interests as well as a pair of fine horses. These steeds were to be O'Brien's downfall: he lost everything to his unbridled passion for racing, forcing him to mortgage his home—and ask his brothers to do likewise—to keep him out of the Debtor's Prison.

O'Brien decided to try his luck in London, and it was there that he first heard of the independence struggle in South America.

It captured the imagination of his romantic soul. Returning to Ireland immediately to bid farewell to his family, he secured passage on a Portuguese vessel bound for Rio de Janeiro, taking with him letters of introduction from friends.

Standing on the deck as the ship cut through the large waves of the open Atlantic seas, his dreams of opening a merchant house in Buenos Aires close to fruition, O'Brien was entitled to feel a certain amount of nervous optimism about his future. However, his fortunes were about to change once again.

The ship had an uneventful journey until it was dashed on rocks around the island of Fernando Po, off the coast of West Africa. Only O'Brien and a handful of crew survived. Stricken with fever, his luggage turned to flotsam by the ocean, he made his way on foot through the jungle. It was two days before he found a populated cove and vital medical assistance.

After recuperating, he talked his way onto an English packet ship to resume his journey to Brazil. Among his fellow passengers were a Quaker couple and their young daughter, Rebecca. O'Brien fell deeply in love. She, in turn, was besotted with his roguish charms and tales of adventure. Sick of the subterfuge required for their relationship to flourish, O'Brien approached Rebecca's father and made his intentions clear: he wished to marry her and sought the Quaker's approval. A few days later, after some pressure was exerted on the ship's captain, O'Brien was forcibly disembarked onto a passing Brazilian ship.

Heartbroken but in one piece, O'Brien eventually made it to Rio de Janeiro and set about tracking down some of his contacts. A retired English general, an acquaintance of some of O'Brien's friends, had promised a job that could provide him with the means to earn his passage to Buenos Aires and set himself up in business. However, bad luck had not yet run its course for the Irishman: the general had passed away three months previously.

His relentless determination and indefatigable spirit saw him through and he was able to secure a loan, allowing him to continue to Buenos Aires and begin fulfilling his dream of opening a merchant house. Like many wide-eyed Europeans in South America, O'Brien was swindled early on and forced to seek work in the Army. Enlisting in the newly-formed Mounted Grenadiers, he was made a 2nd Lieutenant, seeing action during the siege of Montevideo, and gaining promotion to Sergeant Major during the victory.

He was rewarded with a much-coveted place in the honor guard to the general who led the assault. An easy life lay ahead for O'Brien. This prestigious post would clear a path for rapid promotion. But, by 1816, he was disenchanted with the general's politicking and resigned, making his way to Mendoza to join up with his old commander, José de San Martín.

* * *

San Martín remembered O'Brien as a promising young officer. His service record was impeccable, and his instincts, in having misgivings about his last post, were commendable. It was time to get the measure of this man. San Martín gave him the difficult task of defending the Portillo Pass, giving him command of twenty-five men. There, he would be faced with the probing sorties of the Spanish raiding parties. It was essential to defend these incursions resolutely, preventing the enemy from returning with valuable information regarding the size and readiness of the Argentine forces. But O'Brien and his men would face a greater enemy: the Andean winter. After six grueling months, bedding down in the rocks and the snow, O'Brien would return with just eleven men. As a reward for the completion of his mission and the capture of a Spanish Colonel, O'Brien would be made Aide-de-Camp to San Martín—a great honor for the young foreign officer.

40: The Price of Freedom

In July 1816, after dispatching O'Brien to his icy guard post, San Martín met the new Supreme Director of Argentina, Juan Martín de Puerreydón, in Cordoba. He was seeking authorization for his plan to cross the Andes, take Chile, build a navy, sail to Peru, and capture Lima. Puerreydón approved, immediately sending him the troops he requested, and the Army of the Andes was formally inaugurated with San Martín named commander. Two hundred raw recruits were sent from Buenos Aires, followed by the former 7th Infantry from Tucuman, now comprising four hundred men and two hundred Mounted Grenadiers.

Now that San Martín's plan to cross the Andes was public, more and more recruits poured in to Mendoza. Refusing to let Argentine independence become a brief footnote in history, men signed up in droves. The women of Mendoza were not found wanting either. Inspired by San Martín's fiery young bride, they organized collectives to sew flags, dye cloth for uniforms, and plough fields the men had abandoned. María de los Remedios cajoled the wealthier women to donate their diamonds and pearls, which were pawned to purchase weaponry. And the hardest-working women in Mendoza—the girls of Madam Feliz's Gambling House—were never busier.

*   *   *

Eventually, Diego returned to the brothel, but Catalina refused to accept his custom. Esmeralda took pleasure in telling her Diego and Jorge were brothers who had fallen out over her. She didn't want to compound the family feud by sleeping with Diego again; besides, she couldn't stop thinking about Jorge.

Most men threw themselves at her feet, promising her the stars. Every day someone would leave a poem, a gift, or a flower. So frequent were the demonstrations of love that the other girls were getting jealous, and Catalina was getting tired of it. Jorge had been different. That night, he had poured his heart out to her, telling her about the death of his parents. When they finally undressed, he was so tender that Catalina thought she felt something for him—something she had never felt before. Jorge, unwittingly, had slipped past her defenses, puncturing her numbness and awakening feelings within her that she had been afraid to allow herself to feel.

The problem was: Jorge didn't remember a thing. He didn't remember their conversation, and he certainly didn't remember his tears. All Jorge remembered was that he got drunk and slept with a whore, and that he felt such shame he couldn't meet anyone's gaze for fear they would peer into his soul. Matters of the heart are often the playthings of capricious deities, and this situation was no different—for Diego loved Catalina, and Catalina loved Jorge, but Jorge loved no one, not even himself.

*   *   *

Zé was transferred from Tucuman along with the rest of the 7th Battalion and was surprised to see that most of the Mendoza infantrymen were black, unlike his mixed unit of whites, blacks, *indios*, foreigners, *mestizos*, and *mulatos*. While he enjoyed meeting them and swapping stories, Zé was disappointed to find they were exclusively second-, third- or even fourth-generation slaves. None of them could re-invoke the sights, sounds, and smells of his lost African youth.

Training was hard, harder than it had been in Tucuman; the *comandante* kept the troops on a near-constant state of alert. They were all part of the Army of the Andes now, and everyone knew the plan: they were going over the mountains to liberate Santiago. Every battalion was being trained for various eventualities, but nobody knew through which pass they would cross or where they would strike into Chile. Everyone had their theories and preferences, but whether they were being kept in the dark because the *comandante* hadn't decided yet, or because of the rumored Spanish spies, nobody knew.

Zé knew he had been lucky to escape action so far, missing the disaster at Sipé-Sipé because of a timely bout of fever. He also knew his luck was about to change. His superiors left him under no illusions—there would be no avoiding this fight. Every able-bodied soldier would be making the crossing, and all of them would see action. Many were expected to die—the officers were quite open about this—but they also said that the best way to guarantee survival was to kill as many of the enemy as possible. The same message was drilled into them constantly: when the enemy is in your sights, never hesitate, doing so could cost you your life or those of the men around you. Zé had enough practice with his rifle now to feel comfortable with the weapon. He proved a reasonable shot, although he knew the battlefield would be very different. Zé understood that hesitation could endanger his unit, but he didn't know he if could pull the trigger—if he could take another life.

This time, desertion never crossed his mind. Zé knew that if he served out his time—if he survived—he would be a free man. A citizen. For the second time, it seemed, God was asking him to kill to win his freedom.

41: The Archimedes of the Andes

The Army of the Andes had swollen considerably, now numbering more than five thousand men, but San Martín could not ease up. Men needed provisions and uniforms, guns and bullets, tents, blankets, and ponchos. Cavalry support required horses, saddles, sabers, lances, and muskets. Artillerymen demanded cannons and ammunition. And they all needed huge numbers of mules to carry supplies. On top of everything else, San Martín still had to figure out some way to sneak all of this across the five mountain ranges that separated Mendoza and Santiago. Getting the men, mules, horses, and supplies across in one piece, in some semblance of order and ready for battle, would be tricky enough, without having to reckon with the artillery pieces, cannons and howitzers. He decided to go down to the foundry to see if Padre Beltrán had any ideas.

San Martín had begun to enjoy the priest's company. Being from a poor family in Mendoza, the man had no formal education yet he proved himself a natural at mathematics and the sciences. Padre Beltrán could make fireworks and watches from scratch and had a working knowledge of everything from carpentry to medicine. He designed and constructed the foundry himself, and even built the custom machinery necessary for the manufacture of the bullets, horseshoes, knives, daggers, and bayonets the army would need. His inventiveness was matched by his resourcefulness—melting church bells for bullets and turning cow horns into water canteens. In addition to all of this, he coordinated the manufacture of uniforms, saddles, knapsacks and skis. To San Martín, he was a genius—if a somewhat unstable one.

The last time San Martín visited the inventor's workshop that posed as a sacristy, Padre Beltrán had shown a worrying new interest in phrenology, measuring the respective concave and convex indentations of his skull for some obscure purpose. San Martín was only able to escape when a jar containing some mysterious iridescent blue liquid that had been bubbling away in the corner, exploded, emitting a hissing cloud and forcing them to evacuate. Fearing a more serious accident, San Martín had requisitioned a series of abandoned buildings to house the priest's experiments.

San Martín approached the foundry to the industrial clang of hammering metal. The room was filled with acrid smoke that struggled to escape from small holes in the roof. Through the haze, he could make out scores of monks, all stripped to the waist in the stifling heat and with only leather aprons to protect their modesty and shield them from sparks. It made him slightly uncomfortable, watching men of God make weapons of destruction. He decided he would repent after the war.

Padre Beltrán appeared through the haze. "General, how kind of you to visit. Let's step outside."

San Martín followed him out into the fresh air.

"How can I help you?" The priest wiped his dirty hands on his robe.

San Martín grimaced. "I never quite know until I get here, but you always come up with something. I've been thinking about the crossing—obsessively. It's not the strength of the enemy that spoils my sleep, but how to get across these huge mountains." Their eyes were drawn to the snow-capped peaks that towered over them. "It's not the men I worry about; I will have them well-prepared. It's the damn artillery. It's so difficult to transport. But we can't go into battle without artillery. We wouldn't have a chance."

"I might be able to assist, General. I've been thinking about this."

"What have you got in mind?"

Padre Beltrán grinned. "Archimedes."

"I don't follow."

"One moment." Padre Beltrán disappeared into the foundry, returning with a large scroll. "I like to say, 'whenever there is an intractable problem, start at the beginning.'"

"Wise words," said San Martín, amused and intrigued.

"And in the beginning there was God, and then there was Archimedes. Do you know him?"

"Not personally, Padre."

"What a mind he had! I'm sure God gave me history books just to test me, knowing the satanic urges of pride and envy are strong within me."

"Padre..."

"Oh yes. Sorry! Archimedes, Ancient Greek genius. 'Give me a place to stand and I will move the Earth,' and so on." Beltrán stopped, his explanation complete.

San Martín thought for a moment, remembering something from those interminable mathematics lessons. "Levers?"

"Exactly, General." Padre Beltrán took the scroll from under his arm. "Archimedes was an advisor to the Greeks who had colonized Sicily. They were under threat from the Romans, who were just beginning to assert their power and vastly outnumbered the Greek settlers. The Romans attempted a naval assault of Syracuse, but as they approached the harbor, Archimedes had a few tricks up his sleeve. He had designed a series of giant mirrors, made from highly polished copper, arranged along a cliff. These acted collectively as an adjustable parabolic reflector..."

San Martín held up his hand.

"Sorry, General. The copper mirrors were arranged at different angles to focus the sun's rays on a single point. It was adjustable, so they could aim it at a Roman ship: boom! And another! And another! You can imagine the panic it caused."

"Indeed. You don't mean to build one of these contraptions to melt the snow, do you?"

Padre Beltrán looked puzzled.

San Martín tried again. "Or focus the rays on their cannons? Their men?"

"No, but that's very interesting. Hold on let me just make a few..."

San Martín put his hand on the priest's arm. "Why don't you show me the scroll?"

"Ah yes. Sorry, I got distracted there. Interesting idea, though. Another of his inventions for that battle was a giant subaquatic claw. You see, there was only one navigable channel into Syracuse's harbor, which ran near the base of the cliff. Archimedes constructed this claw to leap up out of the sea, flinging the boats in the air, dashing them and their unfortunate crews against the cliff-face." Padre Beltrán smacked his hands together with glee. "Smash!"

"How?"

"An intricate system of pulleys and levers." Padre Beltrán unfurled the large scroll on the ground, securing it with his feet at two corners and instructing San Martín to do the same. Aside from a few wine stains, a streak of jam, and what San Martín hoped was chocolate, the page was filled with a series of detailed designs. San Martín had no idea what it all meant, but it was beautiful. He made a mental note to add draughtsmanship to the list of Padre Beltrán's talents. The priest turned to him. "What do you think?"

"Can you talk me through it?"

"In the corner there, near your left foot, I have designed a portable suspension bridge—not for the troops, but to take the artillery across rivers and gorges. It can be broken down into sections so the load can be spread across several wagons. As soon as the cannons are across, you disassemble the bridge and move it to the next ravine."

"So the artillery won't slow the march of the troops."

"Exactly."

"This will certainly expedite the journey. What's the rest?"

"The portable bridge will be suitable in some instances, but it won't always be possible to deploy it."

"I was thinking that. Are these block-and-tackles?"

"Yes, with some slight modifications. There will be a robust leather sling at the bottom, and you should be able to use these to swing any of your howitzers or other pieces across chasms or any other obstacles."

"Superb."

"I'm sure it will work. They were invented by Archimedes, after all."

"Proceed, Padre. This is exactly what we need."

"Thank you, General."

"Does this make you my Archimedes?"

Padre Beltrán blessed himself. "Heavens above, don't say that."

"What's wrong?"

"Despite Archimedes, the Greeks lost the battle and Syracuse fell—there were simply too many Romans. When the legionnaires stormed the citadel, they discovered Archimedes in his room trying to solve some intractable theorem. He was ordered to leave but refused, and an excitable soldier killed him on the spot. The Roman commander—General Marcellus—was a man of science and had issued strict orders that Archimedes be brought to him, unharmed. Marcellus summoned the murderous soldier and ran him through."

"Fascinating," said San Martín, helping Padre Beltrán collect his scroll. "Let me know when you have made progress. Is there anything else you need?"

"More church bells."

"The Father Superior was not amused when he heard?"

"Tell him you are confiscating all church bells in case of a Spanish invasion; that they could use them for signaling purposes."

San Martín chuckled. "If you insist. More church bells!"

As San Martín walked away from the foundry, Padre Beltrán called to him. "Before you go, I had another idea."

San Martín turned to face the excited priest.

"We could position wagons along the mountain passes in advance of the crossing so the men would have less to carry. We could fill them with horse feed and fresh blankets and medical supplies and spiced beef, and when the troops have unloaded the supplies they can chop up the wagons for firewood. Oh, and we could transport parts of the bridge up to the points we want to cross, in advance."

"I'll send someone down to get a list of what you need." San Martín walked away, shaking his head in amazement.

42: The Man of Many Titles

In August 1816, in the middle of the Mendozan winter, María gave birth to their first child—a girl they christened Mercedes. San Martín was happy to have some time with the infant before he left. The snows of the mountain passes were at their deepest; it would be January before his army could cross without freezing to death. Five months to prepare everything and to finish training the men. It was enough time—just.

In September, in the south of Chile, a guerrilla leader associated with the Carrera brothers launched a rebellion that was easily crushed by the new Captain-General of Chile, Marcó del Pont. San Martín sent a letter of thanks and encouragement to the guerrilla leader, arranging for it to fall into enemy hands in the hope he could trick the Captain-General into thinking the Army of the Andes intended to strike through the Mapuche lands to the south. It was vital that his forces didn't face the might of the Spanish all at once, so he needed to solidify this false impression in the Captain-General's mind and draw battalions away from their defensive positions around Santiago. To this end, San Martín had several ideas.

The Captain-General was pompous and arrogant, but he was no fool; San Martín knew he would have to employ the black arts of deception to give his men any chance of victory. He recruited among the Chilean refugees, instructing them to return home and spread false rumors emphasizing the southern route. An unexpected boon was that these agents were, in turn, recruited by the Spanish. The enemy tasked them with infiltrating the Chilean camp in Mendoza to ascertain troop numbers, preparedness, and the time and point of attack; however, it was all a grand ruse as these men were loyal Patriots. On their return to Mendoza, they were able to provide crucial information to San Martín and identify the genuine Spanish spies in the camp. As a final twist, any Royalist supporters were then "turned", forced to send home letters dictated by San Martín that hinted he would attack to the south.

Even with these measures, San Martín knew it wasn't enough.

"I want him to be convinced! I want them to be so sure that we can creep into Santiago in the dead of night and slit their throats as they sleep," San Martín told his Chief Engineer, Major Alvarez, when he arrived to inspect the saltpeter factory. The major had been brought down from Tucuman to exploit Cuyo's abundant nitrates, and San Martín knew him well.

"After I complete my mission," said Major Alvarez, "you will have all the information you need."

"It's the information they have I'm concerned about."

They walked on in silence, past the beds where the wood ashes and straw were being heaped with manure, both men holding their noses. "He has to be considering the possibility," Major Alvarez said when they reached the area where water was being leached to remove the soluble nitrates. "That should be enough to draw a couple of battalions away." He paused, considering. "Have you thought about contacting the Indians?"

"That's it!" San Martín snapped his fingers.

"What?"

"We'll sign a treaty with the Mapuche. Something official. An alliance. We'll give them whatever they want in exchange for permission to pass through their lands."

Alvarez began walking again, toward the entrance, his hands clasped behind his back. "That's sure to filter back to the Spanish, they can't keep quiet about anything."

"Exactly," said San Martín. "Although, I can't really blame them. This was their land after all, and it's in their interest to cover both sides so they can say they backed the winner."

Alvarez nodded. "You'll need an emissary, preferably an *indio*."

Now outside, San Martín beckoned to his orderly, who approached with his horse, handing him the reins. San Martín put one foot in the stirrup and hauled himself into the saddle. "I have just the man—an *indio* from Potosí. He's tough, and resourceful."

Alvarez tightened his stirrups. "Can you trust him?"

"I don't need to. I'll tell him what he needs to know, no more: we want to sign a treaty with the Mapuche. If the worst happens, all he will have done is let the Spanish know we are seeking permission to pass through the south."

"Excellent."

"I have to get over to the miller," San Martín said. "We're running low on cloth and I want to see what the problem is. When do you leave?"

Alvarez slapped the horse's flanks. "Monday."

San Martín reached into his saddlebag and handed Alvarez an envelope bearing his seal in red wax. "Make sure he knows it's from me. He knows my background."

"Of course."

"Take your time, and don't move too fast. I want this done right. Remember: don't commit anything to paper until the way home."

"Don't worry." Major Alvarez tapped his head. "I never forget a thing."

"You have someone here to keep an eye on things?"

"Just my assistant, but this place almost runs itself now—everyone knows what they are doing, and Padre Beltrán said he would call in now and then."

"You know, he taught himself everything: mathematics, physics, chemistry."

"I heard," said Major Alvarez, "but sometimes I think he has a firmer grip on science than religion."

San Martín laughed and wished him good luck, and then cracked his reins and left in the direction of the mill.

* * *

When San Martín had resigned as head of the Army of the North, Pacha believed their deal was forgotten, so he was most surprised to receive a message from San Martín saying he would send for him. Several months passed without Pacha hearing anything and his thoughts turned again to trying his luck and striking out on his own. Several things, however, gave him pause. First, the penalty for desertion was death, and the army had become a lot better at catching deserters, even hanging them in public in the main square of Tucuman in front of a baying crowd. That was not how Pacha wanted to go. Second, he would have to cross that barren wasteland again, with no support, few provisions, and little chance of being rescued. He knew how lucky he was the last time; he probably would have died but for the sword.

The sword—Pacha hadn't thought about it in a long time. When he first recovered in Tucuman, he tried asking about the sword, but they all thought he was crazy and he soon learned to shut up. An older Indian in the army was more sympathetic, but warned that leaving the sword behind was a terrible mistake—one that would cause Pacha great hardship, haunting him for a long time to come. He asked the old man if there was any way to avoid this, but the old man just shook his head.

When Pacha received San Martín's summons to join him in Mendoza, he was angry. San Martín was moving him far to the south, in the opposite direction from Potosí, away from any future reinvasion of Upper Peru. But, after some consideration, he accepted it with a certain fatalism, thinking it his punishment for abandoning the sword. Those first months in Mendoza passed uneventfully. He ate. He slept. He defecated. He let time wash over him, waiting for the sword to finish punishing him, waiting for the day he could rejoin his family. When he had almost given up on the arrangement with San Martín, he was finally summoned to his office. The *comandante* was apologetic about the delay, and asked Pacha how he was doing.

"Time passes," said Pacha with a shrug.

When the *comandante* outlined the mission, Pacha had to admit he was excited. There was a settlement of Mapuche Indians living autonomously in the south in a region called Fort San Carlos. Pacha was to make contact with them, proposing an alliance. The *comandante* confided that he planned to invade Chile through the southlands and needed the Mapuche's permission to pass through.

When Pacha returned with the Mapuche's agreement to negotiate, the *comandante* was delighted. Still, he asked Pacha not to breathe a word to anyone.

* * *

On the other side of the Andes, the new Captain-General of Chile, Marcó del Pont, was growing impatient. Surely the whole point of being in charge was that you had minions to take care of trifling tasks. He could see an aide in the mirror, shuffling, trying to decide whether to disturb him or not. "What is it?"

"Madrid, sir. They are requesting positive news stories."

"What do you mean?" The Captain-General snapped his fingers. "Re-conquering Chile wasn't enough? Chasing the last of the rebels out of the country wasn't enough?"

"I don't know, sir."

"Well then, ask them! You shouldn't be bothering me with these half-baked requests." The Captain-General dismissed him with a wave of the hand.

The aide didn't move. "If I may, sir."

"Go on."

"The cancellation of General Morillo's invasion was a blow to morale. Those twenty thousand troops would have been enough to quell Buenos Aires, and we could have had all of the colonies back under control."

"I know that. What has it got to do with me?"

"Well, sir, naturally there was an inquiry. Madrid concluded the soldiers had been panicked into mutiny by a series of salacious newspaper articles."

The Captain-General laughed.

"Sir?"

"Most of those idiots can't even read."

"That may be so, sir, but they heard the stories nevertheless, and they refused to even board the ships in Cadiz."

"You're telling me they risked being shot because of some stories in the newspaper!"

"Yes, sir. That's what Madrid has concluded, sir."

"What kind of stories?"

"We suspect they were planted by sympathizers or agents of the insurgents, sir. Ludicrous stuff: fantastical monsters in the Orinoco River; ghosts haunting Inca tombs; wild *gauchos* who fight naked, killing men with their bare hands, and so on. But they were cleverly woven in with mostly accurate accounts of old Patriot victories, Bolívar's War to the Death, and some ancient gypsy prophecies. A potent mix, and one that appears to have been successful."

"These insurgents will stoop to anything." The Captain-General shook his head. "What does Madrid want me to do about it?"

"They want a series of good news stories from life in the colonies: balls, parades, fiestas, peaceful haciendas, profitable mining companies, soldiers marrying beautiful girls, that kind of thing."

"They think this will work?"

"They can't risk another episode like Cadiz. It was very damaging. Obviously, the ringleaders of the mutiny, and their families, will be shot. But they want to be sure."

"Take care of it. What's next?"

* * *

Toward the end of September, San Martín traveled south to discuss the treaty with fifty Mapuche chiefs. He impressed them by addressing them in their own language and by presenting them with gifts as tribute. After a six-day celebration, the alliance was agreed, the treaty signed; San Martín had permission to travel through their

231

territory. All he needed now was for the news to worm its way to Santiago.

* * *

A few weeks later, the Captain-General of Chile received a disturbing report.

"Sir, the Governor of Mendoza, San Martín, has concluded a treaty with the Mapuche."

"I thought we had an arrangement with them."

"We did, sir, but now they have an arrangement with the insurgents as well."

"How reliable is this?"

"Solid, sir. It comes from the Mapuche themselves."

"Covering their backs as always. At least we know which direction the attack will come from. Have my commanders draw up a report. We'll need to move battalions south. But don't leave Santiago completely unprotected; they might send a couple of squadrons of cavalry through the Mendoza passes."

"Yes, sir."

"Now if there's nothing else, I'm going to take a nap. I don't want to be bothered."

Less than an hour later, the Captain-General was woken by his footman. "I do apologize, sir, but you're needed. It's urgent."

Muttering expletives, he stormed into the State Room, where his aide was waiting. "This better be good."

"Sir, we intercepted an Argentine soldier coming through the Los Patos Pass."

"Alone?"

"Yes, sir. His name is Major Alvarez, and he didn't seem to make any attempt to evade capture. He rode directly toward our guardhouse, waving a white flag."

"How odd."

"He claims he came to deliver a message to you, personally, from the Governor of Mendoza, José de San Martín."

The aide handed the weather-beaten document to the Captain-General, who sliced open the seal. It was a copy of

Argentina's Declaration of Independence. The Captain-General thumped the table and spat on the document. "Traitor scum."

"Sir?"

"We trained that bastard for twenty years, and now he fights us. Where is he?"

"Sir?"

"The messenger."

"We are holding him in the city jail, sir. Do you want me to bring him to you?"

The Captain-General paused. "No. Shoot him."

The aide turned toward the door.

"Wait."

"Sir?"

"On second thought, spare him. I will need him to take a reply back to that *mestizo* bastard Governor."

* * *

Major Alvarez was sent back by the shortest pass, by way of Uspallata. San Martín's ruse had worked. No accurate maps existed of the mountain passes between Mendoza and Santiago, so San Martín sent Major Alvarez by Los Patos, the longer pass further north, with instructions to chart the entire route. He calculated that his messenger would be unharmed by the Spanish, knowing that although the Captain-General would be incensed by the independence proclamation, his arrogance would compel him to reply. He also estimated that Major Alvarez would be sent back by the shorter pass, enabling him to map that also as he traveled and providing San Martín with accurate drawings of both passes.

He opened the Captain-General's reply:

Don Francisco Casimiro Marcó del Pont, Angel, Diaz y Mendez, Knight of the Order of St. James, the Royal Military Order of San Hermenegildo, and the Fleur-de-Lys, Member of the Royal Ronda Equestrian Club, well-deserving of his country to an eminent and heroic degree, Field Marshall of the Royal Armies, Supreme Governor, Captain-General, President of the Royal Audiencia, General Superintendent Sub-delegate of the Royal Exchequer of Post, Mails and Couriers, and Royal Vice Patron of this Kingdom of Chile.

San Martín's experience was that men with such overarching self-regard were deficient in other departments. The rest of the letter was a predictable mix of threat and bluster, but the line at the end caught his eye:

I sign as a white man, not like San Martín, whose hand is black.

The taunt was a familiar one, from his days in the Spanish Army. His darker complexion had given birth to many rumors about the purity of his blood. As a younger man, he had responded to these sleights with a challenge, but he was astute enough to recognize that such rumors could only help him in América. San Martín was about to compose a reply, but then stopped himself. He would save his rebuttal for when he saw the Captain-General in person, in Santiago.

43: Release

Even though Cochrane's jail term had been served, he still hadn't been released from the King's Bench Prison. There was the small matter of the fine of one thousand pounds imposed as part of his punishment, and Cochrane refused to pay. For two weeks he held out, extending his sentence in a bid to see who would blink first: him or the Establishment. But the Establishment had nothing to lose. Eventually, Cochrane was forced to concede. On the back of the one thousand pound bill he presented to the jailors, was a note:

My health having suffered by long and close confinement, and my oppressors being resolved to deprive me of property or life, I submit to robbery to protect myself from murder, in the hope that I shall live to bring the delinquents to justice.

Cochrane's popularity in the Radical movement was unaffected, the message showing that he hadn't been cowed by imprisonment. His supporters were glad to have him at large again, hoping he would continue his crusade against corruption and the Establishment. Cochrane had become something of a cause célèbre and, if anything, the social and political landscape in Britain was more volatile than when he entered prison over a year ago. The Establishment's plan was, as ever, unchanged: preserve the status quo at all costs. But at first, Cochrane's attention was on redressing personal grievances. In July 1815, he returned to the House of Commons, this time without having to be smuggled into the chamber. The Navy was finished with him, now he could devote himself to attacking the Establishment, which had robbed him of his career and a year of his life.

One of the first votes on his return was the government's proposal to increase the allowance to the Prince Regent's brother. Normally, such a measure would be straightforward, attracting the automatic support of conservatives, as well as any M.P. who feared being viewed as seditious or, worse, a republican. However, the blueblood in question was the Duke of Cumberland—a particularly despicable character, even by Royal standards—who followed an indecent assault on Lady Lyndhurst with a series of incestuous relations with his sister, Princess Sophia, resulting in her impregnation. A few years before, his royal status had entitled him to a monumental cover-up after he murdered his valet in Kensington Palace. This was no man of the people; he would go on to oppose Catholic Emancipation and the *Great Reform Act*, found the Orange Order, and, after a bizarre set of events, become the King of Hanover. Cochrane had the deciding vote. He cast against.

His next mission was to seek an impeachment of Lord Chief Justice Ellenborough—the judge who had presided over his stock exchange fraud trial. He failed, being supported in the House only by his friend, Radical M.P. Francis Burdett. Cochrane came home that night dejected. The whole time in prison, all he dreamed of was revenge and redemption, the two inextricably linked. If he could have shown his trial had been corrupt, perhaps he had a chance of being reinstated in the Navy. If the vote had been close, or even garnered some level of support, it would have shown some of his parliamentary colleagues believed in his innocence, and he could have built on that. But one supporting vote? It was a devastating blow. He sipped his tea, cursing as it burned his lip. He glared at Kitty.

"I told you it was hot."

Cochrane grumbled to himself.

Kitty sighed. "Thomas, I know you have all of this energy that needs some kind of direction, but I wonder if you are approaching all of this in the right way."

Kitty's words washed over him. He was too angry. They sat in silence. Then, out of a desire to humor her more than anything else, he responded a little more sharply than he had intended, "And what do you suggest? Give up?"

Kitty walked out and Cochrane scolded himself. He shouldn't be so hard on her; she was only trying to help.

It was a period of adjustment for them both. Their idealized versions of each other, perfected in their time apart, collided with the vicissitudes of day-to-day living. Kitty, for her part, felt her husband could still do something great. She saw the regard people held him in. He certainly still had the passion, there could be no question about that; it just needed an outlet. After he recovered from this setback, he decided to change tack, realizing, at last, that he was spending his political capital on fights he could never hope to win. He needed a new approach.

The end of the Napoleonic wars had brought Britain great joy, but it was short-lived. England's economy was in a tailspin, battered by long wars and lost trade. It was further exacerbated when thousands of soldiers, resentful after risking their lives for Britain and watching their friends die in unimaginable ways, returned home to find there was no work. Contempt for the Royal Family was at unprecedented levels, fuelled by intrigue, scandal and a growing sense of disenfranchisement. These were the dangerous days before the *Great Reform Act*, when the Establishment realized—almost too late—that it must cede some semblance of power to the masses.

Cochrane led the protests against the regime, clamoring for universal suffrage. Packed meetings all over England had the Establishment worried. They hit back, charging Cochrane for his escape from the King's Bench Prison the year before. He was found guilty, but the jury showed clemency, refusing to incarcerate him further and instead fining him one hundred pounds. Naturally, Cochrane refused to pay, and a public subscription was required to prevent him from being interred again.

Undeterred, Cochrane organized large open-air meetings, at which he publicly castigated the government. By the beginning of 1817, he had collected petitions containing four hundred thousand signatures from people demanding universal suffrage. At several meetings the mood turned violent, but Cochrane did everything in his power to calm proceedings, urging a peaceful solution. The government's response was predictable. Doing what governments always do when people demand more rights, they took some away, suspending *habeas corpus* and clamping down on the press.

The temperature was rising.

44: The Crossing of the Andes

San Martín was one of the last to leave Mendoza, staying back to send his final messages to Buenos Aires and to ensure his agents in Chile had been alerted. It was essential that his network of spies was ready to propel the populace into open revolt as he simultaneously mounted his initial assault. Aside from the Captain-General having to commit soldiers to quelling these disturbances, his troops' movements would be impeded. And already they were scattered across the country, protecting the southern passes and the ports on the Pacific coast—San Martín's disinformation campaign having been singularly successful.

One week earlier, San Martín had watched the Army of the Andes parade through Mendoza on its way to the mountain passes. It had been a grand celebration, which boosted his men ahead of the difficult ascent. His army now numbered some six thousand troops, but recognizing that it would be essential to maintain the element of surprise as long as possible, even after they entered Chile, he had split it into several detachments which would travel through different passes.

He laughed when Padre Beltrán saluted as he passed, recalling the conversation he had with him about him joining the crossing.

"Padre, I have something to ask you"

"Is it wings for the cannons, General? Because if you want them, you shall have them."

"No," San Martín had said, laughing, "although, that would be useful. I wanted to ask if you would like to become the chaplain of the Army of the Andes."

Padre Beltrán smiled. "Well, then ask."

"Will you?"

"No."

"Why not?"

"I don't like the sound of it."

"But you're perfect for it."

"I think it's distasteful."

"For God's sake, why?"

"I presume the Spanish will have their own chaplain."

"I'm sure they do. What's your point?"

"You are asking me to lead six thousand men in prayer to our all-powerful God, asking him—through me—to help our soldiers kill the seven thousand Spanish on the other side of the Andes."

"If you put it like that, well, yes."

"Presumably their chaplain is doing the same. So it's a battle of the priests. Who has God's ear? General, if we lose, I will take it very personally."

San Martín thought for a moment. "But Padre, they don't know we are attacking."

"So..."

"So, you have God's ear..."

"...exclusively," finished Padre Beltrán, smiling.

"And just think of all those confessions."

"Do I have to wear a uniform?"

"I would prefer you did."

"Thank God for that! This wool is so itchy it lends itself to blasphemy."

One week later, San Martín sent off his last dispatches, made an emotional goodbye to his wife, and galloped ahead to join the

A Storm Hits Valparaíso

rear of the army. The first part of the climb was steady but unrelenting. Vineyards and small towns gave way to the stark, brutal landscape of gigantic broken rocks and ash-colored shale. The thinning air and sharp light created a sinister ambience, exacerbated when men began falling ill and animals started dying. As they continued their climb, the glaciers were ever present, looming over them, promising worse ahead.

During the second week, the sick began dying, and the animals were expiring at such a rate that bullets could no longer be spared to hasten their pathetic demise. The icy mountain rivers were bridged where possible, but often the heavy artillery pieces had to be unloaded from their wheeled wagons and carried by hand, with the help of ropes and block-and-tackles, across canyons, gorges, crevices and ravines. No such artifice was needed to cross the furious Mendoza River, which overflowed with melting winter snow; it was spanned by the Puente del Inca, a natural rock bridge ninety feet wide and sixty feet long. The Army of the Andes had now reached eight thousand feet, and the temperature was consistently well below freezing—this for men whose coldest winter rarely dropped below ten degrees.

Three weeks and one hundred and twenty miles into the journey, San Martín began to despair. His doctor had warned him about the effects of altitude—how it could play with a man's mind. He reverted to taking opiates every day, and grew weaker and weaker as they approached the summit. Everything had been meticulously planned, but his men were still dying. More bodies lay frozen in the snow with every passing day, and ahead lay the full might of the Spanish Army.

* * *

As the exhausted, frostbitten men of the 7th Battalion reached the summit of the crossing, a realization set in: there was no going back now. It had taken them three weeks to get this far, climbing to a height of twelve thousand, six hundred feet; the trail fell sharply away to Chile below. The relief the men felt at beginning their descent was tempered with the knowledge that retreat would be impossible. It was victory or death.

For the infantrymen, most of whom were black, it meant something else again. They were newly freed slaves, courtesy of San Martín strong-arming the plantation owners around Mendoza. As part of the deal struck with the landlords, and to remove the temptation of desertion, manumission would only come into effect after they crossed the Andes. But there was no celebration as they crossed the summit, one by one on their mules, only a solemn appreciation of the task ahead; their freedom would be worth little if they couldn't live to enjoy it.

Zé was one of the first to cross the marker. Like most of the men, he found the climb debilitating. In his backpack, he had carried two weeks' worth of army-issue *charquiscan*, a spiced, ground beef that could be added to melted snow to make a fortifying soup. Zé had never seen snow before—now he was surrounded by it, and eating it. It was important to maintain strength during the ascent. If he weren't careful, he noticed, a fog could descend over his brain, and he found himself out of breath at the most curious moments. There was something bewitching about these heights, something that befuddled a man. It was difficult to keep his wits about him, and dangerous not to. Most of the trails were so narrow that only one man could pass at a time. It was torturous to watch the columns weaving slowly down one side of a gorge and then up the other. The men were borne by mules, which were more surefooted in the terrain. As many of the men had never before ridden a mule, the muleteers were kept busy calming the recalcitrant beasts and reassuring the reluctant men.

It paid to keep an even temperament. For one, there was less vitality in the air, and getting excited often led to panic when men's lungs struggled with the altitude. Firewood was severely rationed, as there was no replacement fuel until they reached the lowlands of Chile. Many men experimented with different systems in an attempt to prolong the invigorating heat from the campfire, but the end result was always the same: a biting cold that plagued the extremities and left sleep short, fitful, and unsatisfying. At the beginning of the journey, the troops collectively indulged in a variety of nourishing fantasies: a crushing defeat of the Spanish, a victorious Liberators' parade in Santiago, a *chilena* to bounce on your knee, a quiet farm with good soil. But as the march progressed, the soldiers fantasized about more basic desires: food, warmth, and rest. For some, like Zé, the cold would never leave their bones.

The animals fared even worse. Horses were largely spared the burden of a heavy load, but even still, less than two-thirds of the sixteen hundred horses that left Mendoza arrived in Chile. Mortality was even higher among the mules; less than half of the ten thousand mules completed the journey—which could have explained their initial reluctance to move. Zé, like the rest of the infantry, was fitted with warm clothing, a knapsack made from the hides of the cattle killed for the *charquiscan* he ate, and a pair of covered rawhide sandals called *tomangos*. But when the men stopped for the night and their sweat cooled, the dampness would seep into their skin. Many of the men caught a chill and their tortured, snuffling snores echoed into adjoining valleys.

When they finally made their way down into the lower hills of the Andes, breathing in the thicker air, spirits began to rise. All they wanted was a freshly cooked meal and a long rest. They weren't going to get one.

45: The Battle of Chacabuco

Diego and Jorge were fortunate, as part of the detachment commanded by General Las Heras, they traversed the shorter, less arduous Uspallata Pass. This relief was tempered with the knowledge they would be first to fall on the enemy. On February 2nd, they attacked a Royalist outpost at the exit of the pass, north of Santiago, and then feigned a retreat into the mountains. A few days later, they descended again, capturing the town of Santa Rosa while the contingent traveling under General Soler captured the town of San Felipe. These were mere skirmishes; everyone knew the real battle lay ahead.

Diego was worried about Jorge. His brother had avoided him during the crossing and had been acting erratically since they arrived in Chile—increasingly manic, sleeping little, urging his commanders to attack at every opportunity, and volunteering himself to lead frontal assaults and raiding parties. When Jorge spoke to Diego, which was rare, it was only about how many Spaniards he would kill. Diego knew that some men have a darkness in their souls that only awakens on their first taste of blood. Such thoughts made him nervous. And he was already on edge, heading into his first real engagement.

***

San Martín had a decision to make. By February 10th, the majority of the Army of the Andes had exited the mountain passes, congregating a few hundred feet above the plain of Chacabuco. Below lay the farmhouse of the Chacabuco ranch—the Spanish headquarters. San Martín's spies informed him that the enemy consisted of fifteen hundred men and five hundred cavalry, including the feared Talavera Regiment, which had been responsible for much of the bloody aftermath at Rancagua. San Martín had more—almost four thousand had exited the passes so far—but, despite the best efforts of Padre Beltrán, most of the artillery was still two days behind. San Martín only had a few light guns at his disposal. The question was: should he wait for his artillery and risk the Spanish reinforcing, or should he attack now?

San Martín decided to strike. Two paths led from the hills above Chacabuco down to the plain below, arriving at separate points about two miles apart. San Martín decided to split his forces, sending one contingent, fifteen hundred men under the command of Bernardo O'Higgins, down the right-hand path to engage the center of the enemy's forces. General Soler was to lead two thousand men down the more obscure path to the left, outflanking the enemy while they focused on the initial assault. San Martín was explicit in his instructions to O'Higgins: he was to engage the enemy, but not to advance until Soler's troops had arrived. The remaining men were to be kept in reserve for the final push, which San Martín hoped would tilt the balance.

***

A couple of hours after midnight, February 12th, the Army of the Andes set out in two detachments, following the paths down the bluff toward the ranch of Chacabuco. Zé picked his way down the path, almost losing his footing a couple of times. Bright moonlight shone on the faces of the infantrymen, who were packed together as they marched, but the ground was not very solid. Zé didn't like his chances of getting back uphill in a hurry if things went against them, and he could see the others were thinking the same.

It was daybreak when they finally reached the plain of Chacabuco, immediately coming under heavy fire from the Spaniards, who had pulled back beyond a muddy stream that bisected the plain. Taking up defensive positions, the infantry strung themselves out in a line, returning fire. The Spanish advanced. More artillery fire scarred the plain. More men added their blood to the quagmire. Despite that, O'Higgins' men were still pouring out of the pass to take up positions.

The Spaniards used their temporary numerical superiority to press hard, picking the Patriots off. In between firing rounds, Zé and the rest of the infantrymen scanned the plain to the left, willing General Soler's troops to appear. No relief came. Eventually, O'Higgins gave the order to charge, which seemed to surprise the Spanish, who were on the back foot for a moment. When Zé and the others reached the stream that crossed the field, their progress was slowed by the thick mud. They began to be picked off again until the order to retreat to the foot of the path was given. Zé was desperately trying to extricate himself from the mud when he felt something slam into his body.

He slumped backward.

It is said that the dying see their entire lives flash before them, but Zé didn't experience anything like that. He was spared memories of the slave ships, and the cold, dead eyes of Robado Vivaldo. Instead, the mortal moment when the bullet entered his chest stretched out interminably. It seemed he would be caught in that painful second for eternity, until oblivion's sweet relief claimed him forever.

* * *

A few hundred feet above the battlefield, San Martín shifted in his saddle, despairing as O'Higgins advanced. "Why isn't he waiting for Soler?" He turned to Major Alvarez. "Tell Soler to speed his arrival." He called over Major Zapiola, "Take a detachment of Grenadiers and capture that damned artillery!" Turning his horse toward the battle below, San Martín charged down the hill to join the fighting.

Having encountered some resistance on the path down the hill, General Soler's detachment finally appeared. O'Higgins and his infantry charged again. The Spaniards fell back under this combined assault and attempted an orderly retreat, but were soon surrounded. Some units broke away to take refuge in the farmhouse and hand-to-hand fighting spread to the olive groves and vineyards surrounding it. Soon, it became one-sided slaughter. Five hundred Spanish soldiers were killed and six hundred were taken prisoner. As San Martín received his final reports, General Soler rode up to O'Higgins. "You could have cost us the battle!"

O'Higgins ignored him. Turning to San Martín, he requested permission to pursue Spaniards who had managed to escape, including their commander, General Maroto. San Martín refused.

"With respect, sir, they are making their escape. If I leave now I can catch them before they make it to Valparaíso."

San Martín stood firm. "We hold back and enter Santiago in an orderly fashion."

"I only need two squadrons of Grenadiers."

"The men are tired."

O'Higgins raised his voice. "For God's sake, José, a couple of squadrons!"

"Your impetuousness almost cost us the day." San Martín snapped. "What the hell were you doing? You weren't supposed to charge until Soler appeared."

"I had no choice."

"You could have held your ground."

"I drew my men into a defensive line at the end of the path, but as soon as I did, the Spanish began to advance. Our position was untenable under their fire. I sent for reinforcements—none came. If we had attempted to retreat up the path we would have been cut down. I had no choice but to attack."

San Martín nodded. "Dismissed."

O'Higgins turned angrily and strode off toward the farmhouse.

"O'Brien, come here," San Martín told his aide.

O'Brien approached sporting a huge grin and waving a red and yellow flag. "I captured the colors, sir."

"Well done. But there's no time to rest. Take two squadrons of Grenadiers and go after the stragglers, and send Escalada over here."

San Martín's brother-in-law, Manuel Escalada, saluted in front of him. "I need someone to take the news of our great victory to Buenos Aires."

Manuel smiled. "Yes, sir."

"And I want you to give something to María for me." San Martín handed him a letter and several ounces of gold. "Make sure she is seeing a good doctor. I'm worried about her. Tell her I'll be back to see her and Mercedes soon."

* * *

O'Brien was unsuccessful in his pursuit of General Maroto, who slipped onto a ship at Valparaíso before he could be overtaken. However, he captured a far more valuable prize. On the roadside, among some discarded satchels, he discovered saddlebags stuffed with gold and silver. About thirty thousand pesos worth—a fortune. Under the rules of war, O'Brien was entitled to keep one-third. Recognizing that the nascent Chilean state would be in dire need of funds, he handed the lot to San Martín, accepting only a letter of thanks so he could claim his prize at a later date.

* * *

The Captain-General of Chile, Marcó del Pont, hadn't taken any chances. On the eve of the battle at Chacabuco, he sent his baggage to Valparaíso, where he had a ship standing by. After news of the Royalist defeat reached him in Santiago, he fled, only to be intercepted on the road to the port. The day after the battle, San Martín received the Captain-General at his palace. "Señor General, let me shake that white hand," said San Martín, with the faintest hint of a smile. Defeated, the Captain-General grudgingly offered San Martín his sword, a symbolic gesture of the transfer of power.

"Let that foil remain on the belt of Your Excellency, Señor General." San Martín refused it. "Because that is where it can do me the least harm."

San Martín sent del Pont by armed guard to Mendoza. He would be killed attempting to escape, two years later.

Vincente San Bruno was captured fleeing the battlefield at Chacabuco and bound to a mule for the journey to Santiago, where he was sentenced to death. On his way to the gallows, the seething, spitting mob worked itself into a frenzy, first throwing mud and stones, and then overpowering his guards, beating him and gouging his eyes before order could be restored. Back in the hands of the guards once more, his face bloodied and swollen, he was brought to the plaza, and shot. The crowd trudged away, disappointed with the realization that a man can be killed only once.

Three days after the victory at Chacabuco, San Martín issued a proclamation drawing together delegates from Chilean provinces to appoint a head of state. The assembly was unanimous in declaring San Martín the Governor of Chile, but he refused the appointment, asking them to reconvene and select an alternative; Bernardo O'Higgins was duly elected Supreme Director. His first act was to appoint San Martín as General-in-Chief of the combined Argentine-Chilean Army.

San Martín began planning the next stage of operations: establishing a training school for new recruits in Santiago and building a navy for the attack on Lima. All of this would cost money, which the new Chilean state didn't have. Anxious to capitalize on the goodwill surrounding his recent victory, San Martín, with only O'Brien for company, set off for Buenos Aires to secure the necessary support. The *Cabildo* of Santiago offered him ten thousand ounces of gold to defray the cost of his journey, but San Martín refused it. When they insisted, he donated it to the establishment of a public library.

On his way back to the Andes, he passed the site of the Chacabuco victory. A giant mound of earth covered the remains of the fallen Patriots, most of them newly emancipated slaves from Mendoza. San Martín reigned in his horse and lit a small cigar, watching the mound in silence. Zé, beneath the mound, rapidly decomposing, was quieter still.

46: The Return

When news of the comprehensive victory at Chacabuco filtered back to Mendoza, Madam Feliz announced she was returning to Tucuman. She was taking many of the girls, including Esmeralda, with her, prophesying that the war would return to the northern front. As she had taken out a long lease on the building in Mendoza, she came to an arrangement with Teresa to take over the business there. The name would remain the same—Madam Feliz's Gambling House—in one of South America's first franchising agreements.

Many *chilenos* decided to wait before returning, to ensure the Patriot's hold on the country was secure before undertaking the arduous crossing once more. Others decided to remain in Mendoza permanently—they had fallen in love, opened businesses, or married, or were just weary at the thought of packing up their lives again. The rest went at the first opportunity, anxious to return home, seek out loved ones, breathe the air of a free Chile, and exploit the numerous business opportunities that a large army camped outside Santiago would bring. Catalina was one of the latter; after all, most of her former customers were now on the

A Storm Hits Valparaíso

other side of the Andes, among them the one she couldn't get out of her mind: Jorge.

"What will you do in Santiago?" Teresa asked. When Catalina confessed her plans, Teresa grew angry. "You have your whole life ahead of you. This isn't the life for you."

"It's not such a bad life."

"You're a fool. You've had it easy here, but it's different out there. Here you had Madam Feliz to take care of you; on the streets, you will have no one. And even if you find a safe place to work, what kind of future will that be? If you're lucky you might get ten years out if it, and then you'll be finished. Your looks will be gone, and no man will want to touch you, your insides so destroyed from disease you won't be able to bear a child to look after you in old age. You have a chance in Santiago—a fresh start. Take it."

After a tearful goodbye with Teresa—with promises of future visits that would never be fulfilled—Catalina departed, once again in a column of refugees. However, this time the journey seemed to pass more quickly, the reigning mood being one of nervous optimism rather than desperation. As Catalina walked the streets of Santiago she saw the *Reconquista* had given birth to a new generation of vagrant itinerants, fatalistic beggars, miserable widows, and bewildered orphans—and on everyone's lips was the name Vincente San Bruno. The lame, the sick, the mad, and the grief-stricken invented ever-increasing curses on his line.

Catalina braced herself as she walked toward Café Malquerida. Her fears were well founded: the windows were smashed in and Royalist slogans were daubed on the walls outside. The café had been completely ransacked, the looters leaving nothing but a mess behind them. She stooped to clear up shards of broken glass, and then stopped herself. Struck by the pointlessness of it, she turned and left. Using some of the little money she had saved from Mendoza, Catalina rented a small apartment until she could figure out her next step. She spent some time trying to hunt down Jorge, hoping he had survived the crossing and the fighting at Chacabuco. Posing as a relative, she eventually discovered he had been transferred to the south, where the fighting continued, making travel impossible.

Drawing up a small client list—regulars from Madam Feliz's Gambling House with whom she had made contact in Santiago—Catalina turned her new home into a house of ill repute. But her conscience was troubling her, and her nightmares had returned. She was haunted, too, by Teresa's words when she had left Mendoza. Her warning rang in Catalina's ears. After she slept with her first customer, the voice became quieter.

47: *Homecoming*

San Martín's decision to leave Chile was a mistake. He believed Spain's spirit had been crushed after his audacious mountain crossing and resounding victory, and all that was left to do was to finish them off in Peru. He was wrong. His natural cautiousness had stayed the vengeful hand of O'Higgins after the Battle of Chacabuco. Fifteen hundred experienced troops escaped by sea to Lima; they would be seen in Chile again.

He left his subordinate, General Las Heras, in charge of mopping-up operations. The primary target was the port of Talcahuano in southern Chile, which afforded the Spaniards an easy means of reinvading the country. San Martín ordered the port taken and then set off for Buenos Aires to secure financial backing for his naval expedition. Royalist support was still strong in the south and General Las Heras' progress was slow. Frustrated, Bernardo O'Higgins joined him with a further eight hundred men. One month later, the Spanish survivors of Chacabuco landed at Talcahuano. The Patriots not only failed to take the port but were badly beaten further north at Talca shortly afterward.

O'Higgins, recognizing the need for reinforcements, began recruiting heavily in the provinces and appointed a much-decorated

French mercenary to command operations around Talca. General Michel Brayer was one of Napoleon's storied commanders—a member of the Legion of Honor and a veteran of Austerlitz, Danzig, and Albuera. He fled France after the deposition of Napoleon and the ascension of Louis XVIII, first taking refuge in Prussia, and then the United States, before turning up in Buenos Aires as a soldier of fortune. Expectations were high, and there was some surprise when he missed a key battle near Talca due to injury.

When San Martín arrived in Buenos Aires, he was appointed Brigadier-General. He refused the promotion, as well as all monetary gifts the government tried to bestow on him, accepting only a pension for his young daughter's education. A parade was staged in his honor, but he was uncomfortable with the pomp and ceremony, reacting angrily when a crown of flowers was placed on his head. He knew he had enough jealous enemies, without being portrayed as seeking money or power, and was anxious to garner support for the final part of his plan. Puerreydón—the Supreme Director of Argentina—was reluctant to commit further resources, wary of separatist chaos in the rural provinces of Argentina, and Royalist action around Montevideo. However, ultimately San Martín was able to secure the promises of support he requested. Agents were dispatched to New York and London with instructions to purchase ships.

After his all-too-brief reunion with María, who was ill and had to remain in Buenos Aires, San Martín commenced the return journey. In Mendoza, he had the relief of meeting his friend, Major Alvarez, who was carrying instructions from O'Higgins to purchase ships in London. But San Martín had another mission for him— one that had to be kept secret for now. On his return to Santiago, San Martín spent several days convalescing in his Spartan rooms in the Bishop's Palace, taking opiates every day now and not rising from bed until he had drunk a vial of the foul liquid. His friends were concerned about his welfare, worried he wouldn't see the end of the war. Back in Buenos Aires, rumors of his ill-health intensified. Puerreydón decided to dispatch General Balcarce, who had recently impressed with victories in the north, to take up position as his second-in-command. The unwritten understanding was that Balcarce was to be ready to take over if San Martín

A Storm Hits Valparaíso

became unable to continue. To make matters worse, San Martín lost a key ally. Padre Beltrán resigned and returned to Mendoza. San Martín begged him to stay, but the priest was adamant. "My war is over."

San Martín grew increasingly unhappy in Santiago. No natural statesman, he quickly tired of the factions vying for control and the sycophants currying favor. His officers were pressing him to take decisive action in the south—where the Spanish still held the port of Talcahuano, the city of Concepcion, the port-fortress of Valdivia and the island of Chiloe—but San Martín was reluctant to commit further troops. An expeditionary force was expected from Lima, but he did not know when or where they might land. When the Patriots had taken on Santiago, Marcó del Pont had to guess the point of attack along a thousand miles of mountains. Conversely, the Patriots now had a thousand mile coastline to defend, he realized. He laughed, but there was no humor in it.

San Martín's pleas for funds increased in both frequency and desperation until he had a rudimentary fleet at his disposal. It consisted of one frigate, two brigantines, and a corvette. A training school was set up in Valparaíso for midshipmen, but recruiting proved difficult; greater prizes lured sailors to the pirate ships of the Pacific. Funds were a continual problem, and a deepening depression, induced by his increasing laudanum addiction, kept San Martín away from the troublesome campaign in the south. Besides, he was obsessed with planning his assault on Peru. Fighting the remnants of the Spanish was an unwelcome distraction, one that could and should be handled by the Chileans, he believed. He dispatched O'Higgins to impose some kind of order and to tease the Spanish out to fight. The bulk of his troops he stationed around Santiago, fearing an attack on Valparaíso by sea, which was now blockaded by Spanish ships.

48: The Surprise of Cancha Rayada

In January 1818, the Spanish—under the command of General Osorio, who had led the bloody *Reconquista* of Chile four years earlier—landed in Talcahuano with a huge detachment of reinforcements from Lima. The Royalists now had five thousand experienced, well-equipped troops ready for battle. San Martín sprang into action, the impending peril banishing the narcotic fugue that had plagued him for months. He ordered O'Higgins to retreat so they could concentrate their forces south of Santiago. Despite the increase in troops, San Martín was worried. These men were green. The Spanish, on the other hand, were experienced, ruthless, and thirsting for revenge. To bolster the spirits of the people, San Martín formally proclaimed Chile independent and had O'Higgins do the same in the south. As O'Higgins raced northwards, San Martín frantically raised reserves around the country, armed militias, and equipped the civilian population of Santiago with fourteen thousand lances, before moving south to take command.

He met O'Higgins in mid-March. Combined, they had six thousand men at their disposal, and San Martín called together his commanders. He calculated that a single huge cavalry charge could shatter the Royalists' forces. The entire contingent of Mounted Grenadiers—seventeen hundred horsemen—set out to attack the Spaniards. However, their advance was hindered by the plains of La Cancha Rayada, where a large field scarred by a series of natural ditches impeded their assault. The Grenadiers were forced to retreat, camping that night with the rest of the troops. A few hours later, a spy brought San Martín disturbing news: the Spanish commanders were considering a night attack around the back of Talca. To his horror, San Martín realized that the rear of his forces was exposed. Hurriedly, he issued orders for his men to change position.

* * *

Pacha stared at the fire, relieved the attack hadn't gone ahead. Since he had transferred to the south, all they seemed to do was race from one skirmish to another. These small battles resulted in minor victories or defeats but only served to maintain the status quo: the Patriots held Santiago and the north; the Royalists, the coast and the south. While there was some joy among the men that they were to finally fight a decisive battle, many worried they hadn't had sufficient time to prepare, or to rest. An extra night's sleep would make all the difference.

Startled by the sound of shouting in the distance, Pacha leapt to his feet. Everyone around the fire jumped up, straining their ears, scanning the darkness, their hands on their weapons. The fire hissed as someone threw a bucket of water over it, and smoke filled Pacha's face. Drowning out his coughs was the thunder of hooves—thousands of them—bearing down on him.

"Cavalry charge!"

The men scattered, lost in the darkness. Bullets tore the night, seeming to come from all directions. Pacha threw himself to the ground as a musket ball whizzed over his head. The sound of galloping intensified. Sure he was about to be trampled, Pacha raised his head to see a pack mule hurtle past. They had been released somehow, running terrified into the night. Pacha felt a moment's relief, until he realized something or someone must have disturbed them, and was immediately knocked to the ground by a fast-moving shadow. Scrambling to his feet, he leapt out of the path of another marauding mule. Despite the confusion, he could make out shadows running in all directions. Who or what they were running from eluded him. He swung around, desperately seeking the leadership of an officer, but none could be found.

He heard voices coming from the row of officers' tents: Spanish soldiers. Soon enough, he could make them out through the smoke and the darkness—small groups creeping toward the edge of the camp, every so often pausing to take aim at his comrades. Pacha didn't understand. *Had no sentries been posted? How had they managed to sneak in undetected and attack the camp?* He made his way toward the command tent, seeking anyone who could tell him what to do. As he got closer, he spied the Chilean leader, Bernardo O'Higgins, screaming orders and gesticulating wildly. Then he heard a crack. The general went down, clutching his stomach.

Pacha wanted to run to his aid, but something directly behind him caught his attention. As Pacha turned, someone grabbed him. Before he could even struggle, a cold blade met the warm folds of his neck. Raising his hands to his sliced throat, Pacha fell to his knees, unable to stem the life pouring from him. His assailant crept forward, toward the doubled-up form of Bernardo O'Higgins. Summoning his remaining strength, Pacha cried out, pointing at his killer. Then he slumped forward. The last thing Pacha saw, as he fell, was the sword, just out of reach, its copper-edged blade glimmering in the moonlight.

* * *

In Santiago, news of the defeat caused panic. Memories of Spanish retribution after Rancagua were still fresh. The people abandoned their houses, cafés, and shops. Rumors flooded in with the retreating troops: O'Higgins was dead; San Martín had been captured and was to be shot; the remaining Argentines had fled to Mendoza, saving themselves, leaving the Chileans at the mercy of their conquerors. Looting was widespread. Fear and anarchy reigned. Five days later, O'Higgins and San Martín appeared in the capital, dispelling the worst of the rumors. Together, they attempted to restore order, letting it be known that the losses weren't as bad as feared, and that the Army had been scattered rather than slaughtered. The truth was, the Patriots had been lucky. The Royalists' cunning night attack had hindered them too. The Spanish had been unable to follow up their victory in the darkness, instead deciding to sack Talca and regroup for the final assault on Santiago.

A large crowd gathered at the Palace, anxious for concrete news.

"Chileans!" San Martín addressed the crowd from horseback. "It was natural that this unexpected blow and the consequent uncertainty should make you hesitate. But it is now time to take stock of yourselves and to realize that our country's army is holding with glory in the face of the enemy; that your companions at arms are gathering fast and that the resources of patriotism are inexhaustible. The tyrants have not advanced a single step in their entrenchment. I have put in motion a force of over four thousand men. I give my word of honor that I shall shortly give a day of glory to América!"

A great cheer rose up as San Martín led his horse out of the crowd, his mind composing his final orders.

The men were to be issued with a limited supply of cartridges and a ration of *aguardiente* before the battle. The rules of engagement were strict: every enemy advance was to be met with an attack. Wounded would be left where they lay; mercy would have to wait until the battle's end. The ultimate sanction would be applied against would-be deserters, and commanders were to ensure all men were aware of the penalty. This was a battle they had to win. After making sure each of his commanders understood, San Martín left Santiago to join his men. It was time: the Spanish were approaching the Maipú River, only two miles from Santiago.

49: The Battle of Maipú

San Martín arrived just before his senior officers retreated to the suburbs of Santiago. He told them that they would engage the enemy on the open plain of Maipú instead. General Brayer, the French mercenary, thought this suicidal.

"We have barely four thousand troops, the confidence of whom is shattered, and you want to pit them against six thousand well-drilled Royalists on the back of a victory. This is madness," he insisted, advising O'Higgins to cut and run.

San Martín dismissed his objections.

The next day, the Spanish crossed the Maipú River unopposed, taking position on the southern end of the plain. At the opposite end, San Martín began devising his strategy. That night, he slept in a mill beneath Loma Blanca—the hill where his forces were massed. At daybreak, he was woken; the enemy was moving. San Martín, dressed in a poncho and farmer's hat, rode southward with O'Brien. Soon they saw a rider coming toward them at speed—General Brayer. San Martín drew up his horse.

"General," the Frenchman seemed surprised to see San Martín, but then recovered his composure. "I'm afraid I must retire to the baths at Colna, with your permission, of course. I fear my rheumatic leg will not allow me to fulfill my duties and your orders."

San Martín's mouth dropped open. "With the same permission with which you granted yourself at Talca, General, you may go to the baths. Within a half-hour we will decide the fate of Chile. You could remain, if your illness allows you to."

"It is impossible. I must insist on requesting again."

San Martín's lip curled. "The last drummer boy has more honor than you." Spurring his horse, he rode on. "If we are still alive tomorrow," he told O'Brien, "and we can find our rheumatic General, I want him shot."

A couple of hours later, the sun had fully risen, gilding the snow-capped peaks to San Martín's left. A church bell pealed in the distance. He took out his telescope and looked south. "How stupid are these Spaniards?" he said. "Osorio is a bigger fool than I thought. Victory is ours today. The sun is my witness."

"General?" O'Brien was confused.

"They're moving." San Martín pointed. "They're taking the Santiago road, trying to cut us off. Tell Las Heras to occupy the passes ahead of them. We'll see who traps whom." They galloped back to Loma Blanca.

With San Martín's maneuvers, the Spanish were forced to march back and retake their position on Espejo Hill. The battle would take place on the plain of Maipú—as San Martín had hoped. From his vantage point on Loma Blanca, San Martín surveyed the enemy. Their elite troops, the Burgos Regiment, were lined up on his left, with the Infante Don Carlos Regiment on his right and four heavy guns on a hill to the east. San Martín lined up General Alvarado's men—predominantly freed slaves with far less training and experience—on the left, and General Las Heras' experienced troops on the right. He just hoped his plan would work.

With a cannonade, San Martín ordered General Alvarado's troops forward. The Spanish responded by sending the Infante Don Carlos Regiment forward to attack General Las Heras' troops. Simultaneously, Colonel Manuel Escalada led a group of Grenadiers in an assault on the heavy guns. They took them easily, turning them back on the Spaniards. General Alvarado's men soon ran into trouble and were being pushed back by the elite Burgos

Regiment. On the other side, General Las Heras' men were pushing back the Spanish advance.

San Martín's plan was working. The enemy's line became stretched and skewed, turning anti-clockwise. San Martín sent in the reserve Grenadiers to wheel around and attack the flank of the Burgos Regiment. A thunder of hooves gave way to the clash of swords as the Grenadiers cut swathes through the Spaniards. Soon, the Patriots were advancing amid cries of "*Viva América!*" The Royalists broke rank and retreated. San Martín sent the rest of the cavalry after them to cut them to pieces as they fled.

* * *

"We have completely destroyed the enemy, sir." General Las Heras saluted in front of San Martín later that day. "Perhaps two thousand dead and the same number taken prisoner. We have captured their stores and ammunition, and the Grenadiers are giving chase to any survivors."

"Our casualties?"

"High, sir. Perhaps one thousand dead or seriously wounded, but Chile is ours."

A Grenadier appeared. "Sir, excuse me," he addressed Las Heras. "We have some trouble at the Espejo farmhouse. I think you should come."

"Go." San Martín nodded at Las Heras. "Send a report back. I'll be over with the surgeon."

Las Heras jumped on a waiting horse and galloped off down the hill while San Martín hurried toward the field hospital. The stench was overpowering and inhuman screams filled the air. With so many injured, only the most serious cases were receiving any kind of attention. San Martín found the surgeon—grim and blood-spattered, and holding a hacksaw. Around him, men lay moaning on stretchers in every direction.

"General," said the surgeon, "please tell me we won. Please tell me all of this was not for nothing."

"The day is ours, doctor."

The surgeon allowed himself a brief smile. "As you can see, I am completely overrun. I fear the worst."

"What do you need?"

"Everything." He shook his head. "We are running low on everything. Most of all, I need clean bandages and clean water, and all the doctors in Santiago."

San Martín called O'Brien over. "You heard him. Put a call out. Anyone with any medical training is to report here immediately. Send a rider to Santiago—no, send one to each hospital. Tell them to get all the supplies they can and to send as many of their people as they can spare."

The surgeon turned to San Martín. "Thank you. Now forgive me but..." He gestured to a young man who lay groaning on a stretcher with one leg a mess of pulp and exposed bone. "We can't save it. An infection has already set in."

San Martín followed the surgeon over to the stricken infantryman, noticing he couldn't have been more than seventeen or eighteen. "What's your name, son?"

"Frederico, sir."

"The doctor here is going to have to amputate your leg."

Seeing the hacksaw, Frederico clenched his teeth, wincing. "It's going to hurt, isn't it?"

"Yes. It's going to hurt."

"General," said the surgeon, "if Frederico doesn't mind, I'm going to ask you to hold him down. It's best he doesn't move."

"One moment." San Martín called in O'Brien and whispered something in his ear. The Irishman ran out of the tent. "Frederico, have I met you before?"

"In the stables, at Buenos Aires, when you were the *comandante*," the boy managed with difficulty.

"Ah, yes, I remember now."

"I always wanted to join the Grenadiers."

"Can you ride a horse?"

"Yes, sir."

"Well then, Frederico, consider yourself promoted."

O'Brien returned, handing San Martín a vial containing a viscous green liquid.

"Drink this, it will help with the pain," said San Martín.

Frederico emptied it in one swallow, and then grimaced.

"Hold it down. I know it's disgusting, but hold it down."

Frederico swallowed.

San Martín nodded at O'Brien and they held the boy in place. After placing a small block of wood in Frederico's mouth, the surgeon lined up the hacksaw. Frederico's ear-splitting cries were cut short by his lapse into unconsciousness.

When the surgeon finished dressing the stump, he used the remaining bandage to wipe the blood from his face and hands. "He won't last the night."

San Martín bowed his head.

After a moment's silence, he picked up a piece of bloodstained paper from the floor and wrote a message: *We obtained a complete victory. Our cavalry pursues to finish them. The country is free.* Handing it to O'Brien, he instructed, "Take this to O'Higgins. He's at the civilian barricades in the suburbs. Doctor, let me know if you need anything else," he said, and then he rode back to the top of the Loma Blanca to view the battlefield.

As San Martín crested the hill, he heard a shout. Bernardo O'Higgins raced toward him and the two men dismounted and embraced.

"Glory to the Savior of Chile," said O'Higgins.

"General," said San Martín, eyeing the bloodied bandage around his chest, "Chile will not forget your sacrifice in presenting yourself on the battlefield with your glorious wound still open."

* * *

Jorge was in pursuit. Two squadrons peeled away to his right to chase down the stragglers, but Jorge brought his unit up the hill toward the farmhouse on top of Espejo Hill, where the Spaniards had been headquartered. His men dismounted and ran to take defensive positions, avoiding gunfire from the windows. The Spaniards had barricaded themselves in. The farmhouse was surrounded by three corrals, but as soon as Jorge's men broke through, a white flag was waved desperately from one of the windows. "Bring up the cannon," Jorge ordered.

"But sir, they are offering surrender."

Jorge grabbed the soldier by the neck. "It's a ruse. Now bring up that cannon or I'll have you shot for disobeying orders."

Trembling, the soldier obeyed.

As soon as the cannon was loaded, Jorge gave the order to fire. The white flag was still raised, and the artilleryman hesitated. Drawing his musket, Jorge pointed it at the artilleryman. "I said fire, damn it."

A large hole was blown in the wall of the farmhouse, from which Royalist troops immediately began shooting. "See." Jorge smiled. "I told you it was a ruse." He gave the order to charge, and his men poured through the newly created hole, sabers drawn. The Spaniards attempted to surrender again, throwing their weapons to the floor, but were hacked to pieces.

* * *

Pulling his horse to a halt outside the farmhouse, Diego dismounted and drew his saber. Bodies littered the ground and blood stained the walls, the ceiling, the floor—every possible surface. A cry rang out from an adjoining room. Inside, he saw a soldier with his bloodied saber drawn. For a moment, Diego thought it was a Spaniard, but when the man's head lifted, he saw who it was. Jorge's eyes were glazed and his uniform was dark with blood.

"Quick, Diego! Some of them got out the back door." Jorge gestured wildly.

Diego froze, barely recognizing his brother, much less what he had done. There were corpses everywhere, but only Spanish. This wasn't war: this was murder.

Jorge ran out the back door, and Diego shook his head, coming to his senses. He chased Jorge out in time to see him run his sword through another defenseless man, who pleaded for mercy.

"Hurry! There's more over there." Jorge turned at Diego's approach.

"Jorge, put down your weapon."

Jorge scowled at Diego. Then, out of the corner of his eye he saw a Spaniard make a break for it, running low between the rows of vines. Jorge took out his musket and cocked the trigger.

"Jorge, no!" Diego threw himself at his brother, knocking him into the mud, the musket discharging in the air.

"Sor—" Diego started to apologize when Jorge's elbow caught him square in the jaw. Jorge wriggled out from under him, and Diego stood back, holding his chin. "Jorge, you can't just—" he was cut short by Jorge charging at him, knocking him to the ground. One blow after another rained down on his face.

* * *

General Las Heras and his men walked through the farmhouse, stunned. These men hadn't been killed; they had been butchered. He opened the back door, leading out to the vineyard. Seeing Diego and Jorge fighting, and assuming Jorge's darkened uniform marked him as an enemy, he gave an order to one of his men. The soldier cocked his rifle and aimed. He couldn't get a clear shot. Another soldier came through the doorway, saw the fight, and charged with his bayonet drawn.

Diego cried out, but it was too late—Jorge was run through. Shoving the soldier away, Diego then propped Jorge up against a tree. Blood burbled from Jorge's mouth and although he strove for words, no sound came.

Eyes flashing, Diego turned on the soldier. General Las Heras ran in to restrain him, noticing, for the first time, Jorge's blood-soaked uniform. "He didn't know he was one of ours. Neither of us did. We thought he was going to kill you."

Diego looked blankly at them, and then turned to Jorge. His brother's eyes had become glassy, losing their vitality. Diego took Jorge's knife from his belt, the knife he had given him, and made an incision across the scar on his left palm, pressing it against the wound on Jorge's chest. Then he bowed his head against Jorge's until his brother stopped breathing altogether.

50: Napoleon

Four weeks after the crushing defeat of the Spanish, Cochrane's career reached a dead end. Many of his Radical colleagues and supporters had been jailed or exiled. The only way he could continue his push for universal suffrage was to lead the country into open revolution, something he was not prepared to do. He had finally accepted that his career in the Navy was finished but he still hankered after the liberty of life on the open seas, and he still felt that he had a lot to offer. He let it be known that his services were available as a soldier of fortune. Shortly afterwards, a Spanish diplomat approached him offering the command of a huge naval expedition to quell their rebellious colonies. The offer was interesting, but he turned it down flat, unwilling to devote himself to suppressing a movement he sympathized with, in the service of a government he considered reactionary. It didn't feel right.

At the beginning of June, Cochrane gave a speech in the House of Commons that stunned those present. "As it is probably the last time I shall ever have the honor of addressing the House on any subject, I am anxious to tell its members what I think of their conduct."

Jeers rang out. Cochrane waited for the noise to subside, then cleared his throat. "It is now nearly eleven years since I have had the honor of a seat in this House, and since then there have been very few measures in which I could agree with the opinions of the majority." He had to raise his voice to be heard over the shouts of his peers. "I will say, as has been said before by the great Chatham, the father of Mr. Pitt, that if the House does not reform itself from within, it will be reformed with a vengeance from without."

Cochrane held up his hand until the tumult died down. "The gentlemen who now sit on the benches opposite with such triumphant feelings will one day repent their conduct. The commotions to which that conduct will inevitably give rise will shake not only this House, but the whole framework of government and society to its foundations. I have been actuated by the wish to prevent this, and I have had no other intention."

It was indeed the last speech Cochrane would give to Parliament, for he had received another offer—one that he had accepted. Major Alvarez had been in London negotiating the purchase of ships for the new Chilean government. Under orders from San Martín, he approached Cochrane and offered him the role of Admiral to build Chile's navy.

However, the Establishment was not finished with Cochrane just yet. The Government hurriedly produced a bill prohibiting Britons from fighting for foreign governments. Before it could be passed, Cochrane, Kitty, and their two young sons, Tom and William, raced to the serene harbor town of Rye, departing in a small fishing boat for Boulogne. By the time the bill passed Parliament, Cochrane had left British waters. Technically once again a criminal, this time he was beyond the reach of the law. Cochrane had another reason to speed his departure, for he had concocted a fantastical plan that involved springing from prison the very man he had spent years fighting: the exiled Emperor of France, Napoleon Bonaparte.

Napoleon had followed Cochrane's career closely since his performance at the Basque Roads—dubbing him *Le Loup de Mer*, The Sea Wolf—and had despaired at his treatment after the Stock Exchange scandal. Cochrane had always admired Napoleon's daring, and was sympathetic to his liberal outlook. Napoleon had sent secret messages of support to Cochrane during his incarceration in the King's Bench Prison, and once the level of Cochrane's support was established, made the Scot aware of his plan to place himself on the throne of a confederation of South American states.

A group of Bonapartist officers, marines, and exiles had agreed to rendezvous on the Fernando de Noronha archipelago—two hundred and twenty miles off the coast of Brazil. They were to be joined by a frigate, two gunboats, and a decorated French General named Michel Brayer. From there, they would sail on to St. Helena, free Napoleon, and commence their expedition. However, some months previously, the Bonapartist officers had been driven out of their base in northern Brazil, and the plan had to be altered.

Cochrane intended to sail directly to St. Helena—unbeknownst to his Chilean employers, who would be present on the voyage—spring Napoleon from prison, travel on to Chile, and place him at the head of the Patriot independence forces. It was an audacious plan, but one that was to be foiled for now. As Cochrane's vessel approached St. Helena, he received news from another ship that the Spaniards had landed an army in the south of Chile. He was ordered to proceed at full speed to Valparaíso. Cochrane had no choice; his madcap scheme would have to wait.

51: The Coward San Martín

After Maipú, San Martín rode out of the city, feeling the wind in his face. He threw back his head and roared. With Chile free, Peru was next, and no one would stand in his way. A Grenadier drew alongside him, pointing and they both banked to the right. San Martín picked up the pace, anxious to see why O'Brien had sent for him. His aide had been chasing General Osorio, but the message he received said the Spaniard had slipped away.

They approached El Salto, where O'Brien had found a secluded spot away from the farmhouses and under the shade of a tree. As San Martín dismounted, O'Brien dismissed the Grenadier. "Take my horse to water and leave yours. I'll see you back at the barracks."

San Martín greeted O'Brien warmly. "Don't tell me you have Osorio hidden here somewhere."

O'Brien shook his head. "I wasn't quick enough. But the general was so desperate to get away, he threw everything else in my path."

"And that was prize enough, O'Brien. There were twenty-five officers among the four hundred stragglers you rounded up. But that's not why you brought me here."

"No, sir. This is." O'Brien led San Martín to the rear of the bushes where he had hidden several saddlebags and a large trunk.

"More gold?"

"Let me show you." The saddlebags contained various maps and confidential dispatches. San Martín noted with amusement the inaccurate estimates of his army, but the real treasure was in the chest. "General Osorio's luggage," said O'Brien, flipping it open.

Apart from clothes, medals and other personal effects, San Martín found a series of secret orders signed by the Viceroy of Peru, Joaquin de Pezuela.

"That's not all," said O'Brien, reaching in and handing San Martín a file. "Osorio's personal correspondence."

San Martín opened it and started reading, slamming it shut after the first few pages. "This is explosive!"

"That's why I called you here."

"You did the right thing. Thank you." San Martín opened the file again and read some more.

"What are you going to do?"

San Martín stared at O'Brien. "I don't know."

* * *

The sky darkened; San Martín and O'Brien piled the last of the firewood in the center of the stone circle. When it was lit, San Martín sat to read the letters once more. After the disaster at Cancha Rayada, when the Spanish began closing in, several of Santiago's leading citizens had decided to switch sides. Several letters professed support for the King of Spain, urging Osorio to bring an end to the reign of this "gang of thieves." Others disclosed the movement and composition of San Martín's troops, with detailed notes and, in some cases, maps. One supposed Patriot even pledged to have a horse shod in silver for Osorio's triumphant arrival. San Martín read all of the letters with care. When finished, he burned the lot.

O'Brien seemed surprised. "Is that the end of it?"

"No. Make it common knowledge we captured Osorio's luggage. I want to make things a little uncomfortable for these …

patriots. If we make them sweat, perhaps we might find them more helpful in the next round of public subscriptions."

Over the following days, as San Martín re-imposed order in Santiago, a coup attempt by the traitorous Carrera brothers came to light. On the day the news of his victory reached Mendoza, Juan José and Luis Carrera were tied to a bench and shot. Only the third brother, José Miguel, remained at large.

San Martín was recalled to Buenos Aires by Supreme Director Puerreydón so the people could celebrate their victory and laud their hero. He acquiesced, but only because he wanted to secure the remaining funds needed for the invasion of Peru while his stock was high. Puerreydón only agreed to a limited version of San Martín's plan: an expedition to capture the ports south of Lima and encourage rebellion among the local population. San Martín was forced to accept. He left Buenos Aires to spend a month's leave with his wife and daughter in Mendoza while he awaited funds.

* * *

It was the first time María had spent any real time with her husband since he crossed the Andes. She knew about the opiates, having pressed John O'Brien, and resolved to wean her husband off them. It was difficult at first, but gradually he seemed fitter, healthier and happier, now that the suffocating cloak of chemically induced depression had been lifted from him.

"María! Remeditos! Come here, listen to this." Her husband called to her one day.

"José?"

"We've got our man. Our Admiral!"

"What are you talking about?"

"Major Alvarez is in London purchasing ships. I told him to sniff out a commander, and we got him."

"Who is it?"

"A man named Cochrane, a British sailor of some repute."

"And why does he want to come here?"

San Martín paused. He didn't have an answer. "The letter doesn't say, but listen to this. O'Higgins says he's, 'one of the most eminent of Great Britain, a person highly commendable, not only on account of his liberal principles with which he has always upheld the cause of the English people in their Parliament, but also because he bears a character altogether superior to ambitious self-seeking.'"

María pursed her lips.

"What is it, Remeditos? This is great news."

"I remember the last time you were this excited."

He wrinkled his brow.

María tried again. "The Frenchman."

San Martín recalled General Brayer's craven performance at Maipú, sneaking off the battlefield before the fighting commenced. He scowled as he opened the next letter. It was from Puerreydón. He was unable to come up with any of the agreed funds. San Martín cursed and banged the table, startling his wife. He crumpled the page and threw it over his shoulder. "O'Brien! Get in here." San Martín dictated a message dispatching his resignation.

One week later, San Martín looked across at his wife's untouched dinner. "María, is that all you are going to eat."

She picked up her fork and toyed with her food. "I don't have any appetite at the moment. It's odd." She put a slim hand on her bulging stomach. "When I was pregnant with Mercedes, I ate like a wolf. But I feel sick all the time now. It's hard to keep anything down."

San Martín took her hand. "Why don't you go upstairs and rest."

María stood, her hand in the small of her back.

"Remeditos, you know I have to leave in a few days."

"I know, José. You don't have to say anything. You have to do this. I know you would rather be here, but we're not going anywhere, and this war will end some day." She patted his face and left, nodding to O'Brien, who stood in the doorway, carrying letters.

San Martín beckoned him in. "Sit, sit."

"I have his reply."

"Hungry?"

"Ravenous."

San Martín traded him María's dinner for the envelope. He held it for a moment before placing it on the table.

273

O'Brien looked up. "Aren't you going to open it?"

"I want to enjoy this moment for a while." San Martín saw the confusion on O'Brien's face. "For the last week I have been a free man. I presume this letter will be Puerreydón rejecting my resignation, coming to some compromise."

"And?"

"And part of me wishes it wasn't so, that he could find someone else. I'm tired. Tired of fighting, of being away from my family. Each time I see Mercedes she has grown another few inches. Who knows how old she'll be when we're finally done." He sighed and opened the letter. "He's giving us two hundred thousand pesos." It was less than half what was originally promised. In response, San Martín seized the funds of businessmen traveling through Cuyo, issuing them with promissory notes that Puerreydón would be forced to cash. After saying goodbye to his wife and daughter, he crossed the Andes once more.

On his arrival in Santiago, San Martín uncovered another plot against his life. The French mercenary, General Brayer, had made common cause with José Miguel, whose band of brigands were terrorizing the Argentine *pampas*, trying to draw San Martín into a fight. A team of French assassins had been hired to cross the Andes and offer their swords to San Martín, before knifing him in the back. Their plan was foiled, much to the annoyance of General Brayer, who began a vicious publicity campaign against "the coward" San Martín. And in the midst of all this, San Martín received the devastating news that María had suffered a miscarriage. He turned to the only source of comfort at hand: laudanum.

52: Cochrane the Pirate

One month later, November 28th 1818, after a stormy, fraught voyage around the Cape of Good Hope, Cochrane and his family landed in Valparaíso. They were welcomed at port by O'Higgins, who later held a ball in their honor. Cochrane returned the favor two days later with a party for St. Andrew's Day, amusing the locals by dressing in tartan. After these pleasant introductions, it became apparent to Cochrane that his appointment had ruffled a few feathers. First was Blanco Encalada, a twenty-eight-year-old sailor who had been demoted to make room for Cochrane. He took it with good grace, but Cochrane was astute enough to notice lingering resentment. In addition, two British mercenaries, Captains Guise and Spry, harbored hopes of the job themselves before Cochrane's arrival. Finally, while Cochrane determined that O'Higgins seemed likeable enough and of a similar temperament to himself, San Martín was another matter. He was aloof, cold and withdrawn. Cochrane couldn't figure him out and did not take to him. One of San Martín's first acts was to appoint an Argentine to act as Cochrane's personal secretary. Cochrane's suspicions were instantly aroused.

San Martín was instantly wary of the Scot. He detested flamboyance in his subordinates. Experience taught him that it lent itself to imprudent risk-taking, and it was already difficult enough reining O'Higgins in. He would have to keep Cochrane on a tight leash, and it did not appear he was used to wearing one.

Cochrane reviewed the rudimentary navy at his disposal. They had just scored two notable victories—ending the Spanish blockade of Valparaíso and capturing a Spanish frigate—but they were hardly ready to dominate the Pacific. He had seven ships—of which four were merely gunboats—to take on the Spanish fleet of forty-two vessels. The inexperienced crews spoke little or no English, and while the officers were mainly British or American, most of the ships had seen better days. Cochrane realized he had a Herculean task ahead of him and set about imposing discipline and organizing the fleet.

* * *

Seven weeks later, at the beginning of 1819, Cochrane was ready to depart on his first mission. Kitty brought her two sons down to the Valparaíso seafront to see their father off.

"Where is Papa going?" Four-year-old Tom had been plaguing her with questions since they left the house.

"On a big ship." Kitty, with her free hand, pointed out to the bay.

"I can't see," complained Tom. "Lift me up." He pulled at Kitty's dress. She readjusted young William on her hip and turned back to pull Tom close to her, but he was gone. She panicked as she lost sight of him, but relaxed somewhat when she saw him up ahead on the shoulders of one of the men. As the sailor continued toward the beach, she could see Tom waving at the larger ships in the bay.

Kitty ducked through the crowd, holding little William close. When she got to the shoreline, she searched everywhere, but Tom was gone. Then William pointed: Tom was in the last rowboat, bobbing his way to the center of the bay. Her desperate cries were to no avail. The boat wouldn't turn around. Her only hope was that her husband would have the good sense to send young Tom back to shore. She should have known better.

* * *

Cochrane wasn't comfortable with the idea of his young son being on board, but the way he saw it, he had no choice. He would look foolish if he delayed the departure of his fleet; besides, he had more pressing matters to deal with. Before they even left the bay, Cochrane had a mutiny on his hands. From his flagship *O'Higgins* he noticed that the crew of the *Chacabuco* were refusing to raise anchor. Cochrane wasted no time, threatening to blow the ship to smithereens unless they capitulated and the ringleaders were put to shore. They complied, and the men were arrested.

While on the outside Cochrane seemed furious, secretly he was delighted by this early opportunity to impose his authority on the ill-disciplined crew. The men were full of trepidation, for Cochrane intended to take the four largest ships of his little navy directly to Callao, the imposing, well-defended port of Lima, which was protected by three hundred and fifty shore guns and the pride of the Spanish fleet, a mighty frigate named the *Esmeralda*. The journey took several weeks, during which the crew amused themselves by sewing a uniform for their new mascot, little Tom, who entertained them with clumsy salutes.

Cochrane chose to strike Callao in the middle of Carnaval. Viceroy Pezuela was inspecting the fortifications as part of the festivities, but Cochrane knew none of this. He slipped into the port on a foggy night, flying the neutral flag of the United States of America. A celebratory cannon-shot was fired in the Viceroy's honor from one of the shore batteries. Naturally, Cochrane assumed his cover was blown and returned fire. As well as the three hundred and fifty shore guns, there were more than a hundred guns onboard the ships in port, all soon to be trained on him. When the firing commenced, Cochrane locked little Tom in his cabin. Somehow, the child escaped and clambered up on deck, busying himself handing powder to the gunners.

Cochrane heard a shot land behind him and a child's scream. Turning, he saw little Tom, his firstborn, covered in blood. He dashed toward him, screaming and grabbing at the boy, looking to see where he was wounded. But Tom was spared; the shot had hit the gunner, whose brains were now splattered all over the child. After this, and with some difficulty, Cochrane maneuvered his ship safely out of the harbor to rejoin his flotilla, which had decamped to the island of San Lorenzo about three miles offshore.

Cochrane set up a laboratory on the island with the intention of creating some of the explosion ships that had wreaked such havoc on the French. However, the only one successfully constructed was intercepted by a Spanish gunboat before it could be detonated. He received orders to return to Valparaíso and captured several prizes, including one ship containing seventy thousand pesos, before returning his son to arms of his anxious wife. Despite his minor successes, the Chileans were beginning to wonder if appointing Cochrane was a mistake.

* * *

Back in Valparaíso, San Martín's plans were thwarted again as fighting broke out between Buenos Aires and the rebellious provincial warlords who controlled much of rural Argentina. Puerreydón ordered San Martín to return to the capital to defend against the coup, fearing the rumored twenty-thousand-strong Spanish force would be sent to exploit the chaos. San Martín felt the invasion was a scare story, initiated only to put the Patriots on the defensive; Puerreydón was sure an attack was imminent. They were both wrong. Soldiers due to make the Atlantic crossing had been decimated by the plague and had mutinied before they even left the harbor of Cadiz. However, the civil war was very real, and San Martín dispatched a portion of the Argentine soldiers under his command to Mendoza, before traveling there himself with half his remaining men.

He was relieved to see his wife and daughter again. María seemed to be recovering from the miscarriage and Mercedes was growing fast. But to his horror, he discovered that the Army of the North had mutinied and General Belgrano had been taken prisoner. His dream of liberating Peru was disintegrating. He spent a lot of time sick in bed, feverish, pale, and thin.

A Storm Hits Valparaíso

When he summoned enough strength to take a walk around Mendoza, he was pressed by various factions to back one party or another, none of which he cared for. San Martín realized that his very presence on Argentine soil could draw him into the civil war. Despite his poor health, he resolved to leave. María and Mercedes were sent to Buenos Aires under armed guard. He left to continue his preparations for the invasion of Peru, so ill he had to be carried across the Andes in a litter.

* * *

After another failed attack on Callao, Cochrane was forbidden to try again. As he was yet to secure a significant victory, some of the Chileans were now openly campaigning for Cochrane's removal. Cochrane turned his attention to the south of Chile, where the Spanish were still holed up in Valdivia, known as Chile's Gibraltar. Now the main stopping-off point for Spanish vessels sailing between Iberia and Peru, it would be a potential staging point for any future reinvasion of Chile. The port of Valdivia was accessible only by a thousand-yard channel of sea, enclosed on both sides by rugged peninsulas dotted with forts. In the middle of the channel was a fortified island. Valdivia was considered impregnable and, as such, had evaded capture by the Patriots; in fact, no commander had been suicidal enough to try—so far.

Cochrane heard that three Spanish ships were due in port, but one had been delayed. A plan formed. Hoisting a Spanish flag, he dropped anchor outside the channel and requested a pilot. The captured crew of the pilot ship was forced to lead Cochrane into the channel where he noted the position of the six forts before sailing back out again, to the confusion of the Spaniards. Safely at sea, he captured a vessel, along with twenty thousand pesos aboard, as it approached the harbor. Then he sailed north to Concepcion to collect a complement of marines.

On his return, Cochrane anchored well out of sight of Valdivia, going over his plan with his officers late into the night. He still wasn't satisfied, but he finally went to bed content, leaving only a midshipman at the helm in the dead calm. He was awoken sometime later by a loud crunch and a violent jerk of his hammock.

Rushing above deck on the listing vessel, he called for the midshipman.

"Sorry, sir. We ... I ... a sudden wind sprang up."

The ship had run aground, and the tilting vessel gushed water into her hull. About him, the crew panicked. There were six hundred men aboard, but it was clear to everyone that the rowboats could only take a fraction of that.

"First things first—to the pumps!" Cochrane bellowed. "Every man who can bail to the hull." It took some time for Cochrane to restore order. In a few hours, the pumps were repaired and the rest of the crew was busy bailing out the hold with buckets. Eventually, the ship heaved off, but Cochrane knew they were so badly damaged that the only port the ship could hope to reach was the one they were trying to capture. He realized his plan to attack now was madness, but he calculated that when the assault began, the Spanish would barely believe it themselves. That alone might just give him enough time.

"Hoist the Spanish colors," he instructed, knowing that enemy guns were trained on the channel. He then beached his vessel on the northern tip of the western peninsula, right below one of the forts.

"Remember, tell them we were escorts for a convoy and became detached from the main fleet," Cochrane told the Spanish-born officer who had been set the task of taking the story ashore.

The Spaniards were not convinced; the alarm sounded.

"Ashore!" Cochrane ordered. His men swarmed from the vessel to take control of the beach. By nightfall, the first fort was theirs. After a vicious bayonet charge, the Spaniards fell back to the second fort. Then the third. Finally, they fled for the protection of a well-defended castle further inland along the peninsula. Before daylight, their alcoholic commander had surrendered too, fearing his men's inexperience in hand-to-hand combat. Cochrane now commanded the western side of the channel leading into Valdivia.

At daybreak, Cochrane ordered two of his smaller ships into the channel to ferry his marines across to the other side. Just as the fighting on the eastern side commenced, he sent his crippled flagship into the channel. It was empty, save for a handful of men; however, as Cochrane had hoped, the Spanish assumed it carried the rest of the Patriot army, for which the marines were but an advance party. The terrified Spaniards surrendered, and Valdivia—the Gibraltar of Chile—was in the hands of the Patriots at last. Cochrane returned to Valparaíso in triumph.

He was hailed a hero, but immediately got into a dispute about prize money. Threatening to resign, along with twenty-three of his officers, Cochrane was calmed by San Martín and O'Higgins, who begged him to remain. Knowing his position was now secure, Cochrane sent a trusted officer around Cape Horn to St. Helena to make contact with Napoleon. By the time the officer arrived, Napoleon's health had deteriorated and it was clear that death was nigh. Cochrane's craziest scheme of all was finished.

53: The Traitor San Martín

After Maipú, Diego got the promotion he had always avoided. He couldn't refuse, but days like today were why he wanted to. It was bad enough to be garrisoned in a nothing town like Rancagua, away from the city lights of Santiago, but now he was expected to fill out reports and discipline his friends. *Jorge would have loved this*, he thought, *an important meeting, all leave cancelled, the* comandante *coming*.

Naturally, thoughts of his brother led to the subject of Catalina. Diego had heard she was in Santiago and although he didn't know where exactly, that wasn't important. He would find her, just not today. Instead of being on leave, he was here—with all the other officers—waiting for some announcement. He glanced around the room, immediately noticing something strange. It was only *argentinos*. Before Diego had time to ask anyone about that, General Las Heras entered the hall. Everyone stood.

"General San Martín has asked me to read out a document. I need you all to listen carefully. When I am finished, there will be a vote."

Murmurs filled the hall. The men had never been asked their opinion on anything before, but now they could vote?

"I know, I know. It's a novelty for me, too, but I suppose we should all get used to it, it's what we are fighting for after all."

Everyone had heard the news from home, but it was still a shock to hear the government had fallen. Apparently, no faction was in control. There was no functioning central authority, nor was there likely to be soon. The Army of the Andes was in limbo. General Las Heras looked up from the document. "Men, I know this is strange, but I need you all to focus. As I said, when I am finished reading, there will be a vote. Everyone is free to decide whatever way they wish, but the majority decision will be binding—on all."

San Martín had declared that, as the government that appointed him no longer existed and none other had taken its place, he was calling on the officer corps to elect their own commander.

The men stood and spoke as one. "San Martín!" No vote was necessary.

* * *

San Martín kept his distance from the meeting, a little anxious when he saw O'Brien's horse. He took the reins as his aide dismounted, smiling. "Good news?"

O'Brien grinned. "You expected otherwise?"

"All I saw was the grim face of an Irishman, what was I to expect?"

"I wasn't worried, sir. I had a solid back-up plan."

"Which was?"

"Shoot the dissenting officers and have a recount."

San Martín chuckled. "Remind me to pack you off to Ireland before you become too much of a threat."

"As you mention it, sir, I've been meaning to talk to you about that."

"Don't say it!"

O'Brien explained that was returning to Ireland to take care of family affairs, but hoped to return before the war had run its course.

"First Padre Beltrán, and now you, O'Brien." San Martín shook his head. "I will have no friends in Peru."

* * *

When a new government eventually took control in Buenos Aires, San Martín was ordered to return with the army. He did not, instead deciding that his authority derived from the men, and not from the government. It was a mutinous act, but one that may have saved the country. The government in Buenos Aires saw things differently. San Martín was declared a traitor and accused of stealing an army, ignoring the troubles in his homeland, and only being interested in the Peruvian expedition to seek power for himself. San Martín sent a blistering self-justification to the people of Argentina in July 1820:

If, obeying the experience of ten years of conflicts, you do not give your wishes a more prudent direction, I fear that, tired of anarchy, you may welcome the yoke of the first fortunate adventurer who shows up, who, far from consolidating your destiny, will only prolong your servitude. Fellow countrymen: I leave you with a deep regret that I experience at the prospect of your misfortunes; you have accused me of not having contributed to increase them, for such would have been the result if I had taken an active part in the civil wars. In such a case it would have been necessary to renounce the undertaking of liberating Peru, and supposing that fate had favored my arms in the civil war, I would have had to deplore the victory along with the beaten themselves. No, General San Martín will never shed the blood of his compatriots, and he will unsheathe his sword only against the enemies of the independence of América.

54: The Expedition to Peru

When Kitty saw the crowds at the waterfront, she was glad she had left the children at home this time. It seemed the whole population of Valparaíso had come to witness the expedition's departure.

The fleet consisted of eight warships, eleven gunboats, and sixteen troop transports. Most of the heavy work had been completed the night before: loading twenty-five cannons, fifteen thousand muskets, two thousand swords and eight hundred horses, along with enough biscuits, beans, flour and salted beef to feed five thousand for six months. Afterwards, the men had been granted one last night of freedom on dry land. Consequently, this morning there were plenty of sailors with sore heads being rowed out to the large ships that dotted the bay.

Aboard the flagship *O'Higgins*, Cochrane led his navy out of the bay. San Martín, in his eponymous vessel, brought up the rear. The distance between their ships reflected the lack of warmth in their relations, which had only worsened over the last few months. Cochrane had been maneuvering to gain overall control of the mission, appealing over San Martín's head to O'Higgins and members of the Chilean Congress. When that failed, he tried to get alternative officers appointed, those who would be more amenable to his views. Cochrane was thrilled to be leading out a force of thirty-five boats filled with troops, but bitter that he had to cede overall command to San Martín. The man was far too cautious, and his plan of attack for Peru merely proved this.

Instead of a direct assault on Callao and Lima—which Cochrane favored—San Martín preferred a slow policy of strangulation, bringing Lima to its knees with minimum military engagement. They were to land at Pisco, one hundred and fifty miles south of the capital, to free and enlist the black slaves. The Andes shadowed the full length of the coast, rising dramatically above the farms that fed the country. San Martín claimed there were fifty thousand slaves working this narrow strip of coastal Peru, which at some points was only ten miles wide. From Pisco, San Martín intended to launch an expeditionary force into the mountainous interior. He estimated that half of Peru's population were Indians, with a further fifth being *mestizos*, and he reckoned that many of the former and some of the latter would automatically flock to the Patriot pennant.

Cochrane wasn't so sure. His experience taught him that people back a victor more than an idea, but his pleas for a more direct approach were dismissed. *At least we won't be staying in Pisco for long*, he thought. They planned to sail on, past Callao, landing at Ancon, more than twenty miles north of Lima. Cochrane was then to blockade Callao, while the troops led by San Martín at Ancon and the expeditionary force heading into the interior from Pisco would encircle Lima. Then the waiting game would begin while the capital's supplies ran dry. It was a good plan, Cochrane had to admit, but it would take all bloody year. A bold attack on Callao could have the matter settled in a month.

* * *

At the rear of the fleet, San Martín was finalizing proofs of pamphlets intended for distribution in Pisco and beyond. He knew his Admiral was straining at the leash, but this was a different kind of war. Nowhere in América was Royalist sentiment stronger than Peru. It had been the heartland of the Incas, conquered by

Francisco Pizarro in the 16th century. Peru's mines funded the Spanish Empire for more than two hundred years, and Lima—founded by Pizarro—was where all the political power was concentrated. All of the other colonies were mere satellites; San Martín knew that taking Peru would end the war.

He was also keenly aware of the need to be seen as a liberator rather than a conqueror. Although he considered that a frontal assault led by Cochrane could well succeed—especially given the Scot's daring and inventiveness—such a victory would come at a price he couldn't afford: making him the hostile ruler of a divided city, his army penned in by superior forces and being eaten away by guerrilla attacks. *No*, he thought, *this campaign had to be different*. Before he entered Lima he had to win the hearts of the people, otherwise everything was in vain. He hadn't come to win a war, but to build a peace.

After two weeks of uneventful sailing past the deserted coast of northern Chile, they arrived. In time to come, Pisco would be famous for grape brandy served with egg yolk—that and a war over bird-shit—but, today, it was where the Peruvian war of liberation began in earnest. Landing at Pisco, the Patriots immediately scattered the Spanish garrison, but San Martín didn't re-board the rest of his troops for another six weeks, despite Cochrane's constant grumbling. There was reason to wait; he was determined to make contact with the secret societies that were scattered around Peru, formed at his behest to foment revolution. Enemy desertions would be key to prevailing against a force six times stronger than his own. In any event, the delay would only make the Spaniards edgy. He was hoping to draw divisions out of Lima before he set sail again.

To San Martín's annoyance, it seemed that the Viceroy had anticipated his plan. Most of the *hacendados* had moved their slaves inland, and he was only able to liberate six hundred, who enlisted readily. However, for San Martín, this only intensified the rationale behind his expedition to the interior. He had chosen the commander of the flying column carefully: General Arenales, a mean-looking bastard with three nasty scars down his face. In fact, his whole body was covered with them; he had been hacked to pieces and left for dead after an ambush in Upper Peru. How he survived, nobody knew. The men feared but respected him, for he never spared himself difficult tasks and always roughed it with the troops. Born in Madrid, his family had moved to Buenos Aires when he was a child. Some of the men called him *El Español* behind his back, but his Patriot credentials were above reproach. After taking part in the abortive Chuquisaca uprising in 1809, he was captured, spending three dark years in the grim jail of Callao before earning his freedom. His incarceration did nothing to dampen his revolutionary ardor, and he enlisted in General Belgrano's Army of the North immediately on release.

San Martín also knew that Arenales had fought this kind of campaign before. In 1813—after General Belgrano's forces had been crushed at Ayohuma and the Patriots pushed back to Argentina—Arenales had been given the dangerous task of keeping the Cochabamba insurrection alive. In enemy-controlled territory, he maintained his guerrilla action for eighteen months, costing Spain thirteen hundred men, disrupting their supply lines, and impeding their incursions into northern Argentina. This mission would be tougher, but Arenales was ready.

"I'm giving you some of my toughest men—from Cuyo and Tucuman, and the survivors of Rancagua—you can depend on them." San Martín met Arenales outside the barracks to explain what was required of him. "Your mission is simple: stay alive and meet me in Ancon."

General Arenales nodded.

"You must avoid all unnecessary engagement with the enemy. When I depart, they will assume you are garrisoning Pisco, possibly awaiting further troops. Leave as soon as is practicable, in small groups to avoid suspicion, under cover of night if possible. And hit the mountains. They won't be able to track you as easily up there."

"What about Ica?"

"You can send a detachment to take the town, but don't dwell there. Once in the mountains, you must make it clear that the men are to refrain from any pillaging or intimidation. If you need supplies, attempt to purchase them at a fair price. Only resort to rustling if absolutely necessary, and try to restrict it to the *hacendados*—they're likely to be Spanish. The force of opinion is even more important than the force of arms. If we win the minds of the people, we get their swords for free."

San Martín handed him a pamphlet. "This is important. I have boxes of these. Distribute them wherever you can. Also, while some of the towns may appear sympathetic to our cause, and may pledge loyalty, always assume you are being watched. Never drop your guard. You will be surrounded by the enemy at all times. I have heard some talk that this is a suicide mission, but if I had no confidence in you, I wouldn't be sending you. In fact, everything depends on the survival of you and your men. The fate of América is in your hands, and I know I can trust you with it."

General Arenales locked eyes with him. "I won't let you down, sir."

San Martín smiled. "Now, go with God, and I will see you in Ancon."

* * *

By the time they finally departed Pisco, Cochrane was sour. Six weeks they had wasted and by now the Spanish had full knowledge of the strength and extent of their forces. After the second week in Pisco, Cochrane had sought authorization to go ahead and launch an attack on Callao. They had a blazing row when San Martín refused.

"If we destroy the port and march in as conquerors, how do you expect the people to react?" said San Martín.

"Who cares!" Cochrane laughed. "You will have Lima. People respect the victory, not the philosophical argument."

"That's where we differ, Admiral. You can achieve your victory and sail away with the plaudits, but I am responsible for the aftermath. I need to build a lasting peace here."

"You can't do that unless you win the damn war, and I can't see your infernal printing press taking Callao!"

Cochrane's protestations had no effect, other than furthering their mutual animosity. But, for now, they needed each other. Instead of attacking Callao, they sailed for Ancon, twenty-two miles further north. San Martín wanted to secure the province of Trujillo and use it as the base for the second arm of the pincer around Lima.

For Cochrane, shipping out brought some relief; at least once the troops were landed he would have something of a free hand. When they neared Callao, Cochrane persuaded San Martín to indulge in a show of force. Having attacked the port twice previously, Cochrane knew the exact range of their shore batteries. To taunt the Spaniards, he strung the fleet out in a line, replete with Chilean and Argentine flags. All the ships had guns out and crew at quarters, and announcing cannonades dropped harmlessly into the ocean. The decks of the transports were packed with infantrymen, cavalrymen, and artillerymen, all wearing the uniform of their respective regiments. Only the volunteers wore the uniform of General Arenales' troops, both as a tribute to them and to confuse Spanish intelligence. There were many onlookers; the cliffs above Callao and the hills behind were filled with spectators. San Martín was delighted. He had been flooding the country with pamphlets and proclamations. As they passed, Cochrane made another reconnaissance of the port that had foiled him twice.

After landing the troops at Ancon, Cochrane made off to blockade Callao, as ordered, but his intentions were a little more ambitious. Now he could act without the frustrating control of San Martín.

55: The Esmeralda

It was approaching midnight when Cochrane looked through the telescope again.

"Did you spot it, sir?"

"I can't see a damn thing, but it's there, I swear it. Just keep rowing and keep your voices down." All Cochrane could see were the harbor lights twinkling in the distance. Now and then, he could make out a couple of ghostly shadow-ships parked in front of the boom; neutrals, he hoped. He looked once more. *It must be there*, he thought. He had seen it with his own eyes not two days beforehand. "Got it!" The rowboat wobbled as Cochrane jumped to his feet in excitement. "Ten degrees to port, boys. I'll keep it in my sights."

Two days before, Cochrane had been reconnoitering Callao from his flagship, the *O'Higgins*, when he noticed two things. First of all, two of the three largest Spanish ships were absent, leaving only the *Esmeralda*—a beautiful ship, sleek and quick and equipped with forty-two guns. The Spaniards weren't taking any chances: the *Esmeralda* was anchored behind a protective boom. The second thing Cochrane spotted was a gap in the boom.

Cochrane's plan was simple, if somewhat suicidal: hijack the *Esmeralda*. To do so, he would have to reach the ship without being detected, board, and then kill or capture the crew. And that would be the easy part. Next, he would have to maneuver the ship safely out of the harbor all the while under ferocious fire from twenty-seven other vessels and three hundred and fifty shore batteries. Even by his own standards, the plan was madness. The only thing in his favor was that it was so reckless and irrational that the Spanish would be caught completely by surprise, at least for a few minutes.

With surprise his only ally, the day before the mission, Cochrane lifted the blockade on Callao and sailed his fleet away. He returned to anchor out of sight of the port, his vessels hidden by the island of San Lorenzo. The Spaniards had been reluctant to attempt to break Cochrane's blockade. His captures along the Pacific Coast and his seizure of the port of Valdivia meant most vessels avoided engagement with the man they called *El Diablo*. The relieved Spaniards celebrated the departure of Cochrane's fleet, toasting their good fortune the following evening with a banquet aboard the *Esmeralda*.

Cochrane put out a call among the fleet for volunteers; his entire complement of seamen put themselves forward. Later that night, after giving explicit instructions to each officer, he led one hundred and sixty sailors and eighty marines in fourteen rowboats toward the gap in the boom. They wore the white jackets, frocks and shirts of Spanish sailors, with only blue bands on their arms to distinguish themselves. The Spanish would not give up their flagship without a fight, so Cochrane's men were armed to the teeth, carrying pistols, sabers, knives, pikes, and tomahawks.

"Now, my lads," encouraged Cochrane, "we shall give them a Gunpowder Plot they won't forget in a hurry." They passed the two neutral ships anchored outside the boom, the British frigate *Hyperion* and another from the United States, the *Macedonian*. When Cochrane's flotilla of rowboats passed the American ship, their sailors hung over the bulwarks, calling out messages of support. The next day, when the Americans rowed ashore for supplies, they would be hung for collaboration.

When they approached the gap in the boom, Cochrane ordered silence as they passed through. It was no use. They had been spotted. The guard boat pulled alongside and the men hid their weapons, bowing their heads while Cochrane stood to offer surrender. The Spaniards realized—too late—that the rowboat was filled with armed men. A stand-off ensued until two more rowboats pulled up on the other side, and their occupants disarmed the Spaniards. With the crewmen of the guard boat bound and gagged and their vessel cut adrift, Cochrane ordered his men to resume rowing, pointing his little boat directly at the flagship of the Spanish Navy. Just before they reached the *Esmeralda*, Cochrane split the rowboats into two detachments: Captain Guise going around port-side, Cochrane coming along starboard.

Grabbing one of the chains that dangled alongside the ship, he made to pull himself up, his blood pumping with anticipation of battle, and of victory. The chains rattled as he climbed, and as he reached the deck he was met with the butt of a musket, which a sentry, alerted by the noise, smashed into his face. Cochrane crashed back into the rowboat. Undaunted, despite the searing pain in his back, he yanked the chains and climbed again, this time shooting the sentry when he appeared over the side. Marines scurried past like rats as he scrambled onto the quarterdeck. His men were taking their positions in the rigging above, both to prepare the sails and to shoot any belligerents who came on deck. From the port-side, Captain Guise appeared. The pair shared a quick handshake before returning fire on two sentries.

With a groan of pain, Cochrane slumped to the deck, blood running from a shot in his thigh. Undeterred, and angry at the pain, he pulled himself up and limped to one of the guns to direct the attack. The fighting was vicious. Lacking the time or space to reload their muskets, both sides soon resorted to hand-to-hand combat, wrestling on a deck made slippery with blood.

After twenty minutes of desperate skirmishing, the boarders had triumphed; however, the noisy battle had aroused Callao's defenders. The alarm gun sounded from the port, alerting the nearby gunboats, one of which opened fire on the *Esmeralda* immediately, killing three of Cochrane's raiders. Captain Guise, in command now in place of the injured Cochrane, ordered the cables cut as their captured ship was subjected to a three-hundred-and-fifty-gun barrage from the shore. In the dark, the Spanish couldn't fix their target, but it was only a matter of time before one of their gunners was lucky and the resultant blaze would make them a sitting duck.

Pot-shots whizzed over the heads of sailors aboard the two foreign vessels outside the boom—HMS *Hyperion* and USS *Macedonian*—which raised the signaling lights of a neutral. Captain Guise, prepared for this eventuality by Cochrane, raised the same lights and steered the *Esmeralda* in their direction. Soon the Spanish guns fell silent, unsure of their true target. By two-thirty in the morning, the *Esmeralda* was anchored safely off the far side of the island of San Lorenzo, along with the rest of her new fleet. Cochrane's mastery of the Pacific was complete.

56: The Long March

General Arenales spent the morning inspecting the troops before they left Pisco, ensuring each man understood the dangers inherent in their mission. Diego stood in line with the rest of his squadron, together with two battalions of infantry backed by a pair of light guns. General Arenales was silent as he passed the line of troops, only stopping occasionally to ask a man his name and where he was from. Finally, he addressed them. "Men, I know how many of you were complaining about seasickness on the voyage from Valparaíso. Well, I have some good news: you won't be going back on a boat anytime soon. The bad news is that you are going there." He pointed at the imposing mountain range behind them.

Their groans were dismissed with a wave of his hand. "When we landed at Pisco, the *comandante* told you we had come to liberate a people, not to conquer them. I want you to remember those words. The Peruvians are our brothers. They are to be treated with respect. Any maltreatment of the locals, any stealing, anything of the sort, will be dealt with severely. I do not expect to have to say this again." Arenales paced for a moment, letting this sink in. "Our mission is to infiltrate the *sierra* and distribute propaganda leaflets."

More groans came from the men.

Arenales stopped and smiled. "If you don't like the sound of that, if it's not exciting enough, consider this: we have fewer than five thousand men in Peru; the Royalists have more than twenty-three thousand."

There was some muttering as Arenales pointed toward the mountains again. "Most of the Indians live in these highlands, and they are no friends of Spain. While the rest of the army sails to the north of Peru, we will be the only ones in the south. To survive, we are going to have to recruit. We will be setting up and arming militias, organizing and training them, assisting them in whatever way we can. If that sounds a little boring to some of you, remember we will be surrounded on all sides by enemy forces vastly superior in numbers to ourselves. For this reason, there will be strict rules on engaging the enemy. In short, avoid it wherever possible. We want to keep them guessing. I will say this once: do not engage the enemy without a direct order from your commanding officer, except in clear self-defense."

The men looked disappointed. "Don't worry," said Arenales. "There will be plenty of action. You may remember that when we got here the Spanish fled. They retreated to Ica, forty miles southwest of here. They have about eight hundred men in total. Tonight, we are going after them."

A roar rose from the men.

Arenales held up his hand. "Some advice: make sure you have a good pair of boots. We are going to be doing a lot of marching. If you don't have a good pair, go to the barracks and get some. I don't want to hear any complaints on the way. We leave at sundown."

But they didn't get their battle after all. The Spanish took flight at the sight of General Arenales' flying column. Two hundred and fifty Grenadiers gave chase, routing them. After leaving a small detachment behind to hold Ica, Arenales set off again, this time toward the mountains. But to get there, they first had to cross the desert.

On the second day of the march, Diego started dreaming of Catalina again. It was the same dream: her face, sometimes blurred and distant, sometimes close and filling his field of vision. The only difference was, this time he was awake. Every time he closed his eyes, her torturous apparition would appear, taunting him with an impotent past, teasing him with an impossible future. Whereas before he tried to banish her from his thoughts to preserve his sanity, now he kept his eyes closed, welcoming her intermittent intrusions. Eventually, his eyelids became so sunburned he was loath to open them again.

The only relief in starting the steep ascent into the mountains was the knowledge that fresh water was not far away. They heard it before they could see it—a crashing white torrent of foam that was difficult to drink from but glorious to try. The General allowed them some rest before they continued their climb. Since scattering the garrison at Ica, they hadn't encountered any enemy troops, but they all knew that would come. The upward trail followed the path of the river, which the General was hoping to cross. It seemed impossible to ford. The water was moving too fast, and after some of the men's canteens were whipped from their hands, no one was game to try.

As they climbed higher, the river fell away, hollowing out a gorge in the rock. They found a rope bridge spanning the chasm. It seemed solid enough and a volunteer crossed with little difficulty. The General ordered everyone across, but with the additional load, the bridge became unstable, swinging wildly with men still more than a hundred feet from the other side. Riders were forced to dismount and calm their horses, driving their mounts ahead of them. Despite a few scares, and some supplies lost to the water, everyone made it across.

The day after they completed their ascent, the topography changed completely. Gone were the sudden inclines, the dramatic ravines and breathtaking streams of water; in their place was a vast, dusty, windswept plain with little vegetation and noticeably thinner air. It filled the group with an inexplicable bleakness, which had not dissipated by the following day when they took the city of Huamanga unopposed. General Arenales ordered his men to rest. They had just completed a march of two hundred and fifty miles in ten days.

On the same day, in Lima, the Viceroy received intelligence regarding Arenales' movements. Huamanga remained free for a month before it was retaken by Spanish troops sent down from

Cuzco. The inexperienced militia of four thousand Indians, put in place by Arenales, proved no match for the well-drilled Spaniards. However, the campaign was bearing fruit: insurrections were breaking out all over the *sierra*. While the Spanish could put them down with ease, it hampered the movement of their troops—a sign they were losing their grip on the country.

At the beginning of December, two months into their march, General Arenales' men fought their first major battle, winning control of the mountain city of Pasco. They were aided by the defection of the six-hundred-and-fifty-strong Numancia battalion. These men, recruited by the Spanish army in Venezuela, had long been targets of San Martín's propaganda. As soon as the dead were buried and the injured were treated, the long march continued.

Like all prisoners of fate, the men of Arenales' detachment had a variety of fantasies concerning what they would do once control of their lives was returned to them. Aside from a desire for gluttony and sexual conquest, a few had the imagination to demand a swim in the ocean, the time and materials to write a letter to their mother, or the underrated pleasure of doing nothing whatsoever.

Diego was more particular. It wasn't that he didn't dream of women or fresh meat, or of seeing the coast or lolling about, but for him, they conflated into a singular, seamless fantasy: seeing the coast falling away as his clipper bested the ocean waves; tasting the finest beef in Buenos Aires, New York or Paris; taking pleasure in idleness on three different continents. His multifarious scenarios of a glorious vagabond lifestyle only fell apart when a woman entered the picture. Then, cruelly, the scales would fall from his eyes. For there was only one woman who could play the part. Only one woman could make his fantasy worthwhile: Catalina. To say his surroundings reminded him of Catalina would be a misrepresentation. Oxygen reminded him of Catalina. Sunlight reminded him of Catalina. Not thinking of Catalina reminded him of Catalina. He was caught in a trap. The only way out that he could see was to get himself as far away as possible, to a place where the trees didn't whisper her name.

Once he had decided to leave, life became simpler. It didn't matter that he had a whole new bunch of complications to consider—how he was going to desert, how to gain passage on a

A Storm Hits Valparaíso

ship when he had no money—he felt lighter. The rest he could figure out. At least now he knew where he was going: far away from here. Two things were easy to deduce. First, if he wanted to get to Europe, he needed a ship—which meant he had to get to Valparaíso or Buenos Aires. Second, he had to get to the coast, and the safest way of doing that was to stay with his unit, for now.

On January 8th 1821, Diego and the rest of the General Arenales' men broke through to Huacho to rejoin San Martín and the rest of the army. They had marched eight hundred and twenty miles through hostile territory.

57: The City of Pizarro

In the chaos following Napoleon's seizure of Madrid ten years beforehand, Argentina and Chile were forced to fend for themselves, giving birth to a self-reliance that readily translated into revolutionary nationalism. Peru had undergone no such transformation. Things were as they had been since the conquistadors had brutally seized the country from the Incas. Peru was a feudal society, even at the time of San Martín's arrival in late 1820. Indians slaved in the mines, and blacks were forced to work the low-lying farms that fed the country. The Spaniards held all the power and the *mestizos* were the working class in the towns and cities, doing all the menial jobs that the Indians and blacks couldn't be trusted with.

There was another significant difference between Peru and the other countries San Martín had sought to liberate: the Creoles were against him. These educated Américan-born whites had a lot to gain from independence—the highest positions of authority would now be open to them, and they would benefit handsomely from the liberalization of trade. Only one thing kept them on the side of Spain: fear. Madrid knew that the best way to control Peru was by pitting sections of society against each other. Out of one million souls, whites numbered a tenth. Since Haiti's bloody slave revolt in 1804, they had even more reason to be afraid. For them, a free Peru meant death.

San Martín knew that to liberate the country, he needed the Creoles on his side. He had to show them he could act as a responsible buffer between them and the masses. San Martín was aware that the liberal ideals of the French and American revolutions had not taken root in Peru; this was the reasoning behind his strict orders to his troops and the propaganda with which he was flooding the country. And it was beginning to work.

Lima had been blockaded by land and sea since San Martín moved his troops to Huacho and Cochrane had captured the *Esmeralda*. All San Martín had to do was wait. Indeed, it was all he could do; his men were stricken by tropical diseases in the stifling heat of the lowlands. Each day, fifty men died, leaving him without enough fit troops to relieve his forward positions. But his strategy was beginning to bear fruit. Royalist soldiers deserted and entire provinces declared for the Patriots. Ica in the south, and then the large northern province of Trujillo in the north, proclaimed independence, soon followed by the desert city of Piura. By May 1821, the whole of northern Peru had sided with San Martín and he began to receive men and money from the Creole elite.

* * *

Meanwhile, Lima starved and San Martín waited, deaf to Cochrane's exhortations to strike, which only intensified the ill-will between the two commanders. Relations had soured after the capture of the *Esmeralda*. Cochrane wanted to rename the ship *Valdivia*, in honor of his victory, but his crew protested—the name being synonymous with the despised Pedro de Valdivia, the original conquistador of Chile. Cochrane refused to back down, threatening the protestors with court martial. This wholly avoidable episode ended with the resignation of two of Cochrane's captains, Guise and Spry, who then joined San Martín's staff onshore.

It was a difficult time for Cochrane. The Peruvian expedition was the first time he had spent a prolonged period away from his wife and children since prison. Kitty had been enjoying herself in

Santiago, attending balls and exploring the countryside, on one occasion even braving the bandits of the snow-covered passes to travel to Mendoza. Despite all of her adventures, by the end of 1820, the long separation from her husband had become too much. Urged on by the despondency in his letters, Kitty and her two young boys embarked on the HMS *Andromache* for Peru.

Kitty arrived off Callao just before New Year's Eve and was reunited with her husband two weeks later, when he rejoined the blockade of the port. However, within a few months she boarded the HMS *Andromache* again and returned to England. Officially, she was going home to begin the process of clearing her husband's name, but privately she was terribly homesick, never taking to Peru as she had to Chile. Just after her departure, Cochrane received news that Napoleon had died on his island prison of St. Helena.

* * *

By the beginning of July 1821, the Viceroy was in a bind. Desertions had multiplied, uprisings had weakened the strength and confidence of his highland troops, and the city of Lima was surrounded by enemy forces on land and sea. The population, short of food, began taking their frustrations out on the soldiery, who couldn't walk the streets of the capital alone for fear of attack. Protests against the Viceroy's administration were growing in number, frequency, and vociferousness. The well-connected citizens, on whose support he could usually rely, had begun suggesting that some deal be struck with the insurgents.

He felt he had no choice but to abandon the city and reinforce his more defendable positions. The Viceroy decided to keep some of his men holed up in the fortress in Callao, and hope that attending to the capital checked the Patriots' advances into the interior. San Martín's patience finally paid off. On July 6th, the Viceroy announced that his army was abandoning Lima for the sanctity of the mountains. Fearing a slave uprising, the city council petitioned San Martín to enter the city and restore order. On the anniversary of Argentine independence, July 9th, San Martín finally entered the capital of América. Nineteen days later, a large crowd gathered in the Plaza Mayor for the proclamation of independence.

This should have been San Martín's crowning moment. He had just mastered a brilliant, patient victory against the Spanish, taking the center of their power without the loss of a single life. He had temporarily assumed the title of Protector of Peru, giving him supreme power in the country and free rein to direct the war effort as he chose. Having liberated three countries from colonial rule, he was in his prime, and at what seemed to be the peak of his career. But San Martín was about to lose everything.

58: The Protector of Peru

While San Martín entered Lima in triumph, Cochrane, in another daring raid, broke through the boom at Callao, cutting out a further three ships from the Spanish fleet. Cochrane entered the capital to a hero's welcome. Just over two weeks later, he paid a visit to the Government Palace on the Plaza Mayor, in which the Protector of Peru was now ensconced. San Martín had promised Cochrane's navy their pay plus a large bonus once they entered Lima; Cochrane had come to collect, but San Martín was evasive. "I'm sure you are aware, Admiral, that there was not a single peso left in the treasury when we took control."

"My men have been promised their pay. I intend to get it."

"From where, Admiral? The coffers are empty. Merchants are fleeing Peru. I'm instituting a new system of taxes, but it will take time. We have some control over the mines, but security is an issue, as is keeping supply lines open. We will be able to regularize this, but it will take time. Your request is not unwarranted, but it could have been made at a more judicious moment."

"You have had plenty of time, General."

"Besides, the debt is due from Chile, whose government engaged the seamen."

"What!"

"Calm yourself, Admiral. There is a solution to hand."

Cochrane glared at San Martín, waiting for him to continue.

"I can write to the Supreme Director of Chile, asking him to provide the necessary funds."

"Pah!"

"Or..."

"Or what?"

"We can settle this dispute in a more reasonable manner, which will benefit all concerned."

"Go on," said Cochrane, suspicious.

"Peru is offering to purchase your squadron and incorporate it into the new Peruvian Navy in exchange for all arrears in pay and prizes owed."

Cochrane was stunned.

"And you, of course, would be promoted to 1st Admiral of the Fleet."

"And what of your duty to Chile?"

"I am Protector of Peru."

Cochrane bristled. "Then it becomes me, as senior officer of Chile, and consequently the representative of the nation, to request fulfillment of all the promises made to Chile and the squadron."

"Chile!" San Martín lost his temper. "I will never pay a single *real* to Chile, and as to the squadron, you may take it where you please, and go where you choose. A couple of schooners are quite enough for me." San Martín began pacing the room. He stopped in front of Cochrane, calmed, and caught Cochrane's hand. "Forget, my Lord, what is past."

"I will when I can," said Cochrane. He shook his hand free and stormed out of the palace. It was the last time they would speak.

* * *

A few weeks later, San Martín was in the theater when he heard the Spanish were marching on the capital. There was immediate panic. He stood, calming the crowd, assuring them that preparations had been taken for just such an event and that he was confident of victory. San Martín ordered the deployment of the citizen militia and the raising of barricades, and joined his force of seven thousand just outside the capital. There were still two thousand Spanish troops in control of the fortress of Callao, but they were running out of food. The Viceroy had twelve thousand troops descending from the *sierra* with the intention of relieving Callao.

San Martín rejected his commanders' advice to attack, instead drawing his troops back into defensive positions in the suburbs of Lima. He watched as the Viceroy's men crossed the dustbowl that separated the mountains from the city. Estimating that the Spaniards had only fifteen days' food, he decided to wait it out, confident the Viceroy wouldn't risk the bulk of his army in a street battle with the dug-in Patriots. His suspicions were confirmed when the Spanish stopped short of the suburbs, attempting to taunt him out instead. San Martín's fellow commanders again urged attack, but the Patriots were vastly outnumbered and again he decided to wait for the Spaniards to exhaust their food supplies. After a few days, the Viceroy, cognizant of his supply problems, withdrew. As soon as the Spanish began their retreat, San Martín ordered General Las Heras to pursue them; however, he soon faced the same food shortages, and the Spanish and the Viceroy escaped.

The Spaniards were still barricaded in the fortress of Callao, where the men had resorted to eating their horses, and the Viceroy's retreat demoralized them completely. On September 19th, the defenders of Callao surrendered. Six hundred prisoners were slaughtered that day when the Patriot forces lost control; it took the commanders some time to restore order.

* * *

The butchery at Callao was the last straw for Diego, reminding him too much of his brother's death. Initially, he had been sidetracked by the pleasures of Lima and the promise of a quick end to the war. Now, it was becoming clear to everyone that they had a long, drawn-out fight on their hands. Like the other men, he had received some of his pay when they took the capital; but unlike the others, he had avoided the gambling houses and brothels. He heard

A Storm Hits Valparaíso

that some Chilean sailors were selling passports to Spanish civilians who wished to return to Europe. The sum was beyond his reach, but he found he could get smuggled onboard for far less. When Diego received an urgent message from the sailor arranging his passage, which alerted him that he had to go that night, he was still short the fare. It was his last change to get onboard.

Not two hours before he was supposed to meet the *chileno*, Diego raced to the cockfighting coliseum on the outskirts of the city. He took a seat on the wooden bench two rows back from the ring. The referee announced there would be three more fights, and two birds were brought forward. Handlers restrained the two gamecocks inside the circle as runners took bets. Diego placed his wager: one hundred pesos, all the money he had. The first fight turned out to be a mismatch. The victorious rooster, when held aloft, was barely bloodied. Diego collected his winnings: two hundred pesos. One more victory and he had his fare. The second fight began ten minutes later, and the arena was becoming overcrowded. The handlers held up their roosters, the sharp metal spurs gleaming in the lamplight. A frenzied round of betting began; Diego laid his winnings down.

All noise in the room ceased as the crowd leaned forward to see the first blow. Once released, the gamecocks flew at each other instantly—flapping, pecking, thrusting, and kicking. Diego strained his neck to see, but it was just a blur of feathers. A roar rose from the other side of the ring; one of the birds had landed a mortal blow, but Diego couldn't make out which one. The losing handler retrieved his dead rooster, presenting it to the winner. Diego had lost. He did not stay for the last fight, setting out instead on the long walk into town.

"I cannot pay the fare," Diego explained to the *chileno*, desperate to be taken on board anyway.

"It's of no consequence," the sailor told him. "I can't arrange passage to Valparaíso. The Protector of Peru has ordered Admiral Cochrane to return to Chile—some dispute over pay."

Cochrane, in retribution, had seized San Martín's treasure ship, distributing the proceeds among his men. He had then announced that he was going north to the Mexican coast in pursuit of the two remaining Spanish frigates. He left it up to his men to choose whether to join him or not. Many decided to stay and fight in Peru; after all there was an opening for crew. Diego hurried down to the port with the *chileno*.

* * *

San Martín, now in complete control of Lima and its environs and with no enemy on his doorstep, set about righting the city. He freed the slaves, decreed equal rights for Indians, created the Peruvian Army, and overhauled the tax system. He had now secured Argentine independence, won the freedom of Chile, and taken the capital of Spanish America itself, the City of Kings, Lima.

It should have been the happiest time in his life, but he was still saddled with a laudanum addiction, and he missed his wife terribly. His early successes turned to frustration as the white, Spanish-born nobility of Lima began to mobilize and agitate against him. He found he was the ruler of a divided city after all. Most of his troops were required to keep order. He could only send limited men on forays into the surrounding countryside. The *sierra*, Upper Peru, and Cuzco remained out of reach due to troop shortages. San Martín only had one card left to play.

Simón Bolívar had heroically turned the tide of the revolution in the northern part of América, freeing Colombia and Venezuela. Now, Bolívar was locked in a desperate battle for control of Quito. The port of Guayaquil, just over the border from Peru, had already declared for the Patriots, placing itself under the protection of San Martín and Bolívar. Sensing the importance of momentum—even though much of his army was tied up keeping the peace in Colombia and finishing the Spaniards off in Venezuela—Bolívar decided to press on to Quito.

The two Liberators had been corresponding since Maipú, and Bolívar, knowing San Martín had a large army in northern Peru, requested his assistance in the battle for Quito. At the start of 1822, San Martín agreed to this request. He was swayed by Bolívar's promise that once Quito was brought under his control, he would return the favor and dispatch four thousand troops to San Martín, enabling him to finally bring this conflict to an end. They agreed to meet in July, in Guayaquil, to discuss the conclusion of the war.

59: The Guayaquil Conference

San Martín had been preoccupied for the entire voyage. Since they cast anchor at Callao, he had been making plans, devising stratagems, and debating ideas with his officers, but it all came back to one thing—men. He didn't have enough to end the war, not before his fragile political alliances fell apart. Since that scurrilous Scot stole his navy, no supplies or reinforcements had been forthcoming from Buenos Aires or Santiago. San Martín had been left to fend for himself. His only hope was the Liberator of the North, Simón Bolívar. He prayed Bolivar would come good with his promises of troops—and soon.

On July 26th, San Martín reached the port of Guayaquil. When the ship docked, Bolívar came aboard and embraced San Martín, the two Liberators of América meeting for the first time. After the formal introductions, Bolívar explained where San Martín would be lodging and where the meeting would take place. "I'll have my aide bring you up. His name's O'Leary," said Bolívar.

"Irishman?" said San Martín.

"Yes, why?"

"Curious. My last Aide-de-Camp—who has returned home, sadly—was Irish too. O'Brien."

"Interesting."

"Fearless bunch, these Irish. I pity the English when these lads seek their own independence."

Bolívar laughed. "True, true. O'Leary is from Cork. He says they are so bloody-minded there they will probably want their own Republic!"

* * *

In a private office on the first floor of the City Hall, San Martín and Bolívar, alone so that they could speak frankly, had been talking for more than an hour. In short order, the conversation became heated.

San Martín's eyes narrowed. "Being at war is no justification for suspending moral precepts."

Across the rosewood table, Bolívar raised an eyebrow. "Easy to say, General, but every military commander has to order their men to their death at some point." Bolívar paused. "Including you."

San Martín shifted in his seat. "I don't order anyone to their death; I take great care with the lives under my command."

"What about Maipú?" said Bolívar.

San Martín frowned. "What about it?"

"It was a great victory." Bolívar held up his hands. "Possibly the greatest in all the battles of this war of liberation—along with my victory at Carabobo of course."

San Martín nodded.

"It was the perfect example of a parallel attack that becomes an oblique attack. But to achieve this, you had to put your weakest troops, your reserves, against the Royalists' finest, knowing full well they would suffer heavy losses."

San Martín was silent as Bolívar continued. "Indeed, you needed them to suffer heavy losses and fall back so that the Royalist line would be stretched and you could attack their flank."

"Every strategy will incur some losses," said San Martín, ensuring his voice remained calm, "but our job is to mitigate them."

Bolívar pursed his lips. "Of course, but you knew those particular men would die in disproportionate numbers to achieve your goal of victory. It was necessary. A means to an end."

"That analysis is somewhat unfair."

"Being a commander involves making these decisions, choosing one man to die so two can live. It's not the normal rules of morality, because war is different."

San Martín had enough. "It doesn't justify the excesses, General."

"What excesses?" said Bolívar.

"Your campaign, Liberty or Death; the butchering of prisoners in Caracas and La Guaira."

"Your hands aren't clean, José. What about the slaughter after Maipú?"

"That was not something I ordered or condoned."

"But ultimately, you, as commander, are responsible."

San Martín bowed his head. "Yes. Yes, I am."

"I accept I made some bad decisions, but war forces a leader to, especially war conducted by the Spanish. I'm not proud of everything I've done, but in my position, I suspect you would have done the same."

"I doubt that, General," said San Martín.

"You didn't face the set of circumstances I did. How many swamps and jungles did you have to hack your way through? Oh, how I wished I was fighting on the rolling plains of Argentina. You had the Generals, and the politicians, and the people on your side. I faced treachery and deceit and betrayal and dissent at every turn. I had to fight my own people as much as the Spanish, and you judge me!" Bolívar thumped the table.

San Martín paused before responding, his tone gruff. "My homeland is torn apart by civil war. I am denounced as a rebel and a traitor in my own country. My own country! My Admiral, Cochrane, made off with my navy and my treasury. The Chileans are plotting against me, and the Peruvians? They are Royalists or Patriots depending which way the wind is blowing. My alliances are crumbling, my men are deserting, and my funding has disappeared. Don't talk to me about circumstances."

"And now we are here," said Bolívar.

"Now we are here."

"I have finally crushed the dissent and have united Gran Colombia behind me. Quito and Guayaquil will be part of that federation."

"That's not what was agreed."

"It's what the people have decided, and who are we to stand in the way of the people?"

"I'm sure the decision would have been different if it had been my army at the gates, and not yours."

"But it wasn't your army at the gates. It was mine." Bolívar thumped the table again emphatically.

San Martín said nothing for a moment. "General, this is getting a little heated." He decided to change his approach. "If I have said anything out of turn, I wish you to disregard it. We are both on the same side, brothers in the struggle for the emancipation of América. You have done a remarkable job, and I want you to know that you have my utmost respect."

"Thank you," said Bolívar, taken aback by the change in tone. "And, of course, you have mine."

"The Spanish are almost vanquished. I am sure that once the Highlands of Peru are subdued, Upper Peru will fall readily to us. Then we will have complete control, and I doubt that the Spanish will ever return.

"How are things progressing in Peru?"

"Slowly, but only for lack of men. That's why I'm here."

Bolívar raised an eyebrow.

"We have complete control of Lima and mastery of the Pacific," said San Martín, "and the Spanish only hold the Highlands, Cuzco and Upper Peru. However, as it stands, my forces are insufficient to complete operations."

"Yes, that's what my information is also."

"But with four thousand of your men, I could finish this war in three months."

Bolívar paused, meeting San Martín's gaze for only a moment before turning away and rising from the table. He walked to the window and stood with his hands clasped behind his back. "I'm afraid that's impossible."

San Martín waited for him to continue.

"I could only spare, perhaps, one thousand men, maybe a little more."

"But General, that is barely enough to garrison Callao and keep the peace in Lima," said San Martín.

"It is all I can offer you."

"That would be entirely insufficient. The Royalists have twenty-three thousand veterans between here and Upper Peru. I have barely eight thousand under my command, almost half of which are struck down with dysentery and the plague. With more men, I could have this war finished in three months."

"But it's all I can give."

"You have the bulk of your army between here and Quito."

"I cannot give you more without taking command of the men myself; there are rules."

"General, please. If you wish the glory of the final battle for yourself, I would willingly serve under your command."

"I'm afraid that would be impossible also. To leave the soil of Gran Colombia, I need authorization from Congress."

"You didn't need authorization when you raced down to annex Guayaquil."

"That was historically part of our territory."

"Well, couldn't you get it? I'm sure there is little Congress would deny you."

"I could, but it would take time. And I don't think it would change anything."

"Why not?"

"I couldn't bring myself to give orders to you, General. It would be beneath your dignity as a hero of the liberation struggle to act as a subordinate. I can't do it, and I won't."

San Martín gasped. "General, let not my dignity concern you. I would be honored to take orders from you."

Bolívar turned away from the window. Still avoiding eye contact with San Martín, he paced the room, his hands clasped behind his back. "We have covered much ground today, General. I think this would be an opportune moment to break for the day and reconvene tomorrow."

"As you wish, General." San Martín nodded.

313

"Before you leave, I received some disturbing news this morning and have been waiting for the conclusion of proceedings to relay it to you, which I am sure you will understand."

"Go on," said San Martín, concerned.

"It seems your new Peruvian deputy has turned against you." Bolívar stopped pacing and faced San Martín. "Yes, I'm afraid things are even more fragile for you in Lima than you realize."

"How did you hear this?"

"I have friends in the Patriot forces there. They have informed me that he is talking to the Spanish behind your back. A conspiracy to oust you as Protector is underway."

"If this is true, then the logic behind ending this war is only strengthened, but I need your assistance."

"That is apparent," said Bolívar, "but your proposals are unworkable. Let us reconvene tomorrow to see if we can find a more practical solution."

San Martín stood and Bolívar came around the table to embrace him awkwardly, before walking to the door and holding it open. With a nod at Bolívar, San Martín walked out.

That night, two things became apparent to San Martín. First, Bolívar would not commit the requisite level of troops unless he assumed command. Second, he would not tolerate any rivals. It became clear to San Martín that there was only one obstacle to Bolívar's troops coming to Peru: José de San Martín.

This realization came as something of a blow. Standing, he opened a window to let in some fresh air. Was he really considering this? Resigning? Handing everything over to Bolívar? Whether Bolívar's story about the plot against him was true or not, the situation in Peru was fragile. Some of his men he could count on for anything; their loyalty was unquestionable and they had been with him since his first battles. However, a lot of the Chileans had not endured the harsh crossing of the Andes that had forged the men, or the Battle of Chacabuco that had made them his. They were loyal Patriots, but they had no special connection to him as commander. San Martín was astute enough to see how a charismatic leader like Bolívar could appeal to them over his head, as well as sway the new Peruvian recruits. He saw only one conclusion—to do otherwise would prolong the war and possibly even lead to an unthinkable conflict with Bolívar's troops. There was no other way—he had to fall on his sword.

The following day, at their second meeting, San Martín informed Bolívar of his decision. "On my return to Lima, I shall convene Congress and resign as Protector of Peru. They will appoint their own leader."

"Your services will never be forgotten." Bolívar shook his hand.

"The future is more important," said San Martín. "Now a new field of glory awaits you, in which you will place the final seal on the freedom of América."

Unable to leave until later that evening when the tide was favorable, San Martín had to endure an official banquet. After he and Bolívar had taken their places at the top table, Bolívar stood and brought the rowdy room to order. He raised his glass. "To the two greatest men in América—San Martín and myself."

There was a loud cheer. Bolívar sat and indicated to San Martín.

"To the early end of the war, the organization of the various republics of the continent, and to the health of the Liberator of Colombia," San Martín said.

The dancing started soon afterwards, handing San Martín an opportunity to leave. He signaled to a servant who led him out a back door. As he walked from the building, he heard a voice behind him.

"General, are you leaving so soon?"

It was Bolívar.

"I hope you don't think it an affront to your hospitality, but I must retire. My ship must catch the tide. I wished to bid you good evening, but saw you were occupied with the waltz. I was loath to disturb you."

"Well, before you ... retire, I have a present for you." Bolívar clapped his hands and a servant appeared, carrying a painting. "A memento of my sincere friendship." He turned and walked away.

San Martín looked at the painting. It was a portrait—a portrait of Simon Bolívar.

60: Return to Valparaíso

On September 20th 1822, San Martín convoked the first Congress of independent Peru and formally resigned as Protector. He sailed for Chile the next morning. After crossing the Andes for the final time, he looked down on Mendoza, feeling no regret about the path he had chosen. On his arrival, he received word that his wife was still in Buenos Aires and was gravely ill with consumption. San Martín was considered a criminal in Argentina, with Buenos Aires still aggrieved by his refusal to return with his army after the Battle of Maipú. By the time he received permission to travel, it was too late.

María, his Remeditos, was dead.

* * *

Diego made it as far as Acapulco before Cochrane and his men gave up the chase for the two Spanish frigates. Cochrane discovered they had taken refuge in the port of Guayaquil and surrendered to representatives of San Martín. Avoiding Callao for fear of arrest, Cochrane decided to return to Valparaíso, where

A Storm Hits Valparaíso

Diego planned to secure passage to Buenos Aires or Europe. Cochrane agreed to let him work on the boat until he found a berth.

On his return, Diego began asking around the port, looking for work.

"There's a small bar off the main square. Messages are often posted there when ships are seeking deckhands," one captain advised.

Diego found it with ease—a small place on the seafront, set back slightly from the street. Ordering a drink, he asked if any captains had been in posting notices. The barman said he would check with the owner and disappeared into the storeroom.

"One moment," said a woman's voice.

"Take a seat." The barman nodded toward the tables behind Diego.

Sipping his *aguardiente*, he examined his fellow patrons. Few seemed interested in idle conversation, their only movements being to signal for more drinks or to wave away the ever-thickening clouds of tobacco smoke.

"You're looking for deckhand work?"

Diego knew that voice. He turned. "Catalina!"

Before he could say anything else, she excused herself and returned to the storeroom. She returned minutes later with a bottle of *aguardiente*, her eyes puffy and red.

"Another?"

"Please."

She sat. "What are you doing here?"

"Looking for a ship." Diego stared at her, trying to make eye contact, but Catalina just stared at the back of her hands. "He's dead, you know," he finally said.

"I know." Catalina called the barman, who passed her a glass. Her hand shook slightly as she poured. "How did he die? They couldn't tell me. They wouldn't tell me."

Diego paused. "In my arms."

* * *

He returned the next day to meet the captain of a ship. It was sailing only as far as Rio de Janeiro, but from there, Diego should be able to organize another. Catalina avoided his table—and his eyes. When the captain left, Diego waited, patiently watching the bar.

Eventually, she came and sat down beside him. "You're leaving?"

Diego nodded.

"When?"

"Day after tomorrow."

Finally, Catalina's dark eyes met his. "Come with me," he urged, taking her hand.

She shook her head.

"Why not?"

"I can't. This bar ... it was my father's." She freed her hand from his. "I rebuilt the whole thing. It cost me ... it cost me a lot. I couldn't leave it now."

"Sell it then."

"No, Diego. I can't. I don't want to. I'm sorry."

Diego came the following day and tried again. This time, Catalina was even more adamant.

"Just pack some things and meet me at the church tomorrow at one o'clock," he pleaded.

"I told you already, I'm not going. I don't want to go with you. I'm sorry."

"Meet me anyway. To say goodbye."

Catalina paused. "Very well."

The next day, Catalina left the bar just before one o'clock. As she stopped to gaze out at the bay, she realized she had been so busy she hadn't been outside for days now. That's when she saw it: the *Esmeralda*. It was the same ship that had carried the sailors to Valparaíso on that stormy night, the sailors who had murdered her father. She froze, feeling suddenly light-headed. What was that ship doing here? It didn't make sense. Her thoughts were cut short by a chunk of masonry hitting the ground behind her, as the ground began to heave and shake and cracks split the road ahead.

* * *

Following the first aftershock, the captains of ships at anchor in the bay began ferrying people aboard. Despite the tidal waves that followed, the people of Valparaíso felt that dry land was more dangerous. Cochrane, aboard his flagship, watched with frustration the demolition of his newly built house. In that moment, he decided to leave Chile and forgo all claims of outstanding prize money. He was finished here; his last tie to the country had collapsed into rubble. Before he left, he provided one more service to the Chilean nation: having victims rowed to his ship for medical treatment.

Despite arranging to meet Catalina at the church to say goodbye, Diego realized his heart could not bear the burden of her rejection. Instead, he boarded his vessel with no one to wave him off. From the bay, his eyes searched the city for the place where the church used to be, seeing only rubble and dust. Commandeering a rowboat, he headed for the beach as quickly as he could in a sea still choppy from the tremors. Injured and bloody refugees lined the shore. Helping as many as he could into the rowboat, Diego then handed the oars to a volunteer and pointed to the ship. He dashed toward the church. The belfry lay in a crumpled heap in front of the door, having squashed several congregants who had gathered outside to converse. Diego helped to clear away the debris from the stricken. They were all dead, but Catalina was not among them. He ran to the bar.

Catalina was sitting on the low wall opposite. Shaken but unhurt, she turned to him as he approached. "I thought you were gone."

He took a place on the wall beside her. "I thought you were dead."

They sat there in silence, Diego stealing the occasional glance at her profile as she stared at the splintered remains of the bar. Eventually, he summoned the courage to speak. "What are you going to do now?"

Catalina laughed humorlessly, the sound quickly strangled in her throat like an aborted bark. She looked at Diego then turned back to the bar "Somewhere far away from here. Somewhere I don't have a past. Somewhere quiet."

Diego thought for the longest time. "I know somewhere."

* * *

At first, Diego wasn't sure he was in the right place. It wasn't just that it was overgrown and in severe disrepair, but that things seemed wrong. The distances between objects seemed off, perspective seemed skewed, everything seemed smaller. His instinctive reaction, which he tried to keep to himself, was that he was making a terrible mistake. Hiding his feelings, he dismounted and helped Catalina from her saddle.

"Is this it?"

Diego nodded.

Catalina was about to say something but stopped and took the reins from his hand. She led the pair of horses toward the remains of a fence.

Diego walked around to the front of the main building. Taking a machete from his belt, he began to hack the bushes that had swallowed up the doorway. A few minutes later, he could see the outline of a door. As he stopped to wipe his brow, Catalina appeared at his side. Something caught his attention, and he cleared a few more branches to get a better look. A name had been carved into the doorframe—Jorge.

With the index finger of his right hand, Diego traced the outline of his dead brother's name. He thought of Inez and Miguel, of crossing the Andes, of jail, of Jorge's death in his arms. When he got to the end of the outline, he started again. Catalina, watching, said nothing. She worked her little finger into his left hand, resting it against his scar. Diego stopped, and closed his eyes.

Epilogue

After San Martín's departure from Lima, Peru tore itself apart in a series of coups. Order was restored only when Bolívar arrived with his army to finally take the fight to the remaining Spaniards in the *sierra*.

San Martín swore he would never spill the blood of a Patriot, but this promise was to give him no peace. He returned to Mendoza, seeking only solitude, but was soon petitioned by various factions, politicians, and veterans of the Army of the Andes to join the civil war. Just as in Guayaquil, he knew the only solution was to remove himself. After the death of his wife, he collected his daughter Mercedes from Buenos Aires and sailed to Europe, eventually settling in Boulogne-sur-mer. He died, his only child by his side, on August 17th 1850.

His aide, John O'Brien, returned to América—the land that had captured his heart. He rejoined the army, fighting with Bolívar's troops in the Battle of Ayacucho in 1824. The victory was complete, and independence was secured forever.

Cochrane left Chile, sailing back around Cape Horn to Brazil. There, he joined the service, taking part in several decisive engagements that secured Brazil's independence. After helping

Greece free itself from the Ottoman Empire, Cochrane returned to England. King William IV cleared his name, and his honor and titles were restored. He died in 1860, aged sixty-four—an Admiral of the Red, still agitating for combat. Sixteen years after his death, the Government gave his grandson forty thousand pounds compensation for his unjust conviction in the stock exchange affair. There must have been something in that blood: his great-grandson, Sir Ralph Alexander Cochrane, went on to command the daring Dambusters raid during World War II.

The treacherous General Brayer's legacy was nobler still. The French forgot his cowardice at Maipú and his name was inscribed on the west side of the Arc de Triomphe. Napoleon left his faithful general one hundred thousand francs in his will.

As for Mendoza, it was leveled by a severe earthquake in 1861, destroying the city and killing half of the inhabitants. However, Mendoza was rebuilt and is still there today, surrounded by fine vineyards and towered over by the imperious Andes. The white thumb of Aconcagua still glowers at travelers who pass on the road to Santiago and make their way down toward the glittering coast and the curved bay of Valparaíso.

Acknowledgements

I would like to thank my editor, Karin Cox, for her expert contribution. This book would never have made it without her skilled intervention. She gave crucial advice at numerous stages before taking my final draft and whipping it into shape. Any remaining errors are due to my own intransigence. My sister, Kate Gaughran, has come up with another beautiful, creative cover that captures her strong vision and attention to detail. Jared Blando created a stunning map, and put up with numerous revisions. Brian Newman and Austin Maguire at Ambient Project provided excellent web design, Finbarr O'Mahony gave great advice on social media, and Heather Adkins did sterling work on the print edition.

The idea for this novel came from a nine-month trip around South America in 2005. I first started work on the book the following year, and I would like to express my gratitude to all the people of South America who made me feel so welcome the first time, and who assisted me with my research on my return in 2008. I read everything I could lay my hands on regarding the subject, but particularly helpful were *Liberators: Latin America's Struggle for Independence* by Robert Harvey, and *Cochrane: The Life and Exploits of a Fighting Captain* by the same author. Of additional assistance were *San Martin: Argentine Soldier, American Hero* by John Lynch; *Colonial Lives: Documents on Latin American History, 1550–1850* edited by Richard Boyer and Geoffrey Spurling; *The Autobiography of a Seaman* by Admiral Lord Cochrane; *Tales of Potosí* by Bartolomé Arzáns de

Orsúa y Vela; *The High Place* by John Demos; *Open Veins of Latin America: Five Centuries of the Pillage of a Continent* by Eduardo Galeano; *The Emancipation of South America* by Bartolomé Mitre and William Spilling; and *General O'Brien: West Wicklow to South America* edited by Donal McDonnell and Chris Lawlor.

I completed the first draft in 2009, during a summer spent in the Czech Republic being looked after by the Vostrovský family. I'm eternally grateful for their kindness, generosity, and hospitality. Countless friends suffered through innumerable drafts over the last five years and provided intelligent criticism and invaluable support. Thank you, sincerely.

The publication of this book was made possible through a crowd-funding initiative, and I would like to express my gratitude to everyone who participated. I hope this book goes some way toward repaying you for your vital assistance in making this happen. In particular (and in no particular order), I would like to thank: Ali Maguire, Michael McMahon, Julia Scott, Jessica Gaughran, Donna Tipping, Michelle Considine, Marc Rafferty, Kate Gaughran, Gary Coghlan, Holly Grant, Mary Gaughran, Lisa Ruth Elliot, Gavin Reid, Cpt. Tommy Marum, Stephen Flanagan, Dashmore, David Llewelyn, Gareth McKenna, Rory O'Callaghan, Pauline McNair, Ciaran O'Muirthile, Kio McLoughlin, Ann O'Brien, Christopher Marcus, Emmet Saunders, Finbarr O'Mahony, Austin Maguire, Cillian O'Briain Fallon, Peter Holland, Michelle Ní Fhearail, Bernard Gaughran Jr., J.J. Toner, and Edel Hughes.

I would like to thank my family and friends for their endless support and their continuous help, and in particular, my parents, Mary and Benny Gaughran. Finally, I want to say something to Ivča Vostrovska: I'm still working on that island.

Historical Note

Every effort was made to make this book historically accurate, but as a work of *fiction*, it should be understood that many elements are invented. The historical record is imperfect, and a novelist must go to work in these gaps. We are not free to invent as we choose, we must preserve the authenticity that is a crucial part of the bond between writer and reader, and great care is taken to ensure such inventions tally with the known record. In some places, however, minor alterations were necessary to make the story function, and they are fully listed on this website: bit.ly/valstorm

About the Author

David Gaughran is a 34-year old Irish writer, living in Sweden, who spends most of his time traveling the world, collecting stories. *A Storm Hits Valparaiso* is his debut novel, but he is the author of several short stories and a popular guide to digital self-publishing. To sign up to his new-release mailing list, please visit: www.bit.ly/valpolist

If You Go into the Woods, a collection of two creepy short stories. The title story was chosen to appear in the *Short Story America Anthology, Volume 1*, a collection of their best stories of the past year, published June 2011. The other—*The Reset Button*—is published for the first time in any format.

"There are definite shades of HP Lovecraft in both stories … punchy, entertaining reads with a bit of mental gymnastics thrown in, you can't go wrong with this one."—Jenny Mounfield, *The Compulsive Reader*, author of *The Ice-cream Man*.

"Two very well-constructed and thought-provoking tales from an author I know I will be keeping my eyes on. 4.5 stars."—Heather L. Faville, *Doubleshot Reviews*.

"This is the most professional design—both inside and out—that I have seen since I started reviewing at *SIFT*. The writing in this story is top-notch. The writer has a strong, clean voice. He's able to sustain an air of mystery and suspense without it feeling cheap." Sarah Nicolas, *SIFT Book Reviews*.

"I heartily recommend this masterful piece of work to any and all that thoroughly enjoy the art of the word, and especially to those that have a special place in their hearts for short stories, as I believe this to be a fabulous exponent of the genre."—LE Olteano, *Butterfly Books*

If You Go Into The Woods is currently available as an e-book from Amazon, Barnes & Noble, Apple, Smashwords, Kobo, and Sony for $0.99. A paperback collection of David Gaughran's short stories will be released in 2012.

Transfection is another short story, but this time with an old-school science fiction vibe.

"I recently bought and read *Transfection* and I'm happy to say it is terrific, and well worth the 99 cents."—JA Konrath, bestselling author of *The List*, *Stirred*, and *Disturb*.

"I laughed out loud at some of the antics as I was reading. Transfection is well worth the price-tag ... yet another well written and, dare I say again, thought-provoking, tale from David Gaughran."—Heather L. Faville, *Doubleshot Reviews*.

"Well written ... a polished product."—TC, *Booked Up Reviews*.

"Very strong images ... a haunting quality ... I totally did not expect that ending. I really didn't see it coming ... I recommend this to people who enjoy well written sci-fi."—LE Olteano, *Butterfly Books*.

Transfection is currently available as an e-book from Amazon, Barnes & Noble, Apple, Smashwords, Kobo, and Sony for $0.99. This story will be part of the same paperback collection of short stories released in 2012.

Let's Get Digital: How To Self-Publish, And Why You Should is the top-rated guide to self-publishing on Amazon with over fifty 5-star reviews. It contains over 60,000 words of essays, articles, and how-to guides, as well as contributions from 33 bestselling indie authors including J Carson Black, Bob Mayer, Victorine Lieske, Mark Edwards, and many more.

It covers everything from how the disruptive power of the internet has changed the publishing business forever to the opportunities this has created for writers. It gives you practical advice on editing, cover design, formatting, and pricing. And it reveals marketing tips from blogging and social networking right through to competitions, discounts, reviews, and giveaways.

If you are considering self-publishing, if you need to breathe life into your flagging sales, or if you want to understand why it's a great time to be a writer, *Let's Get Digital: How To Self-Publish, And Why You Should* will explain it all.

"Let's Get Digital is a must read for anyone considering self-publishing."—JA Konrath, bestselling author of *Trapped, Origin,* and *Whiskey Sour.*

"Credible and comprehensive. I'd recommend it to any writer who is considering self-publishing or anyone interested in the current state of publishing."—*Big Al's Books and Pals*—5 Stars.

"Even with my background as an indie writer, I picked up several valuable tips… this is simply the best book about the e-book revolution I have read."—Michael Wallace, bestselling author of the *Righteous* series.

"It should be THE starting point for anyone considering self-publishing today. This book is a Pixel Pick, and should be considered required reading for any Indie author"— *Pixel of Ink.*

Let's Get Digital: How To Self-Publish, And Why You Should is available as an e-book from Amazon, Barnes & Noble, Apple, Smashwords, Kobo, and Sony. A paperback edition is also available from Amazon.

Say Hello:

David Gaughran blogs about writing and the book business at: davidgaughran.wordpress.com

He also runs *South Americana,* which shares curious incidents from the history of the world's most exotic continent:
www.SouthAmericana.com

Alternatively, send him an email: david.gaughran@gmail.com

Or follow him on Twitter: twitter.com/DavidGaughran

Word-of-mouth is crucial for any author to succeed. If you enjoyed the book, please consider leaving a review where you purchased it, even if it's only a line or two; it would make all the difference and would be very much appreciated.

Sample: *Transfection*

Dr. Carl Peters prided himself on being unconventional. He stood out among the eccentric, doddering, forgetful professors of his faculty, who grimaced at the prints of Dalí, Tesla, and George Best that decorated his office, and was happy to. He knew he could not count any of them as friends. Dr. Peters didn't mind. He knew most of the truly great scientific discoveries were made by outsiders; the only way to shift the paradigm was to reject it in the first place.

His only real friend on the staff was his assistant, Jim Glover, a PhD candidate helping him with his research. His wife regularly joked she was jealous of Jim, who spent more time with her husband than she did, but beneath the teasing Dr. Peters suspected she harbored real resentment.

"Why don't you move into the private sector?" his wife asked, when he came home from work on time for once and complained that his grants were being cut again. They'd had this conversation, in one form or another, frequently—ever since she had spotted her dream summerhouse on a realtor's webpage.

"It's always the same bullshit choice," he said. "Fire Jim and scale back my work, or take the hit in my own salary. I'm sick of it."

She barely looked at him. "I hear there's lots of money in the private sector."

They had stopped talking with each other years ago. Now they just talked *at* each other.

Dr. Peters turned up the volume on the TV. A special report showed an interview with a team of medical researchers, who were announcing that animals fed exclusively on genetically modified foods were six times more likely to develop cancers than those given organic feed. Dr. Peters shook his head, absorbed. He didn't even notice his wife leave the room.

His phone rang; it was Jim. "Are you watching this?"

"I just switched it on. I can't believe it."

"They'll be throwing money at us now to fix it. Anyway, I'll let you get back to it. I just wanted to check."

Dr. Peters put down the phone and switched over to the business channel. It predicted plummeting shares in big GM producers, coupled with surging food prices. He switched the TV off and went into his study to think.

Dr. Peters had jumped at the chance to work at the university—not because they paid the most or had the best facilities (they didn't), but rather to live in a city with a grid-system, allowing endless ways to walk from one point to another without getting bored. Novelty was important to him—new things, new ideas, new ways of looking at old, intractable problems.

He first became interested in genetic modification because it was a radical way of solving an age-old problem: the price and availability of food. Since the Great Economic Collapse a few years back, commodity prices had been rising, helped in part by extreme weather conditions. GM food finally took off. People still had concerns, but when GM food became considerably cheaper their concerns seemed to matter less. This news, however, changed everything. Lost in thought, Dr. Peters did not even hear his wife's car reverse out of the driveway.

Dr. Peters got more money to solve the GM food problem, as expected, but the following year was still a frustrating one. He had been an advocate for GM food, and still saw an important future for it if these problems could be resolved, but he didn't have the medical background to build on the cancer research, although he understood enough to guess that tampering with cell structures was having unintended consequences.

Genetic modification was a complex process, but Dr. Peters knew that the root cause of the problem would likely be the foreign DNA that was being inserted into the host. He suspected the answer lay in the transfection process.

While walking to and from the university, always by a different route, he struggled with the problem again and again. As he did so, he noticed the city changing around him. Vegan cafés and bakeries were opening on every corner. The meat trade had been hit hard–steakhouses and burger joints were closing down. More and more people became vegetarian. Each week another company was forced to admit their products were not–as advertised–GM-free. Farmers' markets were springing up in every park and square across the country. Around the nation, people were fastidiously checking the organic claims of every product. Even so, Dr. Peters didn't find any of these developments threatening. Change was good, he thought; it created opportunities.

His wife saw things differently, and their marriage suffered. He knew it was his fault. The fanaticism he applied to his work left little room for anything else. He was aware of that, but did nothing about it, so he figured he deserved whatever came his way.

The day after his wife left him, Dr. Peters was in the lab as usual. He was relieved, in a way. He had disappointed his wife for the last time. Although sad, on some level, that it had come to this, his obsession with his research allowed him to ignore his emotions.

"My wife left me. Now I'll be able to spend more time here," he told Jim, just like that, as soon as he came to work. Cold. Matter-of-fact.

Jim did not seem surprised. After an awkward silence, Jim attempted to change the subject by showing Dr. Peters a small handheld Geiger counter he bought off the internet.

"Really," said Dr. Peters, "I'm fine, don't worry about me. See if you can pull up the chart from yesterday, I'm going to begin the transfection this morning."

"Do you want the biolistic gun?" asked Jim. "I don't think we have any cartridges prepared."

"No. I'm going to do this one manually." Dr. Peters pulled the Eppendorf tube and the tissue culture flask from the incubator. The first contained the host cell, the second, the desired gene. Under his specialized optical microscope, Dr. Peters injected the gene into the host cell membrane with a glass micropipette.

3

A squawk surprised him from behind. He dropped the pipette, the glass shattering into tiny fragments on the polished concrete floor.

"What the hell was that?" Jim rushed out of the office, which was separated from the lab by a glass door.

"I don't know, but it came from behind me somewhere."

They both peered along the workbench. "The Geiger counter!"

"No way," said Jim, "I mean—"

"—don't say anything. Let's do another. This time I want you right beside me, holding that thing."

It was confirmed: a short burst of radiation occurred at the moment the transfection process began. It didn't make any sense. Radiation came from radioactive isotopes and while all living things had trace amounts, the numbers the Geiger counter produced were way off.

"I don't know." Jim frowned. "There's something not right about this. Maybe it's coming from the lab downstairs. Perhaps some of their machines are leaking radiation."

"Impossible! They have all sorts of monitoring systems down there. Besides, the Geiger counter only picked it up when we began the transfection."

Jim shook his head. There was no plausible scientific explanation for what they had witnessed. A burst of radiation could trigger mutations, which could be the cause of increased cancer rates. But what was causing the radiation bursts? Dr. Peters made Jim swear to keep this quiet, then went for a short walk to clear his head, murmuring the same thing over and over: "This is *huge*."

* * *

Over the next few weeks, as Dr. Peters conducted his secret experiments, three things became clear. First, while all plant cells emitted a short burst of radiation at the moment of genetic modification, he could not replicate this process in animal cells. Second, the pattern of radiation varied from species to species but also altered with each iteration. Third, once the cell had been genetically altered, further DNA injections failed to produce the same reaction.

Dr. Peters began recording radiation bursts and feeding them into computers, then combed the printouts for commonalities. There didn't seem to be any. The same sample with the same stimuli could produce different levels of radiation on different occasions. There was no logic to it.

When his research grant came up for review, Dr. Peters was forced to share his findings with the faculty. Naturally, there was skepticism, but after Dr. Peters replicated the results his team was expanded to include radiation specialists, nutrition experts, oncologists, and three prestigious molecular biologists. Dr. Peters began to feel marginalized. He lacked the expertise to follow the direction the project was taking. He was relegated to trying to discern patterns in the radiation bursts. He recorded them, spliced them, and looped them. He translated them into pictograms, sound files, and binary code—anything to make sense of what everyone else had already written off as unintelligible nonsense.

* * *

One morning, Jim Glover arrived at work to find his boss stone-cold drunk. He must have been there all night. Jim could smell him from the other side of the table, on which pizza crusts were scattered beside an empty quart of scotch. The otherworldly cackling of a Geiger counter filled the room. Even stranger, Dr. Peters was tapping the desk in time with the beat.

"Carl?"

He didn't answer, just stared straight ahead.

Jim went over to the computer and stopped the sound file. When he came back, Dr. Peters was smiling.

"It's a code."

"What?"

"It's a code. Don't you see?" Dr. Peters made a series of taps on the desk.

Jim didn't get it. "Like Morse code?"

"Not quite. I haven't figured it all out yet, but it's definitely a code."

"But what you're saying is..." Jim paused, trying to understand.

"...crazy, I know, but it's the only answer. It has to be."

"I don't think it's the only answer." Jim chose his words carefully. "It could be nothing. It could be random. Could be gibberish."

Dr. Peters started tapping the desk again. "Don't you see? They're trying to communicate with us."

* * *

Transfection is currently available as an e-book from Amazon, Barnes & Noble, Smashwords, Kobo, and Sony for $0.99. This story will be part of a paperback collection of David Gaughran's short stories released in 2012.

Made in the USA
Charleston, SC
11 April 2012